BLADE'S Edge

SATAN'S DEVILS #10

MANDA MELLETT

Disclaimer

This is a work of fiction. Names, characters, businesses, places, events and incidents are either the products of the author's imagination or used in a fictitious manner. Any resemblance to actual persons, living or dead, or actual events is purely coincidental.

Warning

This book is dark in places and contains content of a sexual, abusive and violent nature. It is not suitable for persons under the age of 18.

ISBN: 978-1-912288-39-7

Road Name	Role/Status	Other Name
Drummer	President	Rick Felis
Wraith	VP	Scott Remington
Heart	Secretary	Dale Norman
Dollar	Treasurer	Todd Bishop
Peg	Sergeant-at-arms	Ronald Rinter
Blade	Enforcer	Jack Sharples
Joker	Road Captain	Josh Wilkinson
Mouse	Computer expert	Tse Williamson
Adam	deceased	
Beef		
Bullet		
Buster	deceased	
Dart	transferred	Colin Lowe
Fergus	Prospect	
Hyde		
Jekyll		
Lady		Scott Flintstone
Marvel		
Matt	Prospect	
Paladin	transferred	
Roadrunner		
Rock		
Slick		Jeff Andrews
Shooter	(was Spider)	
Tongue	deceased	
Truck	Prospect	
Viper		

Cast List of Characters

Old Lady	Children
Sam	Elijah (Eli)
Sophie	Olivia
Marcia	Amy, Jacob, Isabel
Darcy	Noah
Mariana*	
Carmen	
Alex	Tyler
Becca	
Ella	
Sandy	

Drew: brother to Mariana

SATAN'S DEVILS MC

Contents

Prologue

"Jacky boy, get your ass moving."

Startling, then turning sharply, I pout at my older brother, Jonah. I hadn't heard him come in, being far too engrossed in what I was doing. Whining like only a twelve-year-old can, in my still high and unbroken voice, I plead, "Do I have to?"

"Money doesn't make itself." Impatiently he swipes back his hair. "Look at you. Wasting all your time drawing pictures. Fuckin' pansy." But his expression and wink belies his words. His frustration is at the situation and not with me. "Dad left. It's up to us now. You're twelve for fuck's sake. Love you Jacky, you know that." He shakes his head. "I know you've got dreams and I'll do what I can to help you follow them, but there's a limit to how much time you can spend playing with pencils and paper like a fuckin' three-year-old. Need you to come with me now, lil' bro."

Glancing down at my handiwork, I know the drawing I've just completed of a rearing stallion looks nothing like the scribbles of a toddler. It's not that Jonah doesn't appreciate the finer things in life, it's that it doesn't put bread on the table. A two-dimensional image holds no practical interest for him, while all I want to do is commit the pictures in my head to paper. He's right, it doesn't help now, but I've been led to have expectations that it will one day bring me in money. Even at my age, encouraged by my art teacher, I already have dreams of being an illustrator. Despite his lack of aesthetic appreciation,

Jonah's proud of me though he doesn't always show it. There's no doubt, due to the way we are forced to live, he'd be happier if I was more like him instead.

There couldn't be a greater difference between Jonah and myself. Six years older, he spends all his time at the gym, doing odd jobs there for free membership. He's muscular and athletic, while I'm pasty and thin from spending all my time huddled over my artwork.

"You want to eat tonight?" He gets right to the heart of the matter. I'm twelve. Of course I do. As he's reminded me, Dad's long gone, and we can't rely on Mom. Searching for a replacement man to look after her is all that's on her agenda. Most of the time she prefers to forget she has two sons, a betrayal of her true age. In her view, we're old enough to be both an embarrassment to her, and to be able to fend for ourselves. But she reappears often enough to eat the food we've begged for or stolen. Or bought with the money Jonah manages to come up with from time to time.

I always blame her, thinking a parent should be someone you can depend on. Jonah shushes me when I complain about her. Some women, he tells me with the wisdom his age has taught him, aren't able to function without a man. We're her children. We should be enough.

Reluctantly, I carefully put aside the pencils I'd been using, tidying up the stack of paper, leaving the picture of the horse on top. Giving it one last glance, appreciating that in my view, the anatomy is just right, you can see the movement, know he'd reached the zenith of the rear, and was about to come crashing down. Standing, I hesitate.

"Will Mom be home tonight?"

He huffs. "Haven't seen her for a couple of days, have we? Fuck knows, lil' bro."

Our eyes meet in sympathy. His read sorrow, for me growing up without adequate parental guidance, mine holding pity for him. He's doing what he can to look out for the burden of a younger brother, teaching me, as best he's able, the ways of the world. His expression suggests he shares the fear that's at the back of my mind, that this might be the time she's left forever. That my one parent will never return home.

Jonah's not a bad brother, I muse as I follow him out of the house, and unchain my bicycle as he does his. Two rusted and just about serviceable modes of transport. He might yank my chain, but he has my back. Though he doesn't understand my hobby, and I'm not a fan of doing the more physical activities he enjoys, he does his best to make sure I'm clothed and fed. He could have upped and left by now, but he hasn't. He's stayed, and I know it's only to care for me in the absence of our mom. Even when she's home, she's little more than a figurehead. In return, I do what I can to support him albeit, reluctantly at times.

We ride to the city centre and then turn into the seedier part of town. Stopping at the end of an alley, I hold out my hand, grabbing the handlebars of the bike he's just dismounted. It's my job to stand and guard them, ready to make a quick getaway if we need to. Turning so his body's in the shadows, I hear the familiar sounds of him checking that his gun is loaded. Then, with a nod at me, he moves away, the darkness quickly swallowing him up.

A standard pick-up. A collection round I've accompanied him on a hundred times before. My job—to wait until he's completed his business. It's cold, I'm bored. My fingers itching to get back to that drawing, the unfinished hoof needing shading. I'm seeing it in my mind's eye when I hear a shout. More than one.

Then my brother's voice. "What the fuck, man?"

A startled oomph as though someone's been hit. *Was that Jonah?* Nah, even at eighteen he's big from working out at the gym. No one could take my brother down.

Scuffling noises make me grow scared and less confident in Jonah's invincible abilities. I stand, frozen, not knowing what to do. Jonah said stay here and not move. Would he want me to go see if he needs help? I can't call out; my shout might draw attention. Jonah's business doesn't need interested onlookers around. If anyone's going to help him, there's only one person who can provide assistance.

The sounds of a definite brawl decide for me. Gently and quietly I rest both bicycles against the wall, then keeping my back against the brickwork, make my way into the alley. *Fuck.* My eyes analyse the scene. Jonah had come prepared to meet one man. Instead there are four. Two holding him by his arms, one bouncing on his feet, prepared for any attempt at escape, a fourth standing menacingly in front of him. It's this one who speaks.

"We've warned you before, Sharples. Ain't going to be payin' you anymore."

Jonah spits blood and a tooth out of his bleeding mouth. "Nothing to do with me. I just collect."

"Well, you've made your final collection."

Unintentionally, as I try to move closer, my foot kicks a stone. It draws the speaker's attention to me. His eyes widen, whites showing in the weak overhead light. "Get out of here, kid. This isn't any of your business."

"He's my brother," I protest, my voice high and squeaking. "Let him go."

The man whose features I'm drinking in, shakes his head. "Sorry, kid. But we can't do that." His eyes go back to Jonah's. "You understand, don't you? This is just business. Nothing personal."

Jonah seems to understand alright. His shoulders slump, his face toward me, his expression blank, he instructs tiredly, "Go home, Jack. I'll, I'll see you later."

Even to my twelve-year-old mind something isn't right. Something tells me I won't be seeing any more of Jonah after tonight. I clench my hands into fists, knowing I'm no fighter, but comprehending there's only me here to save my brother. As I start to step forward, another man puts his arms tight around me, holding me back.

"Warned you, kid," the man facing my brother says. There's sadness, reluctance in his voice, but also, finality as he takes a wicked-looking knife off his belt, the light strong enough to glint off the sharpened blade as he holds it pointing toward Jonah.

"No," I scream, but a hand quickly covers my mouth. I struggle, but I can't get loose. Have no idea how to get out of the hold I'm in. Don't know what to do. Try to ineffectually kick but it does no good as I watch the knife enter and twist in my brother's neck, believing I can hear the grisly tearing of flesh and muscle. Jonah stands, a look of shock on his face, then a horrific gurgling sound comes out of his mouth before he falls back against the wall, then slips slowly, surely, down to the ground.

I'm released. Their job done, the men disappear into the black of the night, as I fall to my knees, trying in the dim light to find life in my brother's eyes, but they're open staring at nothing. Blood's pooling around us as I scoop up and hold my brother's dying, maybe even now dead body tight against me.

"No," I wail into the darkness. "No, no, no no no!"

I can't move. I can't leave him. I cry, useless tears, pleading and begging that the universe corrects its most dreadful mistake when I know it's already too late. I sit there for hours. Eventually the sky begins to lighten as daylight arrives. When the sounds of the world waking up start to reach me, a man appears with a bag to throw into the dumpster. Seeing me, recognising a bloody dead body, he backs quickly away. Shortly after there are sirens.

"Stand up. Put your hands in the air. Step away from the body."

Two police officers are standing, their guns drawn.

Tears still streaking down my face, I do as instructed, reluctantly and gently placing Jonah's body down. "He's my brother. They, they… killed him." Sobs wrack my undeveloped frame as I try to explain.

It's the first time I'm questioned by the cops. Those hours of non-stop intimidating interrogation marked the point where my hatred of authority began. My brother was already associated with a criminal gang, me, obviously involved too, as I'd been with him. It hadn't helped I'd told them all that I knew, it hadn't been enough. I must have known more even though I didn't.

I'd described the man who I'd seen clearly. When they hadn't brought in the police artist to sketch my description, I'd done one myself. That they recognised my technically perfect drawing had been easy to see. That they weren't going to act on it, equally apparent.

I'd been taken home, told they would investigate, even though I somehow knew they wouldn't. They'd told me they were watching me. I'd entered my room, torn up the picture I'd drawn of the stallion, broken my pencils and shredded my paper, vowing I'd never draw again.

If I had been bigger, stronger, more streetwise, I could have saved Jonah. The one talent I did have hadn't been able to help him. Not even to get retribution for his death.

My mom collapsed when the cop had told her what had happened. I'd tried to help, but I sensed somehow she blamed me, even when I was the one wishing most I'd been able to save him. The day after Jonah was killed she'd gone out and didn't come back.

I mourned Jonah alone, for days. Eventually hunger drew me out. I found the gym, the owner took pity on me, allowing me to take over the jobs my brother had done. My mom never reappeared and I wasn't particularly interested in what had happened to her. Jonah's duties at the gym weren't all legal, but sufficient for me to be allowed to bunk down in a storeroom when my home was eventually repossessed.

Years later I'd learned it was a group of police vigilantes who'd killed Jonah, when it emerged he wasn't their only victim. Bodies had piled up until they were no longer able to continue to hide their involvement. It had been a big case at the time. Jonah, just one name in a long list of victims. Another reason for me to hate the cops.

My mom? I presume she'd found a man who hadn't wanted to be saddled with kids. She hadn't even turned up at the funeral for her elder son, nor, it appeared, gave a damn about her younger.

I became an adult with a hatred of authority, and a deep suspicion of women. I didn't trust either.

It was the former that led me to join the Satan's Devils MC. The latter that led me to live my life alone, getting urges satisfied by the club bitches.

CHAPTER 1

Blade

My mouth twists as I stare critically at the picture in front of me. Prez is kneeling, his hands reaching under his bike, the muscles in his face clenched as he fights with an overtight nut. His old lady, Sam, is standing watching him, baby Zane in her arms, a slight quirk to her lips as if she's itching to get hands-on and show him how it's done. Toddler Eli crouches with a serious look on his face, his eyes fixed on what his father is doing. There's life, movement and emotion that's been created by my fingers. I don't need to be told it's some of my best work, the figures look like they could move, a moment captured in time, a drawing that needs no words of explanation.

One more moment to admire my creation, then I pick up the sketch, take my lighter from my cut, and set fire to a corner. When I feel the heat of the flames getting too close to my skin, I drop it into a metal trash can to mingle with the charred remains of other pieces.

For some reason, I've never been able to stop drawing, but nothing ever remains of what I produce. Every burned piece a memorial to the brother I lost so long ago. He was right. There are more important things in life. Each picture I burn a reminder of what can go wrong if you make the wrong choice, take a wrong direction in life, trust the wrong person.

My phone vibrates in my pocket. Without looking, I stand, stretch, then slide on my cut. Time for church.

Thunder rolls in the distance as I walk down the incline from my suite to the clubhouse, pausing to light a smoke, taking a moment to admire the view I never get tired of. The desert punctuated with saguaro surrounding the compound, the mountains rising in the distance. I check, but can see no signs of tell-tale smoke, unable to forget just a year ago my MC, the Satan's Devils, had been threatened by an enemy we had no control over. A *wildfire*. I eye the firebreak we now keep well maintained, hoping we'll never be faced by such flames again.

Ironically, it's how this old vacation resort became our home in the first place, decimated by fire, only a group of bikers wanted to buy it up and restore it. The home we've got now is the envy of all our other chapters.

Though clouds are assembling and a summer monsoon will probably not hold off much longer, as I enter the clubhouse I hear excited screams and splashing from the pool out back. Yeah, it's no wonder our fellow bikers are jealous.

Our facilities don't make us soft though. Far from it. I should know. I've been the enforcer for the club since Drummer took the helm as President, fourteen years or so back. My role to keep discipline amongst the brothers and to deal out retribution for those who cross us.

My thoughts have kept my steps slow. The clubroom is empty except for Paige who's pulled bartender duties this afternoon and is wiping down the surfaces. She looks up and grins. "You're late."

I shrug. Only by a minute, and I'll probably be forgiven for that. Not dignifying the sweet butt's observation with an answer, I start walking to our meeting room when the door behind me opens and closes. Swinging around, wondering who was tardier than I, I spy a man who I hadn't expected.

I still. He stops, hovering in the doorway, seeming unsure of his welcome, so I force myself forward with one hand outstretched, the other preparing to slap him on the back. "Fergus!"

"Blade. Er…"

My hand contacts with the back of his tee. "Fuckin' good to see you, man. You back to stay?"

He half shakes his head, his eyes flick to the bar, then down at his feet. "I don't know, I should have called, I, er…"

"Prospect!" Drummer's loud voice sounds from behind me. "Get me a beer."

At the words, Fergus's head snaps up. His feet are moving before his brain processes Drummer's instruction. Paige passes him a bottle, and he returns almost at a run, holding it out to the prez.

Taking it, Drummer winks at me, then glares at the prospect who hasn't been in the clubhouse for twelve months. He'd left a year ago to look after his mother who, the last we'd heard, had been dying of cancer. That he's here now, probably means she's dead. "You back to work?"

"Yeah, Prez." Eagerly, Fergus bobs his head. His face smiles, but his eyes look haunted.

Drummer nods. "Got church now. I'll talk to you later." Before moving away, his eyes soften. "Your ma gone?"

A sharp nod.

"Later," he repeats.

I raise my eyebrow at Drummer, but we say nothing more until the meeting room door closes behind us, and I take my seat at the left hand of Wraith, the VP.

Drummer bangs the gavel, then huffs a laugh. "You'll never guess who just walked in." As eyes go to him, he continues with a nod at me, "Fergus has returned to the fold."

"Just like that?" Peg rears back. "Nice of him to have warned us."

"Yeah." Prez takes a moment. "Man looked lost. Reckon now he's alone, he's come back to what he feels is home."

Man looking for a family. He wouldn't be the first.

"We going to let him pick up where he left off?" the sergeant-at-arms asks, for the moment not relinquishing the floor. "Or, considering the time he's already got under his belt, patch him in?"

"Not happy giving him his patch," I object. "Yeah, Peg, I know what you're gonna say. Kid prospected for us nearly a year before he left. If he'd stayed, I reckon he'd be around this table now. He put his family over the club. Needs to prove himself all over again."

"Fucker's ma was dying," Wraith rebuts. "Think that was a good reason for leaving."

In my experience moms don't have much to commend them. I wouldn't feel the need to attend my own mother's funeral, if I even knew where she was, or anyone bothered to inform me when she eventually goes. But perhaps, I'm biased. Getting out my knife, my hands itching as normal for something to keep them occupied, I spin it in front of me. "That may be, VP, but he left us in the lurch."

"Blade's got a good point," Drummer backs me up. "I, too, am not comfortable bringing him straight to the table. Let him prospect again, maybe only for a few months. I want to see if his recent life experience has changed him."

I don't comment. Losing my mom wouldn't be any hardship. For all I know, she may have been six feet under for years. My knife spins faster.

Drummer bangs the gavel. "Need a vote? Fergus to come back into the fold as a prospect, review in six months?"

"Or he's out if he fucks up before then." For stating the obvious, Prez gives Rock one of his steely stares.

"Shall I record it?" Heart, our secretary, asks. Prez looks around, everyone seems in agreement, so he raises his chin.

"Let's see how it goes. Six months is a long fuckin' stretch. Leave the time open. He does a good job? Bring him on board. If not," Peg acknowledges Rock's observation, "we part ways."

A raised eyebrow from Drummer. Everyone seems in assent. Heart scribbles in his notebook.

"Moving on," Prez resumes, with a glance toward Viper. "Viper and I went to the Chamber of Commerce…"

"Suited and booted?" Beef roars with laughter. "Or did you go wearin' your cuts?" He holds his belly as though it's a source of great amusement that the Prez and Viper have been mingling with the wealthy and respected businessmen of Tucson. He's not the only one. There are a few twitches of lips from other brothers. I find I'm grinning myself.

"Shut it!" Drummer snarls. "You're like a bunch of fuckin' pussies more interested in what we were wearing than what we discussed."

Viper's shaking his head as he looks around. I can understand his annoyance. He and Bullet have worked hard to get SD Construction to be a respected business in Tucson. Now their team's got the foundations laid, the biggest enterprise we've ever taken on is beginning to take shape. They've employed a number of locals too, giving us a respectability we've worked hard to gain for years. Hence the invitation to the Chamber of Commerce.

Drummer bangs the gavel twice. "Ladies, can I have your fuckin' attention?"

A few quips at his wording, but it soon quiets down, and he's got all of our attention. "I was approached while I was there. A question asked—do we offer security services?"

I purse my lips and tilt my head, while stroking my short beard. It's Peg who voices what I'm thinking. "Do we?"

"That's what I'm asking. The gig is providing protection for a local politician."

"Who? Affiliation?"

"Don't think it fuckin' matters, Rock," Viper, who'd presumably been party to the discussion interrupts, then gives a glance at Drummer who nods. "If we decide to branch out into this kind of work, should it matter to us what who we're protecting stands for? I, for one, don't give one fuck about citizen's politics. Yeah, got to abide by their health and safety shit, but outside of that, what they decide and the views they hold is up to them."

"You're saying we would provide muscle for someone whose policies we don't agree with?" Shooter looks concerned.

Joker laughs. "Whatever platform anyone gets elected on, they do what the fuck they like once they get their feet under the table. Who can name one politician who's ever delivered on their election promises?"

There's silence. Seems nobody can.

"Bunch of liars," Hyde grumbles. "Say what they want to get the job, then do what they darn well like."

"So if it doesn't matter what they say to get elected, shouldn't bother us who they are," Peg sums up. "All a bunch of dicks in the end."

"Or pussies," Beef observes. "Women are steppin' up to the plate nowadays too."

"The question is, is this the kind of work we want to take on? Get more involved in the citizen world?" Drummer asks. "Money could be good."

"Why us, Prez? Don't the feds provide protection?"

"Only for senators and the like. Not for anyone running at the local level," Prez responds to Heart, "and us, because we've got brothers who look like they know what they're doing."

"That leaves you out," Jekyll punches Lady's arm.

"Hey, he scrubs up well. Put him in a black suit and shades, he'd look the part," Joker defends his man, hugging him, right there at the table.

"Put each other down," I rasp out, spinning my knife and stopping it so it points their way.

Lowering his head into his hands, Drummer grumbles, "One fuckin' day I'll ask a question and get a straight answer."

"Not from Joker or Lady," Shooter gets in fast, quicker than I can open my mouth to say something similar.

"Fuck me!" Drummer roars, his fist meeting the table with a loud thump.

"I wouldn't suggest that to Joker or Lady," Shooter's ready again.

Prez just stares at him. Shooter starts slowly sliding down his seat, slipping under the table.

Again, I automatically spin my knife. It's my job to keep order after all. "Prez asked a question. I'd like to respond. Don't give a damn about the shit citizens do, but do give a fuck about the club. More money in the coffers is always welcome. If the price is right, I don't mind standing lookin' pretty and glaring. That's most of what this bodyguard shit would probably involve."

Prez raises his chin at me in appreciation. "Summed it up well, Blade. Sebastian Lawson is the fucker's name. There'll be a meet to go into the details, but from what he said, his campaign manager will give us a list of venues, we'll provide an escort for him, and stand at his back while he's making his speeches. Our message, don't mess with him."

"Sounds simple enough," Slick nods. "I can do that. The most danger we'll probably be in is being bored to death."

"Or getting hit with a rotten egg," Rock laughs.

"Why us?" Wraith asks, glaring across the table.

"Why, VP? 'Cause we're intimidatin' motherfuckers and we're relatively cheap."

Dollar takes off his glasses and polishes them on a cloth he's taken out of the case. "Not too cheap, I hope. You talk rates, Prez?"

For an answer, Prez takes a piece of paper out of his cut, and passes it to the treasurer. Dollar puts his glasses back on, reads it, then whistles through his teeth. I lean over to look at it; it's a healthy amount.

"Getting that for standing and lookin' pretty?" I ask.

"Yeah, Blade. Think you all can manage that?"

For that sum, it seems we can. As I nod, Hyde raises his hand. "I'm up for it, Prez, if you want to assign someone regular."

"Me too," Jekyll supports his friend. The pair prospected together, though they were six months apart patching in. "I can be there when Hyde's at Sarah's beck and call."

I smirk as does everyone else. Though he's still not officially claimed her, Hyde and Sarah are fixing up the property nearest to us that got destroyed in last year's wildfire. It was owned, and left to them, by Sarah's grandmother who'd seen the way the wind was blowing between the young couple.

Prez ignores Jekyll's additional comment, just focuses on his offer. "Anyone object to Jekyll and Hyde doing most of the legwork? Under Blade's watchful eye?"

"I want to be involved too," Peg puts in. "An advisory role."

Mouse hasn't spoken up to now. Mind you, he hasn't really been able to get a word in edgeways. "Need me to check him out, Prez? If anyone's already gunning for him? Like groups who don't want him to be elected?"

"Anyone putting their head above the parapet is bound to have folks against him," Prez agrees. "That was going to be my next point. We need to know who we might be going up against. Don't want to be blindsided."

Our computer guy raises his chin. "I'll get on it, Prez." He jerks his head toward me. "I'll let Blade, Peg, Hyde and Jekyll know what I turn up."

I nod at him. Fuck knows I haven't a clue what's involved in something like this. But it sounds pretty straightforward.

"This Lawson fucker wants to meet with whoever's heading this up. Blade and Peg, that will be you. Hyde and Jekyll, they'll call on you first, anyone else, as and when needed. Okay?"

Peg and I exchange smirks at each other, and when no one objects, I take it that it is, indeed, okay.

Chapter 2

Blade

What do you reckon about the politician guardin' gig?" Beef nods at Fergus, who promptly has two beers in front of us.

Eyeing the prospect, I reckon Drummer's breaking him in slow. Since he'd left, leaving us pretty damn low on prospects, the sweet butts have added bartending to their other duties more normally performed on their backs. But it's something he knows, a familiar task to ease him back into the club. Prez might be going easy, I'm not. "When you've finished here, Fergus, my bike needs a clean."

"Mine too," Beef interjects.

"Mine as well."

As Fergus's face drops, I grin at Peg who's just joined us. "Be good to be up to strength with the prospects." Matt and Truck will be pleased to have another pair of hands.

Instead of answering, Peg's face twists as though he knows something I don't. Instead of prying, I let it drop. Something I need to know? Well, I'll learn about it soon enough.

"We were discussing this protection we're supposed to be providin' for Lawson," I inform the sergeant-at-arms.

Peg nods. "Not got much time for politicians. Bunch of liars in my view." I tend to agree with him, but he doesn't give me a chance to tell him as he continues, "I'll be interested in what

Mouse turns up. There might be something in his closet he doesn't want to get out."

"Could be he's already upset the wrong people," I suggest.

"Could be, Blade. Could be." Peg raps on the bar, within seconds he's got a beer. "You doing okay, Prospect? Glad to be back?"

Fergus dips his head. "Fuckin' good," he agrees.

"Need to talk to him. Drummer's right. What he's been through, might not be the same lad who left." Peg's eyes follow the prospect as he serves someone at the other end of the bar.

Shaking my head, I know Peg's more the right man to discuss shit with Fergus. Knowing my mom was dead would be a relief. Not that she's likely to want to find me, unless she learns I've made bank since becoming an adult, that is. I turn around, leaning my back against the bar, for a moment, lost in the mists of time. I'd been twelve the last time I'd seen her. Twenty-four years have since passed. Doubt I need to worry about her rearing her head. If she'd been around, trying to make a life for her children, my brother Jonah wouldn't have been on the streets trying to collect a debt. He'd still be alive. Looking down at my beer, I frown. Wonder what he'd have done with his life? And, what mine would look like. I doubt I'd be the enforcer for a one-percenter club if he was still around.

No point dredging up the past and thinking of what-ifs. Finishing my beer, I push away from the bar. "I'm off to the Wheel Inn," I say, to no one in particular.

"Take the prospect with you," Peg overhears and makes a suggestion. "There are a couple of new waitstaff who've joined us since he was last there, be good for them to see his face."

Personally, I think the word Prospect on the back of his cut would be enough to identify him as one of us, but it's no skin off my nose to let him tag along.

Fergus is ready in an instant, and we're soon riding down into Tucson, him slipping into place behind me. We're heading for the restaurant and bar which the Satan's Devils own. It's managed by Sandy, Viper's old lady, and is a thriving business. There's usually a brother or two hanging around, and while the food has a good reputation, one draw for customers is probably that they dare to walk on the wild side of life, if only for a short interlude, eating surrounded by men in black leather and wearing cuts. Our presence does tend to ensure there's no trouble. No one ever skips out without paying their tab.

Tonight is no exception. The people standing in the newly extended bar area are happy but not overly drunk, and the restaurant is loud with the sound of cutlery on plates. When we enter, Martha, the assistant manager, comes across.

"You here to eat?"

My stomach rumbles. "Yeah, why not? I'll just take a burger at the bar, Martha, thanks." Turning to Fergus, I raise my eyebrow.

"Burger sounds good," he agrees.

Beers in front of us, burgers in our hands, I raise the loaded bun to my mouth and groan. Fuck, no wonder this place is popular, this is darn good shit. From the look on Fergus's face, he's enjoying it too. In fact, he demolishes it as though he hasn't eaten for weeks. As he chomps on his chow, I examine him. Yeah, he's lost weight. Must be the grief.

"When did your mom die?" I try my best to wear a sympathetic expression.

"Two weeks back. Funeral was last week."

Hmm. I thought he'd take time to get things sorted. "So you came straight back?"

The drink, the food, seems to have relaxed him. "Fact is, Blade, her medical bills were sky high. Took all the money we had and then some. I had to sell the house, everything's gone to paying off the debts."

"Any fall back on you?"

A quick shake of his head. "Her estate was declared insolvent, luckily anything else she owes has been written off. I've got a clean slate."

"But with nothing behind you," I surmise.

His eyes glaze over. "It's as if she never lived, Blade. She inherited the house after my Pa died, always told me the property, and everything she had would come to me. Not that I wanted it, but that was the way she saw it, her legacy, you know? Fucking forty-five years old and cancer took its toll. Spent the last days when she was coherent trying to convince her that leaving me nothing didn't matter a damn. She'd been a good mom, the best. That's all I could have asked for. Started me off right."

Better than mine, that's for sure. Even a hard-hearted bastard such as me has to feel some sympathy for a woman who'd wanted to provide for her son, and then left nothing as he made sure she'd lived every day that she could. It also explains why he'd turned up so quickly after her death. He'd had nowhere else to go.

"Hate our fuckin' health system." Quickly I snap my attention back to the prospect as I realise he's still talking. "Other countries don't ask you to pay for treatment when you need it. Don't ask you to choose between a drug that could be effective and one that barely works."

Having no answer, I just place my hand on his shoulder and squeeze. "Should have asked the club."

"Why? I'm not a member. Perhaps never will be." As I tilt my head he continues, "I know the score. No guarantees, Blade, I might not make the grade."

"You were close before you left," I observe, honestly.

"Bad timing, for sure," he miserably agrees.

"Blade?"

"Martha?" At the unexpected interruption and due to the tone of her voice, I'm already tapping my cut to check my knives are there. From her expression, something is bothering her. Glancing around I see no drunk acting rowdy.

"I know you're not working tonight, but there was a crash out back. I wondered if you could go look to see what caused it." She looks apologetic. "Might just be a cat trying to get at the bins, but…"

"No worries, Martha. I'll go look for a thieving feline and shoo it away, alright?" I grin to show I'm really not bothered.

I don't have to give Fergus an instruction. Good man's there at my back as I make my way to the rear, passing through the kitchen and lifting my hand to the chefs and staff working there. Switching off the alarm, then pressing down on the bar, I step outside. The night's still warm, the ground damp after the downpour earlier. Cars are rumbling along on the distant freeway, the noise carrying through the still air. Night birds hoot. My arm thrown out to halt the prospect's progress so I'm not distracted by the sound of feet on gravel, I stand and listen.

"Rustling," Fergus says quietly. "Over there."

"Martha's probably right, and it's a darn cat." Or rats. I shudder, not being particularly fond of them. Or it could be a snake. We can get anything here. Comforted my knives and gun are within easy reach, I take out my Maglite. "Watch your step," I warn unnecessarily.

Light is coming out from the kitchen; the yard isn't completely dark. Illuminated enough that Fergus can see my hand signals as I point him to the other side of the row of bins. I hear a sound. The Wheel Inn's signed up to the food waste collection service, where most of the edible waste is collected to be turned into compost, and the sound seems to be coming from that bin.

Cats, rats. Seems my earlier thoughts were right on target and it's just an animal helping themselves to a late-night snack.

The crash had come from the bin being turned over.

I approach, cautiously. A shadowy shape starts to rise making me jump back and grab hold of my gun. At my movement, the figure gasps. A very feminine sound.

"Stand up," I snap. Annoyed for a second I'd been taken by surprise.

"I'm not doing any harm," a female voice replies. There's a quaver in it.

"Stand," I repeat.

She obeys. A lithe figure, about five foot six if I can estimate correctly, comes into sight holding a lump of stale bread in her hand. Fergus takes a step toward her.

Thoughts go fast through my mind. A vagrant, if the condition of her clothes and hair are anything to go by. She's filthy, dirt smudges on her face, her hair frizzed up and awry. Not old, in her twenties perhaps? My artist's eye takes in her features, her perk nose that turns up at the end, over-large, and scared looking eyes. Cheekbones well defined. If she was scrubbed up, she'd probably be quite attractive. But as she is? Fuck, I can smell her from here. Guess this isn't the first food bin she's raided tonight.

"Get lost," I sigh. Taking something could be considered stealing, but a lump of stale bread that had already been thrown away? It's the thought of her being driven to find food this way that I find most disturbing.

"You're hungry," Fergus addresses himself to the girl, unnecessarily stating the obvious.

In my view, women are good for one thing and one thing only—fucking. When they've served my itch, apart from the sweet butts in the clubhouse who know the score, I have no further use for them. My female friends are limited to my brother's old ladies, expecting their old men to keep them in line. I've never looked out for my one, never wanted to find her. Women, I learned early, can't be trusted.

What the hell do I care if she's hungry or not? Doesn't matter one fuck to me. But I can bend a little. "You can take the bread," I offer, to my mind, magnanimously, "and anything else you want from in there. But you've got just one minute and then you're off our property."

A flinch as though I've spoken too harshly. Fergus's eyes plead with me, but what the fuck does he expect? Take this, this smelly bitch who's probably got fleas into a high-end restaurant and feed her? Get a reputation for that, we'll have all the vagrants in Tucson queuing up to be fed.

I stand impassively, ignoring the tug inside me as she takes me up on my offer, rummaging again and coming up with a half-eaten cake and a couple of sad-looking pancakes.

Then, with a toss of her long frizzy hair over her shoulder, she straightens her back. "Thank you," she offers graciously as though I had bought her that meal I'd just been thinking about.

She unsettles me for some reason. I can't read her, she looks one thing, but a sixth sense warns me she's something else. A sense that's kept my brothers and I safe before, a warning causing the hairs at the back of my neck to prick.

"Don't come back." If she's indeed trouble, I don't want her anywhere near the club.

A short look spared for me, a longer one settling on Fergus. Then, with her prizes clutched to her, she bends her head and shuffles off into the night.

"There's a story there," Fergus tells me, showing he's on the same wavelength. That woman hadn't been what she appeared.

"Don't think you're wrong," I agree, "but whatever she's hiding, has nothing to do with us."

CHAPTER 3

Tash

At least he let me take the food that I'd found. Even the throwaway items had been upmarket from the Wheel Inn. I'd known it by reputation before in my previous life, though never have stepped a foot inside. My gut feel had been right. What they'd discarded earlier that evening had still been perfectly edible. Well, to me, at least. Someone so desperate for food, they'd go down a bin.

I'm new to this. I should have got out of town, but I'd left it too late. By the time I realised the danger I was in, I couldn't go back for anything. Not my phone, my clothes or my money. I'd just run in what I was wearing. Now, I'm being hunted.

Three weeks ago I'd been living in a comfortable apartment, not having any idea I was living a lie and that everything would come crashing down around me. It was when it all caught up with me I'd found I'd become a liability, something to be discarded, dealt with, removed.

When the men had appeared by the trash cans, at first I'd been terrified, scared they would recognise me for some reason, frightened they'd come to take me. When I realised they were actually there just to stop me thieving, I'd been relieved, then worried all over again. Technically I was stealing from the Satan's Devils MC. You can't live in Tucson without knowing who they are, or their reputation.

One of the bikers seemed friendlier than the other, the one with Prospect written on the back of his cut. The man who'd spoken most, well, he clearly wasn't pleased at finding me there. Handsome son of a bitch, long brown hair which he'd swiped back from his forehead. I'd noticed, though his attractiveness should be the very last thing I should register. I've just about escaped the frying pan, certainly not the right time to jump into the fire. Definitely not to be attracted to a man wearing a flash denoting him as Enforcer. Not worth worrying about. Something told me, when I walked out of the parking lot, I was already out of his life and mind. Doubt if he'll give me a second thought, I won't be giving him another of mine.

Walking cautiously through the streets, keeping to the shadows, I try to find somewhere that's safe. Coming to an alley, I glance down it, listening hard, as I check it out carefully. Wouldn't be the first time I've sought refuge only to find an inhabitant already there, and one who didn't appreciate company. At least a growl, and not the use of his fists, had had me leaving him alone. My fear, being a woman on my own, was finding someone who wanted to take advantage, either offering to share his cardboard box in return for favours, or, offering nothing at all and just taking what he wanted.

I never expected to be in this position. I had no warning of becoming homeless, or not having a cent to my name. I'm not prepared, had never considered it before. What do I know of street etiquette? Zilch. Nothing at all. I've learned a few hard lessons over the past twenty-one days, survival instincts kicking in, the need for self-preservation preventing me giving up. Homeless shelters aren't for me. Not if I don't want to be found. Probably the first place anyone would go looking.

Satisfied from what I can see it's unoccupied, I slide down the alley. It's damp from the recent rain, but the night air's at least warm. Folding to my knees, I gingerly feel around with the hand that isn't clamping my stolen food to me. No broken glass or discarded needles, it's probably safe to settle down.

"Whatcha doing?"

Shit. I should have expected it. Nice hiding spot like this is probably already taken.

"Is this your place?" I ask apologetically. Staying polite as I've learned to be. Tempers flare easily over territorial rights.

A man steps closer. He probably smells, but as I do too, I don't notice. My clothes quickly became torn and disgusting having been in them for so long. Slipping in the mud caused by one of the monsoons really didn't help. As for my hair, well, without straighteners, the rain does it no favours. It won't be rescued until I'm back in civilisation again, and I can't see that on my horizon anytime soon.

"Whatcha got?" Instead of answering my question, he asks one of his own. My eyes, getting accustomed to the dim light, show there's a vacancy in his. My flight or fight impulse comes to the fore. He could be friendly or violent. I've already met both types. That he's blocking the end of the alley makes me concerned.

I can do friendly. Best to get him onside. "Some bread. Cake. Pancakes. Want to share?"

"Fuck yes." He lurches over, pulling up when a little scream of fright leaves my lips. "Sorry, sorry. Tommy clumsy. Sorry lady." Grubby hands sweep back through his shaggy hair. He makes no move to come closer, just stands rocking side to side, repeating, "Tommy clumsy."

He looks so contrite, so worried, I rush to reassure him. "Tommy? That's your name?"

"Uh huh."

"Well, Tommy. Here, I'll tear this in half, okay? And we'll share."

"Share. Good. Tommy can share."

"That's right." The man in front of me must be six feet tall at the least, muscular and well built, but I'm fast finding he's little more than a child in a man's body. When I tear my meagre offerings in half, I'm tempted to apologise that I haven't been able to wash my hands, but then realise how ridiculous that would sound. His are far worse than mine.

When I hold out the food, he snatches it, and starts stuffing it into his mouth. "Mmm, mmm," he mumbles around a mouthful of cake. "This is good shit, lady. Where d'ya get it?"

Knowing I need to eat; I try to still the churning of my stomach. Before my situation divebombed, I'd never have considered eating food I'd dug out of the trash. Bile rises in my throat. Closing my eyes, I pretend I'm back at home, eating normal food with clean washed hands. The bread clumps in my mouth, I gag as I try to swallow it. *I'll probably die from food poisoning eating stuff like this.*

As I'm warring with myself, the pain in my gut from hunger at odds with my disgust as the morsel I'm trying to get down, my companion is watching me carefully. "Good," he repeats, nodding at me encouragingly. Then, a little hopefully when he recognises my reluctance. "Tommy eat?"

I pass him the rest of the soggy pancakes. Bread and cake I can brush the dirt off. The pancakes seem to have soaked it in. Tommy has no such reluctance, and asks me again, "Where did you get it?"

"The Wheel Inn."

"Nonononono!" Tommy's shaking his head so hard I think it might be in danger of falling off. "No. No. No. They're bad men. They catch Tommy there they run him off." He eyes me suspiciously. "They got guns and knives. They kill. You one of them?"

Quickly I reassure him. "I'm not a biker, Tommy. I've not got any weapons."

Pancakes finished, he rubs his stomach and leans back against the wall. "Did the Devil men hurt you?"

Devil men? Inwardly I smile at the name he's coined. "No, they just told me to take some food and leave."

"They were kind to you, lady."

I suppose that sets the limit of the levels of kindness I can expect now that I'm homeless without a cent to my name. Allowing me to dig leftovers out of a bin. Lucky to get even that from what Tommy is saying. I'll probably have to get used to being turned away.

Tommy shuffles down to make himself comfortable, his long legs stretched out. He shrugs a worn pack off his shoulders and places it behind his head. It looks like he's settling in for the night. I've already guessed I've got nothing to worry about with him, and to be honest, company, even his, feels good. And his size won't hurt if someone with more dubious motives comes seeking a quiet place to sleep.

He's so still, I assume he's dropped off. His voice startles me. "Which Devils did you meet?" he asks "Aw, shucks, lady, I don't know your name."

"Tash," I respond, realising with a start how long it's been since I heard the name I prefer.

"Rash," he repeats.

I laugh. The first time in days. "Tash. Tasha."

"Rasha," he says tiredly with a yawn.

I go to correct him again, then think what does it matter? Names have virtually no meaning when you're invisible. As he goes quiet, I close my eyes.

"Rash?" Again, his deep voice makes me jump. "Which Devils? I love their bikes. All sparkle in the light. Loud noises make Tommy frightened. Tommy covers his ears so he can't hear them. But his eyes see. They look great as they pass." The words come out in such a rush it seems to confirm Tommy does indeed like bikes, even if he's wary of bikers.

Which Devils? I neither know nor care. After Tommy's warning, I've no desire to go back. But I try to recall the details, just to be polite and answer his question. "One had a jacket with Prospect written on the back. The other?" his image appears in my head, it seems I'm all too successful in conjuring those locks which should have looked feminine but weren't, and his startling blue eyes. "His said Enforcer. But I think that's what he does, not his name." I shake my head to dismiss the mental picture.

"What's a 'forcer?"

I really have no idea and tell him so. Another interval of silence. This time he has definitely gone to sleep. He's snoring, loud rasping sounds that at any other time might have annoyed me. But as I close my own eyes, I think that the noise might keep animals and other unwanted visitors away, and it becomes a comforting sound instead. For the first time in three weeks I feel relaxed enough to give in to the rest my body so badly needs.

"Hey, lady. Rash. Hey."

I wake with a start, my nightmare still going around my head.

"You had a bad dream. Tommy gets dreams too. You better now?"

My arm hurts. Looking at it in the dawn light I see that it's grazed. I must have been thrashing and hit it against the brick wall. Tommy's looking so concerned, his eyes widening as he sees the blood, I rush to reassure him. "I'm alright. And yes, I did have a bad dream." I indicate my arm. "Lucky you woke me."

"You were doing this." As he throws his arms around like a pinwheel, I giggle at the ridiculous sight.

"If I was doing that, I could have hurt you."

He grinned when I'd laughed, now he frowns. "Rash hurt, Rash. You got a boo boo."

"I do, Tommy." It needs washing, but there's not much hope of that.

"Tommy's hungry." He pouts as his palm draws circles on his belly. Then he brightens up. "They'll be serving food at the shelter. Wanna come?"

I bite my lip, worried. Food, a proper breakfast sounds good. But I don't want to go out into the open, not with daylight approaching fast. It's too dangerous. There'll be people watching for me. *His* men. My hope is that he thinks by now I've left town, but I can't be too careful. He knows I left everything behind and have no way or means to get out of Tucson. Once he knows I've contacted no one I know, nor been to the bank where I have an account, he'll likely be checking the places where people with no money go.

How did it come to this? All I did was fall for the wrong man. I was completely taken in by him. He'd seemed nice, even a man I could see myself building a life with—until it all fell apart. Even now I can't get my head around that he'd tried to kill me. It was pure luck I got away. He won't give up easily, me being alive is too much of a risk for him. There's too much that I know.

"Food? Tommy and Rash eat?" Tommy's looking at me hopefully.

"You go, Tommy. I'll find something else." The way he tilts his head shows he doesn't understand. "There are a bad man looking for me. I, I need to stay out of sight."

His eyes widen enabling me to see the whites clearly. "Bad man? Badder than the Devil men?"

From what I saw last night, yes. "I think so."

"Bad man come after Tommy?"

"No, no," I reassure him. "Just me, Tommy. He won't be after you." One minute's conversation would show even if I'd told Tommy my secrets, he wouldn't understand the dynamite I'd given him.

Tommy stands, stretches, then burps and farts at the same time. "Sorry," his face reddens and he covers his mouth. His stricken look makes me want to giggle again. In truth, I'll miss him when he goes. He's uncouth, uneducated and slow on the uptake, but I've taken to him. Let's face it, he's now my only friend.

"Don't want to leave Rash," he says sulkily. He kicks at a stone, frowns, puckers his lips, then lets out a slow whistle. "Tommy knows what to do. You shared with me last night. Today I share with you. You come with me, and I'll show you a place to hide. I'll get food and feed you. Yeah. Tommy will share with Rash."

As a plan, it sounds like it might work. Now daylight, I don't know who would be coming down this alley, and at least Tommy's size would be protection by itself. As I go to stand my stiff muscles protest. Tommy holds out his hand to help me up. He towers above me. Suddenly and unexpectedly, he gives me a hug, almost squeezing the air out of me.

"Rash Tommy's friend. Yes?"

When he lets me go and I've replenished my oxygen, I pat his arm. "Rash, I mean, Tash is Tommy's friend."

Daylight's no friend of mine for good reason, but it's interesting Tommy seems reluctant to show himself too. I guess that's what homeless people, especially those like him get used to doing—keeping out of sight and not drawing attention to themselves. When we get to a bridge, Tommy points me to a place where there's room for one person to sleep. It's empty now, but the cigarette butts suggest it was used recently. Then with his finger to his lips, he moves away.

I wonder what his attention span is. Whether once he's faced with whatever breakfast they serve he'll forget all about me. But I've nowhere to be, nothing I can think of to do. So I sit on the dirty ground and settle in to wait. If I need to, I'll stay here until it's dark again.

I'm pleasantly surprised when shortly after I've made myself comfortable, Tommy returns. My empty stomach growls at the Styrofoam cup he's carrying and the food in his hands.

CHAPTER 4

Blade

ey! Congratulations, Brother," I call out as Slick jumps off his bike.

"Thanks!" he returns as he races past, throwing an explanation over his shoulder. "Mother and baby are fine. Just come back to get some shit she wanted."

"What have you called her?" I shout louder as he disappears, almost laughing as he skids to a halt and swings around.

"Faith. Seven pounds six ounces if anyone asks."

Then he's gone. I've not even finished my smoke when he's back, bag slung over his shoulder and with a quick wave of his hand has vanished again.

Well, that's another baby on the compound. The ninth to be born to my brothers; sometimes it seems the Tucson chapter's breeding like rabbits. If we're counting children, there's Joker and Lady's kid Maya as well and I shouldn't forget Drew, but at sixteen, I doubt he considers himself a child anymore. For a moment, I envy Paladin now settled in Colorado. When we'd gone there a few weeks back to celebrate Jayden's birthday, there wasn't a baby to be seen, or not one we hadn't taken with us.

But fuck, we'd been the butt of some jokes when the crash truck had emptied spilling out kids. Yeah, yeah, if I hear the joke about something being in the water one more time the person who says it is going to find themselves at the end of my fist. I, for one, am certainly not going to be repopulating the clubhouse whatever I drink. I'd need a woman for that, and all they're good for is giving me a break from using my hand.

I can be happy for my brothers though who seem to have got what they want. Don't even mind the rug rats getting under my feet. Long as they leave the clubhouse to the adults at a reasonable time.

Stubbing out my cigarette on the heel of my boot, I'm turning to go inside, when Prez comes out.

"Slick's just been back for a flying visit to pick up some shit." I'm grinning as I tell him, "Baby's called Faith, and fuck knows why he thought I'd be interested, but she weighs seven pounds six ounces."

Drummer nods knowingly. "I'll pass it on. Women want to know all that shit. They all doing well?"

"He didn't stop to chat. Just took straight back off with a bag."

I move as though I'm going to go past him. His hand shoots out and settles on my arm. "Need you, Blade."

"Yeah?"

"Yeah. Peg's set up a meet with Lawson. You okay to go along?"

"Sure. Now?" Spotting Peg walking out tossing his keys in his hand, it's a fair bet. I don't need Prez's nod for my answer. I'd been anticipating this since the last church, almost a week ago now.

"Blade, Peg," he includes the sergeant-at-arms as he draws near. "Keep your shit together, okay? Ignore anything he tries to preach about his policies, whatever they are we're not going to agree with them anyway. Just find out why he thinks he needs extra security and assess what we need to do to keep him safe."

"What if we hate the fucker?" Peg asks, seriously.

"Try not to kill him, Peg," comes Drummer's dry response. "You know how much we're being paid. Just do what he wants. Do this well, and it may lead us to other work in this line."

I grin. "Got it. Don't break his arms or legs. Not yet." I get a cuff around my head. "Hey."

"Deserved that, asshole." Drummer sounds amused.

Peg's looking upwards. "Best get a move on if we're going to beat that storm." Raising my eyes, it would be hard to miss the dark clouds gathering. The thought of being caught in the dust storm that often precedes the rain, let alone the monsoon itself, has me moving to my bike quickly.

We make it just in time. Pulling up outside a smart modern office block in downtown Tucson as the wind starts picking up. While litter begins to blow around, dust swarming in circles, I take a moment to scan the external of the building for points of entry and obvious weaknesses, then follow Peg up the steps and inside. At a long desk spanning one side of the downstairs area, the receptionist tells us Lawson has an office on the second floor. We decide to take the stairs rather than the elevator. At the right floor, we open the door to find there's another, much smaller, reception. We're asked to wait.

As the minutes tick by, Peg's eyeing the clock above the desk. It's five minutes past our appointment time when an office door opens behind us.

"Mr Rinter and Mr Sharples? Mr Lawson will see you now." Peg and I exchange glares. I suspect if Peg's like me it's been so long since we've heard our citizen names. I, for one, was tempted to look around for someone else.

Entering the office, I spend a moment taking everything in. A person's surroundings can often provide clues as to who they really are. The walls are painted in that magnolia colour, no attempt to add any atmosphere. A couple of nondescript prints are hanging, just two dimensional abstract modernistic paintings, one of a coloured square, one of triangles. Again, nothing to give any particular personalisation. My guess would be the artwork was chosen by an interior designer, and not the occupant who's currently standing behind his desk, reaching out his hand.

Peg steps up to take it first.

"Sebastian Lawson," he announces pleasantly.

"Peg," the sergeant-at-arms replies adamantly, stressing the name he prefers. By the flinch of the other man's face, I know Peg's squeezing tightly.

Making one final observation that a family portrait is prominently displayed on the desk, Lawson, presumably with his wife and child, I copy Peg's action, my hand as firm as the sergeant-at-arms when I introduce myself, "Blade."

I give kudos that he doesn't rub his hand after he pulls it free.

Lawson then nods to our rear at the man who'd opened the door to us, and who is now standing just inside. "Neil Turner. My campaign manager." As he waves us both to seats in front of the desk, he continues, "Most of the liaison will be direct with Neil. He'll make the arrangements and inform you where we need you."

Peg settles down and stretches out his long legs, his action so smooth you'd never know one of them was prosthetic if you weren't privy to that information. He folds his arms across his chest. "Need to know exactly what you expect us to do." That's Peg. Not wanting to waste time on small talk.

Lawson seems a little taken aback by the direct approach, but recovers fast. "Of course. I'm the nominee in the election; you already know that." He pauses for us to indicate our acknowledgement. I shift in my seat, why the fuck else would we be here? Lawson continues, "Politicians, er, well, we're not viewed particularly favourably at the moment, so I want to make sure someone has my back. I'll be running a few rallies, debates, and generally getting out to meet the voters. I'll need you there to make sure no one gets too close."

When he breaks off, for a second, his eyes meet those of his campaign manager's. Mine, in turn, meet Peg's. His raised eyebrow suggests he's wondering what I am, whether there's something we're not being told.

"People like to invent stories, fake news if you like. It's possible someone will try to smear Mr Lawson's character," Turner speaks from behind us.

"You expect someone to try and air some dirty laundry at your rallies?"

It's Lawson who replies sharply, "I've got nothing to hide. But my opponents will stoop to anything. Yeah, someone might try and come up with some lies. I need you to be on the ball and remove such a person before they can capture an audience."

"You expecting anyone in particular?" Peg growls.

"No," Turner reassures us. "But we need to be prepared. The press are always on the lookout for something they can blow up out of proportion. That's how it starts, fake news."

Turning my head to the side, I don't miss the glance exchanged between the two men. Hmm. My sixth sense is awakening, but the words that come out of Lawson's mouth deny it as he confirms what his campaign manager had just told us. "As I said, there's nothing anyone can pin on me. But there are various factions that would prefer me not to come out the winner. Who knows what lengths they'll go to blacken my character."

That goes without saying. Politics seem to be almost as bloody as anything the Satan's Devils get into. Though it's usually verbal while we tend to be more hands on. "Anyone in particular we need to be aware of? Someone said something to make you nervous?"

Another look shared, and twin shakes of their heads as if they've practiced the movement. An ominously loud clap of thunder sounds overhead. It sounds like the heavens are sending us a warning. Not that we need it.

Risking a quick glance at Peg, his disapproval is showing clearly. Like me, he clearly thinks they're hiding something. "Look," he says, sitting up straight. "If you've nothing to worry about, I'm not sure why you've contacted us. Surely the cops would provide sufficient security at your venues."

"They will. But in the current climate, I like to be certain. Cover all bases so to speak." A wide smile shows all Lawson's gleaming, and probably very expensive white and even teeth. "I believe very strongly in the policies I support. I want to be able to deliver my speeches to promote them without having to worry about interruptions. Another thing you'd be useful for is removing any protestors that are too vocal, so the people who do want to listen have a chance to hear what I'm saying."

"But isn't debate useful?" As far as I'm concerned, politicians are supposed to be able to stand their ground and have the conviction to defend what they're spouting.

"Of course. And I'm happy to address any valid issues raised. But it's possible it might turn to personal attacks."

"Who?" Peg snaps sharply. "And what's hiding in your closet, Lawson?"

It's Turner who steps closer. "Mr Rinter…"

"Peg," my brother quickly corrects.

"Peg. See, Peg, Mr Lawson isn't hiding anything. But even if there's nothing, people might cast aspersions just to put doubt in electors' minds. We want to make sure anyone trying to tout lies is quickly removed, that's all." A jangling sound comes from his pocket. Turner reaches down, grimaces, and looks at Lawson. "Sorry, I need to take this. It's Grant." Lawson waves his hand as though acknowledging he needs to answer the call, then watches his campaign manager leave, his interest appearing to be on him.

But he's polite enough when he brings his focus back to us. "So are we clear on what I need you for?"

My brow creases. I'm not really certain at all. I open my mouth wanting to clarify a few details when Turner bursts through the door. Lawson's eyes shoot to him.

I turn in time to see his campaign manager respond with a rapid shake of his head.

Lawson snaps, "But he told us he had her."

Cautious, Turner just moves his head negatively again.

While I don't understand the exchange, the expressions that cross Lawson's face are telling, though a deep breath seems to settle him as he pulls back his jacket sleeve and looks down at an expensive watch. "Well, I'm sorry, but I'm going to have to leave this for now. I've got another meeting to get to. Neil will be in touch with a list of my upcoming engagements. Any questions please direct to him."

That's it? I frown. Before Turner stepped out to take that call it looked like the meeting would continue. *There was something about his campaign manager's reaction that's got Lawson in a tiz.* Something he needs to act on urgently. Why wouldn't he just say so? *Who am I to question the ways of a politician?*

Standing, Lawson buttons his jacket, then steps around the desk. "It was nice to meet you, Mr, er, Peg. Blade. I look forward to working with you."

"I'll call you," Turner confirms, his hand already opening the door.

Dismissed, Peg and I walk out. Our eyes meeting. It's not until we're outside by our bikes that I speak. "What's he hiding?"

"Fuck if I know," Peg replies, looking thoughtful. "Something, that's for sure." He takes out a rag and wipes his wet seat. At least the storm had passed over while we were inside.

Drying my own saddle, instead of getting on, I lean against my bike. "This is no *Men in Black* job."

"Picked that up, did you?" Peg shakes his head. "We're his hired muscle. Removing undesirables."

"People who disagree with him," I confirm.

Peg's head stills. "I think it's more than that. I think he already knows the direction a threat is coming from. But what, I can't get a handle on as yet."

I raise my chin. "Not sure I like being used. There's a reason he's come to us rather than engaging a normal security team. With the money he's offering, it's not cost."

"Drummer thought it could be the start of a new gig for us, but it won't be if we get the rep for being violent."

My lips twitch. "You think that's why he wants us? Because of our reputation?"

"Don't you?"

The problem is, I've got the same strong suspicion and am concerned about exactly what role he wants us to play. What's he think we're going to do? Rough people up to discourage them? Eject them from his rallies viciously? Send them away with a message they won't forget? Thing is, Satan's Devils won't want to be part of that. It's not that we shy away from showing aggression, but it's on our time and only against those who threaten the club. If Lawson's planning on us causing carnage, he's in for a rude awakening. He wouldn't be able to pay us enough.

As we head home, I'm not sure what happened this morning. Apart from being able to put a face to the name, I haven't learned anything more about the man we're supposed to be protecting, nor have any real understanding of his expectations. I don't particularly like going into a situation blind. Knowing the sergeant-at-arms, I suspect Peg will be of the same mind. One thing's for certain, while Jekyll and Hyde are patched members I trust, first time we're called in to one of Lawson's gigs, I'll be tagging along to check exactly what we're up against.

As the few miles pass, I start thinking that I'll ease my frustrations by sinking my cock into whichever club girl is available. At least with so many men now taken, there's a good ratio of whores to single brothers on the compound. Paige, perhaps? Diva? Backing my bike into its spot beside Peg's, I kick down the stand.

"Blade." Wraith's marching sharply across the lot. "Hold up. Need you to go out."

"Where, VP?" My heel's knocked the stand back up and I'm ready to roll. "Where d'ya need me?"

"The Wheel Inn. Fucker down there causin' a commotion."

What the fuck? "Isn't anyone else there?" There should be. We usually try to have someone in attendance just for situations like this.

"He's asking for you."

Me? "Me personally? Who?"

"Yeah. Sorry, Blade, I don't know. But they can't get rid of him and he's upsetting the customers."

I wave my hand to show I'm on it, and start my engine again, thoughts of sinking into a welcoming pussy having to be put on the back burner for now. The vibration of the engine does fuck all to help my cock which had swollen in anticipation.

Retracing my steps back to Tucson, my thoughts are on getting my dick to accept the delay, rather than the road beneath my wheels or the situation I might be heading into. It won't be anything I can't handle. There are not many men who can best me in a fight, not nowadays. And if a fucker wants to take me on he'll pay for keeping me away from a warm willing woman. This better be something important to cause the delay from relieving the pressure in my cock. If not, I may just take my frustration out on this fucker with my fists. Or one of my blades.

Martha obviously hears me arriving. She's by my side as soon as I park, barely letting me kick the stand down before apologising, "Sorry, Blade. I didn't want to call you down here, but I can't make head or tail of what this man's going on about."

Road saunters up. Fuck, he's a big fucker himself. If he's having problems and needs backup, maybe I should rethink taking this fella on. "What the fuck, Road?" My eyes narrow. He wouldn't be calling for help unless it was serious. At last my cock shrivels as my muscles tense.

Road looks more puzzled than fight ready. As though in answer, he taps his head. "Got an asshole out back. Fucker's not right up here, and is agitated. Kept tugging my cut and saying 'forcer'. Only thing I could think of is he wants to speak to you. Was saying what I think was Prospect too, but I thought you'd be better placed to handle it."

I'm having difficulty processing his words, having to quickly reverse away from the conversation with my fists that I'd been expecting.

Martha butts in, "He's crying, Blade. He's upset about something. Stuck on it, too." She waves her hand in the direction of the road. "We've tried to get him to move on. He's nervous, scared, but completely refuses to leave. He was getting louder and louder, only calmed down when I said I'd call you. Forcer? Road and I could only think he was referring to you."

My curiosity now piqued, I ask, "Where is he?" It seems they're not even sure I'm the one he's after, just making a best guess. But they are right, we don't want the customers upset.

"Out back. In the parking lot."

I follow Road around the outside of the building. It isn't long before my eyes alight on a man crouched on the ground, rocking on his heels. He's muttering to himself and sobbing. "Help. Must get help. Help Rash." He's repeating it over and over.

Approaching, I place my hand on his shoulder.

He moves fast, standing and shrugging me off so violently I almost stumble over. "Not going. Not til I see 'forcer. Or Prospt."

"Hey, calm down," I say sharply, my eyes looking him up and down, noticing someone's given him a black eye. His clothing and odour give away he's another vagrant. Fuck, have to do something to stop them coming here, seems like the place has become a magnet for them. "Tell me who you are, and what you want?"

"'Forcer?" He quiets and looks hopeful.

"I'm the enforcer," I confirm. "Was it me you wanted?"

He nods, his head dipping up and down fast then repeating the action a second, then a third time. For a moment I don't think he's going to stop. "'Forcer. Yeah. You're a Satan's Devil. You were kind to my friend."

Me? Kind? My face scrunches up, trying to think of a mutual acquaintance. Only one way to find out. "Who's your friend?"

"Rash."

I don't know anyone called Rash. Road and Martha had guessed wrong and I'm not the man he's after. Seeing the puzzled expression on his face, Road doesn't recognise the handle either.

If I tell him I'm not the 'forcer fucker he's wanting, he'll just stay on making a fuss. Martha's right. He's scared, but there's something—loyalty to this Rash perhaps—that's greater than his fear. I can't leave it like this. I tap a cigarette out of the pack I carry in my cut and light it. After blowing out a lungful of smoke, I ask, more calmly, "What's your name?" Taking into account this guy isn't only homeless, he's a few cents short of a dollar, I tame down my enforcer persona. While part of me wants to tell him to get lost and walk away, there's a pricking at the back of my neck which warns me to stay and listen.

"Me..." he points to himself, then says proudly, "I'm Tommy."

"My name's Blade," I say as gently as I can. "This is my brother, Road."

"Blade. Road," he repeats, and then again. "Mr Blade and Mr Road." His face splits into a broad smile and he does that bobble head thing again. As I hoped, now we're all introduced, it seems to have relaxed him.

"Who's Rash, and why does he need help?" I coax, trying to move this along. Move him along, away from our premises.

"Not a man. No. No way. Lady." Tommy holds his hands a rather optimistic distance from his chest and moves them as though tracing curves to ensure we know what he means. "Rash a lady. Kind to Tommy."

I know this Rash? Strange fuckin' name for a woman. If it's a handle, I'm not at all interested in learning how she came by it. Seems like someone to stay well away from. "Who is this… Rash?" My face twists in distaste.

"You know her," he says indignantly. "You were kind to her."

Road huffs a laugh. "Better get yourself checked out, Blade."

I punch my fist in his stomach hard enough to make him oomph. Then, turning back, ask, "How, Tommy? How do I know her?" I'm racking my brains, but I still can't place her. Of course, I don't always ask a woman her name. But I do wear a condom and usually ask whether she's clean.

Tommy looks frustrated. "Rash. My friend Rash. You were kind. You gave her food. She shared with Tommy. Good food. From here." He rubs his stomach in appreciation.

I gave her food? That's a strange way of putting it if I'd bought a girl a meal, and that would be extraordinary in itself. I don't date. Girl's hungry? The most she'd get is my cock. But, hang on… *it couldn't be, could it?* My mind summons up a memory of a girl hugging her stale bread protectively to her. "She like you? Homeless?"

At last I've hit the fucking jackpot I realise as Tommy furiously nods his head. To Road, I say in explanation, "Fergus and I found a vagrant, a girl, digging around in the food bin the other night. I let her take some stale food. She might have seen the flash on my cut." Finished with my cigarette, I stub it out on the sole of my boot and toss the end into the nearest bin.

"Explains why he was asking for the enforcer and prospect," Road agrees. "Could be you're on the right track."

But even if I've placed her, why has this guy come to me, and what on earth does he think I can do? "Why, Tommy? Why do you think I can help with whatever problem she's got?"

"Antibiotics, Brother," Road suggests out of the side of his mouth. "Perhaps you need to take some yourself."

He gets my elbow again; this time it makes him turn and bend over.

Ignoring him, I watch Tommy who doesn't seem bothered by my horseplay with Road. Instead, he looks sly. "I told her we didn't come here. Tommy frightened of Devil men. But she said you were friendly. 'Forcer and Prospt."

It's like pulling teeth. What he doesn't appreciate is that I know all the best methods of extraction. If he doesn't hurry up with an explanation, what I've done to my brother, who's still trying to catch his breath, will be nothing. I might have to resort to a bit of torture. Thought of pussy—a clean one—enters my head and my cock twitches impatiently.

"Tommy," I say sternly. "For fuck's sake, tell me why does this Rash," *fuck that's a strange name*, "need help? And why are you looking at me to give it? If you don't spit something out quickly, you can go. There's nothing I can do to help if I don't understand what you're asking."

Now his bottom lip quivers. "She's my friend," he insists, his voice trembling. "I, I, I..." Sobs begin to punctuate every attempt to speak. I start thinking how a little pain might help him focus when suddenly he gets it out. "I wanted to be her friend. Made her come to get food. She, she… she didn't want to go out in daylight again, but I made her. I *made* her. Tommy's fault. I made her. It was okay before, not today. Tommy did wrong."

As his voice trails off, this time it's Road who prompts him, glaring at me when I huff with impatience. "You made her do, what? What did you do wrong, Tommy?"

Road's more reasonable tone seems to get through to him better than my gruff one, and now it all floods out. "She came to the food truck. Was nearly there. A big car stopped. Two men got out. They *hurt* her. *Hurt* me." He points to his discoloured eye. "They took her. Bad men." Another loud sob. Grabbing hold of the bottom of his dirty tee, he pulls it to his face and wipes his nose on it. Then he sniffs, brightens, and with a smile, asks me, "You'll find her, won't you? 'Forcer find Rash. Make her safe. Set the Devil men on the bad men."

Road raises an eyebrow at me while I stand bemused. A homeless vagrant with a handle that's probably not even her real name. A simpleton the only person to witness her abduction—if that's what it was. I step closer to him, he's almost my height, bigger built, but he still flinches. "Make of the car and description of the men," I rasp, not even knowing why I'm bothering to ask.

He shrinks back, almost folding in on himself. "Tommy don't know cars. Just it was white. Bad men driving. They were bad men. Bad," he wails.

"Blade," Road growls menacingly.

I throw up my hands and turn on my brother. "For fuck's sake, Road. We've got info from someone with no light on upstairs. He can't give any details to go on. Rash can't be her real name…"

"What does she look like, Tommy?" ignoring me, he asks.

"Pretty. Very pretty."

Again, my hands open wide. But Tommy has reminded me —if the dirt had been washed off—she probably would be attractive. My artist hands twitch, remembering every detail. But that handle, I can't get past that. Where exactly is the rash for which she's named? I have strong suspicions I'd rather not find out. I don't recall spots on her face.

"Tommy," Road's attentions still on the other man. "You haven't given us much to go on. But we'll do what we can, okay?" His dark eyes find mine, an unspoken message managing to convey he comprehends, about as much as I do, how trying to find her would probably be harder than searching for a needle in a haystack, but not wanting to say it out loud. *Give the man some fucking peace.*

"Tommy?" a female voice asks. I'd forgotten Martha was standing there. When she's got Tommy's attention, she continues, "You can leave it to Blade and Road. They'll try to find your friend." Like Road, she throws me a look of warning. *Give the asshole some hope.*

"'Forcer find her?"

Giving in, I confirm, "I'll try."

Suddenly I'm enveloped in a bear hug, so tight I worry my ribs are going to break. "Tommy," I gasp.

I'm rescued by Martha. She's probably seen my plight from my face turning blue. "Tommy, put Blade down. How about we get you something to eat before you go on your way?"

He immediately releases me. I cough to get my lungs working again and send her a grateful chin lift.

"Tommy could eat." His head bobs up and down rapidly. Then he turns and starts walking to the garbage bins. He pauses, considers, then turns with a beaming smile, saying, "Thank you," before continuing in the direction he was heading.

"No, Tommy." I can tell Martha's half shocked, half trying not to laugh, as Tommy thought she'd given him permission to raid the bin. "You come with me to the kitchen door, and I'll get some proper food for you to take." His eyes open so wide they seem to take over his face. Especially when Martha adds, "You come back here when you want, okay? I'll get you some food and you can hear if Blade has managed to find, er, Rash." Her hesitation over the name suggests she shares my misgivings.

Then, fuck me, her words sink in. "Tommy, I can't promise anything." The likelihood is, he'll never see her again. Woman picked up off the streets? Never ends well in my book. Washed, scrubbed, a pretty thing like her? She'll probably be used and discarded, or sold.

CHAPTER 5

Tash

There's not a bad bone in Tommy, he's like an overgrown child. My heart breaks for the way he's forced to live, he shouldn't be on the street, he should be in some sort of assisted living somewhere. That said, he's got more street smarts than me. His whole education seems to have been learning how to survive living rough.

I've tried to ask him about his family, not knowing whether he understands, or if I'm right to assume they're dead when he simply answered, gone. He doesn't know how long he's been homeless, it's been forever in his eyes. Those same eyes which had glazed over when I'd asked how and where he'd lived before. He'd shaken his head. It was either so long ago he couldn't remember, or put to the deepest depths of his mind, as protection against hope of something unattainable.

Tommy gets food and brings it back to the alley. When another man followed him and tried to take it, he saw him off. People might try and take advantage because of his limited mental capacity, but he's got an innate ability to defend himself, and muscles to back up his posturing. In fact, I'd read real fear in the intruder's eyes—Tommy's lurching approach and mumbled words making him more afraid than he'd have been of a similarly sized normal man. He'd fled from the unpredictable and dangerous looking vagrant.

I know Tommy would never hurt me. He calls me his friend. It hadn't taken long before I numbered him among mine, though right now, that doesn't mean much. He's in the company of just one. It's a weird relationship. I'm older I'm sure though he doesn't know his age, and have all my wits about me. I should be the adult here, but I take his lead as he knows this life so much better than I.

Currently, I'm looking at him while pointedly moving my head side to side. Even if I told him the whole of my story, I doubt he'd understand. His whole existence revolves purely around surviving. Food, a safe sheltered place to rest. He's no knowledge of intrigue and betrayal, cruelty of men only expressed by unthinking teasing and chasing him off. I break it down into basics, keeping it simple. "Tommy, I prefer to only go out at night. I think there are bad men looking for me." To be honest, I'm not even totally sure of that. Even if they had been, the threat must diminish day by day. He must eventually turn his attention away from Tucson. Still, I remain worried enough to take precautions and keep hidden. "I don't want to come with you during the day."

"But they'll give you food." His mouth twists. "More food for Tommy and Rash."

Poor man is hungry. He's been sharing his rations with me. His valid point being, if I tagged along, I'd get my own allocation.

"Look. You go and eat. Don't worry about me. I'll scavenge around tonight. I'll find something. Maybe bring some food back for you, too?"

He looks crestfallen, then it's almost possible to see the gears whirring in his head, making a hopeful lopsided grin form on his face. "From the Devil men's place?"

"I thought you said it was too dangerous to go there." My run-in with the bikers hadn't exactly made me want to hurry back. I shiver slightly, remembering the intense man who'd let me get away with stale bread and cake.

Disappointed, he frowns. "You said they were kind to you."

I'm not sure that's really the word to use. They hadn't killed me, that's a plus. But they'd certainly run me off, the only kindness the food I'd been allowed to take with me. "I met the enforcer and the prospect, Tommy. They let me take bread they'd thrown away…"

"Good men," he nods emphatically. In Tommy's book, letting him have food is his definition of being a decent human being. Not for the first time I look at him and wonder how he can remain so cheerful and optimistic when he has nothing at all. If I ever get out of the predicament I'm in, I'll do my best to reverse our positions, and find some way I can help him.

Problem is, right at this moment, I don't have a clue when that might be, or how I could achieve it. Haven't even thought of moving forward. My sole focus has been on staying safe and taking one day at a time. The only long-term plan I've got is leaving the state and changing my name. Starting from the beginning all over again. But at the moment, such dreams are far beyond me. With nothing to my name, where do I start?

Tommy's tug on my sleeve breaks me out of my reverie. "Come on," he whines. "Tommy hungry." Giving me a shrewd look, he widens those puppy dog eyes. "Tommy keep you safe. Tommy fight bad men."

He's wearing me down. As my stomach growls loudly, I can't deny surviving on less than half a man's rations isn't enough for me either. I gaze at him again. He's tall, muscular enough, but would he be a match for anyone who's been sent after me? Could he take Grant on, if it's Grant who's been sent out to search? That's if I'm not paranoid and there's no one coming for me at all. It's been well over three weeks now. Maybe he's not even looking, has assumed I've just run, as any sensible person would, as far away from him as I could.

"Please?" It's as though he can see me weakening. "Rash hungry too." His hand rubs circles on his stomach, and his head tilts to one side.

Completely uncertain as to whether or not I'm doing the right thing, I press my hands to the ground and begin to stand, only to find myself aided by strong arms hauling me up. He hugs me tight, before letting me go, then takes hold of my hand, pulling me along behind him. "Hurry. We'll be at the back of the line."

I'm out of breath as I try to keep up with him, trusting he's taking me in the right direction. These are unfamiliar streets and I can only hope he knows the shortcuts he's taking me down. He seems to be heading somewhere different to where he'd taken me before.

As we go from street to street, my focus is on my feet, hoping not to trip. My hand's still held tightly in his big mitt. I'm being spun around corners. "Hey, Tommy. I can't keep up."

"Got to get there," he says, firming his grip. "They'll run out."

I would like to get there in one piece. Another tight turn. If I was a car I'd be over on two wheels; I throw my hand against the wall to push myself back upright when a loud squealing of brakes hurts my ears. Before I can turn, car doors slam and I'm being wrenched away from Tommy.

Tommy's not a seasoned fighter, he only looks the part. But his face darkens as he reaches to take back my hand. One of the men is faster, punching him hard in the face. Whatever's in Tommy's past, it wasn't physical abuse. He looks so shocked as he goes down, his hand touching his face, seeming puzzled when he pulls his fingers away and finds blood on them.

I try to escape the hold I'm in, wanting to go to him, comfort him as you would a child. But instead the second man puts his fist in my stomach, causing the air to rush out of me. Winded, I'm lifted off my feet and thrown in the back of the sedan. Both men get in the front seats fast while I'm recovering from the blow. The driver puts his foot to the accelerator, and then we're speeding through the streets of Tucson.

The man, who'd been behind me, now turns. I've been protectively bowed over my aching belly. As I straighten, I see a phone held to his ear, and that his face is one I recognise only too well.

There's triumph in his voice. "Got her, boss. Bringing her in now."

No!

What I'd been trying to avoid has happened. He had been searching. Now he's found me.

"Grant," I breathe out the fixer's name. "Let me go, please. I won't do or say anything. I'm no threat. Or give me some money and I'll get out of the state. I'll never show my face in Tucson again."

Grant shares a chuckle with the other man. "Those aren't our orders, sweetheart. We're taking you back. Shouldn't have run, now it will go worse for you."

What could be worse? Grant tried to kill me the last time I saw him. I stay silent, not wanting to know.

Grant leers back at me. "Your apartment was trashed. Word is, you were running from something, a debt unpaid, drugs perhaps? Thing is, you've disappeared. No one's looking for you, so no need to be careful now."

"Yeah," the driver, who I don't know, calls back over his shoulder. "We can have fun before offing you. As long as your body's not able to be found; dead women tell no stories."

"You can bet your bottom dollar we're going to have fun," Grant proposes. Fun for him, not me. I'd seen him leering at me before. He disgusts me.

Bile rises in my stomach at the suggestion of the apparently short future I'm facing, and what they'll put me through before ending my life. I'm shaking with fear, adrenaline making my heart beat so fast, I feel it thumping in my chest.

If they get me to their destination, I won't be leaving alive. The information I have could destroy everything Grant's employer has worked for. The promises I'd made to keep my mouth shut, completely worthless. As long as I'm alive, I'll be a threat.

My death warrant has already been signed. I won't have a chance to run again. Sentence will be carried out unless I find a way to escape.

Grant thinks he's got a terrified woman in the back seat. He's right. What he hasn't counted on is my sheer desperation. There'll be no talking my way out of my fate, no opportunity to plead my case, therefore anything would be better. As we start driving along streets I do know, in my head I plot the route. There's a turn up ahead; the car will have to slow. Every muscle is tense as I prepare to make my move, praying they've not engaged the childproof locks. This is it. I start counting down in my head… *Five, four, three, two…*

On one, I throw myself to the side, opening the handle, curling up, my arms protectively over my head. I hit the ground hard, jarring my shoulder badly but ignore it. My legs are fine so continuing my impetus I come out of the roll, get to my feet, and run.

I've found a good spot, an alley, a maze behind a row of shops. I keep pounding the ground, hearing footsteps coming after me. Bins I toss aside hoping to impede their progress. A chain-link fence. One arm's hanging useless by my side, using only the other, powered by sheer desperation, I climb over it. The thought that it's my life at stake making me Superwoman for the moment.

"There's the bitch!"

Shit! I haven't lost them. Spurring myself on, I ignore the pain, knowing I'll hurt worse if they catch me. *A road.* It's busy, but… I aim for a gap between the first two cars, the one in the outer lane slams on its brakes and I bounce off the hood, lurching myself into the opposite stream of traffic. *I'd rather be hit by a car than go back.* The gods must be with me. I'm over the opposite side. I don't look at what might be behind me.

Limping now, I continue to run, and run, and run. Finally, I come to a drainage ditch and let myself fall down.

It's a dangerous thing to do. Lightning flashes, thunder crashes and rumbles and large drops of rain are starting to fall. *I've got to get out of here.* Rain comes down harder. Puddles are forming at my feet. I try to stand. My initial adrenaline having worn off, I now realise, as well as my left arm hanging useless, my right leg is starting to seize up. *Must be one heck of a bruise from that car, but at least I don't think it's broken.* The sides are too steep to climb with one arm and one leg. I try to summon up my inner superhero again, but she's deserted me.

I start dragging myself on, hoping to find a place where the sides are less sheer and I can get out before a cascade of water that's almost certainly going to soon be charging down the wash, approaches me. Barely able to see through the near solid wall of rain now falling, I stumble and slip as mud forms. I go over hard, almost stunning myself on a rock.

Telling myself, if I'm going to drown, it's still got to be better than whatever Grant had planned, I stagger on. *There's a road ahead.* For a moment I hesitate, if I don't get out… I inch forward, the water up to my knees now. Cars are moving slowly past, still able to get through the water covering the road. *The sides are no longer vertical.* If I use all my remaining energy I can probably get out. *But what if Grant and his sidekick are in one of those cars?*

Give up. What have I got to live for now? *Stay here and drown.* I'm unable to see a future in front of me, whether I survive this or not, whether Grant captures me again. I've got nothing, and he won't stop looking. *Except… I won't, can't give in.* If I die, there will be no one to tell my story. He deserves the world to know what he's done.

Pain makes my fury worse.

With a sudden shout, I throw my injured body at the side of the wash, trying to gain traction with just one hand, my good foot digging into the soft earth. I make progress then, at last, I'm at the top, leaning over, heaving the contents of my near empty stomach onto the ground.

Knowing I've got to find somewhere to hide, knowing I've got to stay out of sight, I start moving again.

I was just in time. Cars are now coming to a stop, halted by the wash flooding the road. I don't even think of the narrow escape I've just had, instead check the cars lined up either side, hoping my luck has turned.

It appears that it has. There's no sign of the sedan.

Dragging myself I carry on, barely noticing the rain has eased off, now only a gentle drizzle is coming down. My brain working enough to formulate a plan. *I'll find somewhere to hole up.* Then, under the cover of darkness, I'll make my way back to the place I've come to think of as my temporary home.

CHAPTER 6

Blade

"We going to take this to Drummer?"

"Take what, Road?" I turn off my engine and leave my bike. "That a fuckin' vagrant's gone missing?"

"I liked the kid, Blade. Don't like giving him hope if we're not going to act on it."

"Kid?" I snort. "Fucker must be in his twenties. And what the fuck do you think we should do?"

Road waves his hands in exasperation. "I'm referrin' to the way he acted. What's his mental age do you think? Eight, ten? Not much fuckin' more. He shouldn't be on the streets. Should be being cared for somewhere."

"Lots of people like him live independent lives," I advise him.

"Yeah, with help. What fuckin' help has he got?" Road scoffs. "Now his friend, possibly his only friend, is gone." He pauses and looks puzzled. "You met her, Blade. Is she like him too?"

"Simple?" I think back. "Nah. But I didn't talk enough to ask what her level of education was," I reply drily.

"Knowing you, you probably scared the shit out of her."

Knowing me, I probably did.

"So you're just going to leave it." Road sounds disappointed.

I swing around. My fast step forward has him taking one back, presumably to get out of range of my fist. "I ask again,

Road, What the fuck do you suggest I do? Tucson's a fuckin' big place. She could have been taken anywhere."

"What about the car?"

I throw up my hands exasperated that my brother won't let this drop. "Tommy didn't know the model, let alone get a read of the license plate. There's more than one fucking white car in the city. We've nothing to go on, Road."

"I'd go looking myself, but I don't know what she looks like." He sounds angry.

"She's not on the streets any longer," I remind him. "Someone's snatched her."

He stares at me for a moment. "A woman. Young. Was Tommy right, was she pretty?"

I close my eyes, remembering her features again. "Yeah, he got that right. But she's not that young, late twenties, early thirties perhaps."

Road kicks a rock as though it's offended him. It rattles away over the gravel. "Still young enough to have a few years left in her. Homeless, presumably no kin. Pinched off the street. Yeah, reckon we know exactly what's going to happen to her."

I'm on the same wavelength. She's likely to become some man's toy. Maybe already has been played with and discarded. The thought makes me burn, but there's nothing I can do about it.

"If only we had a photo," Road says, half to himself.

"Yeah, well, we don't," I snap. Then realising I'm more annoyed with myself than with him, and all I'm doing is using the closest target to take out my pointless anger, I slap my hand on his shoulder. "I'll join you for a beer, later, Road."

Remembering my plan had been to sink my cock into a warm and willing pussy, I realise the turn the evening had taken has removed such impulse from my mind. There's something I'd rather be doing instead, something Road's last statement has triggered. My feet automatically turn in the direction of my suite.

Like most of my brothers, I have a room on the compound. Not that that description does it justice, it's a large bedroom, an adjacent bathroom, and a fucking balcony with views out across the desert and over to the Tucson Mountains. What I call my accommodation is more than many other bikers could ever dream of.

Entering my room, I put my keys down on the table, and walk to my desk. I stand, waiting a moment before sitting. *Do I want to do this?*

Since Jonah was killed, I haven't been able to suppress my desire to draw. It's like a beast raging inside, wanting to get out, my compromise being every drawing I've ever done has been destroyed. No one has ever discovered the useless talent I have. The time I wasted when I could have been learning to fight beside my brother. The guilt I've not shaken over the past twenty-four years hangs heavy on me.

What does it matter? There's no chance we'll find Rash. She's just become another statistic, not that anyone except Tommy would miss her. Another girl stolen from the streets. Another body to be used. Whatever I do is a waste of time. *Fuck it!*

If I don't do this, anything to help, will I just be abandoning one more person? If by using my talent, there's even a minuscule chance it might save her, shouldn't I do it?

If I'd possessed then what I do now, an ability to protect my brothers, Jonah would be alive. If I exercise my talent to do what hadn't helped then, could I now make a difference to someone else's life?

And why the fuck am I getting riled about a woman called Rash? I kick the wastepaper bin away with my foot, seeing it fall and scattering my burned drawings over the floor.

As thoughts war in my head, my hands move automatically. Without having made a conscious decision, I find I'm opening the drawer, sliding out my sketch pad then throwing it across the room with a roar. *I can't.*

I must.

Could I live with myself if I didn't do something to help, however useless it might appear to be? As if in preparation to start sketching her, details of Rash's face come into my mind. Three strides take me to the stricken pad full of blank pages, then I'm picking it up, going back to my desk, now taking a seat. A pencil finds its way into my hand without my brain issuing an instruction.

Leaning my head back, I close my eyes, summoning up the image in my head. It's as if the picture in my mind flows out through my fingers and onto the paper. After half-an-hour I pause, looking critically at what I'd produced. Another line here, a shading there. Squinting I see the vision of the woman I'd met so briefly. It's her. A perfect likeness. No police sketch artist could do better.

Picking it up, I hold it in both hands, considering the vision in front of me. Take away those stress lines, feed her so she'd lose that pinched look in her cheeks, and she'd be quite beautiful. I smile briefly. That snub nose, yeah, I'd captured it perfectly, it's cute. Under the dirt and in better light, I wouldn't be surprised to learn she has freckles.

My cock twitches. *What, now you're interested?* Better pipe down. Ain't letting you get anywhere near someone with that handle. No way. Uh uh.

I think of the club whores who I could drag out of bed if I so wish, any of them would be willing to service me. It's what we give them room and board for after all, and they're girls who'd ride biker cock all day long if they could. Diva? Nah, not in the mood. Paige? Not tonight. Allie? Pussy? My cock deflates as I think of them.

Fuck. I must be tired. An early night perhaps. That's what I need.

Not even bothering to go and have the promised drink with Road, I slide under the covers. The picture I'd drawn where I'd left it, on my bedside table. I'd like to say I tossed and turned all night worrying about her, but I don't. I sleep like an innocent child as though reproducing her likeness had worked to get her out of my head.

When I wake, refreshed, I narrow my eyes as I spy the drawing. It's done. Now what do I do? If I burn it like so many others, the reason why I'd drawn it becomes worthless. But how could it help find a proverbial needle? Feeling on edge, I fold it, and slide it into my pocket.

Deciding I might as well get an early start, I'm down at the shop before anyone else, getting ahead on some of the cars which have been brought in for service. I change filters, top off oil, replace parts. Directing the work of others and sorting out customers. Enjoying the camaraderie of working alongside my brothers, the hours pass fast. I barely seem to have gotten here when it's time to put up tools and after grabbing a much-needed dinner, join my brothers in church.

The normal business is discussed, then Drummer asks for an update from Peg and myself about our meeting with Lawson.

I let Peg take the lead, giving a factual representation of what went down. Then I add my interpretation, "There's something dodgy there, Prez. Lawson isn't being straight with us."

"'Spect he's just being a politician," Beef quips. "They can never tell it as it is. If they did, they'd never get votes."

"Yeah, point right there," Rock nods across the table toward his friend. "Vote for me and you'll pay higher taxes, and when you get sick, I only ask that you go into a corner and die quietly 'cause you'll get no fuckin' help from the state."

I let those and other comments work their way around the table, then enlighten them. "It's more than that. We hadn't really got a handle on what he's asking us to do. Then his campaign manager got a phone call and the meetin' was abruptly cut short."

"Got a bad feelin', Prez," Peg takes over again, his features drawn into a frown. "There's a reason he came to us. Oh, I know that you're the businessman around town nowadays, but I don't think that's influenced him. My gut feel is that he expects us to use force, and maybe not keep it the right side of legal."

"Or, he's scared for his life, and wants someone prepared to do whatever it takes to protect him."

"Ain't being paid enough to take a bullet, Prez," Hyde observes.

Prez's steely gaze fixes on the brother who'd last spoken. After a few seconds, he gives a sharp nod. "I signed a contract that we'd be there at his gigs to provide additional security and crowd control if needed. Nothing more, nothing less. That's all we do, okay? I'm not asking anyone to put themselves in danger. Fucker's not worth more than one of us."

"And there are a hundred more where he came from," Jekyll observes.

As the conversation winds down about Lawson, and everyone's ready to move onto something new, I notice Road's watching me. He mouths a question. My brow creases, then I sigh and raise my chin toward him. I suppose it wouldn't hurt to let my brothers in on what went down yesterday.

Just when I'm about to open my mouth, Prez raps his fingers on the table. "I wanted to get your impression of him before I brought this up. Lawson's been in contact with me."

I sit up. "Complainin' about us already, Prez? Hardly saw him for five minutes."

"Blade didn't even get out his knife," Peg's eyes gleam. "He behaved himself."

I shoot him the finger, then feel the need to get out my knife and start spinning it. As intended, it stops when it's pointing toward the sergeant-at-arms.

"Nah, Blade." Prez ignores Peg and addresses my question instead. "You said you felt there was something he wasn't sayin'. Turns out your gut feel was right."

That makes me straighten my back. I tilt my head at the prez.

"Lawson is apparently a happily-married man."

I interrupt, "Assumed that. Saw a pic of the wife and kids on his desk."

Drummer nods. "Yeah, well, there's a bitch, he thinks she's going to make trouble. He thought he had it handled himself, but she's gone off the radar."

"Bitch?" Peg queries.

"Bitch who's coming up with a different story about him. Spreading what he calls lies about his fidelity or otherwise as she sees it."

I scoff. "Lies?"

"That's how he tells it."

"Smoke and fire," Peg states.

"You should know," comes from a few of the brothers. Yeah, a good analogy when he's married to a firefighter.

Peg's snarl gets them shutting up pretty damn fast. "As I was sayin'," he roars, "where there's smoke, there's usually a fire. What if Lawson's trying to shut this bitch up, and what she's sayin' is the truth?"

Drummer's eyes shutter, it's impossible to know what he's thinking. "He's asked us to find her, explain a few of the facts of life, and that it's not worth her while to make waves."

"Just talk to her?" That doesn't sound right. There must be more to it than that.

Prez's eyes meet mine. A look of understanding passes between us. Then he says, firmly, "Whatever Lawson might expect, want, us to do, I want to find this woman before he does. I don't give a shit whether there's truth to what he's worried she'll say or not, but I just rather we get our hands on her than his goons. I reckon we can make her see the benefits of keeping quiet without hurting her. Lawson? I'm not so sure."

Peg looks at me. "Reckon he'd be ruthless enough to harm her?"

I roll my head around, loosening the kinks in my shoulders, thinking what I know of the man which is very little. Remembering that impersonal room. "He wants to be elected, Peg. He's hungry for it. Haven't got a handle on how far he'd go yet."

"You think," Beef's looking serious for once, "he came to us to make her disappear? For good?"

"That's my concern, Beef," Prez confirms. He picks up a folder I hadn't paid much attention to before, and extracts some printouts, passing them around the table. Sitting next to the VP, I get mine early, and am staring at it in amazement while the rest of the photos are going around. Prez taps his copy and repeats, "I want to find this woman before he does."

Beef snorts. "If I'd seen her I'd certainly know it." As he's leaning back in his chair, it's clear he's clutching his dick.

Rock whistles. "Nice lookin' bitch."

"Hey, man. You're expecting a fuckin' baby any day now. Shouldn't be lookin' at bitches."

Joker nudges Marvel. "He's probably not gettin' any nowadays. Have you seen the size of Becca?"

"What would you fuckin' know about it, anyway?" Bullet leans forward and quips, causing a burst of good-natured laughter around the table.

"I can appreciate a good-looking piece of ass. Even if I wouldn't be touching it," Rock observes. "And there are various positions you know." The last he directs pointedly toward Joker.

"Bitches get horny when they're about to give birth," Wraith smirks, sharing a grin with Drummer.

Rock's lips curve up, then he grows serious again. "All I was going to point out, is that if any red-blooded male—of course, not you, Joker—came across a girl who looked like this, it would be hard to miss her."

"Well," Drummer closes his folder again, "just keep your eyes open. If you do come across her, Lawson wants to know where she is, and he wants to take it from there. I want her brought here instead."

"We got a name?" Mouse asks.

"Emmalina Fielding," Drummer tells him.

"I'll start looking," Mouse confirms. "Woman like that shouldn't be too hard to locate. She's not someone you'd forget easily. Good lookin' bitch."

"What has she got on him?" I ask, my teeth gritted. For some reason, I don't like the way my brothers are talking about her. I'm trying to sort out a puzzle in my head. *The name doesn't fit.*

"That they had an affair, perhaps?" Prez replies, looking at me strangely. "Lawson wasn't very forthcoming. That seemed to be what he was suggesting, and that she could come up with a pack of lies that could put his campaign off the rails."

Now it's me who catches Road's eyes. He's looking puzzled, clearly having no idea of what I'm about to say, or, rather, do. Bowing my head, I take a couple of seconds to send up a silent apology to Jonah, then slide my hand into my cut. Taking out the thick piece of paper, I unfold it, then slide it, wrong way up towards Prez.

Curious, he turns it over. His eyes sharpen, his brow furrows. Then he picks up a copy of the photo he'd just passed around and lays it next to my drawing. After a minute, he raises his head and stares at me. "Where did you get this? Was drawn by a fucking artist, I can tell that." His eyes narrow. "Did you take it from Lawson's office?" He looks down at it again. "Must have been done by a professional. Christ, it's fuckin' quality. Can almost hear her speaking. Wonder if she was in fancy dress. Halloween, perhaps?"

"I drew it," I say quietly.

While the other brothers look on, their faces displaying varying states of confusion, Prez's face goes black. "Credit me with some fuckin' intelligence, Blade. Now tell me the fuckin' truth. There's no doubt this is a picture of the woman Lawson is after. We've spent the last half-hour discussing that we've got to find her first. Seems you've got info you're not sharing. So, tell me straight. Where did you get this fuckin' picture?" His fist meets the table with a thump, an emphasis he wants an acceptable answer to his question.

"I drew it." My voice is louder. My knife spins fast in front of me.

Drummer lurches forward. "Never fuckin' doubted you in all the time I've known you, Brother. But I want the fuckin' truth. Where. Did. You. Get. This?" he thunders, his tone increasing to the extent the whole room reverberates with his words.

"I. Drew. It," I yell back. Reaching around Wraith, I grab Drummer's folder, snatch the pen that Dollar's still holding, and quickly start to sketch. Within seconds I've drawn a credible likeness of Drummer.

Drummer's stare widens in disbelief. He shakes his head, his fingers tug on his beard as he's forced to re-evaluate all that he knows of me. He snarls, his voice menacingly deep, as if I've kept a dead body from him, rather than this secret. "I've known you for getting on eighteen years, Blade. Thought I fucking knew everything about you. How the fuck have you hidden talent like this? Why have I not seen any of your artwork before?"

I'm riled. Upset I've had to out myself. My knife hits the table point down as I blurt out, "Because I normally fuckin' burn them." The blade quivers in the silence that follows, all eyes appear to be on it, and not me.

There are a hundred questions they'll be itching to ask, but are wise enough to hold them back. Drummer slides my sketch to Peg, who examines it, then passes it around the table. When it reaches Road, his eyes open wide and the brief spell of quiet is broken when he asks, "That's her, isn't it? The woman from the Wheel Inn. You must have drawn this last night. She's not in fancy dress. She's a vagrant." He's leapt to the right conclusion. I nod to confirm he's correct.

Beef snatches the paper from Road. His eyes widen as he too matches it to the photo. "Apart from the fact she looks like a scarecrow in your sketch, you've captured her completely, Blade. Ain't no doubt it's her."

"Think one of you better start talking," Drummer growls, looking at me then at Road, finally settling back on me. "Why have you drawn a picture of Emmalina Fielding? And what the fuck is this about last night?"

"He's been having dreams." Mouse is grinning. "Hallucinations. Our brother here's got second sight." He leans forward, tapping the picture that's still in Beef's hands. "His visions must be the clue to where we're going to find her."

"I haven't been having any fuckin' dreams," I say, menacingly quiet. A warning I'm close to the end of my tether. While they wait for my explanation, I take out my smokes and light one, pulling the ashtray closer to me before I commence, "I met her at the Wheel Inn the other night. The day Fergus came back, and Peg sent him along with me. Martha asked us to investigate a crash out back. Went out to check, and that's when we found her. She was a vagrant, wasn't doing much harm, just robbing the food bin. We had words. I sent her on her way."

Drummer isn't the prez for nothing. There's not much he misses. His gaze moves to a man seated further down the table. "So where do you come in, Road?"

"I haven't seen her. But Blade was called down to the Wheel Inn yesterday afternoon as a fucker was making a disturbance and asked to see him."

Wraith nods, Drummer looks surprised. "What fucker? And why, Blade? What has this woman got to do with him?"

It's Road who answers, "Prez, I was at the restaurant. When he appeared, he was on his own. I wasn't even sure that it was Blade he wanted to talk too. All I got out of him were the words, 'forcer and Prospt. Needed to get him off the premises, he was making such a commotion. I thought it worth a shot it was Blade he wanted, so got the VP to pass on a message."

"Why didn't you just run him off? He pull a gun on you or something?"

"Nah," Road taps his forehead. "The fucker's simple. Hard to make out what he was sayin'. When Blade appeared, seemed I'd interpreted him correctly." He pulls my drawing away from Beef, and taps it. "He was calling her his friend. He was distraught, almost unintelligible, but we finally got his story out of him. Said she'd been pushed into a car and taken. She was punched, apparently, and when he tried to stop whoever it was, they gave him a black eye." He raises his chin in my direction. "For some reason she'd told him Blade and Fergus had been kind to her."

Yeah. Kind. Right. I don't understand why the thought the extent of my kindness was only to let her keep hold of some mouldy bread makes me feel guilty. As I look down at my hands, wondering whether I should have done more to help her, Prez keeps up his inquisition.

"Go on."

Road shrugs. "That's all really. He could give us no info. Only a name. Must be a handle. Didn't call her Emmalina or anything like that. He called her Rash."

"Fuck! Don't want nothing to do with a bitch with that handle." Jekyll shudders. "Reckon Lawson wants her to stop her spreading diseases?"

"He's just found out she's given him the clap." Marvel's grinning.

"Or crabs," Hyde suggests.

"Shut the fuck up!" Drummer glares. "Road, continue."

Road shrugs. "Blade worked out it was the girl he let take the discarded food. Tommy, the fucker I'm talking about, thought letting someone have leftover shit was a sign this 'forcer was a good man.'"

"She must have read your cut," Wraith nods at me. I raise my chin back. Yeah, that flash is still just about readable. My name, well, over the years that's had dirt and grease smeared over it.

"And?" Drummer prompts.

"He wanted Blade to find her." Road shrugs. "We hadn't a clue where to start. No idea who had taken her."

I step in. "The quickest way to get him out of our hair was to tell him we'd try to locate her. He was satisfied with a half-assed promise we'd do what we could."

Drummer indicates; Road slides my drawing down the table. He picks it up and looks at it. "For whatever reason, she's in demand. Wanted by a politician and a retarded man."

"Aren't they one and the same thing?" Peg raises his eyebrows.

Peg's got a point. I grin as Prez turns to me. But before he can speak, Peg continues, tapping his fingers to his beard, "That phone call, while we were with Lawson…"

Fuck. He's connected dots faster than me. "He's lost her." I offer an explanation at the blank looks coming my way. "We said the meeting ended abruptly. Turner spat out that they'd lost a 'her'. Fuck me. If that was about this woman, *Rash* or Emmalina as it seems they're one and the same, they had her, but she got away. What's the timeline? When did he ask you to look for her, Prez? After our meeting?"

Prez is catching on too. "It was," he says, grimly. "If you're right, I don't like it." Prez has got that look that suggests he's thinking. His brow is scrunched; his hands push back through his salt and pepper hair. "Okay. As you know, he didn't give me the reason why he wanted her, but if the fucker you met was right, he's not after a peaceful sit-down conversation. Otherwise, why was she hit? Don't fuckin' care for fuckers who hurt women." He raps his fingers on the table. "She got to you, didn't she, Blade? Enough for you to come out of the closet with your drawing." His eyes meet mine. "So what happened? You met this asshole, drew this picture to help you find her?"

I stiffen. "Like you, don't much care for assholes who punch and take women off the street. Especially those already down on their luck. Yeah. We hadn't anything to go on, so I came back and drew her as I'd remembered her." I don't tell him about the strange compulsion that led me to commit her features to paper.

"I want to find her." He looks down the table. "I want all of us looking for her. I want to know what hold she has on Lawson and why he wants her so badly. Mouse, dig up all you can find on Emmalina Fielding, and also look at who Lawson's got work-ing for him. It wasn't a friendly pick-up, so we're looking at rough types. And you, Blade, you know how to find this Tommy again? Got more questions to ask him. She might have told him why she's so important to Lawson."

"You won't get much out of him, Prez." Road shakes his head.

But you never know what might have got trapped in Tommy's brain. We hadn't pushed him hard at the time. Getting rid of him had been our priority. "I'll get in touch with Martha. I'll warn Sandy too. I think it's a pretty fair bet he'll go back to the Wheel Inn. Martha offered to feed him." My mouth twists remembering how the poor fucker had gone straight to the trash. He would have been happy enough, given permission to paw through what had been thrown out. His look of delight as Martha promised him real food had twisted something in my gut. *People really live like this?* That feeling of guilt deepens. I'd hesitated before allowing Rash to take that shit. I'm an asshole. Wouldn't have been much skin off my nose to get her something fresh to eat. But then, I hadn't wanted to encourage the likes of her to come back.

"Yeah, have a word with Martha and Sandy, Blade. I want to know as soon as he turns up." Prez's stare goes around the table. "The rest of you—let's get out there and start asking around. Find her."

"We giving her to Lawson?" Hyde's mouth has dropped open.

"Have you even been listening?" Prez roars. "I want her brought back here. I need to know what the fuck is going on before she goes anywhere near him. If Lawson thinks he can use us and play us for fools, he's got another thought coming. And, Blade? My office. Now."

CHAPTER 7

Blade

I place a quick call to Martha, asking that she keep Tommy there should he turn up, then follow Prez into his office.

"Blade," he nods, once we're both seated. He reaches behind him for the scotch that he keeps ready and pulls down two glasses. I'm not going to turn that down. It's the good shit.

"Whatcha want to know, Prez?" I have my suspicions, which make me sit awkwardly in the chair.

His eyes fix on me as he pushes a full shot glass over. "I want to know why I've known you getting on for eighteen years, and you've never let on what a talent you have. And," he raises his hand to show he's not finished, "I know you spat it out in there, probably wouldn't have gone there if you hadn't been pushed, but why you fuckin' destroy everything you draw."

I'd known this was coming from the time I opened my mouth, had known Prez would have picked up on that. It's hardly the actions of a rational man, is it? Sitting forward, I clasp my hands between my knees, wondering whether there's any way I can avoid this coming out, but I can't refuse Prez. I sigh. "You know I had a brother." I don't wait for his confirmation, he knows I had, and that he was killed. "Well, Jonah was strong. He worked at a gym, learned martial arts. He was streetwise too."

"You were, what, twelve when he died?"

I was. I nod. "I wasn't like him at all. I spent all my time drawing. A scholarship to art school was already being spoken about. I had a talent."

"Fuckin' saw that for myself."

I shrug off the compliment. "Didn't do me much good. When it counted, I knew I'd been wasting my time. Jonah was killed in front of me because I didn't have a clue how to help, nor the strength to act on it if I had. If I'd gone with him to the gym, learned to fight like he'd wanted me to, I might have been able to save his life."

Drummer indicates my whisky; I take a sip. "So you burn your drawings…?"

"I can't stop it, Prez." An automatic response, akin to a shudder goes through me as I try to explain. "It's like I'm possessed or something. Sometimes I just need to get my thoughts out on paper." I rub my hands through my hair. "Then I feel so fuckin' guilty that I've been wastin' time."

He refills his glass, I put my hand over mine in case I need to go out again tonight. Might need my wits about me. "How many set upon you and your brother?"

"Four."

"Four," he repeats. Then asks, sharply, "And you could have taken them on? At twelve years of age?"

"I could have done something. Fought them," I respond, just as tersely. "Had I worked out with Jonah as he'd wanted me to."

"Then I wouldn't have an enforcer sitting opposite me. You'd have been dead along with him. Way I see it, the only reason you were left alive is that you weren't a threat."

"I tried, Drum, I tried."

"I'm sure you did, Blade. But you've been punishin' yourself all these years for something that wasn't your fault."

"But I could have done more if I'd had the skills…"

"Four against two ain't good odds. You probably weren't even grown."

I hadn't been. "I was a weed. Small, no muscles. Did my growin' late."

"Here's the thing, Blade. You're still seeing what happened through the eyes of a child. Fuckin' shame you lost your brother. Fuckin' terrible it happened in front of you. But no one could blame you. You've got to stop blamin' yourself."

"I still miss him, Prez."

He nods. "Know you do." He waits a moment, then changes tack, "Art scholarship, eh? Bet your brother was fuckin' proud of you."

I huff a laugh. "He was on me to do my homework often enough." Thinking back, I add, "Yeah, he didn't think much of my drawings, but thought I had a ticket out of that slum."

"Then honour his fuckin' memory, Blade." At my sharp indrawn breath, Drummer replaces the bottle behind him. Then turns back. "What would he have wanted? Way I see it; you've tried to step into his shoes and made a fuckin' good job of it. Fuck knows you're the best fuckin' enforcer I could have by my side. No one knows better than I how hard that role is." I'm listening, Drummer was the enforcer before he became Prez. "Takes its fuckin' toll on you. Now I know what's lying underneath—an artist's sensibilities—can fuckin' see, for you, it's even harder. Would Jonah have wanted you to go through life pretendin' to be something you're not?"

"I'm not pretendin'. If you're saying I'm not good at what I do..."

His hand slaps down on the table. "Did I fuckin' say that? Were those the fuckin' words that came out of my mouth? Not saying that for a minute." My mouth snaps shut. Drum's hand smooths his beard. "All I'm sayin' is perhaps he wouldn't have wanted you to suppress this side of yourself. It's no crime to want to let out your emotions on paper. You can do both, you know. Knock heads together and paint."

That's a lot to lay on me. At twelve years old all I'd let myself feel was the crushing guilt that I hadn't been able to do anything. That my hobby which kept me locked up inside had been wrong and had led to my brother's death. Left me with the overriding urge to protect and defend, which in turn had brought me to the position I hold now. What would Jonah have wanted?

I'm sitting in front of my prez, not speaking. But he's giving off no vibes he wants me to leave, just giving me the space to digest what he's said.

When my phone pings, I'm filled with relief. A welcome interruption, sending me back into the world I've adopted since my brother's death. A world where I don't need to do much more than just react.

The text is from Martha. I read it, then tell him, "Prez, Tommy's at the Wheel Inn."

He raises an eyebrow and queries with a quirk of his mouth, "Why you still here?"

I grin, stand, and turn, but before I get to the door, Drummer calls out, "And stop burning those fucking drawings, Blade."

Crossing the clubroom, I put my fingers to my mouth and let out a loud whistle. It attracts the attention of the man I wanted, Road, and also, Marvel. "Tommy's back," I shout. Both men get to their feet. I nod. Yeah, Marvel can come along if he's volunteering. The more the fucking merrier.

The journey seems to take no time at all. Riding on autopilot my thoughts swing back and forth from finding Rash and answering Drummer's question about why she's stayed on my mind, and, whether I'm dishonouring my brother's memory by not allowing the artist in me out.

"Fergus has got Tommy out back," Martha rushes over as we park. "He thinks he's done something wrong when we asked him to wait for you. He's a bit agitated."

"For fuck's sake."

"Blade, keep it down. Calm's the way to go with Tommy."

Road might be right, but I don't do calm very well. I take a deep breath, walk around the outside of the building, out back to where Tommy's crouched on the ground, his head in his hands rocking back and forth on his heels.

"Didn't do nothing, didn't do nothing. Tommy didn't do nothing."

"I never said you did." Fergus's frustration comes through in his voice, and his face shows his relief when he sees me approaching. "See, Tommy. Blade's here. Blade's a good man, isn't he?"

"Blade?" Tommy looks up suspiciously, then sees me. He leaps to his feet, lumbers over, puts both arms around me and shouts gleefully, "'Forcer!"

"Got you a new handle," Road mutters out of the corner of his mouth, unable to suppress his mirth. While I'm just trying to breathe with this monster of a man/boy crushing me, Marvel chuckles by Road's side. I regret allowing him to tag along, he's doing nothing to help.

"Tommy, let go," I rasp out with my last bit of air. Thankfully he does, allowing me to take in sufficient oxygen to re-inflate my lungs. I lean over, gasping, checking none of my ribs are broken.

Road goes to speak; I wave him down. He told me to handle this; having seen Tommy's reaction to me, I know I need to step up and take the lead. For some reason, the kid trusts me. I indicate a waist-high wall; Tommy follows and sits beside me. Both Road and Marvel hang back.

"Tommy, we think Rash might have escaped from the men who took her."

His face goes blank. For a moment I don't think he's heard me. I'm just about to repeat myself, when he grins. "Rash, free?"

"We think so." I can't guarantee it. We've only got Lawson's connection and that blurted out phrase to go on. "We need to look for her. Can you think where she might have gone?"

Again, Tommy's face goes blank. Reasoning he doesn't understand me, I open my mouth to try to ask the question a different way, when Road's hand on my shoulder stops me. "He's thinking," he mouths.

Analysing Tommy's expression again, my brother might be right. Slowly the vacant look disappears, and his face screws up instead.

"Tommy knows," he says at last. But he's shaking his head and doesn't look happy. "Rash and Tommy stayed in an alley. Safe there. No one came. Tommy didn't want to go there alone. Tommy stay somewhere else."

"But you think she might have gone back there?"

His eyes close, his hands open and shut. He's struggling to find the right words. "Rash not know streets. Not like Tommy."

I exchange a look with Road. Interpreting what he's saying, he might be onto something. If she's not been living rough long, she might head for a place she had felt secure.

"Was that where they found you? The men with the car, Tommy?"

A negative gesture of his head. "No. Far away."

It seems like it could at least be somewhere to start. "Can you take us there, Tommy?"

His face brightens, his rapid mood swings taking me by surprise. "Forcer stay with Tommy there?" he asks, hopefully.

"Might be an idea, Blade. If she's not there now, she might return at some point." My eyes narrow at Road, expecting to find him grinning. I do not want to spend my night sleeping in an alley with Tommy, waiting for a woman who may or may not turn up, and who's probably diseased. Far better things I could be doing with my time. My brother, however, is looking serious, though beside him, Marvel snorts a laugh.

But Road certainly isn't fucking around. Rather than reject the idea, I begin to embrace it. I'd been charged with finding this girl by my prez, however slim a chance it is, I'll have to take it. In the morning, Tommy can show me where she was taken if she doesn't turn up.

I resign myself to an uncomfortable night. "Where's the alley, Tommy? What street?"

He's in thinking mode again, closed down. But this time, he doesn't know the answer. The sad shake of his head indicates he can't identify it by name. Then, as swiftly he brightens. "Can take 'Forcer there."

'Forcer is getting mightily fed up with his new name, and right now, regretting he hasn't got a cage. Only one thing for it. "You ever been on a motorcycle, Tommy?"

"No," he replies, again looking sad, as if he's missed out on the finer things in life. "No motorcycle ride for Tommy."

"Look at the size of him," Road speaks quietly into my ear, quickly cottoning on to my thinking. "If he mucks around, he could have you off balance."

Marvel whistles air in through his teeth and shakes his head.

I can't see another option, and surely, it can't be too far. "Tommy. Would you like to have a ride on mine? You can direct me where to go."

It's like the sun has come out. He leaps up, jumping with excitement the way five-year-old Amy does. "Tommy ride motorcycle. Yay." Both hands are in the air waving over his head. His reaction brings a smile to my face. To be honest, though I don't express it the same way, it's about how I feel every time I ride.

"Come on then."

Road walks behind, shaking his head. "Gonna end in tears," he mutters.

Marvel slaps his hand on my back. "Good luck, Brother." He sounds like he means it.

I mount my bike, tell Tommy to get on behind, then I instruct him carefully, speaking slowly. "Move with me, okay? If I do this," I tell him, leaning to the side, "you do the same. Can you do that?" I'm pleased when Tommy leans at the same angle as me. "No further, or we'll both fall off."

"Move like you."

"That's right." To see if he'll copy me again, I lean the other way. Tommy does too. "You're a natural," I tell him. "Now, hold those handles, there and there." I wait until he does. I don't instruct him to put his arms around me, unwilling to be subjected to one of his bear hugs while I'm riding. "Hold tight and don't let go."

"Tommy won't let go."

Looking down, I see he's already holding so tight, even under the weak light of the street lamp his knuckles are white. "Now put your feet on the foot rests." As I point them out, he does. Planting my feet firmly to take his not inconsiderable weight, I can't prevent my concerned glance toward Road and Marvel.

"You going to be alright?" Road tips his head.

I nod. I'll have to be. "Tommy. I'll ride slow. You shout the directions, okay?" This isn't going to be easy, a bike's harder to control with someone of his size behind me at slow speeds. But hey, I like a challenge.

"We'll follow. Pick up the pieces," Marvel smirks as he goes to his own bike.

I start the engine, feeling Tommy jump at the loud rumble from the pipes. Then he's hollering with pleasure as I put it into first and ease off, correcting the wobble by shifting my weight.

He shouts instructions into my ear. Sweat's pouring off me ten minutes later when he's calling out, 'slow down', then 'stop'. The alley is barely visible from the street. I tell Tommy to get off, struggling to hold the bike steady as he does. Then, balanced again, kick down the stand and throw my leg over the seat.

Road's walking to the gap between the buildings, a Maglite in his hand. He lights the pavement down the alley. "Can't see anything," he calls back. Marvel approaches with a second flashlight. Even with two, there's no woman in sight.

Tommy isn't fazed, just pushes past us, feeling his way down with a hand against what is clearly a familiar wall. As he disappears, I realise it's longer than I'd first thought. Taking out my own small flashlight, I follow him down, having to squeeze past a large industrial garbage bin.

"Rash?" Tommy hisses.

There's no response. I'm turning to my brothers to say this was a bust, when suddenly Tommy gives an agonised squeal.

"Rash!" He turns, comes running back to me and tugs urgently on my cut. "Rash hurt!"

"Road, take Tommy." Tommy's more than upset, he's visibly agitated. I want to get in and see what we're dealing with. As I squeeze past him, my light beam lands on what at first looks like a bundle of rags. I start to think Tommy's made a mistake, when I take one step more, and see the shape of a human. A female.

"Rash?" I drop to my knees, while from behind me I can hear a frustrated Road and Marvel.

"Settle down, man. Let Blade see what's wrong." That from Road.

Then from Marvel, "Tommy, settle for fuck's sake."

Ignoring the commotion behind me, I look down to see startled, scared eyes, looking into mine. Christ. He was right. She is hurt. And quivering with terror.

"You're alright, sweetheart. We've got you now," I murmur quietly, soothingly. Or at least that's how I hope I sound. "You're going to be alright."

CHAPTER 8

Tash

Cradling my useless arm, trying to ignore the throbbing in my leg, once darkness had fallen I'd forced my stiffened body up from the place where I'd hidden all day, using the wall and one hand to help me. Wondering whether Tommy would even be there, I crossed the city slowly, carefully, eyes and ears open for anyone who might be on the lookout for me.

The alley I'm heading for had felt safe. *But maybe that was only with the big man/boy to protect me.* He hadn't been able to stand up to the thugs Seb had sent, but then, not many people would. He got hit. *He'll be hurting.* How would he deal with that? Perhaps he'll be long gone, faraway. I'm pinning my hopes on him being there, waiting for me, hoping I'll return. I need time to heal. Tommy would look after me as best he can, at the least, being able to scavenge for food. While he couldn't take on Seb's men, his very size is enough to discourage most people from interfering with us.

My head says he's my only friend or the only person I can trust to hide me. Of course I know other people, but Seb will be aware of my contacts and will be watching for me to seek help from them. I can't draw anyone else into my problems. Problems, of my own making. My own stupidity. Why had I gotten involved with the man in the first place?

Eventually, I find the alley. I ease my way down, past the garbage bin and find the cardboard we'd been using, wet from another summer monsoon. With my good foot, I kick it out of the way, then sink down, trying to convince myself, just because Tommy isn't here right at this moment, doesn't mean he won't be returning. I'm out of all other ideas.

My stomach growls, but I used all my strength coming here. Now, as I sink to the floor, acknowledging how much I'm hurting, I know I won't be moving again anytime soon.

Sebastian Lawson. Seb. Why did I ever get mixed up with him? Oh, he's good looking in a clean-cut way, respectability oozes off him. He's got money, manners and charm by the bucket load. I didn't realise it was all a cultivated façade until I really got to know him. By then, I was trapped. I was never the partner I thought I'd been, instead, I was just his plaything. Now I'm worthless to him—I'm a liability he wants to dispose of. I can't let him get his hands on me again.

Which means, I've got to get out of Tucson. But how do I do that? I've no money, not even enough for a bus fare. He's so powerful, I'm living a daydream if I think I can continue to evade him.

I could bring him down.

But who would believe me? He's got far more backing than I would have, and I know some of the cops are in his pocket. Many people are banking on him being elected, have paid good money to see him in power. It's not only him to whom my existence causes a problem. I trusted Seb, he turned out to be the wrong person to put my faith in. Who's to say my obvious poor judgement of character wouldn't mislead me again? Keep my head down, my mouth firmly shut and try to survive until things die down and I'm at a safe distance, then I'll destroy him. That thought keeps me going and not giving up. That I'll get my vengeance eventually.

I try to get comfortable, moving to ease my stiffening muscles, stifling the cry when I knock my injured shoulder. I never believed I would sink this low. Hell, I'm an educated woman with a degree, how is it that I never saw what Seb really was? How could he have misled me so easily? And how did I let him have such control over my life?

Had I really ever loved him? If I had, that emotion had been killed stone-cold dead when he'd taken so much from me.

Now the rush of adrenaline has faded, I start to feel weak both from the pain, and as a result of my exertions. I'd always considered myself fairly fit, but have never run as much as I had to today. Those long daylight hours I'd stayed out of sight, I hadn't allowed myself to relax for a second. My eyes close. I snap them open, scared of someone creeping up on me. Worried Grant and perhaps Seb's other men will still be searching and won't take long before they discover where I'm hiding. I won't be able to escape again, I'm finished. I haven't the strength to run anymore. I'm banking everything on Tommy returning, not daring to allow myself to consider what I'll do if he doesn't appear.

Despite my efforts, I drop into a fitful sleep, startling myself awake at every night sound piercing the darkness.

When I awake it's daylight, and I'm alone. I can't move my arm at all, and my leg feels swollen. *Tommy hasn't come back.* The tears uselessly falling show me how much I'd vested in my companion finding me. I try to get up, I can't. Falling back against the brickwork, I realise there's nowhere to go, even if I could get myself moving. The danger of exposing myself too great. Right now, my options are limited.

The alley feels safe though. No need to move if I don't have to. Tommy may still come back.

I spend the day going between worrying and dozing, ignoring my hungry stomach growling. Finally, as night starts to fall, I slide into sleep once again.

An agonised squeal wakes me, and heavy footsteps move toward me. "Rash!" Then the sounds move in the other direction. "Rash hurt."

My immediate relief at hearing Tommy's voice dies as I realise someone's with him, and then another man's deep tones reach me.

"Road, take Tommy," he snaps quickly in a voice that sounds vaguely familiar, but I can't place it. *There is more than one I hear.* A large shape drops to his knees in front of me. He's shining a torch blindingly into my eyes, I raise my good arm to shield my face from the beam, unable to see the features of the man who's spoken. *One of Seb's men?* Despite the warm evening, a chill floods through me.

I hear Tommy's scuffles as he tries to get free, and someone, trying to calm him. "Settle down, man. Let Blade see what's wrong. Tommy, settle for fuck's sake."

Blade? Who the hell's Blade? Quickly I run through the names I know of Seb's men, but I can't recall anyone called that. But sensing a trick, believing they've conned Tommy into giving away my location, thinking how stupid I've been to pin my hopes on a man with the mental faculties of a child, I fold in on myself, all my hopes of staying free, and alive, leaving me.

"You're alright, sweetheart. We've got you now," the man called Blade murmurs in a low, gruff voice. "You're going to be alright."

I dredge through my memory, trying to remember when I've heard that tone before, but nothing comes to mind. It's just that it sounds as though I've previously heard it.

"You're going to be okay, Rash." His hands come out to soothe me.

"Ow!" I flinch away, knocking my arm again, and for the second time my useless arm makes contact with the brickwork behind me, and the jolt to my shoulder causes an additional involuntary protest to escape my mouth.

The flashlight plays over me, blinding me, as he sucks in a sharp breath. "How badly are you fuckin' hurt?" he rasps.

"I'm fine," I lie. "Please, leave me alone."

"You're about as far from fuckin' fine as you could be, darlin'. Now tell me. I don't want to hurt you when I move you."

Move me? Move me where? And who is he? Seb's men wouldn't care whether they hurt me or not.

"Who, who are you?"

But it's Tommy who gives me the answer as he cries out, "'Forcer! Tommy wants to see Rash!"

I look at the shape hunched down before me. "Enforcer?" I say, wonderingly, as where I heard that voice suddenly falls into place. Why on earth is he here?

"Blade, Enforcer for the Satan's Devils," he confirms. "Now will you fuckin' let me help you, woman?"

"Why, why would you help me?" I can't stop being suspicious. Not just like that. I'm nothing, a nobody, no value except to Seb. Why would someone from an outlaw MC want to give me any assistance?

His answer isn't particularly comforting. "That," he begins slowly, "I don't rightly know myself. All I know is Sebastian Lawson has an interest in you."

If I could make myself any smaller I would. I whimper. I've fought so hard to get away, now it seems it was all for nothing. "Please don't take me to him. Please, please just go and forget you found me." If I'd had anything I could offer, I'd try to bribe him. But I've nothing.

"Tommy! For fuck's sake. Rash is okay. Blade won't hurt her. Fuck, Tommy, that hurt. Blade, move this along. This fucker is strong."

I want to cry out not to hurt the man who helped me, but my attention is brought back to my own predicament by the biker when he says hurriedly, "We're interested in why Lawson has a hard-on for you." When I wince, as much in response to the name he keeps using as to the pain I'm in, he continues with a snarl, "Fuck, woman. You're hurt, who did this to you? Was it Lawson's men? Tommy said you were punched, but this is more than that." He takes his phone out of his pocket, again I try to shrink back. "Prospect?" He proceeds to give the location of the alley and makes a request for a truck.

"Please, just leave me. Please, don't take me to him. Please, please don't." I'm begging. I don't, can't trust him. How can I trust a man who turns up out of the blue? How does he know Seb? How does he know Seb wants me? Is he working for him?

"Listen," Blade says, tiredly but forcefully. "Obviously can't say this fuckin' enough. But I, *we're* not going to take you any-where near Lawson. I can't leave you here, so you're comin' back with us."

Back with him? "Where? I can't go to the hospital." That that's where he's proposing to take me is a reasonable assump-tion, but Seb's men will be watching for that.

"Nah, you can't. We'll get someone to look at you back at the compound." Having answered my question with a response which leaves me confounded, he stands up. His light now falls on the three men, Tommy still struggling to get free. "Tommy," Blade starts firmly, "listen to me carefully. You can come sit with Rash, but don't touch her, okay? She's hurt."

In the light, I see Tommy go still. "Tommy sit with Rash. Not touch. Tommy not touch Rash."

"That's right." I watch, scared as Blade's hand rests on my friend's shoulder, but the gentleness of that action makes me feel easier. Seb's men would more likely hit the mentally challenged man rather than take the time to talk patiently to him. The last thing I want is for Tommy to get hurt on my account.

But patience with the retarded man doesn't mean they're not going to give me up.

"Is Sebastian Lawson paying you?" I call out. A dread settling in my gut, all of me convinced they wouldn't have come for me otherwise.

Blade's quick response is chilling and confirms my worst suspicions. "He is."

While I'm trying to process what to do with that answer, those two words which seem to seal my fate, Blade's companions let the struggling man go. Released, Tommy approaches, and carefully sits down by my side, his hands held up as if to show he's not going to place a finger on me.

Blade also comes back, and squats. He glances at the man so carefully trying not to jostle me, shakes his head, then sighs. I suspect his attention having been taken up with Tommy has led to him being indiscreet as now he tries to explain himself. "We might be takin' Lawson's money, darlin', but that doesn't mean we do anything without knowing the reason. You're hurt, he was responsible. Satan's Devils might have a reputation, but not for abusing women. Don't care what hold you have over him, but we won't be hurting you because of it. You hear me?"

There's a pause. I don't fill it. I might be hearing his words, but nothing makes sense. *Are they working for Seb or not?* He said they are. In my mind, that makes them the enemy.

"Got a truck comin'. You'll come back to the compound. Doc's comin' to look at you, see how badly you're hurt. One thing for sure, you'll be safe there. No one will know where you are."

"Tommy go with Rash." He sounds stubborn. Somewhere in his brain he seems to have processed my reluctance to go with these strangers and wants to do what he can to protect me.

"Tommy not leave Rash," he vows. A promise to me, a warning to them. I swallow, again afraid they might hurt him.

Blade wipes his hand over his face, then turns to look at the man he called Road. They grunt at each other, I can just make out the other man saying, "He'll make a hell of a fuss if we go off with her without him." Then, after raising his chin and considering for a moment, Blade turns back. "Yeah, Tommy. You can come too, if you want."

It's that offer that lets me breathe a little easier. Who would take a man like Tommy casually under their wing? It's not what I expected. Unless… "You won't hurt him, will you?" The idea they were taking him to kill him suddenly hits me.

"Christ woman!" Blade snarls. "Who the fuck do you think we are?" He wipes his hand over his brow as though exasperated. "You'd prefer we walked away now, left you here, like this? How long would you fuckin' last? Even with Tommy here to look after you. But if that's what you want, tell me, and I'll stop wasting my time."

For a second there's a stand-off. I consider my options. I haven't many left. He could easily force me to go with him. Having seen the butt of his gun I know he's armed, Tommy's not. If he fulfilled his promise to walk away, what would I do? I suspect I do need medical attention. While I'd rather not accept his help due to the bizarre connection to Seb, I'm fresh out of other ideas.

"There's something wrong with my arm." Sighing, I make my decision, and begin to answer the question he asked minutes ago, "A car clipped my leg, it's not broken, but badly bruised I think."

"Can you walk?"

"Yes, but a hand up would be useful." No sooner have I requested it, a hand is wrapped around my good elbow, as a gap appears between me and the wall, another snakes around my waist. Quicker, and more gently than I expected, I'm now standing on two feet.

Blade's arm stays around me as I limp to the edge of the alley. When the glow from the streetlight appears on my face, he winces. "You're a strong fuckin' bitch, ain't you? How you got away from that car I don't know, but you paid for it in the process. Most women would have given up."

Not if their life depended on it, they wouldn't. Perhaps he doesn't know that yet, the enormity of the prize I was striving for.

Tommy, not seeming to distinguish the bruises from the dirt on my face, says almost proudly, "Rash is clever. Cleverer than Tommy."

The man who'd not said much up to now snorts, drawing my attention to him. Now able to see Blade's companions clearly, I shrink back. They're both tall, built, and dressed in the same leather as the one Blade is wearing. *More bikers.* Belatedly I realise the compound they've been talking about is theirs. *A biker compound.*

Blade's hand strokes my arm as though trying to comfort me. As if giving names to the men might make them less threatening, he performs the introductions. "This is Marvel," he inclines his head toward the man who had snorted, "and this is Road."

Bizarrely, they grin and offer, 'pleased to meet yous', while I just acknowledge them with a widening of my eyes.

Before anyone can say anything else, Road's phone rings, he answers, "Yeah, I'm here." He steps out of the end of the alley. When he waves, a truck draws up. Another man appears. He, like the man I'd met at the Wheel Inn, has the word Prospect on his cut but he's not the same one as I'd met before.

"Okay," Blade says to me, "let's get you in the truck. No, Tommy. I'll help her." He's quick to see Tommy would like nothing more than to sweep me up into his strong arms and carry me, probably hurting me badly in the process. Then, again to me, Blade asks, "How do you want to do this?"

Accepting I've no option but to go where they want to take me, I might as well make it easier on myself and comply. "Er... If you can give me your hand..." I hold out my uninjured arm.

Blade's surprisingly gentle. He grasps my forearm, as I get my good leg under me and with his aid, start to pull myself up. As I cry out unintentionally, his other arm is quickly around my waist to support me.

"Take it easy, no need to rush. I've got you."

He smells of leather and soap as my head rests against that vest he's wearing. The same one I'd seen the other night, the one where the only word I'd been able to make out was Enforcer. I have my own ideas about what role he plays for the club, but in that moment, welcome his support.

I stagger. He pauses. "Do you want me to lift you up?"

Anything is going to hurt. I grit my teeth. "No." I look up at the truck, it looks like a mountain to climb. Without giving me a chance to protest, he swears under his breath, then I'm in his arms and placed gently in the rear seat.

"Tommy, get in the other side," he instructs as he reaches over me and fastens the seatbelt. "Prospect. Drive fuckin' carefully, okay?"

I notice, now we're in the open, his eyes flick left and right, constantly scanning for danger. "You looking for Sebastian's men?" Even as I ask, I wonder. If he is, I don't know whether it's to welcome or fight them. The only thing I know is that I'll never trust easily again.

"Can't be too careful." Now I can see him in the light from the streetlamps, I notice as I had the other night, he's on the right side of handsome. A short beard and neatly trimmed moustache, at odds with long hair flowing free. Good looking? Yes. Friendly? Approachable? Nah, those aren't words I'd apply to him. "Won't be long now," he turns his attention back to me. "We'll get you safe and sorted, okay?" His nose wrinkles. "Think you'll feel better after a shower."

Then he shuts the door, leaving me with the embarrassing thought that while I was thinking he smelled good, he was having to put up with the terrible odour from me. I wipe my good hand over my face, realising how far I've fallen.

The prospect starts the truck. As it begins to pull away, I realise this is the second time I've jumped out of the pan, and there's no way of knowing how hot this fire is going to be.

Living on the streets was bad enough. Going to the compound of what is known all over Tucson as a criminal gang? I have no freaking idea what to expect.

CHAPTER 9

Blade

I watch the truck pull away, nodding as I see Matt is indeed taking it steady. Fuckin' bitch is hurt and badly, hiding as much of it as she can, but she'll feel every jolt and bump. Her shoulder looks dislocated to me, putting it back in place will ease it some. It's not as if I haven't done it before. Tongue, one of the brothers we'd lost used to have an arm that could inconveniently pop out of place, but I didn't want to suggest it. Hurting her more will scare her too badly. Best leave that to Doc. Knowing Road, Marvel and I will easily catch up, I slide my phone out of my cut before getting on my bike.

"Prez? I've found the girl. She's injured. Can you get Doc to come look at her? Oh, and I think… Yeah, Sam would be great. She's fuckin' suspicious of us." I end the call. Another stray being brought to the compound. It's then I realise I haven't told him about Tommy. Fuck knows what Prez will make of him.

God that girl reeked, almost as badly as the homeless man, but then she's been fending for herself on the streets. Apart from the sweat and filth from her clothes, there was another aroma I know only too well. *Fear.* Lawson had told us she's got something on him, but the person most afraid seems to be Rash. To her, the politician represents danger. It makes me want to find out what he's hiding in his closet, how she knows about it, and what's that information worth. Her life?

Whatever secrets she has, I'm going to ferret them out. I can do that. It's what I do best.

Truck is sliding the gate open. Usually we park the truck at the shop and walk up from there, I nod in satisfaction as Matt has the sense to drive straight up to the clubhouse. I've parked in my usual spot and swiftly go to open her door.

"You okay?" In the light spilling out of the clubhouse windows, I notice how pale she looks.

"I'm fine," she lies as she awkwardly unclasps the seatbelt one-handed before I have a chance to help her. When she goes to swing herself out, she'd have fallen if my arms weren't there to support her. Apart from the pain, she looks completely done in.

I don't allow her to protest, I pick her up and, kicking the door open, carry her inside. Behind me I hear Road instructing Tommy to follow us. Marvel growling something about Tommy being able to check out the bikes later.

Sam, Drummer's old lady, is ready and waiting. "This way."

My lips press together when I glance at the woman I'm carrying. She's barely taking in her surroundings, though she must be curious as to where she's been brought. I don't hang around. Ignoring my brothers looking on in interest, I take her straight back to one of the crash rooms. Rooms, more usually used for fucking, but also come in handy when we pick up strangers who need our help. Something we seem to do quite a lot.

Noticing the clean sheets, I nod gratefully toward Sam. She grins.

Rash sighs loudly as I place her on the soft mattress, her eyes close briefly in relief, then snap open. She looks suspiciously between me and the woman at my side. She looks like she's about to try to sit up, but Sam lays a hand on her uninjured shoulder.

"Hey, relax now. I'm Sam. I'm the president's old lady," she introduces herself. "Got Doc coming to take a look at you. You look like you've been through the wars, but you're safe now."

Looking her in the eye, Rash speaks for herself. "Safe?" Her gaze flits to me, then back to Sam. *She's summing us up.* When she starts again, it's Sam she addresses as if she's less threatening. "I'm sorry, for putting you out, Sam. I'm Tash, by the way, Natasha."

I rear back. *Have we got the wrong fuckin' woman?* My eyes take her in. No, she's exactly how I remembered her. *Has she a twin?* Unlikely. *She's lying to us.* "Your name's Emmalina," I say, tightly. "Emmalina Fielding."

She starts shaking her head, then puts her hand up to the lump on it, stilling the motion. "Emmalina Natasha Fielding. Only my mom, and Seb, ever use my first name. I hate it."

Sam looks between us, then as she gets down to business, telling her it's no trouble to help, I bark a loud laugh, startling them both. "Tash?" I exclaim. "Oh fuckin' hell, that's good."

Sam's lookin' at me oddly. The curious expression on her face has me cracking up more. "Tommy called you Rash. Was wondering how you got that handle." And Lawson had had us looking for an Emmalina. Tash suits her much better. "Rash!" I laugh again.

As I'd noticed when I'd got her out of the truck, up to now, her face had been completely pale. But two twin points of red have appeared on her cheeks as she picks up on the implications. "I might be dirty," she says, "but I can assure you, I don't have a rash. Of any sort."

A fleeting grin crosses Sam's face as she catches onto the joke. "You're hurt though. Blade, go see if you can hurry up Doc, and I'll sort out Tash."

For some strange reason, I don't want to leave her, but no one could miss the relief in her eyes when Sam suggests I go.

She's frightened, and my continuing presence is making it worse. I don't understand why that doesn't settle easy with me, nor why I'd prefer to stay with her. But Sam's right. I should leave. Got better things to be doing in any event. Before I get to the door, she calls me back. But it's not for herself.

"Blade, can, can you check on Tommy? Make sure he's doing okay? All this," she waves at me with her hand, "you and the rest of them. It will be strange. Don't hurt him, please."

I pause with my hand on the doorframe, then, rather than questioning what she thinks we're going to do to the poor fucker we brought back with us, simply respond, "*Tash*, I'll make sure Tommy's okay."

With that, I make my way into the clubroom. Prez is there waiting. When I join him at the bar and ask the question, he reassures me that Doc will be here as soon as he can. When he tilts his head, I see what he's watching. It's Tommy looking freshly showered, and someone's managed to get him a pair of shorts which while stretched tight over his large ass, at least can be fastened. His t-shirt is straining at the seams too, demonstrating again what a big fucker he is. He's gravitated to the pool table, and Drew, the brother of Mouse's old lady, is setting up a game. The homeless man is looking on enthralled.

Drummer's obviously waiting for an explanation. I shrug. "Had to bring him, Prez. He was agitated, would have caused a fuss if I'd just brought Rash, *Tash*," I correct almost to remind myself. At Prez's raised eyebrow I explain, "Her real name's Emmalina Natasha Fielding. She prefers to use her second name, Tash for short." Then continue, "If we'd taken her and left him behind, fuck knows who he'd have told about the Satan's Devils taking her away. He's really fond of her."

Prez stares down at his beer, then looks up. "You were right, Blade." His eyes find the pool table again, and asks almost to himself, "But what the fuck do we do with him, now?"

I've no fucking idea. "At least Drew's keepin' him occupied."

"For now, yeah, Drew's a good kid. Quickly took him under his wing." Prez shakes his head. "But a man like that? Has he special needs? Fuck knows how we'll look after him."

I eye the room, my gaze pointedly landing on various brothers sprawled over the couches and chairs, then turn back to Drummer with an exaggerated wink. "You never know. He might fit right in."

I've startled a laugh out of the prez. After a hard look my way, he shrugs. "Aww, fuck, we'll work it through. How's the girl?"

"Bewildered. Confused. Doesn't trust us. Been knocked around, Prez. Think she caused most of those injuries herself in her desperation to escape, and that's what's worrying. Don't know the whole of it, but part of it was having an argument with a car."

"Lawson?"

"Yeah. She said it was his men. She's scared stiff, and worse, once I admitted we were working for him."

Hearing the door open, I swing around to see Doc heading our way. "First crash room," is all Drummer needs to say. Doc spins on his heel knowing exactly where he's going. It's not the first time we've called him here. He's an ex-Army medic who helps the club. An experienced man, there's not a lot he can't deal with.

Drummer raises his bottle in the direction he'd sent Doc in. "When he's finished, I want a word with that girl. Lawson's hiding something from us, and I've a gut feeling what he's concealing has got something to do with her."

"You and me both."

There's a roar of laughter from across the room. Looking over, I see Tommy giggling and shaking his head. Rolling my eyes at Drummer, I go over to see what's happening. I find Tommy beaming, and Drew looking bemused.

Beef nudges me. "Fucker's got no fuckin' idea how to play pool. Don't think he's seen a table before. Seemed fascinated by all the colours. Drew tried to teach him, but Tommy decided he didn't need a cue stick. Rolling the balls into the pockets seems to have kept him amused."

Casting my eye toward him, I see Tommy does indeed look triumphant. He's also not bothered by brothers laughing at him, joining in with a deep-throated chuckle of his own.

"Blade?" I turn to see Fergus beside me. "Used to know a boy whose brother was like Tommy." I tilt my head and nod for him to continue. "Yeah, obviously don't know if he's going to be the same. Kid was older than us, I'd have been about fifteen at the time. Fucker was easy to please, but didn't know his own strength when angry."

My eyes return to Tommy. Fergus has brought something up I hadn't considered. With his bulk the fucker could do some serious harm if he had a tantrum. Drummer was right, we have no idea of his needs. At least the prospect has some experience and I'm not going to turn that down. "What do you suggest?"

"Keep him happy," Fergus grins. I nod to show I get his meaning. "Feed him for a start. Find out what he likes to do. I don't mind a spot of babysitting if you want?"

Well that would be one thing sorted. "Yeah, Fergus." Wasting no time, the prospect goes to take a step. My hand shoots out and holds him back. "Appreciate it, man."

A quick shrug then I watch Fergus approach. Christ, Tommy's eyes light up like fireworks when the prospect suggests food. Believing I'm leaving him in capable hands I return to the bar, grab a beer, then go sit at an empty table.

Me sitting alone seems to attract attention like bees around honey. Pretty quickly Wraith joins me, then Peg. Drummer, now carrying a bottle of scotch comes across too. As they sit down, we start to go through what we do and don't know.

"So Tommy stays until we know what's happening?"

Giving Wraith a sharp glance, it's clear he's got concerns similar to those of the prez. I'm just hoping we haven't brought a ticking bomb to the compound. "Can't see another way around it, VP. He goes back on the streets; it wouldn't take much for him to start boasting about his new friends—that would be us—or the girl he befriended and helped."

"There would go our chance at this protection gig with Lawson," Peg puts in.

"We still want it?" I query the sergeant-at-arms. "Not sure I like the idea of workin' for him if he's trying to get hold of that girl. His men obviously didn't care how much damage was done to her. As we know from Tommy, they didn't politely invite her back for a conversation with Lawson, first question they asked was with their fists."

Peg shrugs. "It's money, isn't it? As long as we keep her out of his way and prevent him hurting her, who's to say we can't carry on as if nothing had happened."

My eyes open incredulously. "What are you suggesting? We keep her here on the compound?"

"Of course!" the sergeant-at-arms replies sharply. "You can't seriously be thinking of sending her back on the streets."

"Nah," I say quickly. "But there could be other ways to keep her out of his way. While I don't like the idea of anyone hurting her, Lawson might have good reason to fear her. And we can't know whether we can trust her ourselves."

A hand on my shoulder makes me look up. "Mouse," I acknowledge our technical expert, pleased to see him. This is the very man who might be able to help. "Have you found out anything?"

"Not had a chance so far, but I'll make it my next priority, okay?"

"Appreciate that, Brother."

Peg bangs his bottle of beer down. "Agree with you to some extent, Blade. I'd be happier if we knew who she was and what she's got on Lawson."

Too fucking right. Waving my hand in the air, I summon Matt to provide us with another round of drinks. The four of us debate the Lawson/Tash issue for a few more minutes, but unable to approach it from any angle other than the little we already know, we soon deviate off into a discussion of bikes. Prez starts telling us about an old Norton Commando he's thinking of buying to renovate.

While he's answering Peg and explaining the state it's currently in, Doc reappears. Matt runs over with a beer as he drags up a chair and sits down. "That girl…" he begins, and then shakes his head.

"What's the damage, Doc?"

"Well, Drum, she'd dislocated her shoulder. I've put it back in place, but that's gonna be sore for a while. No bones broken from what I can see, but her leg's badly banged up. I'd like her to have an x-ray to make sure I'm right, but she's adamant she won't go to the hospital."

"What about under a false name?" I suggest.

Again, Doc shakes his head. "She's terrified. I wouldn't put her through that. You know what she did to escape?" When we murmur in the negative, he continues, his voice a growl, "She threw herself out of a fucking moving car. Instinctively tucked and rolled by the sounds of it, landed on her arms not her head."

"She said she got hit by a car…" Well, that's what I thought she'd said had happened.

"That was after," Doc informs us grimly. "To assess her injuries, I got her to talk me through it. She crossed four lanes of traffic on the freeway. Lucky for the most part, but was knocked onto the hood of one vehicle. She's got bruising on her chest, but I don't think her ribs are broken. Her leg seems to have borne the brunt of the impact."

While I'm wondering why I want to jump up and strangle Doc having put the image of his hands on her chest in my head, Drummer's observing, "She really was fuckin' desperate."

Clenching my fists to control them, I focus on the words coming out of the medic's mouth. "She was," Doc confirms, his voice equally serious. "I don't know who she's running from, that's your business to know or find out. But she preferred risking a very possible death on the freeway than returning to his clutches." His stare encompasses all of us while he lets that sink in. "I've done what I can with her. Given her a sling to help ease her shoulder. Her bruises will heal by themselves. Though she doesn't think she hit her head, I wouldn't rule it out. There's a nasty lump that she can't remember getting. You got someone who can watch out for signs of a concussion?"

For some reason, all eyes go to me. "Hey," I hold up my hands, "I only brought her here."

"Which makes her your responsibility," Peg shrugs. "How it works, Brother."

"Thought you wouldn't object to a bitch in your bed, Blade."

I glare at Wraith. Bitches and me don't mix. Well, other than to use them for a good fuck, and I doubt she'd be up for that. "Find someone else, Drummer. What about the whores?"

Drummer's looking at me strangely. "After what happened with Jill and Chrissy, you want the whores up in our business?"

He's got a point. I look around the room. Once she's cleaned up Tash will be quite attractive. Surely one of the other brothers wouldn't mind staying with her. Beef would probably jump at it. The thought of Beef and Tash together only has to enter my head once and my hands clench again. "One night," I round on Drummer, snarling as I concede. "One night, Drummer. Then get a prospect to guard her."

Doc's being watching the altercation between us as if he'd been at a tennis match, his head going back and forth. Now a compromise has been reached, he steps in. "I've left painkillers for her. Poor girl doesn't feel comfortable enough to take them. She won't relax her guard. You need to persuade her, Blade. She needs rest to heal. Her blood pressure's high, but that's because her adrenaline's still racing. Got to get her to calm down, okay? Right," he stands. "I'll be off. Give me a shout if you need me. Oh, and I'll send you my bill later."

Drummer acknowledges his final comment, thanks him, then leans forward. "I'll get Dollar to increase Lawson's bill to cover it. Come on, Blade. Let's go see this girl you've brought in."

I finish my beer and get to my feet. In my horror at being made responsible for her, at least for tonight, I'd forgotten the injuries Doc had detailed. Now his description comes back into my mind. Fuck, that girl must have been running from something bad if she'd thrown herself out of one car then risked her life crossing a busy freeway.

Prez is there first, knocking on the door. His old lady opens it. "Great timing." She goes up on her toes to kiss him. "I'm just going to get Tash something to eat. Can you sit with her a while?" A small frightened squawk comes from behind her. Sam immediately swings back around. "Hey, I know he looks a bit scary, but this is Drummer, my old man. You can trust him, okay? Blade, you know already."

Stepping into the room so I'm standing alongside the prez, my eyes immediately open wide. Sam must have helped her have a shower. Tash's hair is towel dried, hanging around her shoulders in a mass of damp curls. Her face, still pale and tight with pain, but with the dirt now gone, I can see my suspicions were way off the mark. She's not just attractive, she's beautiful. My drawing of her hadn't done her justice at all, even the two-dimensional photo had fallen short. To top it off, Sam's given her a Satan's Devils t-shirt. It's too big, covers most of her too thin frame, but I'll be fucked if my cock doesn't twitch at the sight.

"And you," Sam bumps my arm as she goes past, bringing me back to my senses, "go easy on her, okay?"

I'm incapable of doing more than giving a grunt in response, being far more focused on controlling my hard-on before Drummer notices it.

CHAPTER 10

Tash

Two men step in. One I already know, but this is the first time I've had the chance to examine him properly under decent lighting. I hadn't been wrong, he's a handsome man, tousled hair, long, currently held back from his face with a bandana tied around his forehead. His eyes, a vivid blue, draws my attention and holds it, making it hard to look away. As I'd noticed before, his beard and moustache are well groomed, and frame his features to perfection. While I shouldn't be in any state to notice, I can't deny, if the situation was different, I'd find him very attractive, though he's far from the clean-cut man I'd normally go for.

There's an air of danger about him. He carries it wrapped around him like a cloak. If he smiled, it might be different, but his face, set in a scowl which seems to be his natural expression, is scary. I know without being told, this man is a threat to my wellbeing.

With an effort, I drag my eyes away, and take my first look at the second who's entered, the man Sam introduced as her old man. He's definitely older—his salt and pepper hair attests to that—but not what I would call *old*. In his prime of life in my view. Immediately I know this is someone to really be afraid of, a man no person would want to cross. If I thought Blade's eyes were mesmerising, Drummer's piercing grey stare seems to see right down into my soul. Automatically I shrink back onto the mattress.

"Natasha." Drummer keeps his focus on me as he speaks in a deep gravelly voice. "I'm the President of the Satan's Devils MC. I can see you're in pain, and more than anything, need rest. I have fuck all idea what your connection to Lawson is. That may well be something that should stay between you and him." He pauses, and his stare hardens. "What I do need to know is anything that might result in fallback on us." Only an idiot would interpret that as meaning he gives a damn about me. His only concern being what trouble I might bring to his club.

The problem is, I don't know if me being brought to the compound is a good or bad thing, either for him or for me. At the moment, my head is pounding, my eyes hard to keep open. Instead of addressing his statement, I ask the question that's been worrying me, despite Blade's earlier assurances, "Where's Tommy? Is he alright?" It's my fault he's been brought here, I worry these men won't know how to handle him. Not that I know what to do, but I'd hate Tommy to feel lost and out of his depth. I owe him a lot; he'd kept me safe and alive.

It's a relief when Blade chuckles. "Currently stuffing his face in the kitchen. He's fine, Rash." He winks when he uses Tommy's name for me.

Perhaps they can't be bad people if they're helping a homeless man, can they? There's no doubt Blade's telling me the truth, but how long will they tolerate him? That I shouldn't trust what I hear and see is a harsh lesson I've learned. As for myself? The sooner I'm out of here the better. Maybe Tommy too. "I'd appreciate a bed for the night, but I'll leave tomorrow, Drummer. I'll take Tommy with me, we'll both be out of your hair." Any exit will have to wait until morning, I doubt I'm capable of moving right now. Now I've a soft bed to lie on, my muscles have seized and I want nothing more than to give in to the exhaustion that's coming over me in waves. Even that welcome shower had taken it out of me.

If possible, the prez's eyes sharpen. "We'll see about that," he says, ominously.

Pan, fire. The apt words enter my head again. Here with the actual Devils, I might have bought myself a one-way ticket to hell. Now I'm here, if they want me to stay, how am I going to get free? Again I study both men, my eyes flicking one to the other, wondering what instructions they'll have received from the man who Blade admitted is paying them. Instinctively I know, I'm in their hands now, and they can do what they like with me. If they do Lawson's work for him, I just hope they'll make it quick.

But they're not currently looking like men who want to kill me, and, surely, they wouldn't have doctored me if they didn't want to keep me alive.

My head throbs again, my hand automatically goes to my forehead. Drummer doesn't miss it. "We'll talk tomorrow. Blade will stay with you tonight."

What? I glance the enforcer's way. It's him who gives me an explanation. "Doc thinks you may have a concussion. You need someone to check on you while you sleep."

Another conundrum. *Would they try to keep me alive if they were going to kill me?* I'd hoped to be able to hop to the door and turn the key in the lock and feel more secure than I have for weeks, but now it seems my plan is thwarted. How the hell will I be able to relax with this frightening man in the room?

Drummer jerks his chin toward Blade as if he finds the plan completely acceptable, then opens the door just as Sam comes back in carrying a tray. The sandwich she's made me looks like the best thing I've eaten in days, but my stomach churns as she brings it closer, and suddenly I feel nauseous.

As I shake my head, quickly placing my hand to my forehead at the jarring motion, she places the snack on the bedside table. "It's there when you want it," she says, then lets Drummer lead her away.

With horrified eyes, I watch as Blade switches on a lamp beside the bed, then turns off the harsh overhead light. He settles down in a chair and toes his boots off.

"You can't propose to spend the night there," I tell him, hoping to make him see sense and get rid of him. "It won't be comfortable."

"You offering to share the bed?" he lazily enquires with a smirk.

What the hell? "No I'm not," I snap back. "Look, this is crazy. I'll be fine. You must have your own room, somewhere."

"Not leaving you. Don't know your story." He leans closer, I flinch away. "Look, sweetheart, how about you stop worrying about me, and worry about yourself instead?" He picks up the painkillers Doc had left me. "Take a couple of these and get some rest."

"I can't sleep, not with you watching me." I mean, he could be a pervert. If those pills knock me out, as I suspect they will, he could be feeling me up in my sleep and I'd know nothing about it.

His eyes blink slowly. "Look at it this way, you can rest knowing I'm here looking out for you. Ain't gonna let anything happen," he sighs. "Got a feeling you haven't had that security for a while."

He's right. I haven't. But right now, the most danger I'm in may well come from him. I don't trust him, or any of the men here. On the surface, they appear to be helping me, but I mustn't forget, they're working for Lawson.

Easing my head back, I stifle a groan. It feels like someone's using a hammer on my brain and my shoulder throbs. My leg?

Well, even the light sheet covering it presses too hard on the swelling.

"Sweetheart," Blade's voice having dropped, is softer, "you look like death. Ain't nothing going to happen to you. Lawson has no idea you're here, swear to that, woman. You're doing yourself no good fightin' it. You need to switch off for a while. Take the tablets Doc left for you."

It's tempting. What's the worst that can happen? He'll kill me while I'm asleep? Huh, at least I'd know nothing about it, just wouldn't wake up. There's something attractive about the thought of never having to worry about anything again. It's stupid to seriously think he'd molest me, I'd seen myself in the mirror when I'd taken a shower. Blue and purple isn't a good look on anyone.

He offers the painkillers again. Examining his expression, I can't read anything there at all. Seeing it doesn't bother him one way or another decides me. If he'd pressured me, I'd resist. I take them. Then, awkwardly, favouring my left arm, snuggle back down, relishing the feeling of a soft mattress beneath me. There had been times over the past few weeks I never thought I'd ever feel such comfort again.

I feel like I've only just dropped off when I'm awoken. Sluggish from the tablets I've taken, I make no protest as Blade checks me out, then roll over and drift off again. Whether it's because I've been disturbed I don't know, but this time my sleep isn't dreamless.

"Hey, hey. I got you. Whoa, there." Drowsily I open my eyes. The sheets are all tangled around me, my body is drenched with sweat. "Fuck woman. That was a nightmare and a half. Thought you were going to do yourself damage the way you were thrashing around."

A whimper escapes me. The dream had been so vivid, I thought I was back there again, and this time, had been unable to stop Grant.

"Here. Have a drink of water. I was going to wake you anyway to check you weren't dying." My uninjured arm takes the bottle he's holding out. My throat is dry, maybe as a result of the tablets I'd taken, or maybe I'm just dehydrated.

"Are you cold?"

My eyes snap to his, wondering why he's asked. As I shake my head, he tells me, "You're shivering, and you've got goosebumps on your arm." I shrug, not wanting to go into my demons now. When he sees I'm not going to explain anything, he adds, "Go back to sleep."

Using my arm that's not in a sling, I pull myself up. The dream has still got me trapped in its thrall, and I'm unwilling to put myself back there. Looking down, I realise I'm dressed in an oversized tee with the Satan's Devils logo on it. I had been half out of it yesterday, in my pain and confusion, only vaguely aware of the woman called Sam helping me in the shower and dressing me like a child.

"What's the time?" I ask.

Blade consults his phone before telling me, "Five-thirty."

I sit up straighter, half turning to try and prop up the pillows behind me. With only one usable arm, it's difficult, and I wince in pain. He's there, doing it for me. "Take another painkiller."

I refuse, wanting to keep my mind sharp and not fuzzy. I have no idea why I've been brought here; I can't trust these men or anyone. My stomach growls. Turning my head, I notice the sandwich that had been left for me yesterday evening. It's on my left side, so when I try to reach my right hand over to get it, my intention is obvious.

"Fuck woman. You don't want to eat that. It's been sitting there all night." Blade stands, looking disgusted.

"It's better than what I've been eating. Like the leftovers from the Wheel Inn," my lips curve as I remind him.

He has the grace to look sheepish. Then comes over to the bed. "What's your story?" he asks softly, but in a way that suggests he wants no reply, or not at the moment. "How the fuck did a woman like you become homeless?"

"A woman like me?" Now I'm the one who's curious.

"Your hair. It's a fuckin' mess right now, but it's been styled and cut. Anyone could see that. The way you talk…"

His comment about my hair isn't exactly flattering. It might be true, but still. My voice is sharp as I snap, "Anyone can lose their home, their job, and end up like I did."

He frowns. "But not everyone throws themselves in the path of a car as though the demons of hell were after them."

"Isn't that what you are?" I can't resist, glancing back down at the logo on the shirt I'm wearing. "Devils and demons. Aren't they much the same thing?"

One side of his mouth turns up. "That depends," he tells me seriously, "whether you're friend or foe."

The same can be said for him. But as my stomach grumbles once more, I try again to reach for the food that's so temptingly close. Blade picks it up and moves it further out of my reach.

Before I can protest, he's speaking again, "Do you think you can get up and walk?"

I need to as my bladder is telling me. "I think so." As I start to push myself up, he's there, his strong arms supporting me, pulling back the sheet and letting me slide my legs off the side of the bed. I try to ignore that the smell of him up close is like coming home. *He might have brought me here, but it doesn't mean he's my saviour.* It was getting involved with the wrong man that got me into this mess.

My right leg is just about able to bear weight. The medic had confirmed my opinion that I probably hadn't broken anything,

the swelling was just down to bruising. At my detour to the bathroom, when I pull up the tee that hides me down to my thighs, I
see the ugly purpling on my shin and thigh. Having peed, I awkwardly pull up the panties which aren't mine and which I don't
like to think how I got into last night, then wriggle so my tee
falls respectfully down my legs once again. After the rags I've
been wearing for the past few weeks, a garment without holes
seems luxurious. If I'd known I was going to be living rough, I'd
have chosen to wear more than a light summer dress.

We're heading for the kitchen Blade tells me. What I hadn't
expected, was the other people who were up and around at this
time of the morning. A couple of women yawning, already cooking up a storm, and a few men waiting at the table. Misogynistic?
You bet.

Blade pulls out a chair. "Sit, before you fall over." Gentleman like, he holds my arm as I ease myself down. He exchanges
chin lifts with the men seated around me. "Shooter," he points
to one, "he works construction with Viper." He waves to the
next man. "Marvel, you've already met. He works with me in the
shop. That there's Fergus, you'll probably remember him. He's
one of our prospects." He doesn't offer the names of the two
women cooking.

"Tash," I introduce myself, when he doesn't say anything. I
hadn't thought about men in an MC having regular jobs. I mark
it up as something I've learned about them. Explains why
they're up and about so early. I'd expected them to be in bed
with whores or with a hangover—or both.

"Know your name, sweetheart. But that's all we know," the
man called Marvel tells me. He looks suspicious.

Blade speaks over him, cutting him off. "Tommy?"
When he directs the question toward the prospect, I wait
anxiously for an answer. Tommy is worlds apart to these men,
and as well as the obvious difficulties which come with looking

after him, the man/child himself might find it hard to fit in. If he's caused them problems, they could have taken him back to town and dropped him off—or worse. I don't like to imagine what bikers do with someone who's not only different, but who could be a threat to them.

Fergus grins. "Took him back to my room last night and put him to bed. Went out like a fuckin' light. Still sleepin' like the dead. God that fucker snores." He shakes his head, but doesn't seem particularly bothered. "Tried to wake him, but I think he's comfortable where he is for the moment. I'll go get him up after I've eaten."

Inwardly I sigh with relief, and make a mental note to seek Tommy out later, to check with my own eyes he's okay. I feel some responsibility for him. On the streets, he was the one who knew best, here… I glance around, scrapping the thought that I might be able to handle the situation any better than him. I'm probably as much out of my depth as he is, but I am pleased someone seems to be looking out for him. I can well understand how Tommy is enjoying the comfort of a real bed. I did, and I've not spent a fraction of the time my companion had on the streets. For not the first time, I wonder how he came to be there.

Bed and decent food. That by itself is a luxury to someone who hasn't experienced those things for so long. If I'm allowed to leave today as I planned, am I doing the right thing to insist I take him with me? Or would the bikers give him a home? Nah. Can't see that happening.

Suddenly a plate of amazing smelling food is placed in front of me by a pregnant woman. "I'm Becca," she says with a smile. "Not that this asshole here would introduce us." She nudges Blade in the ribs making him gasp. "My ol' man's Rock."

"And I'm Darcy," the other woman, turns. "Peg's mine."

"Fuckin' women," Blade grumbles. "And where is your ol' man, Darcy?"

"Looking after Noah. We had a sleepless night, so he's giving me a break." Darcy looks my way and clarifies, "Noah's our son, he's only two months old and already a handful." Her eyes gentle as she explains.

"Rash!" I know who it is without turning, and my mouth begins to form a smile as I hear the excitement in his voice. "Rash. Tommy had a bed!" Now I do move my head. Tommy looks unrecognisable. He's wearing clean clothes, shorts and a t-shirt which look like they only just fit. He's showered too, revealing his hair's a dirty blonde colour, not the brown I had thought. His eyes are bright and sparkling.

Fergus stands and ruffles his hair, looking down at him fondly. "You follow your nose?" The prospects lips twitch as he sees Tommy's nostrils flare as he tries to seek out where the smell of bacon is coming from.

"Tommy could eat." He rubs his tummy.

"Well, Tommy should sit," Becca grins. "I'll bring you a plate in a moment."

The promise of food appears to be enough. Tommy sits in an empty chair, then leans forward and says conspiratorially, but his whisper is loud so everyone hears, "There's bikes Rash. Bikes and bikes and bikes. Matt said I can help clean them."

Another man has followed Tommy in, I only just notice him. His cut says Prospect too.

Blade growls, "Ain't no one I don't know touching my fuckin' bike."

Marvel, who'd been suspicious of me, seems to be more lenient on Tommy. "If," he points his fork at Matt and then Fergus, "you assholes watch him like a fuckin' hawk, he can polish up mine if he wants."

"Yay!" Tommy claps his hands together and jumps up. Moving quickly for a big man, he's around the other side of the table, his arms circling Marvel in a flash. Vainly Marvel tries to push him away.

"Tommy, for fuck's sake. You're choking me." Marvel's face is going red.

"Here, Tommy." Becca waves a plate under his nose, then pointedly places it where he'd been sitting.

He's back in his own seat in a flash, his eyes devouring the heap of food in front of him. "Breakfast for Tommy," he announces excitedly.

Marvel's shaking his head, but his chuckle shows he bears no malice.

The bizarreness of the morning continues. It's the complete opposite of anything I thought a biker compound would be like.

"You alright, Becca?" Shooter asks, as she pauses for a moment with her hand to the small of her back.

"Yeah. Just a twinge. No need to start watching me yet. Still got a while to go."

"How much fuckin' longer?" Marvel asks, his eyes showing concern.

"Two months." Becca rubs her large belly with a wistful smile on her face.

I look down, swallowing the lump that comes into my throat. I push my half-eaten plate away, Tommy grabs it and pulls it to him, while looking around as though challenging anyone else to take it, then scrapes my remainders onto his.

"There's plenty more, Tommy," Darcy tells him, her words accompanied by a fond smile.

"You finished?"

I have. Blade obviously is waiting for me to stand, but I watch Tommy for a moment. Surprisingly, these men and women seem to accept him. If I'm leaving, would it be right to take him away, if there was a chance he could stay here?

At least there seems no need to worry about him for now. Blade takes me back to my room. I shower, dress in some clothes that have been left out for me—another Satan's Devils t-shirt as if they want to mark me, but at least this time there's also a pair of shorts—then find Blade waiting for me outside the bathroom, leaning against the wall.

"Prez wants to see us."

I raise my chin. I'm not surprised.

CHAPTER 11

Blade

I can't help but admire her. Not once has she complained though she must be in a fuckload of pain. I'd found her some Advil when she again, after breakfast, had refused to take the painkillers Doc had left for her. Instead of playing on her injuries, she's trying to cover them up. Strong fucking woman.

But maybe she's got good reason to keep her head on straight around us. It's obvious she's as suspicious of us as we are of her. Perhaps now we're going to see Drummer, he'll get the truth out of her. I, for one, can't wait to know what it is.

Prez's office is imposing as it's meant to be. A huge heavy wooden desk, behind it hangs the floor to ceiling flag carrying a replica of our patch—Lucifer holding a scythe and standing over three devils. I'm so used to seeing it, it doesn't register anymore, but Tash pauses at the doorway, needing the encouragement of my hand for her to continue on through.

As I come alongside, I notice her eyes go to Prez, then behind him. Not yet having removed my touch from her back, I feel the small shudder that runs through her.

Prez only waits until I've closed the door behind us. "Time to get everything out in the open," he says in a voice that suggests she's got no other option. He stands, waving her to a chair. Again, I hold out my hand to help her into it, but she brushes away my assistance. I've noticed, now she's been moving around, some of the stiffness in her leg seems to have eased. "I want to know everything, Natasha. What there is between you and Sebastian Lawson, and why you were hiding out on the streets."

She acknowledges him with a grim nod, then lowers her head into her hands. A second or so later, she raises her eyes. "Drummer, thank you for bringing me here. Thank you for the medical treatment and the hospitality. But I said I'd go in the morning, and that's now. If you can give me, and," she hesitates, then seems to come to a decision, "Tommy a ride back into town, we'll take it from there."

Prez sits forward. "Not going to happen, Tash. Not until I know what's going on." He waves his hand at her. "You're injured for one thing. I admit I can't understand your rush to leave the safety of our compound. Fact is, though, it would seem you've got information I need, and you're not going to leave before I hear it. Now's the time to come clean. I want to know your story, Tash. Spill."

It's clear to see she's uneasy. Her hands are trembling. But instead of answering, she challenges, "What's your connection to Sebastian?"

"You'll show me yours if I show you mine?" One corner of Drummer's mouth turns up. "Nice try, but I think you'll find we hold all the cards, sweetheart. You're on my compound."

My head tilts as I consider her. On my part I hope she'll start talking. The politician's so keen to get his hands on her, whatever she knows is important. Yeah, we might have accepted a contract from Lawson, however we don't like working in the dark. I'll be fucked if Tash doesn't have the key to intelligence that would be useful to us. Or, on the other hand, Lawson could be right in believing she'd stoop to spread lies about him. If she's dishonest, out for herself, she could also be a risk to us. Can't let my gut feel get in the way of the truth.

Reluctantly, I have to admire the way she's standing up to Drummer. Men normally cower in front of him. She's a strong fucking woman, no doubt about that. I begin to grow concerned about the consequences if she continues to keep her mouth shut.

I know what would happen if she was a man. Drummer would be instructing me to use my particular talents to draw whatever she's hiding out. Not had to apply my skills to a member of her sex before, but if Prez wants her to give up her secrets, he might look to me to force her. I might not get any pleasure from it, but being the enforcer is not only my job, but my calling. If he asks me, I'll do anything to protect the club, even torture a woman for intel.

The club comes first. Always. I'll never put a bitch before that, however much respect I have for her.

It's clear she doesn't understand the position she's in. "I can't tell you anything. That's the point." She looks down at her hand cradling her sore arm, the only sign there's anything wrong with her. "If I tell you anything, Seb will kill me." She huffs a laugh but there's no mirth in it. "He's trying to kill me as he doesn't expect me to keep my mouth shut. If you're working for him, keeping silent might prove to him I'm trustworthy. If I talk, I'm only proving he's right. Safest for me not to tell you anything."

Prez takes a moment to consider her convoluted explanation. That steely gaze fixes on her. "A stand-off, eh?" He raps his fingers against the desk. "My problem is, until I know what you're hiding, I can't reassure you one way or another." He glances at me, then back at her, and proposes in an icy tone, "How about this? If, after you tell us everything, and we think you should be permanently silenced, Blade does it quick and painless."

Her head turns so fast, her hair flies around her. She turns to look directly at me. Her eyes widening as though wondering why I'd be the one to end her, and, I suspect, wondering if I could do it. *Yeah, I could darling. That you can take to the bank.* Something threatens my brothers? I'd do anything it takes to protect them. Not going to watch any of them die, not like Jonah.

I keep my face completely impassive. A trick I've learned over the years. After a moment, her focus returns to Drummer. "And that's an incentive?" she asks, incredulous.

"Darlin'," Prez waves his hand at her, "look at yourself. We chuck you back on the streets, how long would you survive? And what would Lawson's goons do if they caught up with you. Just givin' you options, is all."

With my face set, Drummer wearing the expression few men can stand up to, Tash must know she's not got any other way out.

But she tries. "As I said, it sounds safer for me to stay silent."

Drummer attempts a different tack. He leans forward. "Suppose you don't know anything at all. Lawson believes you've concocted a story that you want to get known. Throw enough dirt it will stick and ruin his chances of winning the election. Wouldn't blame you not wanting to show your cards when what you've got to tell us wouldn't stand up to examination."

"I've got nothing to say," she says calmly, though her hands twist together in her lap, and there's a sheen of sweat on her forehead.

Prez stares at her. "So Lawson's right. It's all a crock of shit. You've got nothing on him. You're just stirrin' up trouble."

It's so hard to read her. I glance at Prez. It's an impasse. On one hand, I can see her point. Lawson wants her as he doesn't believe she'll keep quiet. If she tells us what she's got, or thinks she's got on him, she'll have proved him right. But on the other, her staying silent isn't helping her or us. If Lawson is hiding something, Prez will want to know it. Knowledge is power after all.

Seconds stretch out into minutes. Prez sighs, as though he's given her the chance. "Blade, drop her off where you found her."

The thought of her going back on the streets, particularly injured like she is, tugs something inside me, but I'm not going to argue with the prez. I nod, start getting to my feet, take her arm and cover my inner turmoil by saying unsympathetically, "Look at it this way, at least you've got a hot meal inside you."

Tash gives a resigned look. "Let me get Tommy…"

"That fucker stays here," Prez informs her quickly. "Man like him has no business being on the streets. We'll find somewhere for him."

She startles, not having expected that. I hadn't either. But my lips curve fractionally as I realise what Prez is doing. Tommy is her protector, her provider. Take him out of the equation, she won't last five minutes. Even if Lawson didn't have men out searching for her.

It makes her rethink. "Wait." She jerks her arm out of my grasp and sinks back down onto the chair. "Give me a moment." She curls the hand she can use over her cheek, resting her face into it. "I need to convince Seb I'd keep quiet. I want nothing more than to get far away. Out of state." Her fingers drop away as she looks straight at Drummer. "You're in contact with him. Tell him you've found me. Tell him the truth; that I refused to divulge anything at all. Please, help me get far away from here. Tell him I'm gone and I won't be a problem." She gives a little nod as though she's come up with a good solution. "If he knows I haven't said anything to you, he'll know I can be trusted, and I'll be free and away. I've got qualifications, I can get a job and repay you. Please, just lend me what I need."

Drummer raps his fingers on his desk. Then he lurches forward, making Tash flinch. "Not gonna work that way, darlin'. I've signed a contract to provide security for Lawson. Top of the list of things he wants us to do is make sure you're not in a position to cause him a problem. You suggest you stay quiet. I'd like to know about what. See, I'm a suspicious fucker, like to know who I'm dealin' with. You're implying you've got something on Lawson, something he doesn't want others to know. Lawson says you're making it all up. I want to know which of you is lying. Can't have anything blindside me and shit fall back on the club."

"Then tell him you haven't seen me. But, please, get me out of Tucson. Like this," she touches the sling, "as you pointed out, I haven't a hope of protecting myself. Put me back on the street, Seb's men will find me."

I'm impressed she holds out against Drummer's steely gaze. Most men would already be quaking. I sit back, interested in how this is going to play out.

Prez strokes his beard. For a moment he doesn't say anything, then he leans forward and scoffs, "Doubt if you've really got anything. Lawson could well be right. You're just making up a story to discredit him."

She shrugs, clearly not going to confirm or deny anything.

"Tell me what Lawson is scared of you saying," Prez suddenly roars.

She flinches back in alarm, but quickly recovers. "You're not going to believe me, anyway. I could sit here and come up with anything. Just help me get away, then tell Seb I didn't talk. It's the truth."

"He might not believe me. He might consider you've told me things I could later use before I got you away. Then where would fingers be pointing?" Drum's fist hits the table. "At my fuckin' club." As he examines her, his fingers again tug his beard. "You tell me what you know, think you know, or what you were going to throw at him, then, we'll help you get someplace he can't follow."

She murmurs something. Drummer asks her to repeat it.

"I said, well, he ain't going to heaven, and hopefully I'm not headed the other way, so you're right he won't follow."

Drummer chuckles, it's not a convincing sound. "Tash. Look, despite what I said, we're not going to kill you. We're not in the business of killing women." He pauses, then qualifies his statement, "Not unless you give us just cause."

"That might be the case, but you've signed a contract with Seb as you've just said. How do I know you won't hand me over to him?"

"You don't." She probably misses the look of admiration in his eyes. It's only because I've known him so long that I see it. "Blade, take her out. Get one of the prospects to keep an eye on her. She's not to leave the compound." His eyes hold hers. "One way or another, darlin', I'm going to learn your secrets."

I stand, this time As I reach down to help her, Tash lets me lift her to her feet. As I do so, I notice the look of defeat in her eyes.

Outside in the clubroom, I wave at Matt. When he comes over, I give him his instructions. As I'm doing so, Sam walks in, sees Tash, and immediately takes charge. Relieved of my burden, I'm free to go back to the Prez.

Detouring via the kitchen, I collect two cups of coffee. Both black and unsweetened, just how Prez and I like it. Entering his office, he nods, a fleeting grin crossing his face as he takes the drink from me.

Inhaling the aroma from the steaming cup, he raises his head. "What did you get from that, Blade?"

I take a second to gather my thoughts. "She's so fucking scared of Lawson she won't be saying shit to anyone."

"And she's scared of us because she knows we're working for him."

I grimace. That was my fault. A few simple words that had I thought about it, I wouldn't have said, but which have now caused all this mess. "Sorry about that, Prez."

A shrug. "What's done is done. Sealed her lips for certain. But we know Lawson's got a real hard-on for her. What we don't know is why. Why's she living on the streets? She doesn't belong there."

"That was my point, Prez. Something happened to put her there. She's got no personal belongings, nothing other than the clothes she's wearing. She's obviously shying away from contacting family or friends."

Prez sips his coffee. "Lawson's obviously scared she'll talk to the press, or turn up and disrupt one of his fuckin' meetings. But what's there? What can she say?"

"And is it the truth or a made-up story?"

"What d'ya think, Blade? What's your take?"

I inhale a breath, let it settle into my lungs while I'm thinking. "She's got caught up in something and she's now in over her head. I'd like to know whether it's an empty threat, or if she's onto something."

"You've met the man, Blade. You've seen the woman. Who's likely to be the one lying?" Prez shakes his head, then continues as if not expecting me to answer. "My view? Lawson's one nasty motherfucker. A politician determined to present an image of himself that's far from the fuckin' truth. I wouldn't be surprised to find she knows more than she should about something, and is now collateral damage."

"Why did he contact us, Prez?"

Drummer's eyes narrow. "Because he thought we could find her, when his goons had failed."

"Could be he really thought she'd turn up at one of his rallies." In my head, I go back over the little Lawson had said when we'd met him. "He wanted us to remove any rowdy element. Now it seems he meant her."

"I think we can safely assume that. But there must be more to it. She could go to anyone who'd listen to her story."

"But why hasn't she? She could have gone to the cops or the press already."

"She's too scared of him getting to her." Now Drummer's lips purse. "Normal person? Yeah, that's what they'd do. Which means she knows he's a nasty motherfucker."

"She said he tried to have her killed."

"The only way Lawson will feel safe, is if she's dead." Drummer finishes his coffee. "If she knows what's good for her, she's not going to try to leave the compound. She's got nothing to her name, and can't even fuckin' move without pain. Leave her where she is for today. We've got church later. There's implications to this, Blade. Want the brothers in on this."

I suspect he's thinking along the exact same lines as me.

CHAPTER 12

Blade

"Hey, Blade."

"Mouse." I greet him with a jerk of my head, my eyes still fixed on Tash, viewing her with suspicion, while unable to be anything other than impressed as fuck with the way she's coping with her injuries. Another woman might have played on them, but she gave no indication of being in pain while being interrogated in Drummer's office. She hadn't used them as an excuse for us to go easier on her. Had she groaned, rubbed her arm, favoured her leg; even for two hardened but protective bikers it would have affected how we'd treated her. But no. Though she must have been in pain, she'd ignored it. Hadn't tried to get sympathy.

Was it fear driving her? Suppressing her physical discomfort because she truly was afraid for her life? What hold has she got over Lawson? And is it truth, or made up? Drummer's right. Although she seems to have sealed her fate if she gets into Lawson's hands, there could be something she knows that affects the club. We've got to find some way of ferreting it out.

Of course, we're no strangers to extracting information, but she's a woman. Maybe innocent of any crime, and I'm loathe to bring my normal methods into play. I'd end up hurting her, and that's the last thing I want.

But if it comes to it, I will. I'll do anything for the club.

A cough reminds me my brother's just greeted me. When he catches my eye, he's smirking. "She scrubs up well." Mouse follows my line of vision.

He's right. She does. I'd told Matt to guard her, but the women seem to have taken over. Carmen has obviously helped her with her hair; it's now twisted up in some kind of French braid. Pulled back, it shows off the features of her face, and that cute little nose. I'd been right, now her face is clean, she does indeed have freckles. They're adorable. I'm torn between wanting to shake her to get the truth out of her and drawing her again. My artist's eyes spot things others would miss, the upturn of her mouth, the blush in her cheeks. Then I notice the sharp lines that appear around her eyes when Amy knocks into her arm. I feel her pain as though it was mine. I'm about to intervene when Marcia gently scolds her stepdaughter, telling her she needs to be careful.

This won't do. The fear she showed in Drummer's office has receded. The way she's sitting with the women in a relaxed posture shows she's comfortable in their company, as though she's already become a fixture. A small smile curves my lips as I watch her hold one of the twins for Marcia, awkwardly but competently in the crook of her uninjured arm, then I scowl. It's not good if the women become protective of her, and then I do what my enforcer role says I should do. Extract that information from her in whatever way possible.

But I'll be fucked if even Grunt doesn't seem to have taken to her, the large wolfhound-cross lying protectively at her feet. While I'm examining her, Tash looks up and meets my eyes and I see something I'd missed before. The pain in them hits me. She might look like she's bonding with the women, but she's holding herself apart, keeping something separate as if knowing this is not really her place here. That pain shouldn't affect me. It does.

What's between her and Lawson? How did she get involved with him? How did she get into the predicament she has? Is she really trying to affect a political campaign, or is it something more sinister?

Suddenly I'm asking, "Mouse, have you found anything on her? Her past, where she's come from?"

"Yeah, Blade. Drummer's already asked. I think he'll update everyone when we meet. But there's nothing of substance there. No clues as to what's happening."

At last, turning to face him, I notice he looks tired. "Pull another all-nighter?"

His features rearrange into a quick grin. "Now I've got Mariana? No fuckin' chance, Brother." But then he frowns. As he seems to have something on his mind, I wave to indicate he should carry on, it might take my mind off the girl I'm thinking about far too much. "It's Drew," he enlightens as he takes up my invitation. A raise of my eyebrow encourages him further. "Kid wants a fuckin' bike."

I bark a laugh. "Doesn't surprise me."

"Me neither. I was his age when I got my first. But…"

"Mariana's against it." I chuckle guessing the answer. Fuck, but I like my life. No old lady to listen to, no one to please but myself. I never expected my brother, *my friend* to become led around by his dick, but it seems that's what's happened.

"It gets worse," Mouse says morosely.

"Worse?" I hide my amusement.

"When he's eighteen, he wants to patch in."

"Huh!" Snorting a laugh I continue, "Balloon and lead comes to mind."

Mouse raises his chin. "That's about how it went down," he agrees. "Mariana's got quite a temper when she's riled." He sees me grinning, punches my arm, then gives a self-deprecating chuckle directed at himself. Then, he's back to business. "Well, if you want me to see what else I can dig up before church, I better go get started."

So had I. I might be the enforcer for the club, but that doesn't mean I don't put in an honest day's work. Telling Matt that any issues with Tash he calls me immediately, I leave the woman in safe hands and go down to the shop. At last I manage to get Tash out of my mind, or for the most part anyway, as I get lost in trying to track down an annoying rattle in an engine, finally making headway when Marvel taps me on the shoulder reminding me it's time to pack up if I'm going to make church. Matt hasn't made contact, so presumably Tash is doing okay. In fact, when I enter the clubroom, my eyes quickly confirm the woman I'm seeking isn't there. Seeing my concern, Sophie waves to get my attention.

"Tash was knackered. Her arm and leg were giving her gyp, so she's gone for a kip."

Having known Sophie, the Englishwoman, for a couple of years now, I quickly translate that Tash is tired and hurting and gone to rest.

Engrossed in my work, I'd had a sandwich for lunch but missed dinner. Grabbing a slice of cold pizza, I walk into church, taking my seat between the VP and the treasurer, hurriedly swallowing my makeshift snack in a few bites. I'm just licking sauce off my fingers when Prez bangs the gavel.

"Unless there's anything of vital importance, we'll kick off with Blade's woman," Drummer starts, and is immediately interrupted.

"The fucker's never claimed her, has he? Fuckin' hell. Never thought I'd see the day." Beef thumps his fist down on the table. "Another one bites the fuckin' dust."

Lady nudges Joker. "Told you, there's something in the water. They all give in eventually."

"She's not my fuckin' woman," I snarl, my voice loud enough to drown out the other comments that keep coming. "I just happened to find her. Sheesh. You lot are like a bunch of ol' fuckin' women. I stumbled across her is all."

"Way it works, Brother," Rock nods his head sagely.

"Tell me about it," Mouse agrees.

"About the way of it," Peg raises his chin.

"That does it." Beef shakes his head, then looks seriously over toward Road. "I'm never steppin' foot off the compound again."

Drummer's head is in his hands. When the comments start to die down, he raises it again. "If everyone's finished?" His stare suggests even if they haven't, they'd do well to shut up. He then starts to run through an abbreviated summary of what Tash had told us, or more accurately, what she had not.

"Why won't she just come clean?" Peg sounds frustrated. "We rescued her. Brought her and that half-wit here. Fed her, doctored her. Done nothing to threaten her. Why won't she just talk?"

I suddenly find the knife on the table in front of me very interesting, avoiding Prez's eyes which burn into me.

"You gonna tell them, or shall I, Blade?"

But I don't have to say a thing.

"It was what you said, wasn't it? In the alley?" I growl softly, but Marvel proceeds. "While you had your arms full with Tommy, Road, you might not have heard him. But I did. You told her we were workin' for Lawson."

"Fuckin' idiot." Rock's shaking his head. I spin my knife so it points his way. But I don't try and defend myself. It had been a truthful answer to her question. One I might not have given had I have thought.

"So, there you have it. She trusts us as much as we trust her," Prez sums up.

Silence descends, I ignore the critical looks sent my way. Mouse takes pity on me and raises his hand. "As I told you earlier, Prez, I've looked into Emmalina Natasha Fielding. She's exactly what she appears. Moved here to take up a job when she completed her Psychology degree. Good family background, never had a speeding ticket. However hard I looked, both her and her family back in Cali seem squeaky clean."

"What's between her and Lawson?" Joker enquires. "How did they come into contact? Do... did they have a relationship? And why?"

"Not that you'd notice," Shooter grins to soften his words, "but she's smoking hot, Brother."

I frown, suddenly annoyed that he's noticed. But I have to agree. "You want someone to step out on your arm, she'd probably play the part well enough."

"You suggesting he was playing around?" Prez gives me his stare.

Shrugging, I explain, "It's a likely explanation."

"Says in the blurb about him that he's a happily-married man," Peg reminds me.

Mouse waves his hand. "I can answer one part. Emmalina Fielding was his campaign manager until two months ago. Then the position was taken by Neil Turner. The switch coincided with Lawson getting the nomination."

The thought they might not have been having an affair is comforting. For fuck's sake, I give myself a mental slap around the head. *What does it fucking matter if they were or not?* "So that's her connection with him. Why didn't Lawson tell us?"

Prez runs his hand down his beard. "I ain't happy. Both Natasha and Lawson are too fucking tight lipped. She was his campaign manager. Swapped her out when it became serious, maybe he thought she couldn't cope? Maybe she didn't take it well, threatened to expose him with some shit. Made up or fact, wouldn't matter. He wouldn't want anything coming to the fore now."

"He could have just told us," Peg frowns.

"He could. That's why I think there's more to it."

I raise my chin at Prez. "Don't forget, she's scared for her life. Wouldn't there have been a better way of handling it? Why not pay her off?"

"Might have the answer, Prez, but it means putting puzzle pieces together. The wife and kids. They've only just moved into town."

Now that is interesting. I sit up straighter, as Prez asks, his eyes regarding Mouse thoughtfully, "Where did the wife and kids spring from?"

"Yeah, well, let's first start with Lawson. I read that shit about him that he put out—his biography for the masses—and then did some digging of my own to find the parts that weren't openly disclosed. He was born in Tucson, but has lived out of state for a while. Comes from money. Lots of fuckin' money. Not enough for his family though. About thirty years back they bought a huge beef farm up in Utah, treat their workers like dirt by the sounds of it. Unconfirmed rumours they employ illegals they can pay cents instead of dollars." Mouse pauses and frowns.

Hmm. He knows more than most of us about the immigration situation. He wouldn't have much sympathy for folks taking advantage.

Mouse continues, "The family that's suddenly popped up? These are the facts as I found them. Lawson married about eight years ago. His wife, Louisa, had three children in fairly quick succession. I'm talking one kid straight after the other, less than a year between them. Then, interestingly, her medical records show her tubes were tied."

"Man who doesn't like wrapping his shit up," I nod at Prez.

"Looks that way," agrees Mouse.

"Selfish fucker," Peg growls.

"Could have been her decision," Beef offers an alternative view.

Prez sighs, then prompts, "Go on, Mouse. While the discussion about whether or not Lawson likes to cover his dick may be interestin', it's unimportant. I'm more interested in where the wife's been and why she's not been here, supportin' her husband."

"Could they have been separated, and that's when Lawson had an affair with Tash?" Road asks.

I glare at the thought of that slimy bastard going anywhere near Tash with his cock. *What the fuck does it matter? They're both adults.*

Mouse has been waiting for the chance to speak again. "Getting back to the wife," he glares at Road. "Also from her medical records, was a visit to the hospital two years ago. Busted jaw, various bruises, a broken arm. Explanation she walked into a door."

I suck air in through my teeth, all too familiar with what damage a well-placed fist can cause. I've doled it out often enough. "The injuries read like a beating," I grimly observe.

"What I'm thinking, Blade. Fuckin' door must have got very up close and personal," Mouse agrees.

"She take out a restraining order?"

"Nah, Prez. But there was a good chunk of money put in her checking account shortly after, and it coincides with the time Lawson moved away and back to Tucson. That Tash, and presumably the people who worked with him, weren't aware he was married, suggests something, or somebody, made him leave her and the kids alone."

"You don't think they visited?"

"Can't be certain, of course. But those puzzle pieces can be placed to show a picture of a family who closed ranks. Didn't want to make it official with a legal trail, but indications are they kept husband and wife apart."

I think for a moment. "So Tash might truly have been unaware he had a family. Until he thought it might benefit him to produce a wife and become an upstanding citizen for his electorate."

Drummer taps the table. "If that was the case, and he'd been stepping out with her, it must have shocked the hell out of Tash to find there was a wife in the wings. Could be another reason she wants to bring him down as retribution."

And we're back to Lawson and Tash being a couple again. I don't like the thought of that slimy asshole's hands groping her. "Or," I glare, "she's as honest as the day is new, and just objected to them presenting an image of a happy family when that was far from the truth."

"Brother," Beef reminds me, "have you seen that girl? Wouldn't blame Lawson playin' the single man and bangin' her. Okay, with those bruises her face still looks like shit, but as our brother said, underneath those, she's fuckin' hot."

I inwardly seethe, wishing they wouldn't keep reminding me.

Prez strokes his beard. Just as he's about to speak, Mouse clears his throat. "I did more than look into his background, Prez." He pauses to glance around. "Unless it touches us, none of us here get concerned with what's going on in the citizen world, so this probably wouldn't have registered. Certainly came as news to me as I wasn't followin' what was going on. Lawson originally threw his hat in the ring without any particular hope that his name would rise to the surface. His family pumped money into his campaign, but he wasn't getting support from the political groups. Wasn't particularly liked by the names who matter until things started crawling out of the woodwork."

"Things?" Wraith leans forward, his hands clasped together on the table.

"There were two men, better experience. The incumbent was retiring, so whoever became the nominee would be a new-comer. But everyone assumed one of the other two would get the nomination."

"What happened, Mouse?" Drum's eyes are creased as though he's trying to remember. But Mouse is right, none of us take much interest in the outside world.

"The man in second place, well, he had an accident. Lost control of his car and wrecked it off the side of a mountain. Dead on impact."

"Accident?"

Mouse nods. "That's what they're calling it. I've read the police reports. Well, Marcia got me into them." He nods at Heart who raises his hand to acknowledge the mention of his ex-cop old lady. "There could have been a mechanical failure, but it went down a few hundred feet. Was pretty banged up and exploded. Burnt out."

"Cops investigate?"

"As far as they could with little to go on."

Prez raises then dips his head. Then asks, "And the frontrun-ner?"

"Sex abuse scandal. Oh, he denied it, of course, but it was enough to unsettle his backers. Suddenly Lawson had money pouring into his campaign fund. Cobbs stepped away though he continued to deny it."

Peg's looking like that smoke he likes to mention has just burst into flames. The table goes quiet. Nobody needs to have it put into words, we can all join the dots. Lawson suddenly had what he'd wanted handed to him on a fucking plate. The question is, did the cards just fall his way, or did he mark the fucking pack?

CHAPTER 13

Tash

The words 'biker compound' had summoned up a nightmare scenario in my brain. Last night it had been dark when we had arrived. I'd been aware of the ominous clang as the metal gates had slid closed behind the truck, worryingly reminiscent of a prison. Then, when Blade had carried me through the clubroom, I'd caught glimpses of men in leather standing around, most drinking. In the minute or so before I'd been laid on a bed in a private room, my suspicions had seemed confirmed.

I'd been unable to relax. Sam's presence had made it easier, but all I could wonder was how a nice woman like her, ended up married to the man who must be the worst of the lot. I doubt you became president of a group of criminals without doing something to earn the title. I'd had dire thoughts when I'd been left alone with him, and the man who is the enforcer. *Had they killed? Tortured?* Grant, Seb's fixer had been bad enough, a man with no conscience. Seb wouldn't allow him to use it, not while he was working for him, but Grant Locosta went by the nickname Loco. I'd seen more than enough of him to know it wasn't just a shortening of his family name. Were these bikers just like him? They were taking Seb's money, working for him. Far too many similarities for me to ignore.

The compound of the Satan's Devils, by day, I'd suspected I wouldn't like it, having had an image in my mind of a dark dingy place, foggy with cigarette smoke and full of men drinking and either there already, or well on their way to being drunk. Any women would be scantily clad or naked, and not there by choice. What I hadn't anticipated was the rabbit hole I seem to have fallen into. It had started with that strange breakfast. The kitchen had had a family vibe, men getting ready for a day's work, nothing like I'd expected. The idea in my head they spent all day asleep, crawling out at night to ride bikes and molest or rob unsuspecting citizens had to be quickly re-evaluated.

The women had been a surprise too. They seemed normal. Not unlike the housewives I'd met on Seb's campaign trail. Under their men's thumbs though, they had been the ones doing the cooking. But at least they were fully clothed. What surprised me most had been the relationship they'd each claimed with a single man—I'd expected to find whores.

Nevertheless, I hadn't let my guard down in Drummer's office. How can I trust men taking Seb's money?

When Drummer dismissed me and Blade led me out into a bright and sunny clubroom, I'm pleased with myself that I held my own against the president, but realised the game we had both been playing still had me coming out the loser, whichever way you painted it. I'd kept my mouth shut about everything I know. Without proof, no one would believe me. But Seb might suspect Drummer is now in possession of knowledge he could use against him, even if Drummer denies it.

For a second I wonder whether I should have trusted them, but all I've ever heard about these Devil men of Tommy's doesn't give me the confidence to place my faith in Drummer and his men. *Is Drummer calling Seb even now? Getting his instructions on what to do with me? Will Seb send Grant to collect me?*

I could run, try to escape. But to where, and to what? Huh! How far could I get with one leg barely able to support me, and an arm in a sling. How could I survive on the streets like this? *I wouldn't, not unless Tommy came with me.* That's the thought in my head. The first inklings of a plan as Blade instructs the prospect to keep an eye on me. *Would have to get past him first. Could Tommy take him on?*

That, of course, was how I'd been thinking before Sam had come over, greeting me like I was already a friend. As she takes me under her wing, the feeling of being Alice, presented with an unbelievable wonderland escalates.

"Hey, Tash. Come join us." Us is her and a woman who has an English accent. She's introduced as Sophie, wife of the VP. Sophie has a young baby, only a few months old, who's discreetly suckling under a blanket.

"Girl or boy?" I ask politely.

The question brings forth wide smiles from both president and VP's wives. "Girl," Sophie replies. "This is Zoey," she nods down at the baby in her arms, then at a toddler playing by her feet. "And that's Olivia. My other daughter." She winks. "Wraith near shit a brick when he found out he'd fathered two girls."

Sam chuckles. "While my two are both boys. This is Zane," she points to the baby asleep in a bouncy chair beside her, then at the boy playing with Olivia. "That monster is Eli."

Sophie says thoughtfully, "He's getting more like Drummer every day. Little prez there in the making."

My eyes widen as I view Sam, wondering if she'd be happy that her son, looking little more than two years old, was already being groomed to lead a criminal gang. But she's just looking on proudly as though she has no problem with the idea.

"Want a coffee, Tash?" That sounds great, so I nod.

"Matt?"

"On it, Sam." The prospect, obviously happy I'm going nowhere for now, leaves and disappears into the kitchen. Hmm. So the prospects do the women's bidding? Perhaps it's not so male dominated after all.

"Where's Tommy?" I'm concerned when I can't see my friend from the streets around.

Sam waves toward the clubroom door. "He was helping Fergus last time I saw him." Leaning over she pats my hand. "He's a lovely guy, isn't he? Bit slow, but so friendly. You don't need to worry about him. Fergus has taken him under his wing."

I hope she's right. While Tommy's a great guy, it takes a special person to see that good in him. Another side of the bikers I couldn't have predicted.

Matt's soon back, and steamy cups are placed in front of us. I add sugar and cream, then sigh. The ability to have a cup of the life-giving nectar whenever I wanted was something I'd missed on the streets. I notice Sophie has a different drink in front of her.

"Tea," she explains at my curious glance. "I'm not a heathen like you lot. Give me a cup of char any day. Can't beat a decent brew and Matt's been well trained." She raises her drink toward the prospect. "This is bloody good, thanks."

Matt's quick grin shows his appreciation of her compliment.

The children play. Sophie refastens her top when Zoey finishes feeding and holds the now sleeping baby in the crook of her arm. A lump rises in my throat at the sight, but I try to force that down. As things have turned out, maybe it was all for the best. Doesn't mean I don't regret it, and probably will all my life.

My morose thoughts are interrupted when a woman, slightly older than Sam and Sophie appears and makes a beeline straight for me. She stands to my front, her gaze raking over me, her lips pressed together as though in censure. I brace myself for the expected questions to start. *Who am I? What am I doing here?* Surely they must be curious about a strange woman appearing. I'm surprised I haven't had an interrogation before now.

Her opening words, therefore, take me by surprise. "You poor thing," her hand waves at my sling. "Can't do much with that, can you? You like all that hair around your face in this heat?"

It takes me a second to respond. Raising my sling a fraction, I agree, "Hard to put my hair up with one hand, but you're right. I normally have it out of the way."

"Well let's help with that." Giving me no chance to object, she finds a space for her purse among the coffee cups, rummages inside, and pulls out a small bag which she places on the table. As she opens it, I see it's full of grips and bands. Business like, she goes behind and starts to brush out my hair. An over-personal action for someone I don't know, but her introduction offered belatedly, explains why. "I'm Carmen. My old man's Bullet. I'm a hairdresser." The last sounds like it's mumbled around a few pins she's placed in her mouth. "I'm around most mornings. You want your hair sorted? You come to me. You've had a good trim recently, haven't you?"

"Yeah, about six weeks back." It had been one of the last things I'd done before my life had fallen apart. As my hair is long, and just needs tidying up every now and again, and given a bit of shape around the front, I haven't a style which grows out fast. I'd visited the hairdresser to cheer myself up. It hadn't worked.

"Next time, you come to me. I do all the old ladies hair for free." She tugs a little at a knot, and I flinch. "Sorry."

"I think I hit my head." My fingers show her the sore spot.

Once again, her lack of questioning as to how I came to be hurt surprises me. "I'll be careful," is all she says. And she is, again not prying as to what happened.

Her gentle strokes as she brushes out my hair are like a massage. I find myself relaxing and recall what she said. "I'm not an old lady."

Sam, sipping her coffee, huffs out a laugh, making Carmen pause for a moment. "Who brought her in?"

"Blade," the president's old lady replies.

"Blade, huh?" She starts brushing again, slowly lifting my hair from my nape. "He'll be a tough nut to crack, but don't give up. I reckon he might be worth it."

"Hidden depths that one," Sam agrees. "And certainly easy on the eyes."

"Who we talking about?" Another woman walks in. She's pushing a stroller with twins sitting side by side. A boy and a girl by the look of it. An older child, maybe five or so, is skipping along beside her. My mind goes back to the kitchen this morning and the pregnant woman I'd seen, and Darcy who'd admitted to having a young baby. Christ, I'm already losing track of how many children are on the compound.

When Sam says, "Ten," I realise I must have been musing aloud.

"Eleven if you count Drew, but he's older, sixteen, and wasn't born here. I'm Marcia, by the way." The woman pushing the stroller waves at me. "Mine are Amy," Amy looks up from where she's already sat down with the toddlers and wriggles her fingers, "and here are Jacob and Isabel."

"Asleep for a change," Sam observes with a grin.

"Thank God. They had us up since five."

"Who's missing?" Well, I might as well get the rundown of them all, but I'm never going to remember the kids' names, or who goes with who. *And probably, I won't be here long enough to have a chance.*

"Ella, Slick's old lady and newly born Faith," Marcia informs me with a smile. "Oh, and Maya. She's Joker and Lady's. And Mouse has an old lady, Mariana, but they've got no children. Yet. Drew is Mariana's brother. But let's get back to who your man is. Tash, isn't it?"

"Yeah, I'm Tash. But I haven't got a man." I don't want one, either. One lucky escape was sufficient. A politician was bad enough. There's no way I want to be connected to a biker.

A plaintive cry sounds. Sam leans over and pulls Zane onto her lap, unfastening her top and putting the baby to her breast. *This is so not how I imagined a biker compound.*

"He feeding well, Sam?" Carmen asks as she continues playing with my hair.

"Like a pig," Sam laughs. "He's going to be a big boy."

"I don't know how you did it Marcia." Sophie places another cup of coffee in front of me. "One makes your tits sore enough."

"I gave up and went to bottles after three months," Marcia laughs, getting herself settled next to us, a look of love thrown toward her sleeping twins.

"Don't blame you," the VP's wife observes.

I pick up my coffee which is too hot, to give my hand something to do, and my face an object to hide behind. *That could have been me.* I suffer a quick pang of regret, then tell myself I wouldn't have wanted Seb's baby. Not once I knew what he was.

"Oh, you're all in here, are you?"

I look up to see the woman I'd met in the kitchen earlier. Becca, I think I recall. Again, I notice her swollen belly. *Are all these men super-virulent or something? Do they have super-sperm? Or have they never heard of birth control?* Not that Seb had liked to use it. That's how I got knocked up. *Stupid, stupid error.*

"Is there anyone who's not pregnant or breastfeeding?" My hand goes to my mouth as though to try to push back the words that had come out without me thinking.

"I'm not. There, finished. Not contributed to the offspring yet." Carmen comes around to the front to check her handiwork. "Feel better?"

I nod my thanks as Sam counts off on her fingers. "Sandy, my stepmom, she's definitely not. Neither's Mariana. But Becca's almost ready to drop. What are you now, Becca?"

"Two months to go." She looks wistfully at the coffee. "I suppose that's not decaf?"

"No, but Matt will make some for you." Sam raises her eyes toward Matt who's pointedly not watching her breastfeeding. With only a slight huff, he makes a trip to the kitchen once again. "Now, weren't we discussing Blade and Tash?"

"No we were not," I feel confident enough to say. For an answer, Sam raises her eyebrow, and says enigmatically, "We'll see."

"Rash!"

The mispronunciation of my name signals Tommy's found me and saved me from the awkward turn the conversation had taken. I turn to see him bouncing in, followed by a grinning Fergus.

"Hey. You must be Tommy. How you doing?" Sophie greets him with a wide smile. "Christ, you're built like a brick shit-house."

Sam giggles, "That's a new one, Soph."

The Englishwoman waves Sam off. "Look at the size of him."

Tommy beams, soaking up the attention. "Cleaned alllllll the bikes," he tells everyone within hearing.

When eyes go to Fergus, the prospect shrugs. "All I had to do was supervise. He was surprisingly careful. You like your bikes, don't you, Tommy?"

"Tommy likes bikes," he agrees. Then, a little sneakily, "Tommy likes eating too."

"Matt!" Sam yells out. "Bring a plate of cookies."

CHAPTER 14

Blade

Drummer is the first to break the silence. His eyes sharpen. "Okay, then," he says, slowly. "Lawson, the outsider, becomes the nominee, and it's not impossible that wasn't an accident. It is possible that someone as close to him as a lover…" For a second my snort puts him off his stride, but he quickly recovers with a glare toward me. "Or a campaign manager such as Tash has some dirt about that, or put two and two together. Then there's the other matter. He needs to be a respectable man, so somehow digs up his wife and kids and relocates them to Tucson. How, if what you, Mouse, suspect about the abuse is right, I've no fuckin' idea. But they are here, that appears to be fact. So the girlfriend, Tash, becomes a liability. Blade! Will you stop fuckin' trying to interrupt?" Drummer's stare is now steely, making me go still and shutting my mouth. "Okay, girlfriend or employee, whatever, she's a problem. She's got no folks close by, it's a calculated risk on his part if she disappears. But," he pauses, rubs his hand over his face, "surely there'd be something to link him to her. Then it would all blow up."

"I think we've got a man who can cover his tracks, Prez." All eyes go to our tech guy. "I had to dig deep. They've deleted the files about Emmalina Fielding being his campaign manager. All mention of her salary is gone. She is listed, but only as a volunteer supporter. On the face of it, there's nothing to give any story she produces credibility."

I'm grateful we've got a man on our side who doesn't take things at face value, who can dig into deleted files. Most people don't understand how it's virtually impossible to completely erase shit from systems. We've had that lecture from Mouse more than once.

"I found one other bit of information which might involve Blade's Tash."

"She's not fuckin' mine," I yell out.

Mouse is unrepentant. His eyes lock onto mine, as almost in a monotone he adds, "She visited an abortion clinic in Tucson."

Fuck. In fact, the whole table is stunned into silence.

"His baby?" Marvel asks, but his joking tone is absent.

"Look, hold on a moment." The VP uses a voice he doesn't usually employ. It's not a shout, but loud enough we all take notice. "Sophie has been to one of those clinics. They provide contraception advice and deal with women's health issues as well. In fact, she had a Pap test done there. You're quite probably jumping to the wrong conclusion."

Drummer's lips press together as he nods at the VP. After a second he says, "Who knows? But if she went for the reason Mouse is suggesting, any pregnancy wouldn't have suited his purpose. Even the whisper of an abortion, the conclusion you fuckers have immediately jumped too, would probably not do him any good. That's something by itself. Add her holding potential evidence he was knocking off his rivals one by one. Christ, that's enough shit to unbalance an upstanding politician."

Peg's got a campaign leaflet in front of him. He pushes it across the table to the prez, tapping a line on the paper.

Prez takes a deep breath. "He's running on a pro-life platform."

I can't deny from Mouse's digging, it could very well be, she was pregnant and now isn't any more. "Kid might not even have been his, Prez. Could have been her setting him up. Just fingering him for the dad is enough to sway the election against him." But if he was, it wouldn't have been an immaculate conception, and would mean his cock had definitely been near, fuck, inside her. My skin crawls at the thought.

"I'm surprised he didn't wipe the clinic's records," Rock observes.

Mouse grins. "He's got control over his own systems, but it takes a genius like me to get in anywhere else. But Wraith's right. It didn't give the reason for her appointment, just that she'd been there."

I glare at him. So why had he led me to believe Lawson had put a baby inside her? He's lucky I don't throat punch him.

Beef holds up his hand. "Hate to say this. There are other means to getting rid of a kid. Could have happened naturally, or Lawson might have used his fists." Christ. Beef's suggestion makes me feel sick. In fact, everyone goes quiet around the table, allowing Beef to continue, "If what we're coming up with is the truth, we're being asked to provide security for someone who may well have come to us because of our supposed reputation."

"As we originally feared, Beef," Prez agrees. "And now we're homing in on the possible reasons, and it's not just to eject a few loudmouths from his meetings."

"Tash might have visited the clinic to set up a red herring. A path for someone like Mouse to find." Sitting, listening to everything, has made me angry. "The bitch isn't sayin' anything. She's the fuckin' key to all this." There were a fuck load of things Tash could have told Drummer and I when we were talking to her earlier. If she'd come clean, then we wouldn't be sitting here wasting time, trying to make Mouse's puzzle pieces fit. If she would have told the truth in any event. Christ, out of everyone, I'm a man who knows bitches can't be trusted, my mother was the ultimate example of that.

Lawson could be squeaky clean. She might be the root of all his ills and him totally innocent. If that's so, he might be on the right lines if he's thinking of removing her permanently. Bitches are nothing but trouble. My voice is loud when I ask bitterly, "What if you're wrong about his wife, Mouse? What if there was a perfectly good reason why they were living separate? What if he is an upstanding man, and Tash is trying to bring him down? What if anything she has to say would only be a pack of lies? Safer for her to keep her mouth shut rather than come out with something that could easily be disproved."

"She was living on the streets, Blade," Peg reminds me. "Presumably chased off from wherever she'd been and afraid to go back, or contact friends or family. No one does that by choice. If she hadn't found a protector in Tommy, she might well be dead."

But she'd said that herself. "Losing a job and their home can happen to anyone."

"She did work for him. Joined his campaign a few months back. That's fact." Mouse looks confused that I'm jumping to Lawson's defence.

I continue playing devil's advocate. "He fired her," I suggest. "I dunno. Perhaps she had debts she couldn't pay off, didn't take long to lose her house, everything she had. That's why she could have been living rough. Don't think we should take anything she has to say as gospel." Yeah, I might be getting on a roll here.

"Blade!" Drummer thunders bringing me to a halt. "I sat there and watched her. She's fuckin' scared. As far as Lawson is concerned, she's a loaded gun. I'm not at all sure she was lying when she said she'd leave the state and keep quiet." He breaks off and takes a deep breath. "But you're right. We shouldn't dismiss it out of hand. Lawson would know her better than any of us."

Yeah, in the fucking biblical sense.

"Still got the issue Lawson's trying to find her. Makes sense he's worried she's going to say where his bodies are buried, or at least, make waves so people think they are there. Can't deny that could be good reason to want her out of the way. And that could be why he's come to us."

"What you sayin', Beef?" Shooter's scowling.

"I'm sayin'," he turns to the youngest member. Now Paladin's gone and is playing happy families up in Colorado with Jayden, Shooter's regained that title once again. "He might think we'll threaten, maim or kill on demand."

"Worrying he'd think that of us," Viper puts in. "Doubt those skills would go down well in the Chamber of Commerce. Our reputation would go to shit."

Drummer bangs the gavel to get our attention. "Carry on, Beef. Don't think you've finished."

"Prez. Nah, just wanted to say, if she's threatened to tell lies about him, could very well be putting a slur on a good man, lose the election for him."

"So why hasn't she already come forward?"

Peg shakes his head. "Who'd believe a homeless woman ever had an affair with a politician? She'd need to get cleaned up first."

"Lawson didn't know she was on the streets," I tell him. "He'd completely lost touch. Suspected she was in Tucson, but not that she was no longer such a risk." I remember my initial reaction to Lawson. I hadn't liked him, but then, I've never seen a politician who appealed to me. You have to be a particular type of beast to run for office. Not something I would consider myself.

While I'd been recollecting, Beef's said something else that I didn't catch. I ask him to repeat what he just said.

With a roll of his eyes he does. "If we think there's a chance she's got real dirt to spill on Lawson, we don't want to hurt her. Have to go easy on her until we know. Best way of doing that is to catch her off guard." He's making sense so far, I raise my chin to show my agreement. He continues, "I'm proposing to offer to get close to Tash. Bitches spill secrets when pillow talk is involved."

My seat goes over backwards as I stand, knife in hand, blade quickly at my brother's neck.

Beef's eyes meet mine. They're fucking sparkling. From his end of the table comes Drummer's roar of laughter. Rock gets out his wallet and passes a couple of notes to Marvel.

"What the fuck?" I growl, my blade almost cutting into Beef's skin.

"I think that settles it," Drummer says drily. "Agreed. Need to get the truth out of Tash and not jump to the obvious conclusion that a politician's lyin'. Beef's idea works, fuck the truth out of her, but let's substitute Blade's name instead."

Knife and hand slip away from their threatening position. My jaw drops and my eyes flash. "No."

"No?" Drummer repeats, his hand waving around the table. "It's a good fuckin' suggestion which means someone has to do it. You don't want to? Well, you make the choice. Who do you suggest gets up close to her, Brother?"

I look around. Married men aren't meeting my eye. But fuck ing Dollar's taken off his glasses and is swinging them by one arm. Beef is sitting with his arms folded, his head tilted to one side. Shooter looks like he's just about to put his hand up. Marvel, Jekyll and Hyde all appear overly interested. When my eyes settle on Road, he gives a quick smile and a shake of his head, suggesting he's taking himself out of the running.

"You want them to draw straws?" Drummer prompts.

No I fucking don't. The thought of any of them getting their hands on Tash makes me see red. But I can't do what they're asking. Cosy up to the bitch? I don't mind the fucking part, my cock would be more than happy to sink into her, but talk to her afterward? To get the information out of her, to suss whether she's lying or speaking the truth, I'll have to hold her, pretend to feel affection for her. Yesterday was the first time I'd ever spent the whole night in close proximity to a bitch, and I didn't want to repeat even that.

"I've got another suggestion," I say, my voice like ice. "I'll torture that shit out of her." Yeah, I can do that. I'm already thinking of which knife I can threaten her with. Something long and sharp, slice those borrowed clothes off her, let her feel cold steel against her neck…

"You can't torture an innocent woman, Blade," Prez offers quite reasonably. "And if we need to produce her to Lawson, can't do that with half her skin flayed off. Nah, one of you," he looks at the eager faces around the table, "are going to need to get to her via your dick."

As the murmurs of offers come again, my mouth opens and I rasp through clenched teeth, "I'll do it." Maybe it won't be so bad. She'll be staying in the crash room. I'll just fuck her and go back to my own bed…

"You'll do it?" Fuck me, Drummer's actually smirking. "Right then Blade, we do this right. Move her into your suite."

Wait one fucking moment.

But everyone's nodding as if it's the best plan ever. My blade slams into the table top leaving yet one more mark in the wood. *Fuck!*

CHAPTER 15

Tash

Tommy is surprisingly gentle with the children. As he eats his cookies, giggling and pretending to steal one from Amy, but quickly giving it back when she pouts, I realise he seems to fit in with this strange family. Soon Eli and Olivia are climbing his huge frame like monkeys, and it doesn't faze him one bit. At first the women looked on warily, but quickly seem confident enough to let their offspring play with the big man. After a while I hear zoom zoom noises coming from under the table, Tommy's on his belly lying flat out, looking on and reverently admiring Eli's toy bike. When Matt makes sandwiches for us all, Sam hands him one which he devours without getting up.

As I watch him playing, enjoying himself with no pressure, food being put into his mouth; it hits me Tommy must think he's died and gone to heaven. I've no idea of his story, but this is the kind of place where he should be. With people who seem to tolerate, and even like him. If this is an example of how they're going to treat him, if they offer him a place to stay, how can I think of taking him away? Of using him while I'm getting myself back on my feet

Back on my feet? I don't dare think of a future without any worry. The idea of a house with a white picket fence has to be put right out of my head. Survival at best is all I can hope for.

To survive, I must be careful. However nice these women appear to be, I can't let myself relax. Even now Seb might be sending Grant for me. But Tommy? Whatever happens to me, I hope that he might have found his place.

With bikers? What am I thinking? The women seem normal enough, but they can't be. Not when their men are criminals. Just the type of people Lawson would have on his side. I must not get too involved with them, or allow them to trick me. I've been lulled into a false sense of security. *Was that why no one's been questioning me? They already know why I'm here.* I eye them again, this time differently. It's hard to imagine they're all putting on an act, meant to catch me off guard. Is this just one more way for Drummer's interrogation to continue? Will Sam, nice as she is, drop in a question when I'm least expecting it?

Suddenly a huge dog bounds into the room, followed by one of the bikers who goes straight over to Marcia. The way the leather clad man pulls her out of the chair and to him, angling her head so she's positioned just right, before putting his lips to hers and proceeding to ravish her mouth makes my stomach clench. For a second, I wish that was me. Not with him, I would never take another woman's man, or, not knowingly. But the possessive way he's showing he obviously loves her affects me. I've never experienced anything like that. The men I've been with have all been far too polite.

Eventually the two part. I notice no one else has noticed any-thing abnormal. The pair's intense interaction must be common, or do all the women have men who treat them the same way? Maybe that's the attraction of bikers.

"Heart," Marcia playfully slaps the biker's arm.

"Hey, I missed you." His eyes gleam, unapologetically.

"Daddy!" Amy's voice shouts sternly. "Did you miss me?"

"'Course I did, little one. What you doing?" Heart's eyes find Tommy; they crease momentarily while watching his interac-tion with the children. He's cautious, a good dad. What he sees seems to satisfy him, and shortly he sinks to his haunches, his full attention on his daughter.

A sense of something I'm missing tugs at my heart. Here I am, an outsider, judging these people without knowing them. These people who I believe to be criminals have the kind of life I want. It would be all too easy to get sucked in, to take the front they're presenting at face value. If I stay around them, I might get drawn into the pretence, stop being vigilant, when it's critical to stay on my guard. I can't afford to relax.

When there's a gap in the conversation, I pull myself to my feet. "I'm sorry, I'm tired, and my arm's aching. Thank you for sorting my hair out Carmen, but I think I need to go and lie down."

My comment is greeted with a seemingly genuine outburst of agreement and commiseration, hopes that I'll soon feel better, then I'm free to leave. I notice Matt's eyes carefully following me as I go first to the bathroom, then to the room I'd slept in last night. His attentiveness reminds me I'm under guard here.

Now alone, I admit I hadn't been lying. Talking, watching, learning about the people that live here had distracted me, but now alone my head pounds, my arm is sore and my leg throbs. My brain's fed up with thinking, trying to puzzle everything out. Covering my mouth, even though there's no one here to see, I yawn widely.

I eye the painkillers on the bedside table, I could really do with something to ease my hurts. My hand inches toward the enticing pain relief, then backs away. It's dangerous here, I should remain alert. I lay on the bed, trying to get comfortable, but pull on my shoulder as I turn over and wince out loud. Then I put too much pressure on my bruised leg. Damn it. I pull the strip toward me, then take two powerful painkillers as the medic had prescribed. Immediately, I wonder if I've made a mistake.

Whether I have or not, it feels good to relax, to sink my head back into the soft welcome pillow. The three weeks I spent on the streets was enough to make me appreciate a real bed, even if this mattress seems a little worn with a pronounced dip in the middle. I doubt I'll ever take one for granted again.

With thoughts in my head of despite how uneasy the location makes me feel, I'm feeling pretty comfortable right now, I drift off.

When I come back to my senses, to my horror I find I'm no longer in the cosy bed, but being carried. *What? Who? Don't let it be Grant!* I whimper and struggle, hitting something with my aching arm which hurts both me and the person in whose hold I am.

"Fuck, woman, stop that. I've got you. Don't fight me."

It's Blade's voice. But what is he doing, and where is he taking me?

"Blade? What the hell? Put me down." I panic, thinking he's going to take me away from the compound. Put me back on the streets. Or worse, deliver me to Seb.

What he replies may be even worse. "Calm down, woman. Nothing bad's going to happen. You're just moving into my suite."

No. It's the drugs. They must have really played with my mind, I thought he said… My voice shakes as I ask him to repeat it, "What did you say?"

"I'm taking you to my room. Hold on, let me get the door, we're here." Without putting me down, he shifts me to allow him to open a door, steps into a short hallway, then turns the handle which lets us into another room. When I struggle again, this time he puts me on my feet, steadying me as my drugged-up head doesn't send the right signals to my legs.

Christ, were the women right? Does he think because he brought me to the compound, he's got rights to me? If he does,

I've got to make him see sense. No way and no how, and when hell freezes over, are the thoughts that come to mind.

"Welcome to your new abode," he says. But it's not a welcome I hear in his tone. It's more like resignation.

Shaking my head, trying to clear it, I make an effort to focus my bleary eyes. There's a big bed, a desk, a table. A large closet, and an open door leading to a bathroom. Sliding doors lead out to a balcony. Apart from a few bike parts strewn around, it could look like a hotel room. There's an odd display on the wall that I'll examine later, for now, my vision isn't quite sharp enough. One thing I do notice—*if this is his room, he's quite neat.*

"Where are you going to stay?" I ask, suspiciously.

With his hands still holding my biceps, he replies into my ear, "With you."

As his voice vibrates against me, his warm breath carrying a faint odour of cigarette smoke brushes my cheek. It must be an effect of the tablets or something but my thighs clench together. My body's unwanted physical reaction makes my response sharper than it otherwise would have been.

"No." Using all my strength I push myself away. Free, I stagger, right myself, then swing around. "I'll stay in that room in the clubhouse. I am not going to be your personal sex toy."

His eyebrow rises. "Interesting you went straight there. Who said anything about sex, darlin'?" Chuckling softly, his low growling tone causes my body to shiver in anticipation. "If you were offerin', wouldn't turn you down. A bit of relief? A quick fuck?" His eyes, a startling blue, suddenly look icy cold. "But that's all it would be."

"I don't want a quick fuck." Not with him. Definitely not him. Or any kind of fuck for that matter.

"Let's get this straight, right from the start, woman. I'm not looking for an old lady."

I don't normally swear, but his assumption forces it out of me. "Now it's you going *there*. Why the fuck did you say that? I'm not looking for a man, and if I was, a biker would be the last person I'd want to tie myself to. I've just escaped—or hope I have—from what happened when I last let a man into my life." I push back a strand of hair that's escaped from the braid Carmen did for me. "I don't even like you, Blade."

"That's alright," his shoulders rise and fall. "I don't need to like the women I fuck either. Not if it's just to get some relief."

I shouldn't have raised my eyes to his ruggedly handsome face. I certainly shouldn't have raked them down his muscular body, finding it hard not to pause for a second on the impressive bulge pushing at the material of his jeans. My face flushes as I look away, hoping he hadn't noticed my reaction.

"Like what you see, darlin'?" he drawls.

Fuck these tablets, they're making me indiscreet. I draw myself up, saying as haughtily as I can, "I'm hurting, in case you haven't noticed. You could be the sexiest man alive and it wouldn't have any effect on me." I'm lying, but it must be some strange reaction to the medication I've taken, or something to do with the fact he was the man who rescued me. I didn't lie, I really don't like him. He's cocky, self-assured, and I'm getting the impression he thinks he's God's freaking gift to women, that he only has to raise his little finger to get whoever he fancies to scratch his itch.

"Well, the offer's on the table, just let me know if you change your mind. Make yourself comfortable. I'll go find one of the whores to fuck."

Christ! He really doesn't give a damn where his dick goes. "You do that," I hiss, without turning around.

The door closes loudly behind him. Going to the window I look out, and see him walking down the pathway with mascu-line purposeful steps, watching the way his hips swing and his ass flexes. He pauses, takes something out of his cut, then as he strides on, flicks a lighter and puts the flame to the tip of a cigarette. I watch him until he's out of sight. *Just to make sure he won't change his mind and come back.*

Eyeing a pillow, I pick it up and throw it as a scream bubbles up out of me. *Was there ever a man who was so frustrating? Aarrghh!* What a bizarre conversation we just had. Both of us admitting we didn't like each other. Him offering, what? To let me ride his cock for the night? An hour? Nothing more. I could never be attracted to someone like that. But the pressure between my thighs suggests I may be lying. *No. I'm not.*

I don't need to stay here. But when I go to the door, I find it's been locked. From the outside. Damn!

Huffing, I examine what is apparently my new accommodation, or my prison more like. The feeling of drunkenness fading, I step closer to that display on the wall. Perhaps I've now found the reason for his strange handle, it's a collection of knives. Blades long, short, narrow, all with one thing in common—they look lethal. I feel the beginnings of a lop-sided smile, and going over, take a particularly sharp one out of its sheath. Ha! Blade will get a taste of his own medicine if he tries anything with me. I'll castrate him.

Perhaps I shouldn't be too hasty.

Oh, for goodness sake. I give myself a mental slap. He offered a quick fuck, that's all. I've just left one man who used me. Why on earth would I want to repeat a mistake?

Blade's image, though, is hard to get out of my head. It's the pain meds, it has to be. I've no idea why, but our sparring, the references to fucking, had for some reason aroused me. He's left me wanting. What was in those painkillers? There had to be something.

If the feelings he's caused don't go away when the tablets wear off, what would it hurt if I used him? Just to get some relief? In the same way as he'd use me? Somehow I suspect Heart's demonstration back in the clubroom would pale in comparison to what Blade could do.

This isn't me, is it? I bang my forehead with the heel of my hand, hoping to knock some sense into myself.

Anyway, he must have been joking. This is just somewhere to keep me out of the way and isolated from the friendly women. There's no way he'll be staying in this suite with me. That had just been a poor joke. He said he won't be returning. Nah, he'll be warming the bed of a whore just like he told me.

While I haven't yet seen them, the idea they keep them here doesn't surprise me. Women who are probably locked away, waiting only on the bikers' pleasure.

Blade will be doing to them, what I'm thinking of him doing to me.

Freaking hell, brain! Shut up!

CHAPTER 16

Blade

That woman infuriates me, but it seems I enjoy baiting her. Despite what my brothers had suggested at church, there's no way I'll be fucking her. I did what they said, moved her into my suite, but I won't be doing the deed. I'll find some other way to make her open up to me. I'm the expert at eliciting secrets after all, I just need to find a weakness to exploit.

Let's face it. I'm doing them a favour as well as myself, taking her out of their reach. A bitch like that isn't the one and done kind, nah, she'd be a clinger. One wrong step with her and she'd be trying to ensnare me, or any of my brothers, as her man. I stepped up to save them, not because I didn't want anyone else to touch her.

I do have some sympathy for her. Girl's had it rough enough, she doesn't need one of my brothers pressuring her. Best for her to stay with the one man who doesn't want to touch her. Or won't let her get to him. I know how deceitful bitches can be, one of the first lessons I learned in my life. Someone like Beef would be far too soft. *Not his cock though. Reckon she'd get him hard.*

Fuck that. She's a bitch, and like all of them, can't be trusted. *Mouse thinks she had a fucking abortion.* Tash threw away her baby before it was even grown. What the fuck kind of woman does that? Even my sorry excuse for a mother had given Jonah and I life, not that she'd cared much about us after. Shallow, selfish bitch only thinking of herself. Yeah, Tash is just like my mom.

Fuck but it's funny though. She was obviously turned on. I wonder what was in those tablets Doc left her. Some kind of aphrodisiac it would seem. Hmm, may not be such a farfetched idea, marijuana is thought to be a turn on by some. But as I've been smoking plain nicotine, that doesn't give me any excuse. As I walk, I adjust myself, these jeans are tight, not much room for a swelling dick. Then again, it's not that particular woman herself. It doesn't take much to turn me on. I'm a red-blooded man after all, a nice pair of tits, a perk ass, well, that's all it normally needs to make my cock wake up, and no one could accuse Tash of lacking either of those attributes. I could fuck her and ignore what comes out of her mouth. *Nah.* Not giving her the chance to get her claws into me. Think of her as Rash, that's a good turn off. But even that doesn't seem to help.

I hadn't lied about needing some relief so I run through the club girls in my head. Paige, now she's great at giving head, Diva loves taking it in the ass, Pussy's okay, but, well, let's just say she's been here a long time and is perhaps a little overused. Allie, now she's sweet, will do anything you want. Let's face it, if your cock needs attending to and you're bored with your hand, any of them have pluses and minuses, and all of them are used to me and my ways. I don't kiss, never have, never will. Can't see the need to stick your tongue in a bitch's mouth when it's another part of your anatomy that wants inside instead. Waste of time if you ask me. In other ways, I don't leave them wanting, which is why any of the whores are always willing to service me.

By the time I'm at the clubhouse, my dick is completely under control. Which is strange, considering my thoughts and the main reason I've come down here. So when I walk in and see Drummer standing at the bar, the urgency to fuck having left me, I'm not disappointed when he waves me over to join him.

"Prez." After a nod his way, I glance toward Allie. Wouldn't have been able to have her tonight anyway, she's playing bartender. "Beer."

"Coming right, up." Her smile's wide and genuine as she goes about her simple task, and I soon have an opened bottle in front of me.

"Come, sit." Drummer points to an empty table in the corner.

I follow him over. "What's up, Prez?"

His steely gaze settles on my face. "Just wanted to check in with you. You doing okay?"

"I'm fine, Prez. Why wouldn't I be?" I've got a hot and possibly willing woman left in my bed, which means I can't go near it. Yeah. I'm hunky dory.

He draws a hand down his face, stroking his beard. "Don't forget I know all about it, Blade. Before I became the prez, I was in your shoes. I was the enforcer."

"Someone's got to do it," I reply, philosophically.

Lifting his beer, he takes a few mouthfuls, his throat working as he swallows. "Seems a bit at odds with your artistic tendencies, that's all."

The sides of my mouth curl. "You've never complained about my artistry before. Think I can be quite inventive when necessary."

His response is a quick grin, but then it fades. "Yeah, no complaints there, Brother. But then you puke your guts up after."

My face twitches and I look down. I hadn't been aware that he'd known. "We've all got to do what we have to, Prez."

"Know that, Blade. Know that. It's easy to see something's always been eating you up inside. No, don't stop me. Let me say this. Have you ever considered you can do both? You're one of the best fuckin' enforcers in any of the chapters, always know how to get the best results. It's a fuckin' science to you. But there's no fuckin' reason why you can't allow yourself to be the artist as well."

I go to tell him he's wrong. That in my head I equate sketching, letting my creative side flow through pencil and pen, with weakness.

"Don't tell me I'm wrong, Blade. You've not suppressed it, you draw. You just destroy everything afterwards. What would it fuckin' hurt to show off your artistic skills?"

In my head, I think how much Sam would have appreciated the sketch of her, Drummer and their kids. I'd burned it like all the others. I could have got paints, done a proper job, but no, I'd destroyed it instead. Is that a waste of my talent? I'd never thought about it like that, just the guilt I couldn't stop drawing. Taking a deep breath, I lean forward. "I used to paint. Even at twelve I'd had pictures in a few exhibitions. It's just like I've got this roadblock in my brain, which stops me doing anything now."

"Oil or watercolour?"

His question sends me back to those days. "Both. But I'm better, or was, with watercolour." I wonder, whether after all these years, I could pick it up again.

"What would Jonah want, Blade? For you to torture yourself for the rest of your life? His was cut short through no fault of yours. Your misguided guilt wants to make it up to him? Well live twice as hard. Be the man Jonah would have been if you have to, but be yourself too."

"It's not that easy, Drummer. If…" I falter, not knowing how to express it.

But Prez already knows. "You think it takes all you are to put on the bravado you need to enforce the rules of the club and protect us from our enemies. If you let what you think is the weaker side of you through, then you won't be able to play your role?" His eyebrows raise as though in question, but he doesn't wait for me to answer. "As I said, I've been there, Brother. I know the fuckin' cost on a man. But because it takes a lot out of you, you're in danger of shutting all emotion away. Need to let it out sometimes. I got out, became Prez." His eyes cloud over, he got the top spot when his father, Bastard, the previous president and more than half the club had been killed in a police raid. Not the way he'd have wanted it to happen. Pulling himself together, he begins again, "I became Prez. You got a fast promotion into my old shoes."

"Rather be in my boots than yours. Don't think life became any easier for you. As to passing down your old footwear, the club had been decimated, Prez. You didn't have many to choose from." My lips press together.

"I chose well from the few that I had. No one would, or could have been better, Blade. Never fuckin' doubt that. But it changed you. You've become hard, as you needed to, but I worry you've lost your soul along the way."

He's right. I had. No one can play on a man's pain, know and use those spots that hurt the most while not causing death, understanding how to make a man writhe in agony but still be alive without becoming a monster. My beer's empty. The bottle, devoid of contents, seems a reflection of myself.

"I'd have lost myself too, eventually." Drummer's words make me look at him. "If I hadn't met Sam."

He's softened, changed. For the better? He's not as hard-headed as he was. Still sharp though, a good leader, a man you wouldn't want to cross.

"If you're saying I need a bitch in my life, Prez, you're wrong." Another promise I'd made to myself. Jonah would have been the first to understand. They only desert you when you need them most.

Drummer stands, his own bottle now empty. "We'll see," he responds, enigmatically.

As he raises his chin toward me, then walks off, I shake my head. *He's wrong.*

"Can I do anything for you, lover?"

Paige's voice cuts into my thoughts. I look up and smile. "Sure can, darlin'." Standing, I take hold of her hand, leading her into the crash room Tash had recently vacated. Yeah, these rooms are for other things than housing temporary visitors.

I don't know what's wrong with me. Sure, it's normal to fantasise when you're thrusting into a warm mouth, images coming into your mind from a porn show recently watched or an otherwise unobtainable film star, but why the fuck do I find myself thinking of Tash when coming with a roar down Paige's throat? I look down to see the whore wiping her lips, an expression of achievement on her face, and the remorse I feel is unexpected.

Paige is a sweet girl. One look at me and I don't need to express what I'm feeling in words. "It's okay, Blade. I'll go take care of myself." She winks as she stands.

When the door closes behind her, I let out the breath I hadn't known I was holding. I couldn't even pretend, not tonight, but it isn't me to leave a girl wanting. This life that I live, no one gives a damn if all I do is to take and never give back. My reward for sacrificing my soul for the club. The club girls give and take whatever is offered in return, if nothing, well, the next brother might be more so inclined.

Tash is waiting in my suite. The woman my brothers expect me to fuck. To use my cock as just one more weapon in an enforcer's armoury. Not that I've ever fucked information out of anyone before, but then I've never been called on to use my expertise on a woman.

This pillow is too soft, too uncomfortable and annoyingly still has a faint odour of Tash. I try to punch it into submission, thinking over Prez's words, that Sam had saved his soul in some way. There's no doubt she complements him, stands up to him, doesn't take shit from him, but steps back when it matters. Never interferes with the club, but seems to keep everything running smoothly. Yeah, Viper's daughter from out of the blue had been a good addition to the old ladies. He needed someone strong, and there was not one close to the mark until she'd come along.

But me? Nah, even if I wanted someone, doubt there'd be anyone who'd fit. What woman could live with a man who had violence running through their veins? Who was in love with a cold selection of knives, who knew no other type of lovemaking than how to have a good fuck and get off.

Shit. This mattress needs to be replaced. However I turn, I keep rolling back to that dip in the centre. I try again, my nose making contact with the sheet which also smells of Tash, luckily after the shower not prior. *She'd want to be kissed.* How does that work? Hell, I've used my mouth often enough on a woman, but on that hole between her legs, never her lips north of her waist.

What would it feel like? My lips moving against hers? My tongue sweeping into that warm abyss, meeting hers, gliding together.

Fuck. Now my cock's hard again. My hand reaches down, touching it, wrapping around it, wondering how Tash's hand would feel on my dick. *Would she squeeze hard, like this? Or would she gently slide her palm up and down, my grunts and groans encouraging her until she got the right pace, the right grip. Yeah, she'd slide it like this, faster, faster...*

I come. Covering my stomach with ribbons of cum. Bunching the sheet in my hands, I wipe myself clean, strip it off the bed, and leave it on the floor. Rather than relief, I feel empty.

Fucking woman. Get out of my damn head.

I could go see her. Fuck her. That's what I'm supposed to be doing. Not force her, of course, but somehow persuade her. Without bragging I don't think it would be difficult, not after the way she reacted to me.

She's still hurting. Fucking would have to wait until she's less sore. *But there are things we could do, ways to get around those injuries.*

I don't go to my suite. Instead I spend the night in the crash room, unable to sleep, hearing noises of brothers partying outside with no desire to join them. *What's happening to me?* Why the fuck am I hiding out here and not going back to my own bed?

Admit it, you've got the hots for her. Okay, so I have. But I know how this will play out. This woman would be no different to the hundreds of others. I'd fuck Tash—probably enjoy it— then walk away without even a glance back.

But in this situation, that wouldn't be enough, and I've got the sense to know it. To get her to talk, she's got to trust me. How the fuck could I earn that trust if I just walked away? If I pretend it's anything more than sex, she'll see right through me, she already has. Fuck Drummer, for putting me in this position. *Should have let one of the other brothers have her instead.* My hands clench at the thought.

What will the prez think when he finds out instead of doing what he wanted, getting close to her, I've spent the night here, hiding out in the crash room? Keeping, not closing, the distance between us.

In the morning, I creep out trying not to look like I've spent the night in yesterday's clothes. Stinking of sex as I've not gone to my shower.

Peg shakes his head when he sees me. "You look like shit, Brother."

"It's that bitch keeping him awake," Shooter grins, tilting a cup toward me.

"Yeah, well, whatever," the sergeant-at-arms says. "We've got a meet with Lawson this morning. Gonna freshen yourself up?"

I throw him a nod, then take a loaded plate from Darcy. When I ignore the comments around me, the brothers' ribaldry soon dries up.

I sense her presence before I see her. Looking up it's to find her standing in the doorway as though unsure of her welcome. Before I glance away I notice there's more colour in her face today.

Darcy waves her in. "Hey, Tash. Hungry?"

"I'll see you later, Peg. We leaving at ten?" When he nods, I get up, leave my empty plate on the side. As I walk past her, I hiss, "How the fuck did you get out of the suite?"

"As you seemed to have abandoned me, I climbed down from the balcony," she tosses back, equally quietly.

My eyes narrow as I eye her shoulder, no sling today, but she's supporting her arm with her hand. "Crazy bitch. I'd have come back for you."

"I didn't know that, did I?" she challenges.

Trust. Fuck. Her actions prove it's not just her who's got a long way to go to earn that. She really thought I'd locked her in and forgotten her? Swallowing hard, I push down my temper. "I'll always come back," I reassure her.

The look on her face suggests she doesn't believe me.

I've got somewhere to be. Knowing I'm going to have to make more of an effort later, I go past her, then make my way up to my thankfully empty suite.

Walking into my room, I stop dead. There's nothing different about it. Girl's neat, I'll give her that, the bed is already made, but there's a perfume hanging in the air which wasn't there before. I can't put my finger on what it is. She's used my soap, so that's not what's different. My deodorant too it seems. But somehow it's turned into a heady mix when mingled with her unique musk.

It's not overpowering, so why does it give the illusion she's taken over my suite? *My home?* Why, when she's not even here, is she making her presence known? And why the fuck am I feeling so guilty about that blow job last night? Or how I jerked off to the thought of her hand on my cock?

I throw off my dirty clothes and stride naked into the bathroom, turning on the shower, stepping in when the warm water runs. *I should just have let Jekyll or Beef have her.* Yeah, that's what I'll do. No one will care if I change my mind. Something about her unsettles me. If I can't stand to be near her, I'm certainly not going to be able to discover her secrets. Yeah. Having seen Beef's eyes flare when he saw her, he'd be delighted to have her beneath him, plunge his cock into her cunt, into her mouth…

No! No, no, no and fucking no.

Turning off the water I smooth my hands down my face. *What the fuck is wrong with me?*

As I dry myself off and get dressed, the last item to slide on being my cut, I've still found no answers. Or none which I can accept.

My phone buzzes.

Peg: Get your ass down here. Prez wants a word.

I'm grateful. Action might get the unpleasant thoughts out of my head. So I do, as suggested, get my ass down to the clubhouse. A now familiar scent hitting me as I almost bump into Tash.

"Sorry," she says needlessly. We both go this way and that until we manage to synchronise so I can move past her. I acknowledge her just with a nod, then go straight to Drummer's office.

"Hear you chickened out last night," Drummer says with a smirk.

Can't keep anything quiet in this place. "She's recovering, Prez. Don't want to push her too fast."

"Seems to be coping well enough to me," Peg not very helpfully butts in.

She does. Other bitches with a dislocated shoulder and bruised leg might go fishing for sympathy. She's pretending there's nothing wrong. Doesn't want to show weakness. *Strong fucking girl. She climbed down from my balcony.*

"Peg and I have been talkin'." Drummer gets down to business. "You're visiting Lawson this morning. Wondered about drawing him out a bit."

"Oh yeah?" I stretch out my legs. "How?"

Peg takes over, "Tell him we've found Tash and brought her to the compound."

My legs shoot back under me as I lurch forward. "Are you fuckin' kiddin' me? You suggestin' we hand her over?"

"What the fuck do you take me for, Blade?" Drummer thunders. "He'll ask for her, I'm certain. But we're not going to comply. Suggest we do what's necessary. Try and get him to put his cards on the table."

"If we're right," Peg stares at me, "about what he thinks our services may include, he'll be more than happy for us to take care of his problem." Using his fingers, he pretends to put the last in inverted commas.

"You think he'll come right out and ask us to kill her?"

"He might skirt around it, but I suspect that's what he would want us to do. Peg's idea," Drummer nods to acknowledge it wasn't his, "is that we can cut this short. We get a direct instruction from Lawson, we'll know what we're dealin' with. We can tell him we offed her, but instead we'll give her money, and get her set up somewhere else."

There are holes in Drummer's plan, I can immediately see them. "She's got family, Prez. She'll want to go back and visit. If she's innocent, then she can't be trusted not to speak to them."

"Good point, Blade. I'd rather not lie to her folks. But if she concocted a story, then she'll probably keep her mouth shut."

Peg's unrelenting. "Still think that's the easiest way to play it. Get Lawson to show his hand."

"We'd have to ensure she stayed quiet for ever. Set her up in Vegas or Colorado, get another chapter to keep a close eye on her." I think for a moment. "If we let Lawson believe she was dead, it would mean telling her parents that too and getting them to believe it." Having lost my own brother, I don't feel good about causing anyone else that type of pain. "Is Tash the type of woman who'd hurt her family?"

"Thought that's what you were going to find out, Brother. Instead you spent the night in the crash room. Need lessons on how to fuck?" Peg accompanies his suggestion with a crude gesture more reminiscent of Beef.

Drummer raises an eyebrow toward Peg. "Peg could be right. Admitting she's here might get him to show his hand. There are too many unknowns and I don't like them. How he wants to play it from there will at least get things out into the open." Leaning back in his chair, Prez folds his arms over his chest, then puts forward another opinion. "Of course, if we refuse to give her up to him, there goes our security contract and possibly any other business that might have come our way."

"Would we really want it, Prez? It's a woman's life we're talking about here. Whatever she's done, I don't want to have a hand in offing her." Peg's amusement has faded; his face looks grim.

Prez glares. "Just reminding us all what's at stake."

We go quiet, each lost in our own thoughts. It's me who breaks the silence. What I've got to think about is what's best for the club. "Ok. Let's play it Peg's way."

To my surprise, Drummer shakes his head. "Let's keep that card up our sleeve for now. See if we can draw him out while keeping the woman hidden. We can always 'find' her at a later date."

The wave of relief that goes through me is surprising.

CHAPTER 17

Blade

It's midsummer here in Tucson. That means the weather is fucking hot. Luckily the air-cooled V-twin engines seem to cope well. If anything, I reckon my bike runs better in the heat. Humans though, well we don't fair so fucking good. Not so bad if we can keep moving, but stuck in traffic, as Peg and I currently are, it's a bitch.

There's been an accident at the junction ahead, hopefully they'll get it cleared soon. I undo the bandana I've got wrapped around my head. After using it to wipe the sweat from my brow, retie it.

"Fuck this," Peg snarls after a few minutes, his temper overheating as much as his body. He gets off his bike, waving me to stay where I am.

I watch him stomp off, smothering a smile and choking back my laugh as I see his tall frame towering over the arguing participants and gesticulating. Then, he gets behind one of the crashed cars, and helps to push it out of the way. When he returns, to applause and honks from other cars around us, I raise my eyebrow.

"Just told them I don't give a damn who did what, but to argue it out once they'd cleared the fuckin' junction."

I grin at him. Not many people would want to cross Peg, he's a big, tall fucker. At last the traffic is moving and we're able to complete our journey. The air-conditioning inside the building we enter comes as a shock, causing goosebumps to rise on my arms. Not that I'm complaining, it's a welcome relief. Peg and I remain silent as we take the stairs to the second floor, and then find ourselves in Lawson's reception area again. This time we aren't kept waiting.

"Peg, Blade." Turner steps forward holding out his hand. "Good to see you again. Mr Lawson is ready for you. Can I get you a coffee?"

Both Peg and I shake our heads. We're not here to socialise. I expect Peg, like me, wants this over and done with. Even without the suspicions Mouse's digging had churned up, there's a vibe here that I don't like. Maybe it simply surrounds anyone who has something to do within the political arena. It seems to breed men, and women, who appear to come from the same narcissistic mould. I'm sure there are some genuine folks who selflessly want to help others have a better life, but most seem to be in it for themselves, and whatever they can get out of it, be that money or power. Enjoying the pomp and circumstance and relishing the kowtowing of people seeking favour. Well, if Lawson's expecting us to fall to our knees and lick his boots, he's looking at the wrong men.

We step inside. Lawson immediately raises his head toward his campaign manager and jerks it toward the reception desk that can be seen through the glass dividers. Out of the corner of my eye I watch as Turner has a word with the receptionist, who collects her bag, smiles and then disappears toward the elevator. Hmm. *This conversation isn't for prying ears.* What could he want to discuss in here that he doesn't want overheard?

When Turner returns and we're all seated, Lawson wastes no time on pleasantries. "You have information?" He places Tash's photo on the desk and slides it over to us. "About her."

"Emmalina Fielding." Peg shakes his head. "We've been out searching, but not yet." He's right. We've found a Natasha, but no Emmalina.

Some of the light goes from Lawson's eyes. "I'd hoped you'd have had more luck than my men, with your contacts and all." He adds almost to himself, "Where the fuck can she be hiding?"

"You've tried all her friends, associates, family?"

Lawson nods. "We've asked around, of course. Don't think anyone's hiding her. Grant was doing a random drive by in town and came across her. Said it looked like she'd been living rough." He sneers. "Shame he fucking lost her."

"We'll try the homeless shelters again," Peg offers hopefully. I'm glad he's taken the lead. Me? I don't think I could have kept a straight face when we know exactly where Tash is. "We're working blind, Lawson," Peg continues nonchalantly, leaning back, crossing his legs at the ankles, or, in his case, ankle and prosthesis. "If you tell us what she is to you and what you want with her, there may be clues to help us find her." His eyes sharpen. "Put it this way. If we come across her, what would be her side of the story?"

Behind us, Turner huffs a laugh. "You can bet she'd be filling your heads with all sorts of nonsense. Girl lies as easily as she breathes."

Interestingly, Peg stays quiet. Though he knows as well as I do, Tash hasn't said a word.

Lawson pushes down his eagerness as he appears to have a conversation over our heads. Letting out a heavy sigh, he begins, "She would tell you she used to work for me."

Peg and I exchange looks, but give nothing away. *Let him have the rope and do the job himself.* Our lack of comment gets the words spilling.

"Let's say, though she hid it well, she had different political affiliations. Discovered it when my opponent got a copy of my speech before I'd even given it. Could have cost me the nomination. He took some of my ideas and ran with it. It was lucky I was holding something back."

"And you were lucky when Cobb had to back out," I put it bluntly.

"Who would have believed it? It came right out of the blue. Didn't expect it, but yeah, the fact that Raul Cobb couldn't keep his dick only in his wife's pants was a stroke of pure luck for me."

"So you found you had a leak in your organisation." Peg's trying to move this along.

"Yes." Lawson's face glows. "There was only one person who that could be. Emmalina was the only one who'd seen that speech other than Neil and myself."

"Emmalina was only a volunteer," I refer to the doctored records Mouse had found. "Why did she see the notes of what you were going to say?"

Neil coughs from behind us. "I'm afraid I was a bit indiscreet. She's a pretty girl. I slept with her."

He did? Not Lawson? Not sure what that means. I catch Peg's expression of warning and keep my mouth shut.

"Unfortunately Neil trusted her a little too much."

The danger of doing that I can quite understand.

"You sure it wasn't Neil who leaked the speech?"

An indignant huff comes from behind us. Lawson ignores it. "I'd trust Neil with my life, let alone my career."

"My career depends on Mr Lawson being successful," Neil speaks up for himself. "Does me no good if he's discredited. Best day ever for me when he won the nomination. Now we've just got to win the election."

"Yes, Neil. But I won't win if Emmalina acts on her threats."

"Threats?" Peg asks. "Written?"

"Verbal. And not recorded. She threatened to say she had an affair with me, more than that, that she had an abortion. There's no truth in anything she says."

"The affair was with me," Neil confirms holding his hands up. "Though it could hardly be called that. I slept with her twice, both times initiated by her, whatever she says. The baby? Fuck knows. If there was one, it wasn't mine."

He sounds convincing. The picture they're drawing of one more untrustworthy woman I've been unlucky enough to cross paths with.

Again. Peg sends a cautionary look my way. Jumping in before I can ask anything else, "You sent your men out looking for her. They found her. She must have been desperate to manage to get away from them. Or, not want to talk to you."

"As I said, Grant came across her by accident. He decided to bring her in so I could have a chat with her. I was going to make her see sense, how much damage her lies were doing." Lawson's face falls. "That she ran just shows she's not going to give up. She'd told my wife she was having an affair with me, that I got her pregnant. Luckily Neil stepped up and my wife, of course, believes me. She'll stand by my side if it comes out publicly, but it's not fair on her to hear those lies. She's just… well, she's sensitive. Fragile you might say. This worry is not good for her at all."

Fuck me, but if he's lying, he's a good actor. For a moment, he looks crestfallen. On my part, I'd have thought a strong woman like Tash would be better to stand by a politician's side than the wife he's describing as a delicate flower. I don't dare look Peg's way. From what Mouse had said, he doesn't give a damn about his wife's sensibilities, but I suppose we're to see it as damage Tash inflicted on him. A seed of doubt comes into my mind. Maybe he missed his wife and became a changed man.

"She tried first to get to me." Turner comes around and now perches on the desk. "Tried to tell me Mr Lawson forced her to have an abortion. If that was true, I could no longer work for the man. I'm anti-abortion. But the clinic she named assured me she hadn't been there. Or not to abort a child in any event."

"We need to talk to her," Lawson butts in. "Need to persuade her not to tell her lies to anyone else. That's why it's crucial we find her."

"And how will you do that?" Peg asks. "If she's determined enough, there will be someone willing to listen. I'd suggest it would be best if you prepared to defend yourself. With your wife backing you up, no records at the clinic, you could come out clean and, of course, get public sympathy on your side."

I shoot Peg a quick look. He sounds like he not only believes Lawson, but that he's on his side. Must admit, there's enough in this which sounds credible. But despite what Lawson might think, Tash isn't as loose mouthed as he believes. She's refused to tell her side of the story, though we'd given her the chance. More than that, she hadn't broken when we'd applied pressure.

Lawson sighs. "I've thought of that. But there's always a chance people would believe her. She's a pretty woman, comes across well. That's why I allowed her to volunteer in the first place. Her ability to get people on board with our policies are not so good if she uses those same skills to make them believe her lies. No, keeping her quiet is the best way to go about it."

"Do you think it's money she's after? Could you pay her off?" Peg suggests.

"It would depend how much she's after. Mr Lawson has already invested a lot in this campaign, and to use funds which have been assigned to getting elected would be a misappropriation of campaign funds."

"But if it gets her off your backs…"

"We need to find her first." Lawson waves Peg down. "I suggest that's the first priority. You find her, then keep her on your compound. The election is in four weeks' time. Keep her there until then. Once I'm elected, any slurs would have to result in an impeachment. It won't just be a matter of changing people's minds on how they vote, it would be up to my party whether or not they continue to back me."

If Lawson is running on a platform they support, it could well be they'd ignore any rumours just to vote in the policies they want.

"And," Turner begins with a laugh, "of course, Emmalina would be questioned as to why she hadn't come forward earlier. I can imagine the derision if she says she was kept out of the way on a biker compound."

"We, of course, would counter that she stayed with you voluntarily, happily playing the part of one of your whores, thus clearly putting her character in doubt."

I see Peg's muscles bunching. Clearing my throat to get his attention, I give him an almost imperceptible shake of my head. My turn to send him a warning. A silent message, *Cool it, Brother.* His wife's a fucking firefighter for fuck's sake, and she lives on the compound. I want to put a fist in Lawson's mouth myself.

"First, we have to find her. Then you're talkin' about kidnappin' and holdin' someone against their will. Peg and I can't make this decision, Lawson. We'll need to take it back to the Prez. What you're suggesting is illegal."

Lawson looks like he's suppressing a laugh. "I wouldn't have thought your club would let something like that bother you."

Peg's face, and mine, remain stoic.

"It's a shame," Turner states, "that she can't disappear permanently."

Now Peg can't hold back, asking in clipped tones, "What are you suggesting?"

Lawson's eyes open innocently. "That she moves out of state. What do you think Neil meant?"

I think we're all on exactly the same page, though some of us don't so much like what we're reading.

"Let's just make this clear," Lawson states. "I would be happy if I never saw Emmalina's lying face again. If you don't think the Devils can find her and keep her out of the way for a time, locate her and bring her to me, and I'll take it from there." He shakes his head, his eyes going to his campaign manager's face. "Money might be the only thing to make this go away, Neil." Then, as though a switch has been thrown, his face changes, and the tension lines leave him. "I'll let you take my proposition back to your president. But now, there's something else to discuss. I've got a rally coming up next Friday. It's one of the biggest I've done. I'd like your men to be there as we previously discussed. There may be some dissenters, and, of course, Emmalina might turn up—or someone representing her. If anyone starts speaking out of turn, or monopolising my time and not letting other people talk, Neil will give you the nod." He looks at Peg almost in admiration. "We may need to eject them, discreetly, from the meeting."

"We won't be acknowledging you officially, you understand?" Turner says. "For all intents and purposes, you're just normal citizens."

Yeah. Removing any dissenters or people who ask difficult questions. Fuck, I'm going to need a shower to wash away this stench.

Lawson again consults his expensive wristwatch. "Right, I'm afraid I'll have to cut this short. Thank you so much for coming to see me today. I'll wait to hear back from you about our other problem."

Tucson air might be hot, but it feels fresher than that which had been artificially cooled in Lawson's office. As Peg and I step over to our bikes, I see Peg give a shake of his head. *Yeah, with you there, Brother.* Anything we need to discuss; we'll do back at the compound.

When we arrive, I'm not surprised to find Drummer's impatiently waiting for us.

"I don't like the man," Peg informs Drummer when we've filled him in. "He's the very epitome of everything we hate. Civilians, citizens, fuckin' lawmakers. But strip out all the politician's dressing up, what he said was credible enough. It's his word against the woman's. Is she after taking him down? If so, why? For personal reasons? Political? Would she be working for herself or with someone else? Maybe the other party?"

"Or," I step in taking her side—not for any reason but to put forward an alternative view— "is he lying through his teeth?"

Prez taps the table. "She spent a month living rough. Ran, leaving everything behind her. If she'd had her purse or phone, she'd have gone somewhere more comfortable."

"Lawson's the kind of man I don't trust. His anger and retribution could be as bad if he was trying to stop her spreading lies as exposing the truth. Whatever way around, she's angered him, Prez."

"For fuck's sake." Drummer suddenly stands, kicking at his chair, his hands raking through his hair. "This is why we live outside citizen's rules and don't get involved in how they want to manage their lives." He looks at Peg and I as though we should understand why he's saying this. Our twin confused looks we send back show that we don't. He leans his hands on the desk. "Look. We could keep Tash well away from any danger, whether she's telling the truth or not. That goes without saying. Not killing a bitch for no good reason. Party politics that she doesn't want him elected? She might have planned to go about it the wrong way, but that doesn't deserve a death sentence.

"But if she's in the right, then he's going to get elected on a bed of lies. An adulterer, and one who quite possibly goes against his very own policy of being anti-abortion. Word of that gets out? Election day he might very well be finished."

"So what's it got to do with us? As you said, civilian world, nothing for the club to worry about." My preference is to send her away. Get another chapter to keep an eye on her. Already I'm sick of this shit.

Drummer pulls his chair back into place, sits, and tiredly puts his head into his hands. "I propose we do get involved, this time. If he's dirty, he could affect a lot of lives. We live outside their laws; doesn't mean we don't get caught up in them. Got brothers in prison can testify to that. So, we try to get to the bottom of this shit. If Tash really has got something on him, we'll help her get the information out."

"What if she doesn't want to do that? She's scared already. And she hasn't exactly been forthcoming to date."

"We don't give her the choice, Blade. Too many lyin' politicians without adding one more."

I like the idea less than I like her, which means it's at the very bottom of the fucking list. I might not think much of her, but we'll be putting her in danger. I feel I need to point that out. "We'll be painting a fuckin' target on her, Prez. She blows his ambitions out of the water? Doubt if he'd ever stop coming after her. She'd never be in the clear."

"You're not making this easier," Drummer complains. "Fuck, what a mess. It's not even a case of doing the right thing. This second, don't rightly know what the correct action is." His head moves side to side, then he looks straight at me. "Do what you have to, Blade. Learn her fuckin' secrets. See if you think she's lying. Get to the truth and we'll take it from there."

My reluctance is written on my face. I'm not the right person. How the fuck can I tell if she's honest? In my view, all bitches lie and are guilty.

Prez examines my face carefully, sighs, then slowly nods. "Okay. I'll get Beef…"

"No. This is on me," I interrupt quickly.

Chapter 18

Tash

God, this is a beautiful place. I'm standing, leaning on the balcony outside of Blade's room. In the distance, I can hear kids and some adult cries of pleasure as they splash around in the pool. Straining my ears I'm sure I can hear Tommy's excited shout too, and I smile. With all the fun he's having, he must think he's died and gone to heaven.

If it wasn't for my worry about straining my weakened shoulder joint, I'd probably join them. I'd wanted some fresh air, so resorted to just stepping outside, but I won't be able to stay here long, it's too hot. Already the cooler air inside the suite is beckoning.

The sliding door noisily opening behind me makes me jump. I turn, bump into the table, get my ankle caught on the chair and go down hard on my backside. *Damn! I'll probably have a bruise on my ass now.*

Indignation makes my temper flare. "What the fuck are you doing here?" I hiss.

Blade's biting his lip, probably to stop himself laughing as he approaches, reaching out a hand to help me up. "It is *my* room."

I stare at the hand, wanting to refuse his assistance, but in the end, take it. I'll make more of a fool of myself trying to manoeuvre myself up.

"You want to stay out here, or…?"

For an answer, I huff, squeeze past him, and go inside, the cooler air hitting my skin immediately. I hear the sound of the doors sliding shut and take a deep breath. "What's this, Blade? You come to take back your room?" If he has, I'll gladly vacate it. I'm happy to take a couch for the night.

He's staring at me as though seeing me for the first time. "Nah, Tash." He pinches the brow of his nose, then ceases his scrutiny and looks down at his feet. "Look, I'm sorry."

Sorry? For what? And an apology means nothing if it's delivered to the floor. Just as I'm going to voice my opinion, his eyes rise, and an intense gaze meets mine. "I'm sorry," he repeats.

"For what, Blade?" This man rescued me. Brought me to the compound.

"I think we've got off on the wrong foot."

Up to now he's been full of himself, bossy. The man standing in front of me seems different, softer perhaps. My eyes narrow in suspicion. Has he had a personality change, or is this all a front? "I don't know which foot you expect us to be on, Blade."

He mutters *fuck* so softly; I barely hear it. My doubts he's changed or that I'm seeing the real man are confirmed. He is putting on an act, and I don't understand why. As I watch, his hands twitch by his sides, his fingers curling into his palms, then opening again.

I thought I was prepared for anything, but it seems I'm not. When he moves as fast as a snake striking, his hands are on my arms, pinning me to him before I have a chance to evade him. He pulls me close, his lips hover above mine, such a small dis-tance between us, I feel his exhaled breath on my skin, inhale air tainted with the slight smell of cigarette smoke. My traitorous body responds to his closeness.

He's holding me in an iron grip, not painfully, but tight enough it would be a struggle to make him let go. All I need to do is rise on tiptoe and my mouth would be on his. It's a fight between my brain reminding me I dislike him, and my body desiring to close that small gap.

Before I know which side of me is winning, suddenly, his hands release me. He twists his body around, strides to the door and leans with his forehead on the wood. One hand braced by the side of his face, one hand… I'm certain he's adjusting himself in his jeans.

What the fuck is going on?

"I can't stay here, Blade. Not with you." It's impossible. My head might know how I feel about him, but my body has different ideas. There's the problem. *If he'd kissed me, let's be honest here, I would have responded. What would his kiss be like? Would I enjoy his taste?* For my sanity, I've got to put distance between us. Even Seb never aroused me so quickly, *so intensely.* No, with Seb it had taken weeks of polite flirting, a few dinners, some hints, and then, after a few make out sessions, I'd done the deed. It had seemed almost inevitable by then. But as it turned out, Seb had liked the chase more than the prize.

It wouldn't be like that with Blade. For the first time ever, it wouldn't take me much to jump into bed with a man I don't know. A man I don't like or respect. *He's a criminal.* It would be sex. A bodily function.

I couldn't do that.

It's the knowledge of how close I came to doing just that which spurs me to tell him again, "Open the door and let me go, Blade. I'll stay in the room I was in the other night."

"Can't do that." His voice is somewhat muffled against the door. "Can't let any other fucker have you."

What?

"Look, Blade. I know bikers live by a different code, but surely my virtue is safe?" A horrifying thought comes to me. "Are you saying I've got to pay for staying here with sex? Do you expect me to become one of your club whores?" My voice has been rising, the final word coming out as a squeak.

Still facing the door, he raises his fist and thumps it, and then does it again. There's a pause, then he swings around. "Not fuckin' gonna be forcin' you to do anything." A sly smirk appears as his lips curve. "Don't think I'd need to do much coercin' in any event."

My mouth opens and shuts. It might have been what I was thinking, but for him to put it so bluntly, have it out there in the open. At last words come out, "I am not going to have sex with you."

Like a panther he's moved closer, his movements so stealthy I'd barely noticed. His hand streaks out, his fingers tangle with my hair as he eases my head up to face him. My hands cover his, trying to get him to set me loose.

At his growl, I stop struggling, and look into his blue eyes. Maybe it's the light, but they seem to be glowing.

"I don't want to fuck you," he says, while tilting his hips forward and rubbing a blatantly hard cock against me. "Well, I could. My dick has a fuckin' mind of its own. I will, if I have to, but I'd rather you just start talkin' to me."

I can't understand a word that's coming out of his mouth. I can't even shake my head to show my confusion as he's holding me too tight. "What do you mean?"

"I mean," he leans his face down, "I'm the fuckin' enforcer, babe. I extract the information we need to protect the club. You've refused to tell your story, one way or another, I'm going to get it out of you. You can choose how easy or hard this will go."

Now it's my turn to taunt him, pushing my body against his. "It already feels pretty hard to me."

Oh no. I shouldn't have prodded what I've realised is becoming a very angry bear. He snarls, then angles my head up further and brings his lips to my neck. "You think you're pretty damn clever, don't you?"

"I'm not telling you shit. I don't trust you."

"Then I'll make you."

"You can't make me trust you." He's strong, stronger than me. A shiver of fear which I'm embarrassed to admit also contains anticipation runs through me. My cheeks flush as I ask, "If I don't tell you, are you going to rape me?"

That arrogant smirk appears again. "Wouldn't be rape, babe. You're already begging for it."

Is this my 'Me Too' moment? Or, is he right?

Jeez. There's something about this man. I don't know whether I want to hit that smarmy look off his face, or throw myself into his arms and take him up on what he appears to be offering. I need to remember I'm fighting for my life. I've already run from the man who wants to kill me, and who is paying these men. It would be crazy to start something now, and with him. But, start what? Blade's made clear it would be nothing more than a cheap coupling of bodies, no long-term relationship. A physical relief, nothing more.

As he drops his hand and I'm free to move, I stay frozen, my body still, my mind racing. I'm tempted. God knows, I'm tempted. After the last few weeks, a chance to let down my guard, find solace in a man's arms if just for a moment sounds like a welcome vacation. But I know me. Even while I now know Seb reeled me in with lies and deceit, projecting a man who didn't exist, I went into it with the expectation we'd both work at a relationship. Oh, I didn't expect a proposal on day one, nor a lifelong commitment, but why hook up with someone when you knew from the start it didn't have a fat chance in hell of working out?

That's exactly the reason I should run from Blade. Now I've just got to tell him.

I turn, unconcerned my back is toward him, my pace forward taking me to the window, my gaze looking out to the desert beyond. Deep down I must trust him, knowing despite his words, he won't approach unless I give him an indication. Which is precisely not what I'm going to do.

"You're right," I inform him at last. "Maybe it's the circumstances, maybe it's you. But yes, I find you attractive. But I'm not going to act on it. I'm saying, no, Blade. Whatever you think my body is telling you, my mind is saying no."

I hear rustling behind me, a footstep on the tiled floor. Then his hand touches my shoulder. "Are you wet for me?"

Didn't he hear what I said?

Unfortunately, the answer to his question is probably yes, though I've never had a man ask me so blatantly before. I flush at the audacity, too embarrassed to answer. I can't lie. I can't let him know. As his hand starts to trail down my body as if to find out for himself, I know I've got one chance to act. One opportunity before he takes this somewhere I don't want it to go. Before he makes me feel too much that I lose my ability to stop him.

The flick of the knife as it opens is louder than I expected, like a pistol shot in the room, but I use the split second of surprise to spin and have the blade against his neck before he realises what I'm doing.

"Leave me alone," I hiss.

"Babe," his eyes twinkle with merriment. "You do know I know a hundred ways to disarm you, don't you?" He chuckles softly. "I noticed the knife was missing as soon as I came into the room. Wondered when you were going to try to use it. And, babe, my jugular's here," he moves the blade an inch. "If you're going to do something, do it properly."

As he's repositioned the blade, he's also taken a tight grip on my wrist. When he spots the defeat in my eyes, he uses his superior strength to move the weapon out of harm's reach. My fingers loosen as he easily takes it.

"Man pulls a knife on me? Want to guess what would happen?"

I think I know without having to make a suggestion and letting him confirm it. Lowering my eyes to the floor, I wait for his next move. He bows his head, speaking into my ear, "What did I tell you I was, babe?"

There are many possible answers as to what I think he is, but I stick with the obvious one he's looking for. "You're the enforcer. For a criminal gang."

"Mostly right, but we're not a gang, darlin'. We're a motorcycle club. And we aren't criminals."

"You just haven't been tried and convicted. Yet." Seb would come under that category as well. A man who does illegal shit though the authorities haven't yet caught up with him. Not too far a stretch to think that applies to the Satan's Devils too.

"You know what an enforcer does?" At my shrug, he continues, "I enforce the rules of the club. Do what I can to protect it. Against people who've done us harm, or would do it. I'd do *anything* for my brothers darlin'. Any-fuckin'-thing, and you'd do best to keep that in mind."

Surprisingly, his voice remains soft, his words almost a caress, even as they darken. "I've tortured men before, killed them too. Made them hurt until they were begging for death. Never had to question a bitch before, not in that way. But don't think I won't use all the tools of my trade if I have to."

If he wasn't speaking in a monotone, perhaps I wouldn't have been so afraid. He's not posturing, every word he's said has been the truth. While I couldn't see through Seb's lies, I've no doubt at all that Blade's stating fact. I shiver, and it's not the air conditioning making me cold. It's the atmosphere in the room that's made another change. From flirty, teasing, sexual, to the aura of one overriding thing. *Danger.*

CHAPTER 19

Blade

She's stubborn. She's fighting an attraction to me, and on my part, it wouldn't be any hardship to fuck her. My eyes keep settling on that cute turned-up nose; there's something about it that constantly draws my attention. She's not a classic beauty, but there's character in that face. Her tits are worth more than a second glance, and when she'd turned her back on me, I just had to feast on that heart-shaped ass.

Yeah. My cock is very interested. While I do a lot for this club, my dick's not going where it's not welcomed. I'm not a man who'd get any pleasure from forcing a female who's unwilling. Instead I've spelt out exactly what I can do. Which is why I've now got a trembling woman in front of me, standing so close that her exhaled breath warms my skin.

If my brothers are right, and getting close to her is the way to find out her secrets, perhaps she'd allow one of them in. Maybe I was wrong to try and take her for myself. Maybe they'd have more success. But my cock's interested enough it doesn't want anyone else to have her.

What do I fucking do? It's an impasse. *I told her I'd torture her. Told her I could.* I'm a fucking liar. I could no more hurt a hair on her head than I could one of the club's children.

But I need to do my job.

Neither of us make an attempt to put distance between us. She's giving me time to think, while believing she's having a chance to compose herself. She doesn't know what I'm going to do next, but I've got a plan.

Slowly I reach into my back pocket and extract what I usually keep handy. Could have been a boy scout as I'm always prepared. Before she's got time to exhale her next breath, my arms snake out fast, taking firm hold of her hands and zip-tying her wrists behind her.

"Oh." Her eyes look up to me in confusion.

"More than one way to skin a cat," I tell her. I look into her eyes, needing to check. It doesn't seem like the position is paining her shoulder; I'd find another way if it did. Instead, her cheeks flush with something different. *Fear? Arousal?*

Again, moving fast so she's no time to protest, I push her back, aiming her body so it sinks into a chair that's behind her, easing her with my hands so she hits it, making sure her arms are looped over the back. As she realises what I'm doing she starts to kick out, but I'm bigger, and it's easy to overpower her, taking a firm hold of her uninjured leg and fastening it to one of the chair legs.

"Stop. You'll hurt yourself," I admonish her. I'm trying to be gentle as I attempt to catch her bruised limb, but the way she's still trashing, disregarding the pain, is making it difficult. In the end, I use my weight to subdue her. Standing back, I admire my handiwork. Without being able to stand, she can't free her hands. She's going nowhere.

"Now what?" she spits, her spirit returning. *Fuck me, but she's brave.* I swallow the laugh that wants to escape, as images of men I've had at my mercy begging for me to let them go, come to mind. *Now what? She asks?* Now I torture my first woman.

"Talk," I say.

"Nice weather we're having."

Now the laugh escapes. My cock jerks, admiring her audacity. I've had men piss themselves for less before. Arranging my features into my impassive, unemotional enforcer's expression, I shake my head. "Sooner you start telling me what I want to hear, the sooner you'll be free. And the less you'll hurt."

She tosses her head, long hair swinging around her face. "You can't make me. If I talk, I'm dead."

"If you don't talk, you'll wish you were."

Perhaps I should have taken her to the storeroom. Let her see the implements at my disposal. Problem is, I'd have had to walk past my brothers, let them see I couldn't conduct this interrogation as we'd agreed. That I'd failed—she wouldn't let me get close to her.

Nah. Better here. I think of what I have got at my disposal. I let her see me staring at the display on my wall. *Lucky she only got her hands on one knife. There are others far sharper and deadlier.*

Yeah. Walking across, I select a nice, long, sharp stiletto. Just right for my purposes, getting a sense of satisfaction when I turn back to see her eyes flaring.

Her mouth works, but I respect her when she doesn't ask the question she's obviously longing to. Instead, I remove the necessity of asking for my intentions, when I move close. "Keep very still," I warn as I slide the knife under her t-shirt, slicing it through the middle. Underneath, she's wearing a plain bra.

She gasps in a breath as I slice off the top button of her shorts.

Then she looks straight ahead. "The clothes don't even belong to me." She swallows, I see her throat moving. Christ, every little thing she does makes my cock jerk. My action may have made her feel vulnerable, she's got no fucking idea what it's done to me. I'll leave the threat of exposing her totally hanging, but truthfully, if I dare uncover what I suspect are delectable breasts, I wouldn't be able to control myself. But torture is often about intimidation, a suggestion of what might come left hanging; the victim not knowing if their tormentor is going to carry through. I might be an expert at this, my proficiency honed over the years.

I stand, showing her my back for a second, as I try to bring my cock under control. As if the sight of those covered breasts weren't enough on their own, coupled with the way she's brazenly challenging me is sorely testing my limits. Never known a bitch like her, that's for sure.

Swinging back once I've had a stern mental word with my dick, I warn her, "Let there be no misunderstanding here. You've got information I need to protect my club. I *will* hurt you if you don't talk."

She glances down at the damage I've done, then cocks her head to one side. "Explain it to me. Why you think what I've got to say is so important? I don't understand, Blade." For a second, the strength dies. She's more confused than frightened. "I'm trying to do my best here. My life depends on me keeping quiet, proving I can be trusted. That's what the man who's paying you wants."

I roll my head back, inhaling sharply. *Not this same impasse again.* I'm tired of it. After considering for a moment, I sink down to my ass so I'm sitting on the floor and lift one of her feet, holding it in my hands. Yeah, I'll admit it. I've got a thing about feet, and hers are small, dainty, pretty. I slide my blade underneath, I've no intention of cutting her, but she doesn't know that. I've no idea of how to proceed, I need to play this by ear.

"Blade!" She twitches, and as far as her bindings allow, tries to pull her foot away.

I realise immediately, *she's ticklish.* Although my features don't change, inside, I'm grinning. *Could it be I've unearthed a new torture technique?* Maybe if I'd found it earlier I might have spared the prospects some time mopping up blood in the storeroom.

"Tell me," I say, digging the pads of my fingers into the sole.

"Blade. No. Stop. Please." She writhes but can't get free. "Blade. No." She's blinking rapidly, her breathing speeds up. Signs she's starting to panic.

My pressure on her foot is unrelenting. "Start with something simple. Tell me how you met him." There's no need for me to mention Lawson's name. Once she commences, I'm hoping the floodgates will open.

"I'll tell you that," she screams as my fingers press in again.

I stay where I am. A firm hold on that satin smooth skin on the top of her foot. "Speak, woman."

She sobs, then, in a stronger voice than I had expected, begins, "I met Seb about six months ago. There was a fundraiser for the party he's affiliated with. I'm not a supporter, hell, I don't even bother to vote, I've no particular political leaning. Politicians whatever side they're on are all as bad as each other."

I nod, I have to agree with that. Part of the reason we stay out of the citizen world. "Go on." For encouragement, I lightly run my blade over her sole. She tries to pull away, but the binding won't let her.

"Stop Blade, stop. Please!" I suppress my smile as she begs; I'm barely touching her yet her breathing rate has again increased. She doesn't like her feet being touched. Or not how I'm currently doing it, I reckon I could show her how to enjoy a more sensual touch. I apply my fingers, she jerks again. "Alright, alright! I worked for the venue. It wasn't the first fundraiser held there, but the first for him. It was just an ordinary day for me. I was in charge of the arrangements, making sure everything ran smoothly. I ignored the speeches, they didn't interest me, but getting people fed, waitstaff acting like they were invisible, clearing tables to make a dance floor. Yeah, that was all down to me. I took pride in doing my job." She pauses. "I did it too well it would seem. Afterwards Seb came to thank me."

She gives a quick toss of her head. "I'd told him I was just doing what I was paid for. I was flattered that he'd noticed how well it had gone. When he asked, I told him my background. It wasn't in hospitality, you see, this was just a position I'd fallen into."

Yeah. I remember Mouse saying she had a psychology degree. I could see how knowing shit about people could help in that role. "Go on," I prompt again.

"Seb wasn't a front runner at the time. He admitted it was unlikely he'd rise to the top, but wanted to do everything possible. He explained the campaign manager's job to me, and it seemed something I could handle. Of course I needed my qualifications and references checked out, but I was confident there was going to be no difficulty there. Subject to everything being as I'd told him, he offered me the job on the spot."

"And you accepted?"

A little reluctantly it seems, she nods. "I knew it was a temporary position, but it was good experience to add to my resume. So yeah, I agreed to take it on." Her lips press together. "That he'd actually get the nomination wasn't in the cards this time around, he knew that, but he wanted to raise his profile, get known and set himself up for the next time. He seemed genuine and reasonable as he dangled the job in front of me." Breaking off, she snorts a quick laugh. "Of course, it wasn't just my skills and expertise that he wanted."

"He wanted you." It seems a foregone conclusion. Girl as pretty as her? Yeah, what man wouldn't want to get in her pants. As I glance up I notice her eyes have glazed over as if she's back in the moment, and she's staring straight ahead, rather than looking at me. "Seb is a chameleon. He fits in, wherever he is. He shows you what you expect to see. I found exactly what I imagined I would. A good-looking, intelligent and committed, hardworking man. That's what I saw from the persona he presented to me. He throws his all into getting what he's after, and, for some reason, and at some point, that became me."

"So you started working for him? Giving him other benefits?" I frown at the distaste I have for that thought. She might not have seen through him, but I had. Sure, he presents a civilised front to the world, but I'm practiced at seeing the man underneath. If it wasn't insulting the reptile population, I'd call him a venomous snake.

"We worked well together. He was quiet, very charming. Flattered me." She looks at me directly. "So that's it. I fucked him. The fact I was working for him provided him with cover if he was ever seen out with me socially." She seems to brighten, which makes me suspicious.

"Keep going," I growl.

Her words flow easier now. She checks to make sure I'm listening. "He told me he was single. Of course, I believed him. Well, there didn't seem to be a woman around, and he dedicated so much time to me."

"He's married." If I believe her, she's another woman taken in by a man just out for what he can get. Don't understand men like that at all. If you just want to fuck, come out and admit it. Never stopped me getting pussy.

Tash lowers her face and scowls toward me. "Know that now. Didn't have a clue at the time. He kept that relationship quiet, until it became useful to him, and he shipped his wife back in from out of state."

If I can trust what she's saying, she was conned. *If.* It seems too straightforward and reasonable to me. She has confirmed she was his campaign manager, not some volunteer, which catches Lawson out in a lie. "So, you were the dirty bit on the side. That's all you've got on him?"

"You asked how I met him. I didn't agree to tell you anything else."

No, she didn't. "But you will," I tell her, rubbing the underside of her foot before asking metaphorically, "I wonder if you're ticklish anywhere else?"

She yelps, at just the threat. I start to rise. "Okay," her eyes are leaking. "Okay."

"Okay, what? My hands grasp her just under her ribs and I dig my fingers in. For a second it's like I've got a wild animal thrashing in my arms.

"Stop! Stop!"

I pause, leaving my hands there in threat. She sobs, stares at me, then looks away. "Just before he got the nomination, he got, he got… carried away. He didn't use a condom. He didn't want me to get the morning-after pill. Didn't want me to be seen buying it in Tucson. Said it was unlikely, so to take the chance." She shakes her head as though trying to shift a bad memory out of her head. "I didn't know he had a wife then. Thought it meant if the worst came to the worst, he'd stand by me. I was so stupid. Didn't let it worry me, thought he'd be at my side if I ended up pregnant. I'd tried to stop him when I realised he hadn't used protection, but he'd continued. I thought he'd step up to what was his mistake."

"And?"

She lets out another sob, takes in a breath, then looks back with determination. "I'd suspected and did a home test. I went to a clinic to get confirmation." Her face hardens.

That fits in with what Mouse said. "Go on." I try to be unemotional, if I show sympathy, she'll only break down.

"I found out I was indeed pregnant. I actually thought he'd be pleased, that he'd might even marry me, and show he was a family man…"

"You're not pregnant now."

"No." She glances back at me quickly. Without being able to use her hands to wipe them away, tears are rolling down her face. "He wanted me to have an abortion."

Her delivery of that pronouncement is chilling. "Did you want an abortion?"

"As soon as I knew, I wanted that baby. Even if I didn't have him. I didn't hate him until then."

"You could have said no."

"Yeah," she scoffs. "Sounds easy, doesn't it? But I still saw him as the man he wanted me to see. A man I thought I was going to spend my life with, that side of him he allowed me to see. He did everything he could to wear me down. We'd stopped having any other conversations, he went on and on and on. In his view, abortion was reasonable. It wasn't the right time for him or for me. That time would come later. He promised we'd have a family further down the line, dangled the image of a perfect future, one only obtainable if for now we both concentrated on our careers. Remember, then, I didn't know he already had a wife."

"You bought what he said?"

She seems to find my display of knives on the wall very interesting. "I didn't know what to think. Maybe hormones were already acting on me, but he was relentless. He began swinging from the man I knew and thought I loved to a complete stranger who, quite frankly, scared me."

"Seb knew I'd gone to the clinic. I think even then he had someone following me. He was furious. Told me he couldn't have any paper trails. That because I was working on his campaign, anything I did reflected on him. I told him I'd just gone to confirm it, that I didn't want an abortion." Her voice breaks, and she stumbles over the next words. "But he did. He told me not to be so stupid, that it wasn't a baby, just a few cells. And it wasn't to be done at any clinic, that it didn't need to be, Instead, he'd already got drugs online. Two simple tablets to be taken forty-eight hours apart." Her head bows as a shudder goes through her. "He wanted to make sure it was done. He stood over me, after I'd swallowed the first one, stroking my hair, telling me repetitively how much he loved me. That it was all for the best. To ensure the best start to our future together. That our time would come. He was nice, kind, even loving until two days later and after he'd fed me the second pill."

My eyes are on her. Christ, I'd be upset if I got a bitch pregnant, but even I wouldn't be a bastard and force a woman to do what she didn't want.

"You aborted the baby, what happened next?" It's getting harder and harder to remain cold.

She huffs a mirthless laugh. "Seb was different. I don't know, he'd had a scare. He wasn't coming around quite so frequently. He was excited about something… I lost my job, I was no longer working for him. Oh, he told me it was because of my health, and to be honest, I was quite done after, after…" She shakes her head as though the detail wasn't important. "Things had changed. Suddenly he was in line to get the nomination, I…" Her eyes shift to the side, she's not looking at me, as she changes to say something different. "He said he was worried about me. Left his man, Grant, guarding my apartment, which meant no one could get in, but I couldn't go out either. Every time I tried, Grant would stop me. Oh, he was pleasant enough, always got someone to go and get whatever I needed. But I was a prisoner in my own home."

I interrupt. "You said he was excited about something." Yeah, she thought I'd missed that. I hadn't. "Excited as he knew things were going to happen? Like the forerunner for the nominations being killed in a car accident perhaps, or the next in line being involved in a scandal? You got any information he had anything to do with that?"

She won't meet my eyes. "I don't know what you mean. But you asked how I found out he had a wife." Her voice hardens. "I had the TV on when it was announced he'd got the nomination. Part of his platform was of course, anti-abortion. He was talking about that with glee when he brought his wife and three kids up onto the platform. I still remember the shock. I hadn't known she existed until that point."

"How the fuck didn't you know he was married?"

Her lips press together. "She'd been living out of state for some reason. In front of that cheering crowd, he mentioned she was moving back down from Utah, but not why she was living there, and no one asked."

"What happened?"

She continues in a monotone. "He came to see me that last time. Threatened me. Said he'd got exactly what he wanted, and he wasn't going to let a bitch fuck it up. I had the power to destroy his life, and his career. He frightened me. I realised it was true. If I stepped up, he'd lose everything he worked so hard for. His threats worked, I told him I'd keep quiet. Having seen what I had, I didn't want anything to do with him anymore. He said, he wasn't sure he could trust me." As she breaks off, her face tightens. I realise she's starting to resemble an Amazonian princess. "He frightened me so much, I made a promise I would keep my mouth shut. I didn't realise that wouldn't be enough, nor that I'd end up fighting for my life. Or fighting for anything at all. He left. A short while later there was a knock at the door. When I opened it, Grant pushed his way inside. He…" she gulps. "He started overturning furniture. I stood there, asking what the fuck he was doing. It was then I noticed he was wearing gloves. He stopped, stared straight at me, and told me Seb was done with me. Arrogantly, he said he'd have liked to have fucked me, but that I'd have to forego that pleasure as he didn't want to leave evidence. He'd have to satisfy himself with making it look like a home invasion gone wrong. I became terrified as I realised his intention wasn't to scare me into keeping quiet. He was going to kill me."

I have no doubt this is how it happened. She's paling as she relives the events as they'd happened. My features are tight when I ask tersely, "How did you escape?"

"I ran into the kitchen. I've got one of those big iron skillets, you know? Grant wasn't expecting me to put up much of a fight. I, er smashed him over the head with it. As soon as he went down, I ran. And, well, you know the rest. I was so scared I left everything behind. I didn't even stop to pick up my bag or my phone. And I certainly wasn't going to risk going back."

Even tied to the chair, she'd grown taller when relating how she fought for her life and succeeded. Now the story's out, she seems to slump in front of my eyes. A strange impulse to hold her, comfort her, comes over me. I hold myself back.

Since bringing her here, watching, seeing with my own eyes how she'd coped with her injuries has impressed me. When I'd heard how she'd escaped from that fucker Grant by managing to put him out of action, my admiration for her increased. Most bitches would have frozen. Her? No, she managed to turn the tables on him. Yeah, she'd been fighting for her life, but fuck, had she fought. My hands itch to get hold of Lawson. For what she said he put her through, he deserves death.

I want to believe her. My ingrained distrust of women is holding me back. Perhaps it's wrong that a thirty-six-year-old man is still allowing himself to be shaped by events that happened so many years ago, but my one female role model had deserted me at a time when I needed her support most. A lie, by omission. I never wanted to be dependent on a woman again. It's made me over cautious. Now faced with Tash, having heard her story, I want to, but how can I trust she's telling the whole truth?

I do, and I don't. What she's told me has the ring of sincerity to it, certainly the description of her escape from Grant. For one thing, she had indeed ended up on the street penniless. But was Grant acting for Lawson or did he attack her of his own accord? And did everything else go down as she had said? Would Lawson go so far as to kill her, when instead with the reputation he'd carefully cultivated, he could dismiss her supposed relationship with him as lies? Men get away with providing alternative stories all the time. I grow certain there's still something she's not telling me.

"Who can attest to your relationship with him? Who knew you were seeing each other?"

She confirms my suspicions when she replies, "No one. I told you. We did go out together, his constituents saw us, would come and talk to us. But he only ever introduced me as a colleague working on his campaign."

"And you've told me everything?" My voice has a tone of finality, accepting I'll get nothing more out of her today.

She pales and shrinks back into the chair. "Yes. And I shouldn't have told you…" Her eyes go wide as I pick up my knife. "Blade, I've told you everything. Oh, fuck, I shouldn't…"

She hasn't. There's more. Already I've got ideas of what she's trying to hide. She thinks she's got the better of me, and for now, I'm going to let her carry on believing it. Her accusations about Lawson? So far, could be denied. I'm starting to realise why she doesn't trust us.

She's scared, but I'll lull her into a false sense of security. I reach around her back and cut the tie holding her hands together, then, leaning down I undo each of her feet. As she rubs her wrists to get her circulation going again, I try to pull the sides of her ruined t-shirt together.

For my pains, I get a sharp slap around my face.

I nod. Yeah, maybe I deserved that.

CHAPTER 20
Tash

The echo of the sound made when the palm of my hand makes contact with his cheek, rings in the suddenly silent room. Even the hum of the air conditioning seems to have quieted. My now free hand covers my mouth as I wait to see what he'll do.

Men like him are likely to retaliate. After all, he told me he'd torture me. *And he had.* I hadn't felt threatened when he'd sliced through my shirt, part of me had thought if he tried to use sex against me, he'd fail, as I'd probably enjoy it. It had been how he'd touched me next which had done it.

I'm ashamed he broke me so easily, but I've always been ticklish. It might be difficult for others to believe, but I have nightmares where I'm trapped and can't escape tickling hands.

Everything I told him was true. Seb had started a relationship with me. At the time, I hadn't thought him trying to hide it strange. Sure, I'd been a bit annoyed that he thought I wasn't good enough to be seen on a politician's arm, but thought that would all change once he didn't, or as it turned out, did, get the nomination, which should have come as a surprise.

It's also true that he used every trick in the book to persuade me to have an abortion. I'm madder than hell with myself that I didn't see through him at the time, but I still thought he was a good man, until the blinders had been removed from my eyes. By then, that small bundle of cells which had been growing inside me had gone. All because I'd listened to his lies. All because he selfishly hadn't bothered with a condom. Even though I'd told him no, and asked him to stop, once I'd realised.

You're too adorable, too sexy, it's too late sweetheart… I'm not sure if my eyes are leaking angry or sad tears now. But my emotional reaction, hopefully is having an effect on the enforcer sitting watching me. Men hate a woman crying, don't they? Anything to strengthen my case is a tool I can use.

It's the things I haven't told Blade that would be why he'd kill me to protect the man paying the club for protection. That's why I can't tell him the rest of the information I possess. If I came forward, with what I'd just told Blade, it's probable no one would believe me. I'd just be a jealous woman wanting to put a slur and blemish on a man's character. Seb would brush that off easily, no, it's a joke to think he'd be afraid of that.

It's what else I'd stumbled across that's the reason why Seb would want me to stop breathing.

Seb's paying this club and I'm not sure why. While I've seen none of their nefarious activities, I still suspect some go on, and would be the reason Seb's using them. The question is, how long have they been working for him, and what else has he involved them in. Opening my mouth, well, if my suspicions are correct, what I have to say could take them down too. I can only hope Blade's taken the line I've thrown him. *I don't know anything else. Nothing that would incriminate the club if they've been doing Seb's dirty work for him.*

I realise I've been staring at my hands, rubbing away the red marks the constraints had left. Blade's still on his haunches staring at me. When his hand reaches out, it's not to return my physical attack, but to gently brush away my tears with his fingers.

"I need to go talk to Drummer." He seems confused, as if he doesn't know what to do with me now. Reaching around me, he opens a drawer and extracts a box of tissues, offering them like another man might present a box of chocolates. At the moment, one's just as welcome. Taking it, I blow my nose noisily. Well, it's his fault I'm full of snot. He made me cry. He can deal with the after effects.

I notice him look toward the patio doors leading onto the balcony and see him grimace. Following his eyes, I see he's glaring at the bolt on the inside. Then he turns to me. "Should have left you tied up," he observes. "No fuckin' way I can trust you to stay put now."

He's right about that. He's proved I'm no match for the enforcer, and I'll… *I'll do what? Run?* Leaving aside the how and where, I'm exhausted. Mentally drained having relived my story, totally unable to think. My face is puffy, my eyes sore. "You can trust me. I won't go anywhere." I feel at the end of my tether.

"Babe, nothing personal, but I don't trust bitches."

The introduction to his statement softens it a little. His tone is almost reluctant. "What have women done to you?" I wonder, aloud.

His finger taps me on the nose. "Something you'll never have the need to know," he replies. He stands, holding out his hand. "Come on. You better come with me. Need to make sure you're not going to run off."

"Where would I go?" I scoff as I stand. When I do, I pull my hand free. "Trust works both ways, you realise? How do I know you're not going to run to Seb and agree I can't be trusted? That I told you what had happened." I cross my fingers behind my back. Seb knowing I'm alive would be enough to instruct them to kill me. All I can hope is that they think I'm exaggerating, and I'm no risk to a nominee.

He rolls his eyes. "Can't commit we won't talk to him, but I promise we are not going to hand you over to Lawson."

No. They'll just follow his instruction to make sure I never leave the compound alive. Hasn't Blade just admitted he'd kill for the club? And if Seb tells them what I really know… If they were working for him, it's not just Seb I can bring down but the Satan's Devils themselves. I settle for raising and lowering my shoulders as I point out the obvious again, "You work for him."

"As you've reminded me." Again, his face gives nothing away. He goes to his closet, comes back with another Satan's Devils tee. Unlike the one the women had given me, this one is his size and dwarfs me. Still, after having no clothes to change into on the street, only what Tommy managed to find for me, I can't be picky.

Before we leave, I go into the bathroom and splash cold water on my cheeks, needing a moment alone to try to process what just happened with Blade, how easily he got me to speak to him. I must never let him suspect I know more. Not now I know how easily he can break me.

The first person we see on entering the clubhouse is Beef. He stares pointedly at what I'm wearing, then at my face, then at Blade. "Thought the girls had got her clothes."

"Got ruined," Blade grins.

Beef gives a hearty laugh; it sounds almost congratulatory. "You fuck her?"

Blade's chest puffs out as he replies with an exaggerated wink, "What do you think?"

My eyes open wide and so does my mouth in preparation to utter a protest. Blade tugs my arm and pulls me away. His grin is still on his face as he whispers sharply, "You want every asshole in here to know you spilled everything 'cause I tickled you?"

"The alternative," I snarl back, "is letting them think you've had your cock anywhere near me."

Unrepentantly he shrugs, "While you're here, you belong to me. Everyone knows that. Can see it happening sooner or later. Just give in and accept it."

"Romance is your middle name, isn't it?"

His grin widens to the extent it makes him look younger, and annoyingly hot. "How did you guess, babe?"

He leaves me digesting his impudence, as with his hand to the small of my back, he encourages me down the short hallway, one of the doors I already know leads to Drummer's office. A gruff voice calls permission to enter when Blade raps the wood with his knuckles.

The president's eyes go from me to Blade, then back as he examines my face. He nods at the expression he sees on the enforcer, then his gaze returns to me again. There's a fleeting expression of sympathy in his eyes, confirmed when he says, "Blade would have got the information one way or another, darlin'. You can be grateful that he didn't use some of his normal methods."

I stare back, unyielding. "He may have discussed those with me."

"You tell him everything?"

It's Blade who answers, "Yeah, Prez." His eyes find mine as I'm filled with relief that he obviously believed me. "I'll tell you myself, Prez. Don't want to drag her through it again." That surprises me. After what must have been my convincing crying fit, I'm grateful.

Drummer nods. "Girls should be around. Get a prospect to keep eyes on her, then come update me. Oh, and Tash? You're Blade's after that, okay?"

What does he mean, I'm Blade's? Does he assume what Beef had, or are they going to do Seb's work for him? Clean up the mess he left. Permanently.

As I feel the blood drain from my face, Drummer snarls, "He ain't gonna kill you. If you want to leave the compound when I'm through askin' questions, that's on you. For now, I want you to stay put. May still be gaps I need filling." *Oh yes there are. But even Blade's torture methods aren't going to make me spill them.* Unless he tickles me. *Shit.*

Even before Drummer's finished speaking, Blade has again put his hand on my back. As soon as the last word leaves Drummer's mouth, the enforcer shepherds me into the clubroom. Somehow in the few intervening minutes, it's turned into a daycare. From the number of towels over arms and still damp toddlers running around I guess they've only just come in from where they spent the afternoon—not being interrogated like I have, but enjoying themselves around the pool.

I'd been right. Tommy had obviously been with them. He's shaking his shaggy hair, spraying water around him just like a dog would. But it's the wide grin on his face that has me smiling. God, it's good to see him having fun.

Darcy scolds him as though talking to a child, which in many ways, he is. "Go get a towel, Tommy. Change out of your trunks. Then you can come get some food from the kitchen."

He immediately follows her instructions. Offer Tommy something to eat, and he'll do anything you ask.

I recognise Becca, the woman sitting with her hands over her very pregnant stomach. My conversation with Blade has brought it all back. *That could have been me.* The young children are now being dried and dressed in fresh clothes, Marcia's expertly changing her babies, the dog lying by her side watching on with his soulful brown eyes as if checking she's doing things right.

My gut clenches with regret. This is one place I don't want to be.

"Blade, can I go back to the room? I'll stay there, I promise." Blade's eyes go from me, to the scene in front of my eyes. He passes his hand over his face, and I swear I can see understanding come into his expression.

"Fergus?" He calls, and the prospect comes across the room almost at a run. "Take her back to my suite. Lock the door, then sit outside, okay? Watch that balcony like a fuckin' hawk."

Shaking my head, I exclaim, "It's a hundred degrees out there at least, Blade. Trust me, I'm not going anywhere."

"Nah. He wants to get patched in? He can take the heat."

With that, Blade turns and walks off. Fergus smiles, "He's right, you know. And I've been in Tucson long enough to know I won't melt."

I feel even more guilty when Fergus sees me in through the main door to the two adjoining suites, ushers me into Blade's, then goes outside to position himself opposite the balcony. As I watch him fasten his bandana over his head and polish and replace his shades, I sigh. Definitely no way for me to get out of here today.

What would be my chances of escaping the compound even if he wasn't standing, or, as I check out of the window again, sitting on guard? I'd have to sneak down and then try to get out of the gate. Idly I rub my shoulder, both it, and my leg, seem to be healing. Bruises and sprains, no permanent damage, nothing there stopping me attempting an escape. But the compound is some way from the main road, and then it's a few miles into Tucson. I've no money, nothing. Blade's wrong if he thinks I'll try to get away, and poor Fergus is suffering for nothing.

As I turn back to the room, I smile, remembering seeing Tommy just now. He gets such pleasure from the simplest things. We could all learn a lot from him.

Simple pleasures. How long since I was able to enjoy them? I sit down on the bed, and rest my head on my hands, staring out into space. Even when I'd been 'resting' at home after the abortion, I'd steered clear of pursuing my hobby. Now, while the sight of the children had been upsetting, it also inspired me again. If I don't do anything, all I'll think about is this predicament I'm in. Concentrating on something else might be healthier, allow my brain to take a break, if only for a short while.

My dream? To write children's books. I'd been toying around with a few ideas in my head. Seeing Grunt lying watching over his young charges had put an idea in my mind. My fingers itch, but there's no laptop available. Maybe Blade's got some paper and a pen around here somewhere? At least I could start jotting a few ideas down. I get to my feet and cross over to the desk which seems the likeliest place to start looking. Slipping my fingers inside I feel paper. *Score.* I open the drawer further, it's a notepad of some sort, big.

My brow furrows as I find the paper I was seeking, but it's not the normal flimsy type. No, this is thicker, an artist's drawing pad. I pull it out, wondering whether there will be a blank sheet. Along with the question, who does it belong to? It's unlikely to be Blade's.

Almost eagerly I flip it open. My eyes narrow. Half the pages seem to have been pulled out, those which remain are blank. Now the drawer is fully open, I see a variety of coloured pencils inside. Oh, and a folded-up piece of paper. Curiosity has me opening it, then sitting back hard on the chair.

It's a drawing of me. From when I was on the streets. Christ, but this was done by someone with talent. If it wasn't for the dirt on my face, my sunken eyes from tiredness and hunger, I'd be proud to have such a drawing of me.

Seb. He must have got someone to draw it. But why? That's impossible. He didn't even know I was living on the streets. Blade? Nah, Blade's no artist.

But the contents of the drawer in his room suggest different. It might be that he is.

CHAPTER 21
Blade

Well?" Drummer tugs at his beard impatiently when I return.

I start talking before my ass hits the seat. "Gave me the basics. He employed her, fucked her, got her pregnant, made her get rid of the kid. Dumped her when his name started floating to the top."

Prez's eyebrows rise. "That's it?"

Shaking my head, I refute it. "Nah, but she's trying to palm us off with that shit. Oh, I believe that happened and she was tellin' the truth, but I'd bet the fuckin' ranch it goes deeper than that."

With his fingers drumming on the table, Prez thinks aloud. "What you've already outlined wouldn't look good for a family man."

"He's running on an anti-choice platform too. But if she came forward, who'd believe her story? She was his campaign manager, lost her job, and now she wants payback by throwing dirt."

Prez asks questions, I answer them. His next doesn't surprise me. "So, what do you think is at the bottom of this?"

"Something that smells bad, Prez." I lean forward, putting my elbows on the desk and clasping my hands. "Got no proof, but it's mighty curious how he's emerged the front runner like he has. Luck was certainly on his side getting rid of his rivals. One dead, one has his reputation in tatters."

"She mention anything about that?"

"I asked, but she evaded a direct answer. Fact is, Prez, she knows he's payin' us."

"Shame you ever told her that."

I straighten my shoulders accepting the well-earned criticism. Can't argue with his observation. "What's done is done, Prez. The long and short of it? While we're taking his money, she isn't going to trust us." Breaking off, I sigh. "She believes the reputation we've got, the one we can't shake off. Reckon she's fingering us as havin' a hand in getting' his rivals out of the way. She probably thinks any info she's got could bring us down too."

"No wonder she's scared of us, Blade." Drummer stands, and starts to pace. I give him the space he needs to think. After he's crossed his office and back twice, he starts to divulge what he's come up with. "She's been through a lot. Obviously thought she'd found the man for her, was prepared to have his fuckin' kid. Gave that up for a promise of a future which never materialised."

"Hard to see how someone like her was taken in by him." I'd have thought her more intelligent than that.

Prez shrugs. "Lawson's clearly used to wearin' a veneer. But like anyone acting a part, eventually the mask slips."

When he gives me a pointed look, I reward him with a quick grin. Yeah, sometimes I let my enforcer's mask drop. It's not who I am, it's the role I've fallen into. If I'm honest, my art is my coping method, but getting back to the man in question. "His wife can probably testify to that." I pause, then add, "I think we should get Mouse diggin' deeper." My grin is now replaced by a frown. "Get all the details about what happened to those other politicians. See if there's a way fate could have been given a helping hand."

"I agree." Prez raises his chin. "Get her talking again, Blade. See if you can find a way to get her to trust us. She knows something." Taking it as a dismissal, I stand. But Drummer hasn't quite finished. "Let her in, Blade. Gain her confidence. It's give and take with a woman."

My brow furrows. "Take is about all a woman does, Prez."

His eyes narrow. "Don't judge all women by the actions of one, Blade."

I raise my shoulders. Never getting close, never trusting a bitch, has done me well so far. Don't see any reason to change that now. Finding that one woman and keeping her, well, it's okay for the likes of Drum and my brothers, but it's not in the cards for me. It's not the fact that I'd find it hard to be faithful to one pussy, it's that I'd be waiting for her to betray me at some point. Drummer's invested in Sam, but in doing so, he's given her the power to pull him down. I wouldn't be able to live with that thought. *Drummer's changed since he's found his woman.* Nah, there may be benefits, but the cons outweigh the pros.

"Can't help it, Prez," I tell him at last. "I'm happy the way I am. Comfortable with myself. Not putting my heart on the line." I'm not sure I actually have one. Only person I ever loved was Jonah—apart from my MC brothers of course—and he's gone.

I open the door to Drummer's office to find Truck, our fire-fighting prospect waiting outside.

"He free?" Truck asks.

Not thinking much of it, I hold open the door. "Yeah, he's available now." With my head bowed, my thoughts on the task ahead, I return to my suite.

Dismissing Fergus, only feeling the slightest bit of guilt that he looks like he's been wilting in the sun, I go into what had been my refuge and home, hating that it's been invaded, and it doesn't look like I'm going to be rid of the intruder anytime soon.

Tash is standing, looking out through the doors to the balcony, her body in silhouette against the bright sunlight streaming in from outside. I enter quietly, quickly checking all the knives are in place in the display on the wall. She seems to have learned she can't better me, they're all there. Then I look at her. She must have heard me coming in, must have seen me relieving the prospect from his guard duties. She knows I'm here, but she doesn't turn, giving me the opportunity to examine her profile.

She's beautiful. Or, at least, to me. Everything I could have dreamed of in one package. My head's in line with my cock, wondering what she would feel like wrapped around it. I just want a taste—I'm not going to get addicted to one pussy, no way. But just once, to feel her, to put it into my bank of memories. Yeah, I've already got a special spot reserved for her there. One day, soon, she'll be placed in it.

I'll have had her. I'll be satisfied. The sooner the better, then my questions will be answered once and for all. Whether she's tight, whether those muscles will grip me, squeeze me—whether her lips around my cock will be as good in reality as they are in my imagination.

"Where did you get this, Blade?"

When she speaks, I startle, guiltily lost in thoughts which have made my dick throb. "Get what?" I take the opportunity to adjust myself before she's fully turned around.

"This."

Stepping forwards, I snatch it from her. "Where did you find that?" I hiss. Then realise, "You've been sneaking through my shit."

"I was looking for a pen and paper," she snarls. "You're the one who trapped me in here. Made me a prisoner. If you didn't want me to pry, you should have locked your stuff up."

Why did she want pen and paper? "You going to write a goodbye note or something?"

"None of your fuckin' business."

No bitch has ever spoken to me like that before. I'm wondering what to do about it when she speaks again, her tone still angry, "Who drew this, Blade? Who gave it to you? And why?"

"Why does it matter? It helped us to find you." I stare at the drawing I'd produced what seems so long ago now. At that time, I'd never dreamed one day the two-dimensional image would become real and be standing in my suite.

She taps it. "Just look at it. It's me at my worst. What bastard wanted to draw that?"

"This bastard," I rasp, my temper flaring.

Her mouth snaps shut. Her body goes completely still. "You're lying. You, you…"

"I drew it from how I remembered you, from that night at the Wheel Inn."

"Why? Why would you do that? Oh fuck. It's because you were working with Seb, isn't it? It's the proof that you'd found me. Wouldn't it have been easier to take a picture with your phone?" She's upset, distraught. "You were looking for me even then. Now it makes sense." She starts moving, pacing the room. "I wouldn't have gone there if I'd known it was owned by criminals. Tommy was right. Should have stayed away."

I snap. Her inaccurate description of the club being the last straw. Moving fast I have her pinned to me, then throw her down on the bed, my weight on top of her holding her down.

"Listen the fuck to me, woman," I roar. "We are not criminals. We weren't even working with Lawson then."

She's struggling, her writhing causing my cock to harden. "Why did you draw me, then? Why? I was no one…"

Give and take, Drummer had said. My job is getting her to believe me and trust us. I've never been challenged by a bitch before, and my head really doesn't know what to do with it. "Fuck it," I snarl. "You want to know why I drew you? Because I had to after Tommy had said you were missin'. I can't fuckin' explain it. Your face, your expression," my voice softens of its own volition, "your cute little nose." My face drops closer to hers, I rub mine against her turned up feature that I find so endearing. "This cute little snub nose." My voice, my action, surprises the fuck out of me. It seems to have the same effect on her. Raising my head, I stare down into her eyes.

"I hate my nose." An inane statement. I have no reply, but she continues anyway. "You captured everything in that drawing. My despair… It feels like an invasion of privacy, Blade. You didn't ask, you just drew it."

"At the time, babe, I never thought I'd see you again. Thought you were just a statistic. Another woman snatched off the streets."

"That sounds about right. You wouldn't give a thought to anyone living rough. Wouldn't care how they got there…"

"I'm not some do-gooder, babe. Understand that. My desire to protect and nurture is finite, extending no further than my brothers in this club. Can't spare more of me to worry about the predicament of strangers or how they got there." Her eyes harden. I try to explain it another way. "We've all got our burdens, babe. Yeah, the world would be a better place if we did shit for others the whole time, but be realistic. There's only so much anyone can do, and my job is protecting my club."

"Your club…" she begins, sneeringly.

"My club," I interrupt. "The brothers who I'd die for. Their women, their children as well."

"You're criminals."

Fuck. Why does she keep coming back to that? "You want to know how we got caught up with Lawson?" She nods. I give a harsh laugh. "We earn our money honest, darlin'. You know the new mall being built in town? Well, we're building that. Gave us such a large fuckin' construction contract that Prez and Viper were invited to the Chamber of Commerce. That's where Lawson approached us about providing security for his rallies. Fuckin' joke, isn't it? It's our respectability, not our undeserved reputation for criminal activities, that brought us to his attention."

She's stopped trying to buck me off. My cock's very grateful. Her eyes crease as they stare into mine. "Providing security? That's it?"

"Yeah. Only met him shortly before I first met you. It was a legitimate business meeting I might add."

"You had no contact with him before that?" When I shake my head, she continues, "Why should I believe you?"

"I might be a lot of things, Tash, but I never lie." It's my turn to give her an intense stare. "Want to know my view? Him employing us coincided with him being unable to find you. I think he wanted us to discover where you were hiding."

"Does he know you have?" Her chest stills as though she's holding her breath for the answer.

"No. Not yet."

Now she's trying to get away again. "Yet?" she screeches. "You're going to give me to him? I knew it!"

"He deserve to be elected?" I roar, getting her attention.

My question takes her by surprise. Her mouth opens, then shuts. Eventually she replies, "Do any of them deserve to?"

"Put it another way then." I'm struggling to find the right buttons to press. "He do anything to give him an unfair advantage over the competition?"

Her lack of response tells me he did. "So, darlin'. This is what I think. Yeah, he messed around when he shouldn't as he's portraying the image of a happily-married man, but he's built a defence about that. You've got something else on him. Something your carrying around in your head. Probably too much of a burden for one woman. Time to let someone else in to help."

I pause. Her eyes are wide, her skin paling. "Assure you babe, we've got no fuckin' idea what it is, though I've got my suspicions. You've got yourself into a situation you can't get out of. If I'm right, the info you've got could get him arrested, and that threat will last as long as you're alive. You go out of state? He won't give up searchin'. You've got family? You'll want to see them, make contact with them. He'll be waitin'. For the rest of your fuckin' life."

She's scared, I try once more to convince her. "We're not criminals, Tash. Left that life behind a very long time ago. Do I think our old rep is the reason why Lawson approached us? Fuck yeah. He believes it, clearly you do as well. Promise you, doll, these days we're more likely to work alongside the police and feds. Have done too, more than once. Also, on my word, on my brother's lives, I'll tell you this. Whatever you think we could have been involved in? We weren't. But we can help. If we know what you've got on him." Damn, how can I get through to her? "We're keeping you safe, aren't we? Nah, we haven't told him where you are. And won't, unless doing so helps bring him down. You hear me?"

Her teeth worry her lip, drawing my attention yet again to her mouth. Just when I think she's not going to reply, she does. In a voice, barely louder than a whisper, "What should I do, Blade?"

That's it. I've got her right where I want her. But I need to be careful not to scare her away. I choose my words carefully. "You tell us, Tash. Tell us everything. Let us have your back, and trust us to do what needs to be done."

"And… and what needs to be done, Blade?"

"Justice." I give her that one word, then, seeing hope flare in her eyes, repeat it, "Justice."

CHAPTER 22

Tash

Justice.

Can I believe in that word? Blade is right. The information I have on Seb could bring him down, not just lose the election, but his freedom.

"I ran. I left everything." Blade nods. He already knows that. "Without access to my stuff, I can't prove a thing. It's my word against his. He'd easily discredit me."

"What have you got on him?"

"What do you want? Receipts that prove where he was, recordings showing his plans."

"On his fellow nominees? Proving his part in the accident and character assassination?"

Blade has gone still. I swallow, then take a leap of faith. What I say next is either going to seal my fate, or be my salvation. I commit with one word. "Yes."

He sucks in air through his teeth. "And where is this shit?"

"Hidden. In my apartment." He looks puzzled, so I explain. "When he got Grant watching me, I wondered whether he suspected. So I lifted a floor board, hid everything underneath."

Tugging his ear, his eyes sharpen. "You said Grant ransacked the place. You reckon he was searching?"

"I do."

"Could already be gone, babe."

That's my fear. It might. I watch as Blade raises his head back. Slowly he releases my wrists he'd been holding over my head. He's still lying on top of me, it seems natural for my now freed hands to move down, and lightly rest on his back. His nostrils flare as my action doesn't go unnoticed.

"I need to talk to Prez. You gonna tell him everything, now?"

He's started to convince me that the Satan's Devils are on the right side, but I had lost faith in everyone once Seb had shown his true colours to me. Hell, I don't even trust myself anymore, definitely not my own judgement. But the thought of someone else sharing the weight on my shoulders is welcome.

I bite my lip, moisten my dry lips with my tongue, then commit, "Yes. Okay. I'll tell you everything I know."

Blue eyes stare into mine, intently as though willing me to believe him. "You're doing the right thing, Tash." A strange look comes over his face, and he lowers his head. I think he was aiming for my cheek, but I turned at the wrong, or maybe right moment, and the platonic kiss he was going for lands instead on my mouth.

He flinches, then grunts, but his lips don't break contact. It's almost as if this is new to him. His lips press hard, move over mine, side to side, gradually adding more pressure. It's me who opens and lets him in, aggressively thrusting my tongue into his mouth. He tastes just as good as I expected, and I moan as our lips smash together.

My hands come up and grasp hold of his hair, holding him tightly to me. Thoughts that I've been starved of human affection since Seb betrayed me go through my head. While Blade's touch isn't particularly gentle, it's not tenderness that I need. Savageness is what I want, and, I suspect, if I'm not careful, is what I'm going to get. I've had enough of being pawed by a gentleman, all I want is to wake the beast I'm holding, and use him to get me out of my head.

His cock which had been hard and rubbing against me since he trapped me on the bed, betrays how much he wants me. Knowing I'm not in this alone gives me the confidence to brazenly thrust my hips, admitting he was right all along. I want him to fuck me. Want to feel something other than fear for just a while.

"You don't know what you're asking for, woman," he rasps, putting only a fraction of space between us to let out the words, before he's taken my mouth once again.

"Fuck me, Blade." My own instruction surprises me; I've never asked for sex before. Always let the man lead, let things happen naturally at their own pace. But I instinctively know, if I don't push him, he'll retreat.

Raising his mouth from my lips, his hands clasp either side of my head. "Remember it was you asking for this. Rules are, I don't come back for seconds. No matter how good it fuckin' is. You gonna be okay with that?"

One fuck. That's all he's offering me. One time to explore this crazy attraction between us. Can I do that? Separate my feelings from my body's physical needs? It's not something I expected I'd ever do, I've not even considered having a one-night stand before. There's one thing in favour though; I may react to him like I've reacted to no one else, but I still don't like him. He's arrogant, cocksure, annoying. While I feel guilty admitting it, there's no way I'd want this to turn into a relation-ship.

I can respond with sincerity. "That's all I want, Blade."

"Christ woman, you're desperate, aren't you?" He grins widely, showing me his white teeth. Then the warmth of his body leaves me, as with one final peck to my mouth, he stands and rips his tee off over his head. My eyes feast on his heavily tattooed body normally hidden by his clothes, noting there's no fat on him, he's pure muscle.

My eyes follow his movements as they go to the first button of his jeans. He catches me watching and smirks. Then his eyes darken.

"Need you naked, babe." His head tilts as his hands still. Observing, waiting to see if I'll obey. This isn't going to be a nice sedate seduction. *A quick fuck.* That's all he's offered, and all, I recall, that I asked for.

Normally I'm shy, waiting for a man to politely undress me, unwrapping each piece of clothing as though I was a present on Christmas day. Exclaiming when at last he reveals my breasts, taking time to admire them, before stripping off more. I'm unused to seeing a man, now already naked, his impressive cock jutting out proudly, waiting impatiently for me to reciprocate. Wait, what's that glinting? *He's pierced.*

I can't help it. I lick my lips.

"Like what you see?" Confidence oozes from him. His smirk showing he has no fear that I won't.

I can do this. Sitting up I pull my t-shirt over my head, then, my eyes fixed on his, I unfasten my bra and slip the straps down my arms. The effect slightly ruined by the purple bruising around my shoulder, but Blade doesn't seem to care. His cheeks hollow as he sucks in air.

I lie back, and slowly unbutton my shorts, then, hooking my thumbs inside the waistband, take both them, and my panties off at the same time. Bending first one leg, then the other, I push them off my feet. Then I lay back, like a sacrificial offering, set out for him.

For a second, Blade doesn't move. Then he springs into action, first opening a drawer in the table by the bed, and takes out a pack of condoms. When he opens one and starts to slide it on his cock, I have a moment of doubt. He said a quick fuck. Does that mean he'll get off and not care what happens to me?

But even before that thought can take root in my brain, he's climbed onto the mattress. He glances at my leg, the colouring of which perfectly matches my shoulder, and gently lays his hand on it. "Still sore?"

"Not so much."

He tests it for himself, bending it while watching my face carefully. When I don't react, he pushes both my thighs apart, then lifts my legs over his shoulders and his face immediately goes between my legs.

His nostrils flare as he inhales deeply, then observes, "Fuck, you're wet."

I suspected I would be. For the past half-hour, I've had an incredibly attractive man lying on top of me.

Blade knows what he's doing. His tongue licks, trying different motions, then settling on the one which elicits the loudest moan from me. My hands reach down, my fingers entwine with his hair, trying to, I don't know exactly, get more pressure? Position him? But my puny efforts have no effect, Blade's going to service me how he wants.

When he inserts two fingers inside me, I'm content to let him play. He's not a man who needs a map to find that g-spot, he's there straight away.

My stomach contracts, my muscles tighten, my back bows. I don't think any man has ever brought me close to the peak so quickly. I'm ready to explode, just one more caress.

I'm screaming. White light blinds me as though a flashbulb has gone off in my head. I'm jerking uncontrollably as he extends my pleasure, drawing it out. It's like I'm performing for him. Only when the last few weak shudders rack my body does he pull away. Now he's straightening my legs and pushing them over my shoulders, finding the right position.

He thrusts in. This is no gentle exploration. This is an invasion. He doesn't stop until he can go no further and I feel him against my cervix. He's so big and thick, there's a burning sensation which quickly fades as he holds himself there for a moment giving me time to adjust.

"Open your eyes."

It's only when his instruction comes that I realise I've scrunched them shut. I do what he says, then regret it. His handsome face, hovering above mine, that intense gaze from his brilliant blue eyes which doesn't move from mine as he slowly slides out, then with a knowing grin, hammers back in again, is almost too much sensory overload.

Another slow slide out, then in again. Then he sets up a rhythm, and on each pass, that piercing is hitting the sensitive spot inside me.

Oh my God. He's a master at this. My body feels alive like it never has before. There's a smirk on his face. He doesn't need my moans or gasps to show what he's doing is right, he already knows.

I'm getting close again, I roll my head back. "Eyes," he snaps. Then follows it with, "Touch yourself."

I do, rubbing my clit, sucking in air and holding it. He increases his pace. The friction inside me, the action of my fingers and I've gone again.

He pulls himself out, his arms coming around me while I'm still coming down from my peak, turning me, then positioning me on all fours. Then he thrusts inside again. He's even deeper now, especially as he wraps one arm around me, anchoring me to his chest.

That big cock keeps up a punishing rhythm. I can honestly say I've never experienced anything like this before. There's a brutality that should be scary, but it's not, it's the most erotic feeling I've ever had as he grunts, pounding into me without mercy.

"You going to come for me again?" he rasps against my ear. "Come."

I've never reached release without external stimulation before, but this strong relentless man is controlling me. My body reacts to his command, and soon I'm screaming. Again, he pulls out. I haven't enough breath to protest, even had I wanted to, as he turns me over onto my back, then kneels between my legs, pulling them around his waist and my ass up onto his thighs. Like a homing missile his cock finds my pussy again.

My limbs feel weak; all I can do is lie here and take it. I'd think he was using me as though I was a blow-up doll if it weren't that his eyes are locked on mine, and he's making small adjustments, watching my expression for what gives me the most pleasure.

"You got one more in you?" he asks, with a grin.

Relieved that he's at last sounding breathless—just how much stamina has this man got?—I move my head side to side. But even as I'm telling him no, he's placed his fingers on my clit and starts strumming. It's impossible, I can't... but somehow I can.

Now he starts thrusting faster, leaning forward, gaining as much ground as possible, his cock plundering impossible depths inside me until, at last, a roar comes out of his mouth and he's pumping with fierce, smaller jerks. Then his head rolls back and he holds that position for a second.

His chest is fighting for air, the way his skin ripples makes his tats seem as though they're alive. Coming down from my own high, I watch, entranced.

Then his head comes forward again. His hands carefully hold the end of the condom as he pulls himself out. One palm slaps my ass as he moves off the bed. "Get dressed." Then he's gone into the bathroom.

No cuddles? Christ, after that workout I could do with some aftercare and a shower. The cool air conditioned draft brings the sheen of sweat covering my skin to my attention, and I pull the sheet around me.

I've just had the best sex of my life with a man who then got out of bed and left me with only a cold instruction to put my clothes back on. Who's already warned me he'd only fuck me once. Why would I expect him to be sweet and lovey-dovey afterward? That wasn't the bargain and not who he is. He warned me of that. That's the deal I willingly made.

But, oh God, I think he's ruined me for other men. When Blade says he's good for just one fuck, he makes the most of it.

He leaves the bathroom fully dressed and stands looking at me with a serious look on his face. *I agreed. I all but begged him. I accepted his terms and conditions.* I make myself smile and get in first before he can speak, "I need a shower." Keeping the sheet around me, though realising it's a bit foolish as he's now seen everything I've got, I start to pick up my clothes.

Whatever he was going to say goes unsaid as I negate the need for him to remind me. *He'd only fuck me once.*

"Yeah, well, I need a cigarette." Reaching into his cut, he pulls out a pack and, I'm glad to see, goes to open the balcony door, presumably intending to smoke it outside.

As I wait for the shower to warm before stepping under the spray, I realise I don't know whether I'm pleased or sorry that he was worth it. While I know I'll never experience that again, I'll store up that memory and remember it forever. It was so good I don't regret it.

CHAPTER 23

Blade

Well I've done it now. I've fucked her. It's over and done. Taking a drag of my cigarette, I look out over the compound, barely seeing the mountains beyond. I may just have made the biggest mistake of my life.

Is she going to cling? Try to get me back into bed? Beg me to fuck her again? Well, now she's agreed to speak to Drummer, at least there's no need to keep her close. She can go back to sleeping in the crash room. It will be nice to have my room back to myself.

I take my time, smoking my cancer stick down to the filter, then stubbing it out on my boot. I've finished just as the door opens behind me.

She's towelling her hair, but is fully dressed. She might have washed the scent of me off, but her face still has that after-sex glow. *Down boy* I instruct my cock, surprised he's even twitching. I just came hard, and normally he loses interest after he's been there once.

"What?" I ask, after it seems she's just staring.

"Was that biker loving, Blade?" Her impudent grin worries me a little as I wonder where she's going with that.

"Like it?" I chuckle at her quick nod. "Well, can't speak for my brothers of course, but I've never known anyone to complain."

"Yeah, I liked it," she confirms using words. "A lot. Wouldn't mind a repeat performance."

See? Can't trust bitches. "Once," I growl. "I explained. Once. Not going to do you again."

She waves her hands as though indicating that doesn't matter. "Got me wrong, Blade. I know the score. Just wondered how your brothers would compare."

My fingers curl into fists at my side. I clamp my teeth to stop words coming out that I have no right even to be thinking. *Ungrateful bitch. I just gave her the best fucking of her life, and she wants to move straight on to one of my brothers?*

"Gotta get to church," I tell her, physically moving her away from the door and pushing past. *Fuck. I was right. Bitches can't be trusted.* I'm angry at her, even more furious with myself. Why should I care now I've been there and done that? Why aren't I happier she's showing she can move on? *Should I get Fergus to watch her again?* I can't even be fucking bothered to do that. She wants to leave? Good fucking luck to her.

I'm early. Arriving at the clubhouse, I grab a beer. Beef starts walking across, but I'm not in the mood to talk to any of my single brothers right now, so I make like I haven't seen him, and instead head for our meeting room. I get there to find I have the empty room to myself. Suits me fine. I can do some thinking.

"Blade, you okay?" Wraith slaps me on the back as he walks to the seat next to mine. "Saw you come in."

"Sort of thought that might have suggested I wanted some time alone," I grumble.

The VP chuckles, "Got something on your mind, brother?"

I can't tell him what I'm really thinking about. Instead I shrug. "Got somewhere with Tash."

He nudges me in the ribs. "That well-fucked look on your face suggested that, Brother."

"I don't mean that," I say far too sharply. But I don't deny it, and the VP smirks, noticing my omission. "She's got dirt on Lawson."

"Has she now?"

"You cracked her?" Drummer asks, as he too takes his seat.

"Looks like he fucked her to me." Peg's throaty laugh comes from across the other side of the table.

I get out my knife, raise it up high, then plant the blade into the wooden table top. It quivers for a moment. "Next asshole who says one word about what I may or may not have done to Tash can expect that in their fuckin' head next." I glare around the table noticing everyone else has come in. Joker makes a play of zipping his mouth. Shooter waves his hands as if saying count him out. Mouse is smirking, the asshole. I preferred him when he was moody, before he met Mariana. See? A woman can change a man, and not for the fucking better.

Which one will she go for next? I drop my head into my hands, not understanding why that thought makes me see red. Never minded sharing a bitch before. It's her reaction that's all. Suggesting it was over and forgotten so fast after I'd put so much effort into pleasing her. It wasn't enough? Well, good luck to whoever's next, that's all I can say.

The gavel bangs. "You fuckin' with us, Blade?"

Prez is staring at me. Seems I've missed something. "Sorry, yeah."

"As I was saying. Truck's come to see me. There's a bad wild-fire in California."

"Not unusual, Prez." Road's not making a joke. Far from it. His face looks pinched as he states the fact. But none of us would find it amusing. We had first-hand experience of one this time last year.

"Yeah, well, Truck's been asked to go down there. He'll be gone for as long as it takes."

Peg scrunches his face. "Could be the whole season, Darcy was saying."

"You knew about this?" Prez looks surprised.

"Firefighters talk." Peg shrugs. "Truck wanted to tell you himself."

And, clearly, wives have loose mouths. Bitches can't be trusted.

"What does it mean for his role in the club?" Wraith asks. "Man's done his time as a prospect. Must have been with us getting on for a year now. Should we think about patching him in?"

Frowning I ask, "But what about Fergus? Thought he'd be the next."

"Matt ain't far off either," Peg adds.

Prez strokes his beard, then pronounces, "Truck's announcement makes him a different case. He's leaving us, but it isn't his choice. I've been thinkin' along the same lines as the VP. I propose we patch Truck in. I'd trust that man with my life."

"So would I, Prez."

"You bet."

It's hard to distinguish voices as we're all saying the same thing.

"Fergus?" This time, it's Joker who asks. Like me, he seems to respect the man. "He's had it hard. Needs family."

Nodding down the table at him, I see the changes since he and Lady came out. Having a family around him was the making of him. He would understand more than most what it's like to be without.

"I like the fucker," I say to support him. "What about a double patch party, Prez?"

"Leaves us fuckin' short on prospects," Peg objects.

"Can't keep a man from being a brother just because we don't want to do our own shitty work," Prez observes. "If we keep them hanging, might lose them anyway."

"Kept me hanging for eighteen months," Hyde complains.

"Yeah, well you were a useless twerp." Slick's grin takes the malice out of his words, and he laughs when Hyde shoots him the finger. Any differences there were between them, had been resolved a while back.

"I might know a couple of lads interested," Viper says, nodding at Shooter.

"Yeah, they're on-site with us. Good workers." Shooter works for Viper and Bullet's construction business.

"Well, let's move this on. Proposal is, we bring both Fergus and Truck to the table. Want to vote separately or together?"

"Both," I propose. My suggestion being echoed from all sides.

It takes but a minute before Heart's writing the decision in the book. Two new members will be joining us around the table. Truck already comes with a readymade road name we see no need to change, but we take a few minutes debating what to call Fergus. It's Joker who comes up with it.

"Man's drifted out, then back in. How about Drifter?"

I shrug. Seems as good as any suggested.

"Okay, we'll go with that. We'll tell them the good news at the end of the meeting. Now, Blade. Where have you got to with Tash?" Prez moves on.

"Well he's past first base that's for certain." Beef roars with laughter at his own joke.

"Pretty sure he's made a home run." Rock high fives Beef across the table.

Grabbing hold of my knife I point the blade toward each of them in turn. "Unless you want to feel steel I suggest you shut the fuck up."

"Oooh. He sounds frustrated. Maybe he only got to third." Now Joker is joining in.

Mouse is grinning widely. I gesture toward him. "One word, Brother, one fuckin' word, and you'll find yourself at the wrong end of a scalping."

"Everyone shut the fuck up!" Drummer bangs the gavel bringing us back to some semblance of order. "Don't give a damn what Blade's done or how far he's got. I've got my own woman to fuck, and that's what I'd rather be doing."

Prez's voice and steely gaze is enough to shut everyone up. I swallow down my anger and try to come up with a summation. "She's got evidence Lawson was involved in the accident that killed Ferguson, and that he was responsible for setting up the scandal for Cobb."

"What evidence?" Mouse asks quickly, his eyes narrowing. "Physical?"

I nod. "She didn't go into details, but she seems to think she's got enough. She hid it in her apartment, but Lawson's man, Grant, was last seen in the process of tearing the place apart. He was sent there to kill her, but she got the better of him and ran."

"Fuck," Road exclaims. "No wonder she left with nothing."

"You reckon this asshole Grant could have found what she'd hidden?"

I turn to the VP. "Depends if he was actually lookin'. He told her he was making her murder look like a home invasion gone wrong."

"He'd have looked." Peg's gaze meets mine. "But how clever was she at hidin' it? And can we get in to find if it was missed?"

"And where's this fucker Grant?" is snarled from the end of the table. "I'd like to get my hands on him. Telling a woman you're going to kill her?"

I turn and raise my chin at Marvel. My brothers have done a one-eighty switch. One minute they're all baiting me, the next on my side trying to unravel what's going on, and how we can help.

"Explains a lot." Prez gets our attention. "She knows we're on his payroll. Probably thought we'd take over where Grant left off. No wonder she wanted to keep what she was hiding quiet." He lets his words sink in for a moment.

Wraith fills the gap. "We are on the bastard's payroll. Question is, do we want to stay there or not?"

I inhale deeply, then audibly let my breath out. "Do we give a damn about citizen politics?"

"Those are the two questions we need to answer. In my view, Blade's needs to be addressed first." Again, eyes go to Drummer. "Do we care about one more dirty politician?"

Lady raises his hand; Drummer gives him a nod. "We don't live by citizen's rules. Sort shit out for ourselves. But there are some things they do that affect us, whether we like it or not."

"Fuckin' taxes for one," Dollar, our treasurer interrupts.

"Money, for sure. But it's more than that. Joker and I can be refused to be served because of a fucker's supposed religious beliefs. Politicians say whether they recognise our right to be married or not."

"Hold the cards as far as Mariana's concerned too," Mouse backs him up. "She's got residency, but still needs to wait to apply for her green card. Hate fuckin' politicians myself, but however much we'd like to ignore them, they hold one fuck of a lot of cards. They're able to keep movin' goal posts."

"What are you sayin'?" Prez leans back in his chair. "Spit it out, Brothers."

Viper does the opposite to Drummer and sits forward. "I think what they're sayin' is what I'm thinkin'. Don't get involved in their policies or who they fuckin' support. Most politicians are in it for themselves. But if one's already swimming in the swamp, don't want to help him get more power. He stoops to playin' dirty to clear his path now? Wouldn't sit easy with me to think what he could do with more authority."

Several of us nod.

Prez raises his chin. "So have we a motion to take Lawson down? Expose him?"

"Why not just kill him?" Shooter gets straight to the point. "Treat him like he treated Ferguson."

"While I don't dislike the idea, Brother, there's too much risk." Peg is wearing his sergeant-at-arms hat. "He's too visible."

"We could do it," Jekyll insists.

"Don't want any of us going inside for offin' a fuckin' filthy lawmaker." Prez's voice rings out loudly. "If we can get our hands on the evidence, we take him down."

"If I can get more details from Tash, then I can start doing some digging myself." Mouse offers. "If I know what she's got, that's a good place to start."

Wraith clears his throat loudly. "What are we going to do in the meantime? Try to bring Lawson down while still taking his money?"

Prez's face splits into a grin. "Exactly that, Wraith. We keep close to him. Try and make him slip up. We're holding an ace, remember? The woman."

I glare at him. "Tash has been through a lot. Don't like the thought of him knowing where she is."

A pregnant pause before Prez raises his chin. "If the timing is right, Blade, think we ought to give him that information. Record the conversation, may get him requesting us to take her out. Then we have something to take to the cops."

All eyes open. "You're not fuckin' suggesting we do this legal?"

Prez chuckles. "Why fuckin' not? As the sergeant-at-arms so rightly pointed out, it's too risky to deal with him ourselves."

"So we're gathering evidence." Mouse's eyes light up. They would. He enjoys a good puzzle to solve.

"It will need to be cast iron," Bullet observes. "They won't trust us."

"They'll trust Tash, if she has enough to back her story up, and us behind her to protect her, of course."

"He's got friends in the cops," I remind them.

Heart sniggers, bringing my attention to him. "So have we. Marc will know who to take this to." Yeah, his ex-cop wife will probably still have a few contacts.

"When she ran," Hyde asks, "why didn't she go straight to the police?"

"Because Lawson's a persuasive fucker," I respond. "She knew without evidence; they'd believe him and not her."

"Was she ever going to do anything?" Wraith seems to wonder aloud. "Or was she going to let him get away with it?"

He sounds critical, so I shoot him down. "For the past few weeks she was trying to stay alive. I think that's been her priority."

"Okay. Let's vote. We bring down Lawson." Prez calls an end to the discussion. The vote is quick. All ayes. It's recorded, and Prez continues to hold the floor. "First thing is to get into Tash's apartment, find the evidence ourselves."

"Reckon Lawson will have eyes on it."

Peg grins, shaking his head at Dollar. "We're his security. He wants us to find the girl? Tell him we're looking for shit his man missed."

That could work. "Lawson is desperate enough to try anything," I point out.

"Good point, Blade," Prez acknowledges.

"I'd like to start with Cobb. Hear his side of the story. Might give us some clues as to what Lawson's got." Mouse starts putting puzzle pieces together. "And I'll look into Ferguson's accident."

"Okay. Let's wrap this up. Peg, Blade. You're still leading with Lawson. Meet with him, see if you can press him as to what he wants us to do with Tash if we get hold of her. Just go careful. He's probably as devious as us."

There are the expected offers of help from around the table, then we get to the part of the meeting I always enjoy. Fergus is called in, made to feel six inches tall as if he's in trouble for some shit, then his new patches are slid down the table, and we all slap the relieved and happy man's back.

The meeting doesn't end there. Now it's Truck's turn. The big man enters the room. Unlike Fergus, he's not nervous, but apologetic.

"Look, I'm sorry to leave you in the lurch. I stepped up when they asked for volunteers. Didn't put the club first, I know that. But those fires in Cali are out of control, they really need help."

"Now listen here," Prez snarls. "Yeah, we expect prospects to give their all to the club. Prospecting's when you prove you can be trusted, and you've done that. Accepted you were a firefighter, and that that made you a special case. Not surprised you're dropping everything to go where you're needed. Doesn't mean you've stopped caring about the club."

"When you leavin'?" asks Wraith.

"Tomorrow. Early, VP. Fires don't wait."

"Got time to sew these on?" Drummer stands up, walks around the table, and slaps the patches into the firefighter's hands.

Truck stands stunned, looking down at the Satan's Devils' insignias he's holding. He shakes his head side by side. "Thought you'd be throwing me out. As I told, Drummer, hard to know when I'll be back. If I'm asked, I'll join a hotshot team, and fuck knows where I'll be based."

"You'll always be a member," Drummer tells Truck. "Get those on your cut, leave it with me for safekeeping. It will be here for you when you come back. If you get based somewhere else, you might be able to transfer to that state's chapter."

"Fuck, Prez." The big man's eyes are leaking. "Fuck." Then he envelopes Prez in a bear hug.

Truck might be leaving, but he'll always be part of the brotherhood.

CHAPTER 24

Blade

There's an obligatory patching in party after church. It's a strange one tonight. Fergus, no, *Drifter*, is happy and excited, accepting congratulations from all round, but en masse we're all sad to know Truck will be leaving us, and while now a full member, won't be taking his seat around the table or at least for a while.

The firefighter's also not drinking, needing a clear head when he leaves in the morning. I know I'm far from the only one who's admiring him, knowing first-hand how scary those wildfires can be. Last year's came too close to the compound for comfort. It's due to the efforts of him and his firefighting colleagues that we've still got a home.

I'm leaning back against the bar, drink in hand, watching Truck deep in conversation with the Prez when Mouse approaches.

"Your woman not around?"

"You want a black eye?"

I get a slap on my back. "I was just jerking your chain, Brother. But hey, you look like you've got something on your mind."

"Mariana's good for you, Mouse."

After a moment's confusion while he computes my swift change of subject, Mouse raises his chin. "That she is, Blade. Didn't go lookin' for her, but I found her just the same. Brought me some balance in my life. Can recommend havin' an ol' lady."

"Not for me." I shudder. Can't think of anything worse.

He stares at me for a moment. "What the fuck's up, Blade? You're acting strange."

All the men here are my brothers; Mouse and I go back a long time. But I can't tell him what's on my mind, a situation of my own making which I'm wondering if I'm now regretting. I'm saved when Drummer at last breaks away from Truck and comes over.

"Got a minute, Blade?"

I've got plenty of them. Not going to go back to my room soon, perhaps not even tonight. I follow Prez into his office. As he retrieves his bottle of whisky from a shelf and two glasses, I sit down.

"You and Tash?"

"You up in my business now, Prez?"

"Feel I need to be, Brother. Don't much care whose cock goes where, except when it affects the club. Need to know whether you just fucked her to get your dick wet and information out of her, or whether you're claiming her. With Lawson on the loose, could make a difference to any play we make."

"Who says I fucked her?"

"You going to tell me you haven't?"

I don't want to lie to Drummer. He barks a laugh. "Wraith owes me some dollars."

I'm not surprised to hear they've been taking bets on whether I'd do the deed or not. "Yeah, well. I've been there. But you know me Drum, I won't be going back."

"You fucked her. She talked. Job done?"

I raise my chin. "Yeah. Job done." Then, I add, "Well, that's what I fuckin' hope."

His eyebrows rise. "Strange way of putting it, Blade. She got a magic pussy? You worried you can't keep away?"

"Got a problem, Prez."

"Thought you had." He tops up the whisky that's disappeared from my glass without me noticing. "Why we're having this chat."

"Yeah, I fucked her." *Every which way to Sunday and back.* "Took my time," I phrase it politely. "When I finished, found the condom had split."

"Fuck." Drummer's lips purse. "What she say?"

I shrug. "Didn't tell her."

"What? You don't think she should know? You should talk to her. If you're not prepared to deal with any possible outcome, there's always that pill she can take."

I sit forward, lean on the desk and put my head in my hands. "Remember that convo about Lawson's wife? Jokes about him not liking covering his junk? Well, he did that to Tash, got her pregnant, then promised her the earth and a future if she had an abortion."

"Yeah," he already knows that, "she went through with it." His expression suggests she'd likely be practical again. I'm not so certain.

"He didn't give her much choice. Got the tablets for her, sat over her while she took them. Fuckin' screwed her up, Drum."

He sips his whisky, then nods. "But you're not in a relationship with her. She thought that's what she had with Lawson. A preventative measure isn't the same thing. Brother, unless you can step up if there are going to be ramifications, you need to have that conversation now."

All I can see are the tears in her eyes when she told me what Lawson had done. Drummer's right, the only promise I'd made to her is that I was a one-and-done man. That now I've had her, I won't be going back. For a second I regret that, my cock twitches reminding me how happy he'd felt there, clearly at odds with my brain which is telling me to run.

"What would you do if she ends up having your child?"

It's a reasonable question. I've never for one second considered having a kid of my own. While I don't mind all the babies in the clubhouse, I don't particularly like them. "I'm not like you, Drummer. Never wanted a family."

"You think I did? You've known me a fuckin' long time, Brother. Before I met Sam, I was quite happy fuckin' whores then moving on to the next. The right woman can change you."

Yeah, Drummer got his handle as he'd bang anything in sight. And wearing the president's patch meant he never went wanting. He gave up all other pussy to be with Sam.

"Don't think I've got fidelity in me, Prez."

He barks a laugh. "Neither did I. But when you meet the right woman you know it." He looks straight at my eyes as if trying to see right inside my head. "That's the difference, isn't it? I tried to ignore my attraction to Sam but it was there from the start. Clearly you can't say the same thing about Tash, so you need to be straight with her. Tell her what went wrong. No one's fault. Shit happens. Tell her you won't be sticking around, that we'll sort out this fuckin' situation with Lawson so she can get on with her life. Up to her if she takes the risk it'll have a kid in it."

"Not that easy, is it? She has my kid; I'll have to play a part. At the very least, support it." I frown. I don't remember my dad. My life may well have been very different, had he stuck around. Jonah might still be breathing. What if Tash turned out like my mom? Only thinking of herself and not the kid. Christ. I couldn't just pay up, I'd need to check she was bringing it up right, step in if not. Wouldn't be easy if she was the other side of the fucking country. But if she's nothing to me, she can go where she likes.

"Can't see you've got any option, Blade. Don't think you can blank the possibilities out; small as they might be. Unless you're prepared to step up. You want my advice? Here it is. I can understand you not wanting to hurt her after all she's been through, but if the worst happens, don't you think she'd have wanted to have been given a choice? You have to tell her."

Slowly I nod. Much as I'd prefer not to have this conversation, Drummer is right. I know it will cause her pain, bring all her bad memories back. And probably for nothing. What's the chances that a few escaped sperm could have entered her just at the right time?

"You know what the other chapters say about Tucson, Blade. Maybe there's something in it. One thing for certain, we don't have any problems getting our bitches pregnant."

I chuckle. "You're not wrong there, Prez. Maybe there is something in the water."

I finish the whisky, momentarily glad I'm drinking it straight, and stand, raising my chin towards him. Then, straightening my back and ignoring the party as I walk through the clubroom, I return to the suite for the conversation I'd rather not have.

Tash is so engrossed as I walk in, she doesn't hear me. I stand watching her. Her left arm is resting on the desk, wrapped around my sketch pad she seems to have taken ownership of. Her right hand is scribbling frantically, words flowing out onto the page. She pauses, biting the end of the pencil, *my pencil*, leaving teeth marks there I expect. Then she's back to scribbling again.

Her hair, untamed by a tie today, falls over her face. Impatiently she tucks it back behind one ear.

As I breathe in, that particular aroma she adds to the smell of my shampoo fills my nostrils. I wonder whether I'll ever get her scent out of my room. Fleetingly the question crosses my mind of do I want to? Each time I smell it, it's like coming home.

Giving myself a mental slap I dismiss that thought fast. It's the predicament we're in, the one that I know and which she's ignorant of for now that's making my thoughts fanciful. Me having a woman in my life? Something I've never considered.

She sighs. *Fuck. That's like the sound she made when I first touched her.* My cock starts to swell. *Nah, fella. Down. We've been there, done that. Time to move on.* I'll have the conversation I need to, then go seek out one of the available club girls. I might need to wait in line tonight as there are two more brothers patched in, and who'll be taking advantage of their new status. Truck might be able to turn a drink down, but he may well take his fill of free pussy.

The thought of using a woman who's already been with my brothers tonight suddenly doesn't interest me at all, my cock even deflates at the idea. Leaning back against the door, I fold my arms. Am I crazy? I've got a woman here in my room, I could have all to myself. *She wasn't serious when she said she'd move on to my brothers, was she?* I'll have to warn them all off.

Warn them? Of what? That's she's got an amazing tight pussy that grips your cock just right? That she makes you come so hard you see stars? That she makes you want to keep going and never stop? That she's fit, pliable, fits into your arms as though she's made to be there?

What the fuck am I thinking? Perhaps it's because I didn't kick her straight out. Or maybe, it's because I kissed her. Never done that before. Somehow that had seemed more intimate than fucking. Her taste... My tongue licks my lips. Wouldn't take much to persuade me to go back for more.

Her hand stills, the pencil she's been using, *chewing*, is placed down. "I know you're there, Blade. I can hear you breathing."

"Why didn't you say something?"

"Why didn't you?" she challenges. "Anyway, I was in full flow. The words just kept coming."

Whether it's to put off the moment when I need to start the difficult conversation I'd returned to have, or whether I'm genuinely interested, I'm not sure. But something leads me to ask, "Can I see?"

She hesitates, her hand covers the paper, then she inches it down. Her brow scrunches delightfully as she reads back her own words. "It's still rough, but, okay then." She turns fully and glares at me. "Don't you dare laugh."

I nod to agree. I'd probably feel much the same if anyone ever asked to see one of my half-finished drawings. It had been bad enough having people critique the one I'd done of her. Mind you, their comments had all been positive. I can do the same. As I move closer, I decide whatever rubbish she's written, I'll make an encouraging response.

Placing my hand on her shoulder, ignoring the static electricity, I lean over her and start reading. My lips curve. Then twitch. Then I do what I promised I wouldn't, I chuckle. Then I let out a full belly laugh.

"You said you wouldn't." Her hand covers the paper.

I move it away, with a demand, "Let me read."

"Oh fuck." I'm chortling. "Fuck me, Tash. That's brilliant."

My hand moves down from her shoulder so my arm now imprisons her, pulling her back against me. With my other I take ownership of the sketch pad, flicking through pages covered in her neat handwriting until I get, finally, to a blank sheet. Releasing her, I carry it over to the bed and sit down.

"What are you doing?"

My hand itches, experience tells me there's only one way to get relief. The graphite touches the paper and starts to fly.

"Blade?"

The bed dips as she sits next to me. When she sees what's taking shape, she gasps. Now it's her turn for her hand to find my shoulder, and she's leaning over me. I should feel trapped, suffocated, but so intent on what's appearing on the paper, I ignore her. Her breath feels warm against my ear, but I don't seem to care that she's crowding me.

"Blade. Oh my God. That's what I pictured. Blade. That's amazing!"

She'd told me not to laugh, now she's the one giggling. But it's not at me, it's what's taking shape under my hands.

"It's only a rough idea," I tell her. As my fingers slow their frantic movements, I feel embarrassed she's been watching me. Finished, I tear out the sheet of paper.

Mistakenly believing it's an invitation, she takes it. "That's just what was in my head, Blade. That's how I saw it."

Self-conscious, but somehow relaxed, drawing often removes the tension in me, I shrug. "Give it to me."

Another second or two examining it, then she passes it back. I gaze on it again, my lips curving. Her text had been titled, 'The Adventures of Grunt, the Biker Dog'. My picture shows him sneakily approaching a Harley and attempting to get on. One paw on the handlebar, a hind leg in mid-air being thrown over the seat, his head looking around with that guilty look dogs wear when they know they're doing something they shouldn't.

Already a series of pictures are forming in my head, she's written most of the book from what I can see. A children's book. Fuck me, but the kids in the clubhouse would love this shit.

Now in possession of my picture, I take it over to the bin, flick my lighter…

"What the hell are you doing, Blade?"

I pause. "Burning it," I reply as though it's the most normal thing in the world. And it is. To me.

Her arms are pulling me back, her hand trying to take the paper. "No you're not, Blade. That's too good to destroy. Give it to me."

We both tussle to get custody. It's art paper, it's thick, but not that strong and it's going to tear. Oh fuck, if she wants it that badly. When I let go, she hugs it to her, a look of pleasure on her face. "Could you do more, Blade? Illustrate the book for me? I've used illustrators before, but none have got inside my head."

What the fuck she talking about? "You've had books published?"

Her face reddens. "I self-publish, but yes. I've got one out there."

Well fuck me. I wouldn't have expected that.

"I was going to do a series featuring Grunt. 'Grunt Saves the Day' is the first one. 'Grunt to the Rescue' another, oh, and 'Grunt Gets a New Brother'."

I bark a laugh at that one, wondering whether she knows the double meaning if she's talking about a biker club.

I reach out my hand, stroking her hair, tucking it back behind her ear, the action that had tempted me half-an-hour ago. "You're a dark horse, aren't you, sweetheart?"

CHAPTER 25

Tash

Please don't touch me. Please don't touch me.

Having just seen Blade has hidden talents, him reaching out and caressing me so tenderly makes me go weak at the knees. I told him I was up for a one-night, or to be accurate, one-afternoon stand, but it seems that I lied. I've got to be strong. Got to keep my distance. He turns me on like no one else has ever done. Sex with him was incredible, far beyond anything I've ever experienced. I tried to dismiss it as a bodily function, but to me, it was far more.

Before I'd decided I'd rather occupy myself writing, Blade making love, no, fucking, had been going around and around my head. Half disgusted at giving myself to a man I didn't even like, the other half of me glad I'd been able to find out what it was like. If that's the way all bikers make love, no wonder the women here look so happy. They must be kept well satisfied.

Because he's an arrogant dick, it was all too easy to convince myself I didn't want a repeat performance even had it been offered. If the opportunity arose again, I'd told myself I'd ignore the stupid unexplainable fact that he turns me on, I'd have too. I've a horrible feeling I could become addicted to him and his rough, immensely gratifying, ways. That he'd walk away is an absolute given. But, if he keeps his promise, the question will never arise.

I'm looking at him differently now he's shown there's another side to him, one, the like of which, I never dreamed would exist. He's an artist, and an extremely good one, shown by the way he'd captured Grunt's image. That's not all. He'd read my words, getting the jokes easily, and not only that, seemed to reach inside my head and pull out the exact illustration I'd envisaged to go with the text. It's almost frightening as he saw something that was only in my mind. On the one hand, I'd love him to do all the illustrations for me. On the other, that would be a very bad idea. To work beside someone who understands me so well, and yet is so unattainable, is a terrifying thing. What if there were yet more sides to him? Sides which I could relate to as well. I wouldn't want to let him go. And he's not the man for staying.

I turn away from him. As his hand hovers in place before returning to his side, I busy myself placing my prize, the picture, in the closed-up notebook also containing my words.

"Tash, we have to talk." The tone of his voice tells me it's not artwork or writing that's going to be the topic.

The loose sheet of paper I'd stopped him burning isn't lined up properly. I concentrate on getting it just right, while responding, "I think we've said all there is to say. You made it quite plain, Blade."

"Tash. Put that down and come over here. There's something I've got to tell you." His tone has lost its arrogance. All mirth and playfulness is gone. Whatever he has to say is going to be serious.

I hear him move, looking around I see him perched on the edge of the bed. He's patting a space he's left to his side.

Well, until he lets me have my freedom, I'm still his captive. I do what he says. As soon as I've made myself comfortable, one leg folded beneath me, he starts, "Tash, we need to talk about earlier."

"There's nothing to discuss. I know the score, Blade. And to be honest, I don't want a repeat," I lie through my teeth.

"You don't?" he cocks his eyebrow in challenge, I make myself stare back steadily. Again, the cockiness quickly fades. He shakes his head, starts to speak, then stops. Then tries again, "Fuck, I should just put it out there, shouldn't I?"

"You've got an STD?" My hand covers my mouth as I think of the explanation for something that's clearly so hard to tell me.

"What the fuck? No I haven't got a fuckin' STD!" he snarls. "Why the fuck did you go there?"

"Because you're a man whore?" I suggest drily.

He breathes in sharply, but doesn't try to defend the indefensible. "I could ask the same of you."

Now it's my turn to open my eyes wide. "I'm clean."

He rakes his hands back through his hair, letting out an exasperated sigh. "Tash. This is fuckin' serious. Will you please listen to me?"

Confused, not sure what there is to talk about, I sigh. "Go on."

"There's no easy way to tell you this, but you need to know. The condom split, Tash."

Oh. My. God. It's like déjà vu. It's happening all over again. My hand covers my mouth and I leap to my feet, tearing into the bathroom kicking the door closed, but having no time to turn the lock before I throw up the contents of my stomach into the bowl. There's not much to bring up, and soon I'm dry heaving.

"Fuck, Tash."

"Get out," I scream.

"Tash, Tash." Blade's pulling back my hair as I heave again. "Tash, here." He's pulled off a few sheets of toilet paper. Gratefully I take them and wipe my mouth. He reaches around me and pulls the flush. "You gonna be sick again?" he asks, stroking my back.

I shake my head. "Not a lot to bring up," I tell him crudely, but honestly.

His hand pauses. "Fuck. Shit I'm sorry Tash. You haven't eaten have you?"

"I'm used to it."

"Well you can get unused to it. Sorry. I'm not used to keeping a prisoner. Should have made arrangements to have you fed."

"You make me sound like a dog."

"Never had a pet either."

It's a bizarre conversation, but strangely it's taking my mind off the problem that made me throw up. My mind circles back to it as Blade takes his phone out of his cut.

"Bring some sandwiches up to my room. Tash hasn't eaten." A pause, then, "Oh, fuck, sorry Brother. Totally forgot. Get Matt to… You will? Good on you, *Brother*. Thanks Drifter. I owe you one."

He reaches out his hand to help me up. As I take it, he's shaking his head. "Fergus got patched in tonight. Completely forgot. But he's sorting you out some food, okay?"

"You didn't have to. I don't think I can eat anyway." Angrily I wipe away the tears which have started leaking from my eyes.

"Babe." He pulls me into him. I want, need comfort, so I don't protest. A sob comes, another follows. I breathe in the leather of the cut he's still wearing; its smell already familiar. His hand is stroking my back again. "I'm so sorry, babe. Should have told you earlier, didn't know what words to use."

"It wasn't your fault Blade. At least you wore one."

He chuckles softly. "Put it under a bit of stress though."

My fingers tighten as I remember just how. Then I wail and throw myself away from him as it all hits me. "I can't do this. I can't do it again."

"Babe."

"No, don't babe me." A flash of anger. "You shouldn't..." then my rage subsides as quickly as it had risen when I remember technically it hadn't been him, it had been me. I'd been the one to encourage him. Now I've got to wait two weeks to find out if the worst comes true.

The problem being, it will be my nightmare to deal with, a single woman on her own, but even now I'd never think of a baby as anything other than a gift to treasure.

"Tash." He's come to sit beside me. "Don't hate me, this is only a suggestion." He sighs, "There's always the morning-after pill."

Another emotional swing as I snap, "You'd like that, wouldn't you?"

I wait for him to tell me it's the best option, the sensible thing to do. What I should have done last time. Only with Seb I thought it wouldn't matter, that we'd eventually have a family, and if he wanted to be careful, he'd have worn a condom anyway. We would just have been doing things a bit back to front, that was all. But Blade? Well, it's clear he doesn't want children, or at least with me. Hell, he doesn't even want me. We're not in a relationship. Unlike Seb, he's not pretending. He couldn't have told me the score any more plainly. We'd made a bargain. I accepted it.

I realise he hasn't answered my question. I expect he's thinking how he can persuade me. I'm not sure what I want to do. I'm probably not pregnant. Taking a pill wouldn't hurt in the circumstances, would it?

"I don't know what I want." Blade looks confused at the words that have come out of his mouth. He slides up the bed so his back is resting against the headboard. "Come here, babe." For some reason, I do. "This is a fucked-up situation, isn't it? Let's think this through. I'm not looking for a relationship, I've got my reasons why. It's not you, it's that I've decided I'll never have a woman riding up behind me. Don't need a companion for that, got my brothers beside me. Got the club whores to fuck. Whatever happens, I'm not going to be playing happy families."

"I think I've got that message, Blade."

"Yeah? Well, I wouldn't want you to pin your hopes on trying to change me." He says it in a matter-of-fact way that isn't insulting. Just stating the way that he is. For a moment, I feel sorry for him, then remember, I don't know his reasons.

"I can't hope to have a future, not with Seb after me. You're right. He won't stop until he's got rid of me for good."

"Don't concern yourself about that. Normally wouldn't discuss club business, but don't want that worry in your head. Club's voted to get rid of Lawson."

I sit forward and look at him sharply. "You're going to *kill* him?"

He chuckles, and cups his hand around my cheek. "That was one of the options, but no, babe. Didn't agree on that. We're going to take your evidence, get more, then present the case to cops who are not in his pocket. He'll go down for murder if we do our job right."

If they can do that, it will mean I'll get my life back.

"Until we do, you'll stay here on the compound. I'll talk to Viper; he's been fitting out more suites as the chapter is growing. I'll see if we can get you into one of your own. Come back here." I take the invitation to return into his arms.

I feel his lips against my hair, then he resumes speaking. "Chances are good none of my swimmers reached their target, okay? You want to make sure of that, I'll get you the pill. You want to trust fate? I'm down with that too. You've had a hard fuckin' time of it, and I'm not going to add any more pressure on top. Your body? You do what you want with it."

"I'm as much as a loss as you as to what I want," I admit.

"If, and it's a fuckin' big if, if you're pregnant, well, I don't know how I'd cope. Must admit I tolerate the kids here, never saw myself adding to their number. Don't know how to deal with them, always kept a distance if you see what I mean. But I won't walk away from my responsibilities. I'll have your back, and will help financially."

"But you won't have any emotional commitment." I'm not accusing or judging; just stating fact.

"Don't think I'll be able to, Tash. I'm not programmed that way."

"So you wouldn't see the baby? Or want to be involved in the pregnancy?"

He swipes his hand back through his hair. "No fuckin' idea. I don't think I'd be able to give you an honest answer until it's certain there's a problem to deal with. The chance is so slim; I can't get my head around it right now. I tell you something today? Could all change."

He's right. Last time I thought I'd have a man beside me. This time, if our mistake bears fruit, I've got to accept I won't. I can't accuse Blade of not being honest.

There's a knock at the door. Blade slides out from under me and goes to open it. Fergus is standing there, swaying. A slightly loopy grin on his face; in his hand, there's a plate of sandwiches he looks like he's in danger of dropping.

Blade takes the plate quickly and looks at it dubiously. "You make these yourself?"

"Yup." He nods his head vigorously and places his hand on the doorframe to balance himself.

"Thanks, Drifter. You get back to your party."

"Yesss," Fergus hisses.

"Drifter?"

Blade kicks the door shut with his heel. "Told you. He got patched in. Gave him a road name as he drifted out and back in." He stares down at what he's holding.

I make a gimme gesture with my hands, now realising I'm starving. Blade brings it across. "Not sure…"

There's a huge lump of ham sitting between two thick slices of bread. It looks like a gourmet meal to me. "Honestly Blade? This is better than what I scrounged from the bin at the Wheel Inn."

Throwing himself on the bed, he puts his arm up over his eyes. "Please do not remind me. How the fuck could I have done that? Let the potential mother of my child scavenge in the waste bin for food."

As my eyes widen at the words I didn't expect, I see him wink.

CHAPTER 26

Blade

I don't want the responsibility of a fucking kid for fuck's sake. The thought terrifies me. I want to complain to the condom company, get some compensation or such shit, but maybe I had given it too much of a workout. That was down to Tash. Her cunt had felt so amazing; I didn't want it to end too soon. Knowing it was the only time I would allow myself to go there, I wanted to enjoy the experience every way that I could.

That may be my downfall.

The chances are high she's not pregnant.

There's a slim possibility she is.

Do we pretend there's nothing to worry about? Or decide upfront what we'll do if fate doesn't let the cards fall our way.

Her reaction when I told her was extreme, puking her guts up in the bathroom. I might not have any emotions where women are concerned, finding it all too easy to love 'em and leave 'em, but that doesn't mean I don't feel any sympathy if they're upset or hurting. That pain Tash is going through? I understand it and feel for her.

She'd expected Lawson to step up to his responsibilities, instead he cruelly stepped down and walked away, leaving her devastated. Deep inside I wouldn't be surprised if Tash is hoping she is carrying a baby, her second chance. It's just a fucking shame that the father would be a bastard like myself.

This should have been simple. We'd deal with Lawson for her, make it safe so she can resume her life. Get a job and write those books she wants to, find a good man who is right for her, a house, a picket fence, two point four kids. Not be saddled with a kid fathered by a one-night stand with a biker. Or perhaps the man she ends up with won't mind if she's already got a kid, would be quite happy to take on a stepdad role. My brow creases. I'll have to vet any fucker carefully, get Mouse to look into his background. He'd be raising my child after all. One thing I'd be watching for carefully, any signs of neglect or abuse.

"Why do you burn your drawings, Blade?"

The first words that come to my mind are that she should mind her own business. It's not something I talk about. But lying on my bed with a woman who I may have a permanent connection to isn't normal for me either. I've never engaged in pillow talk. I try to find a short answer that will satisfy her.

"They're not important. Why should I clutter up my room with my art? That would be pretentious, don't you think?"

"Apart from the ones of me and of Grunt, have you any others I can look at?"

"Nope."

"None?" Her shock encourages me to explain.

"Tash. Drawing for me is an outlet. Once I've finished, I don't need it anymore. I don't expect you to understand." I wish we'd get off the subject.

She laughs, a gentle chuckling sound. "That's where you and I are different. I keep everything, all my notes, all my half-started work. Mind you, I don't use paper, I have my laptop…" Her voice trails off.

"What's the matter?"

"Grant smashed it."

"You keep your shit about Lawson on it?"

"Some on paper. But what was on the laptop will be gone."

"Maybe not. Want you to sit down with Mouse. Tell him everything you've got and had. There may be copies of shit he can track down. When we get into your apartment, we'll see if the info on the hard drive of your laptop can be retrieved. Mouse is a fuckin' expert at shit like that."

"How long do you think it will take? To bring Lawson down?"

"We've got what, two months before the election?"

"Seven weeks," she confirms.

"Before then. If we also clear Cobb's name, I presume he'll get the job. What's he like?"

"I was surprised when the accusations turned up against him. He seemed a nice man, but then, so did Seb. I feel like I should never trust anyone again, who knows what goes on behind the faces."

I nod at her answer. Not trusting is a good way to live. It stops you from getting hurt.

"What didn't surprise me was that he immediately stepped down and didn't try to brazen it out."

"That sounds like guilt to me," I retort.

"Not necessarily. He didn't want to drag his family publicly through the mud or bring disrepute to the office. Wanted it handled quietly. He was insistent in his speech that he was innocent, but in today's climate, he wasn't believed."

"Do you believe him?"

"I probably wouldn't if I hadn't seen stuff I shouldn't have. Lawson's got a connection with each of the accusers."

"Sounds like you've got some good shit, Tash. If we can get hold of it."

She's quiet for a moment. "How are you going to play this?"

I tap her nose. "Club business."

She sits up, half turns, and looks down at me. Her eyes flare. "This is my life, Blade. I've got a right to be involved."

"What you don't know can't hurt you, Tash."

Getting off the bed she stands. Tension radiates off her. "It was what I didn't know that got me into this mess in the first place."

I speak to her back, "This is one occasion where you're going to have to have some trust."

Now she swings around. "Trust?" she snorts.

The word hangs in the air. Our eyes lock. Her breathing has quickened; her stance thrusts out her breasts. Her challenging expression makes me want to throw her down and fuck her. *Been there. Done that.* May have been the biggest fucking mistake of my life. But as my cock starts to thicken, I know I'm losing grip on my control.

Quickly I get to my feet. "That's the way it's got to be, babe. Ain't nothing you can do about it. And I'm not stayin' here to argue. Make yourself at fuckin' home, I'll find somewhere else to sleep."

"With a club whore?" she chucks at me.

"Nothing to you whether I do or don't." The thought doesn't appeal at all, but she's not to know that. Sure, we might have forged a link between us, something neither of us want, but it doesn't give her any power over me. None at fucking all.

She huffs loudly, then steps over to the desk, taking out my drawing pad and pencil again, and starts scribbling. *She's ignoring me. I've been dismissed.*

Almost forgetting it was me who instigated it, I leave *my* room furious I'm having to vacate it, and go back to the clubhouse to find a bed for the night. I step around Drifter passed out and snoring, a bottle half full still in his hands. Going to the bar I instruct Allie who's cleaning up for the night to give me a bottle of Jack.

"Want company?" she asks hopefully.

"Nah, sweetheart. Not tonight. Another time, okay?" I probably won't fuck again until I've invested in some reinforced condoms.

With a wave of my hand I wish her a silent goodnight, then make my way to the crash rooms. There are sounds which warn me I don't want to open the door to the one Tash had been sleeping in, not unless I want to join in with Beef and Road and who I think are Paige and Diva. Sharing shit has never interested me.

The next door is open, and even quickly adverting my eyes I see far more of Truck's pasty but muscular ass then I ever wanted to. Good for the newly patched-in member. He deserves to have fun on his last night.

The next room, thankfully, is free. Though it's clearly recently been used. I eye the messed-up bed with substances I don't want to try to identify smeared over the bottom sheet, pulling the bedclothes off, and grabbing a fresh set from the cupboard. That's all I'll need tonight. After removing my boots and jeans, I sit in my boxers and tee, and drink whisky straight from the bottle.

What if I'm going to be a dad?

Should I have tried to persuade Tash to take that damn preventative? If she would, any uncertainty would be removed from my mind. If she hadn't so recently been coerced to do something that was against her nature, I probably would have pressured her more. I may be a bastard, but in the circumstances, not as much as that. Some part of me doesn't want to act in the same way as that fucker Lawson, to be lumped in as the same sort of man. Up to me? I'd get the pill for her. But I'm a man, how the fuck do I know how a woman's mind works? I might know my way around her body, but inside? Her emotions, feelings? I probably know less than any of my brothers.

As I'd sat next to Tash, it had struck me, I'd never had taken the time to have a real conversation with a woman before.

I raise the bottle again, feeling my throat work as I swallow in gulps rather than sips. It's taking a long time to work, my mind's still busy, still racing. Fuck me, but that writing of hers had made me laugh. As I read, the image had come into my head and I'd had to get it out on paper. It was as if someone had been controlling my hand, the ideas needing to get out before they faded. I've only ever drawn in front of one person before. *Jonah.* He used to stand over me, watching in awe as I drew a perfect image of something he'd just described. I smile, remembering. *"Don't know how the fuck you do that, Jack. That's exactly what I saw."*

The whisky must have started to do its job as it hits me, it's the first time I've allowed myself to remember Jonah other than that last day I saw him alive. Now it seems the floodgates have opened, memories coming back so fast, it's hard to separate one from the other.

"Cool, Jonah. I didn't have any paper left. I didn't think we had any money."

He shrugs. "Helped myself. Slipped it into my jacket."

"Don't get caught, not for me. It's not worth it."

"No one will catch me," he jokes, flexing his muscles. *"If you're going to get that scholarship, you're going to need to practice, right? Need anything else, you tell me, okay?"*

"Jonah, I…"

"Hey, kid. One of us is getting out of this slum. That's your ticket right there."

Drummer had been right. He had been proud of me. What would he think if he knew I'd thrown my talent away? Would he be as proud of me being an enforcer as he would have been of an artist?

Perhaps I could do both? A crazy idea hits me. *What if I offer to illustrate Tash's book?* Nah, if she's already published she's probably got an illustrator lined up. That would mean me working with the woman, retaining a connection to her. How could I stay close, and not fuck her? As my cock, unaffected by the whisky I've drunk starts to swell at just the thought of her, I realise that would be a very bad idea. Could her pussy be the one to tempt me to go back for seconds? Fuck no. I already might be in enough trouble having her once.

I just need more drink, that's all. Then maybe I'll get her out of my head and get my darn cock to calm down.

I wake with a start, then rest back on the pillow. Fuck, but there's someone beating a drum in my head. I haven't laid one on like that in years. I wait for the room to stop spinning, then slowly, carefully, pull myself into a sitting position, reaching over to my cut and drawing out my phone. *Eleven am.* Fuck, I've overslept as well. I swing my legs over the bed, kicking at something on the floor. The empty bottle of Jack rolls away. I can't have drunk it all *thank fuck*, as the wet puddle I've just put my other foot in shows. It must have fallen out of my hand when I eventually passed out. I'll have to get a prospect... er, Matt, he's the only one now, to clear the mess up.

Still, I doubt I'll be the only one with a sore head. Everyone celebrates when a brother is patched in.

Christ, I hate fucking hangovers. I pull on my jeans and slip into my boots, then put my cut over my shoulders. My head feels like it's stuffed with cotton wool, every movement sends pain through my head, and I'm in a foul-fucking mood.

I emerge into the over-bright clubroom, rapidly blinking my eyes. It's full of women and fucking kids. Babies are being fed, and oh fuck no. I put my hand to my throbbing temples as Eli trips up and lets out a piercing shriek. As I try to sneak past, wanting fresh air and to indulge in a smoke, Sam soothes her distraught child, then sees me.

"Hey, Blade. You're a dark horse, aren't you?" Toddler held tight on her hip, she comes over and bumps my arm. "How on earth didn't we know you could draw?"

What? Looking around the room, my bleary eyes fall immediately on Tash. Hers meet mine, then immediately dart away, then back, then she looks in the other direction. There's a slight flush to her cheeks. Yeah, she should feel fucking guilty as shit.

Ignoring the pain which pounds with every step, I approach her. "What the fuck have you done?" My voice is so loud it hurts my own head, only serving to ramp up my rage.

"Blade, I didn't know," she explains in a rush. "I thought everyone would have known. I just thought people would like to see…" Her voice trails off at the expression on my face. "I'm sorry," she adds, trying to appease me.

"You fucking cunt," I yell. Ignoring Sam's shout informing me there are kids around. "You come here, letting my secrets out. Fuckin' bitch just like the rest, can't be trusted. And you wondered why I didn't tell you club business?"

"I'm sorry." She's whispering now, "I didn't know you wanted it kept quiet."

Everyone's staring at me. Whether it's because they've discovered my hitherto unknown talent, or whether it's the spectacle I'm making of myself, I neither know nor care. Nor can I stop the words coming out of my mouth, "You're a hateful bitch. Just like the rest. Hope to fuck it turns out you're not pregnant with my kid, you'd make a shit-poor mother." Just like my fucking own.

Her gasp. Her look of horror. The pause as the room goes silent. Then she stands. Even in the state I'm in, I can see that she's shaking, and her face has gone pale. With some semblance of dignity, she turns her back on me, and without meeting anyone's eyes, she leaves the room.

"Blade! My office now!"

CHAPTER 27

Tash

"Can I join you, Tash? Or would you rather be alone?"

I didn't want to return to Blade's suite. In the rage he's in, he might follow me there to continue the confrontation. I couldn't stand to face him right now. But I can't leave the compound, I'm not stupid enough to try to do that. So I came around the back of the clubhouse and sat myself down on the picnic bench. I hadn't realised no one knew about Blade; that he'd allowed me to see a part of him no one else had. When that look of shock had appeared on his face, I immediately realised my mistake, but not the extent of it. For a second I'd even basked at the thought that he'd entrusted me with something only I knew.

I had no idea how quickly his temper would flare, nor how angry he'd be. So enraged, it was the first time I'd seen the enforcer, not the man I knew as Blade, in front of me. He wasn't the man who'd held me tenderly. Those words he'd screamed at me reminded me of another man, another time. Suggesting he's not too much different to Seb after all.

I answer Sam with a wave of my hand to the bench seat opposite. "I don't know what I want, Sam. I'd rather be far away from here, but I'm in too much danger if I leave."

She straddles the bench. "I don't know your story. How you came to be on the streets, what or who you need protection from. Drummer doesn't share club business with me."

I narrow my eyes. "How can you stand that, Sam? Being kept in the dark?"

"Wasn't easy at first. I was used to making decisions for myself, not being told to keep my nose out of things where it wasn't wanted. But then I came to see, it didn't mean that I'd abdicated everything to my man, that I could still have control in areas that affected me. I'm Drummer's equal, I support him. In return, he supports me by making sure I'm protected. That protection sometimes comes in the form of not being told about what goes on in the club. If I don't know, I can't be implicated in anything they do."

"Their criminal activities." The Blade I saw this morning seemed just the type.

"You're wrong. The club runs legit businesses. But sometimes, they have to do things to keep the club, and us, safe, in ways citizens wouldn't approve of. They stamp down threats fast. They can't afford to show weakness. Anything where they step over the line is to keep the club, and those they love, brothers, old ladies, children, and even the sweet butts, protected. That's what we, the old ladies, aren't told about."

"Blade…"

She interrupts. "Would it help if I told you I've never seen Blade like he was this morning? I've never seen him lose his temper before. I'd usually describe him as a man who keeps himself under tight control."

Does that help? Not really. It only shows I bring out the worst in men. Seb showed me his true colours, now Blade has too.

"Shall I address the elephant in the room? Do you want to talk about it?" She leans her elbows on the table and rests her chin on her hands. "If you do, I'm a good listener. If you want to tell me to mind my business, I'll shut up."

"Everyone heard, didn't they? You won't be the only one to ask, Sam." I rub my arms, feeling them burning in the midday sun. "You want to sit in the shade?"

She does, so we do. After we've moved and settled, suddenly I find I'm telling her everything. What went on with Seb, up to and including what happened between me and Blade yesterday.

She's quiet as I tell my story. It's easier getting it off my chest the second time, than it was the first. There's only a small leakage from my eyes. When I've finished, I realise I would appreciate a woman's opinion. Someone to tell me what they would do.

"I got pregnant pretty damn fast after I met Drummer." Her eyes stare into the distance, and her lips curve. "Never regretted it. But then, we already knew what we felt for each other."

"Huh," I laugh sarcastically. "Blade and I already know too. I hate him, he hates me."

She gives me a quick unreadable look. "Sophie and Wraith didn't wait long. Slick, on the other hand, well, at first it didn't appear it was going to happen for him and Ella. They're so happy now. Heart? He was furious when he thought Marcia had tricked him. You hear about that?"

I shake my head. I haven't been around the women enough that they'd tell me their stories.

"Well, she lost her family in a traffic accident when she was eighteen. She was the only survivor and badly injured herself. She was told she couldn't have children. Signs were there, though. Heart made her do a pregnancy test, and well, yeah—she was pregnant." Sam grins as she remembers. "She refused to believe it, or that it would all go to plan, until the twins were born. And that in itself is another story."

"There's so many babies here," I observe.

"Maybe one more?" she queries.

"Probably a long shot."

"It's not too late to do something about it. If that's what you want, I'll help you. I could pop down to the pharmacy now."

Biting my lip, I consider her offer. "Trouble is, Sam, I don't know what I should do. All I know is, if I am, and I have a baby, Blade will have nothing to do with it."

She looks down, then back up. "I'm not so sure you're right about that. But it's probably the best way to look at it. What will you do? Would you be able to cope on your own?"

"I've got family back in California. I could go back there. Maybe they'd help." *Or maybe not.* They've never been particularly supportive. But I'd be okay on my own. "Plenty of single women raise children by themselves. Not how I'd have planned it, but there you go."

"Where in Cali?"

"Near San Diego."

She grins. "Club's got a chapter there. The VP, Dart, well he transferred over from here. He's got a lovely wife, Alex. They'd look out for you. I think you'd get on well with Alex. She's got a boy; he must be eight now. She's the club lawyer."

My head tilts to the side. I didn't realise women in the club had careers. I think I expected that from Blade's reaction, they were all kept women. Sam seems to understand my confusion. "We get the best of both worlds, Tash. Our children, a family there to watch over them, freedom to do what we want. I'm a mechanic, I build and restore bikes. Marcia works with Mouse on some mysterious projects that even the club doesn't know about, Mariana's training to be a nurse. Darcy, of course, is a firefighter. Our men support us in what we do, as much as we are there behind them."

I feel my eyes widen as she tells me what I hadn't expected. It drives me to share. "My dream is to be an author," I tell her. "I've published one book, but I need to do more. I can't support myself writing yet."

She laughs. "You need a biker behind you, hon."

My face drops. The only biker I could see myself being attracted to is the very last man I'd want to have in my life. The arrogant, rude, misogynistic, rage filled dick.

"You want my input? What I would do if I were you?"

I nod. It would be good to have someone tell me what to do.

"If it were me in your position, I'd let things play out. I don't read that you think having a baby would be the end of your life."

"I'm probably not even pregnant."

Her mouth quirks. "You do realise, by now everyone will know there's a chance. They'll be running a book on whether you are or not." She pauses, then gives a genuine smile. "Whether or not Blade steps up, whether you want him to or not, you'll be carrying a Satan's Devils baby. You might have blood family, Tash, but you'll have a biker family too. And family always comes first. You won't be in this alone unless you turn your back on us."

"Until yesterday, I didn't trust the club. Thought they were in cahoots with Seb. That they would kill me." As her eyes widen, I continue, "Hard to get my head around it all, Sam. I was scared. Suspicious."

"Of course you'd be, if that was how you were thinking." She breaks off, stands, and holds out her hand. "Now you know we're not going to kill you, how about you come and get to know us properly?"

"I'm embarrassed," I whisper, staying seated on the bench.

"No need to be embarrassed," a deep voice sounds, making us both jump.

"Well," Sam nods, "I'll just leave you two to sort things out."

No. That's exactly what I don't want. I don't want to be left alone with Blade. But I don't get the choice. As the president's wife walks off, Blade takes her place.

"Hey, look at me."

I've been studying my hands, not wanting to meet his gaze. But I can't pretend I'm somewhere else, I raise my eyes, and immediately cover my mouth with my hand. "Oh. What on earth happened to you?"

Blade touches the reddening and swelling bruises on his face. "Prez objected to me swearing in front of the kids."

"What does he look like?" Blade had been so angry; he would have retaliated.

"What? Nah, Tash. Didn't hit back. I deserved it. I was out of fuckin' line."

I notice him rubbing at his temples and grimacing. "Does your head ache?"

"Self-inflicted, babe. Got a bit too friendly with a bottle of whisky last night." He looks at me sharply. "I didn't go with a whore."

I shrug. "None of my business whether you did or not. You're a free man."

"I'm sorry," the words are rushed. "Fuckin' sorry. I shouldn't have spouted that shit."

I hadn't expected him to apologise. "I shouldn't have said anything about you being an artist."

"You weren't to know."

I smile wanly. "I hear they're going to be running a book."

He grins. "That's my fuckin' brothers for you. Drummer already won when they heard I fucked you..." His face falls. "Fuck, babe. You gotta understand. They know me too well. Saw from the look on my face that I'd just been in the best pussy I'd ever had in my life. Couldn't deny it."

Bristling, I inhale deeply, thinking living here must be like living in a goldfish bowl. Then I replay his words in my head. "Best pussy?"

He groans. "Fuckin' hangover. Shouldn't have said that."

Leaping in, I take advantage, "While you're all guilty and loose-mouthed, can I ask you a question?"

"Guilty and loose-mouthed? Well, yeah, fuck. Perhaps I deserve that. And go on, ask. No guarantees I'll answer."

Once again I look down at my hands, wondering if I'm going to taunt an injured beast, but find no answers there. So drawing in a deep breath, I take a chance. "Why, Blade? Why keep your talent a secret?"

A sharp inhale. A moment's silence. Then, "I was twelve when my brother died. Jonah, well, he was eighteen." It seems natural to reach my hand across the table. It stays there, palm up and forlorn. Just when I'm about to draw it back, he covers it with his. "I was young, but there was already talk about art scholarships. Jonah encouraged me, said it was my ticket out of the way that we lived. He, on the other hand, he worked to muscle himself up. Our mom was next to useless after our father left. Couldn't keep a job, never had money, always looking for a new man to look after her. Jonah took care of us both. Some of the shit he got into to put food on the table, well, it was shit he should never have touched. Sometimes he took me with him as backup." His eyes glaze over as he remembers. When silence stretches out, I'm just about to tell him he doesn't need to dredge the rest up, when he tells me, "I was an artist. What could I do to help Jonah when he was taken down? Fuck all. He was killed in front of me, babe." My hand squeezes his, as tears come into my eyes. "I vowed I'd give all that shit up. Scholarships weren't going to feed me and had done nothing to help him. He was dead. I had to man up and live the life that he couldn't."

"I'm sorry," I say, knowing it's inadequate.

"Yeah, well. Drummer, and you to some extent, have made me do some thinking. Part of the reason I drank so much last night. A decision made when I was twelve perhaps now needs some re-evaluation. Maybe I was wrong."

"What happened to your mom?"

His eyes fix on mine. His lips thin, and his cheeks redden. "Day after Jonah died she walked out. Never saw her again. Didn't even bother to come to the fuckin' funeral. She'd obviously found a new man to keep her and never looked back. Doubt it would have made any difference if she had."

"Blade!" His name is shocked out of me. He'd said it in a cold tone, but all I can think is how that had hurt a young boy. *He doesn't trust women.* He was let down by the one who should always have been there for him. At the worst time of his life his mom had disappeared. Suddenly I realise the size of a mountain a woman would have climb to even begin to earn his trust. After all these years, is it even possible?

"I would never," I start, as forcefully as I can, "desert a child. Ever."

He raises his eyes, pulls his hand away slowly, and gives a small, sad, smile as he shakes his head. Then, making an abrupt change of subject, he says, "Mouse wants to speak to you. Time to get this shit with Lawson put behind you, Tash. So we can both get on with our lives, and things can go back to normal."

CHAPTER 28

Blade

Guilt had made me reveal the history that I usually keep to myself. I'd turned the key, opened the lock and let it out from the recesses of my mind. Yeah, what happened to me had fucked me up, but I'd always thought I was handling it, dealing with it in my own way. Content to live the life I'd chosen; the life Jonah would have been living had he had the chance. Was I a good enforcer? Fuck, yeah. I get results. Would Jonah have done better? Who the fuck knows.

But this is what he would have been doing. What would he be like? Would he have had a wife and children? Maybe. He had that caring side to him, he'd not deserted me, even if he'd have had more freedom if he'd just left me behind. Instead of making a life for himself, he'd stayed, providing both for me and my waste-of-space mom. He'd stayed because he loved us, and eventually, and all too soon, he'd paid the ultimate price.

I feel like I'm standing on the edge of a cliff. I could turn back, retrace my steps and carry on the same as I'd done since Jonah had died. Or, I could lift my foot and allow myself to fall, to trust in fate that I'd survive the drop and whatever lay underneath. The thought of taking a step into the unknown scares the shit out of me. At my age, am I too old to change?

I walk beside Tash as we enter the clubhouse, leading her through to Mouse's office, glaring at anyone who looks like they're going to open their mouths. There can't be a person here who doesn't know now that I've fucked her and somehow screwed up. Even now I see Beef leaning forwards as though to see if there's any sign of pregnancy written on her face. When his eyes settle on her breasts, I know he's going to be feeling my fist later.

As usual, when I open the computer guru's room, a cloud of marijuana smoke drifts out. Looking down at Tash, I frown. As Mouse picks up his lighter, putting it to the end of a fresh joint, I'm driven to comment, "Put that shit out, Mouse."

"What?"

Nowadays we don't smoke in the clubroom as there are so many kids around, but what Mouse gets up to in here is his own business. He's not used to being criticised. As his dark Navajo eyes focus on me, I know he's waiting for an answer. "Because… well, look Brother, in case…"

Mouse snorts a laugh. "In case she's knocked up I think is what you're trying to say, Brother. You want I should look up the odds?"

"Odds don't mean a damn when it's down to fate," I respond.

"It's me you're talking about. Mouse, you go ahead I'm sure…"

"I'm sure," I interrupt sharply, "that Mouse is going to respect my fuckin' request. He can do without a smoke for a while." Surely she can see that she shouldn't be near that shit if there's any chance she's having my baby. Fuck, I've got to make sure she takes care of herself. I seem to have picked up a lot while I've been surrounded by pregnant women and kids in the clubhouse. Pretty damn sure Drum wouldn't have let anyone smoke around Sam.

Holding up his hands as a sign of defeat, Mouse points to the two chairs in front of his desk. I shake my head. "Not staying. You can fill me in later, Brother."

Tash swings around, looking at me in concern, but I've got no worries about leaving her with Mouse. He's recently, and very happily, married.

I shut the door of the office, holding it for a moment as I look down the hallway and out into the clubroom. Not immediately seeing my target, I step down to where my brothers are congregating, pushing through them with one sole aim. Ah, there he is.

"What the fuck?" Beef holds his stomach as he doubles over.

"You were ogling Tash's tits," I tell him, my jaw clenched.

"What the hell does it matter to you? Everyone knows you've already tapped that. You don't go back twice except for the club girls. That makes her fair game brother." As Beef's still trying to get air into his lungs, Road answers on his behalf.

"Yeah, and tits get bigger if a woman's pregnant. I was looking to see if anything's changed." Beef, now straightened, waggles his eyebrows. "I'm aiming to be on the winning side of the bet. Mind you," he adds thoughtfully, "might make a play for her myself. Seeing those tits naked, I could measure them every day. I don't mind going back for seconds myself. Girl like that? Looks like she'd have a tight pussy."

"Until she spits the kid out," Marvel butts in.

"Nah, brother. Doesn't work like that." Wraith winks.

"I heard they can sew it up tighter." Beef's looking far too invested in this conversation.

"Anyway, she's definitely got a nice tight ass," Road observes.

If he's not careful, Beef's going to feel my fist again. As for Road, well, I thought he was my friend. Obviously not. "She's off limits," I growl, making myself clear.

"You claimin' her?" Beef's eyes open wide. As the room goes quiet, it's only then I realise we've garnered an audience.

"Fuck no." I put it out there so there can be no mistake.

"So what's the fuss?" Wraith demands. "If you don't want her, let her go with someone else. You can't have it both ways, Blade."

I backpedal fast, hurriedly trying to think of an excuse that would work. "VP, think about it. There's no way yet of telling if she's pregnant or not. Hell, my swimmers might not even have reached the egg yet. One of you fuck her? What if another condom breaks? Fuck of a mess as we wouldn't know who the father was." There. Let them argue with that. Sounds quite sensible to me.

VP's looking at me, his eyes wide, his nostrils flaring as though he's smelling something off. As he stares without speaking, I shrug, emphasising there can be no comeback.

"Really?" Wraith says at last. "Really, Blade? You're going with that?" Then he's bent double, but it's not caused by my fist, it's caused by his own laughter. "Your fuckin' swimmers might be too slow and be overtaken by someone else's. Fuck me, I've heard everything now."

"Okay," Beef is relentless. "I'll fuck her. If she's pregnant, we'll take a paternity test. See if my fellas are stronger aqua athletes than yours. Hey, they could have a fuckin' race."

"Mine might have a better sense of direction," tosses in Road.

"Joker's would know the best path. Shame he doesn't swing that way." Lady's fucking grinning with his arm around his man, who happens to be the road captain who plans the route on runs. "And, of course, he's mine." Putting his hands on either side of Joker's face, he plants an open-mouth kiss on his man's lips.

Fuck knows how long that would have continued until a little voice says, "Daddy, Daddy, hug me." Maya, only a toddler, already has the female pout and stance down pat as she stands with her hands on her hips, demanding her dads pay her attention too.

Shit. With the kids here, I can't respond the way I'm itching too.

"Perhaps it's time you pull your head out of your ass, Brother." I swing around as someone else joins in to see Rock at the bar, his beer bottle pointed toward me. "Jealousy's a bitch with a fuckin' message. If you get riled at the thought of one of your brother's inside that pussy, then it means you want it as yours."

"Man's got a point," Peg agrees. "Not known you to get possessive before."

"I'm not fuckin' possessive. I just, I…" A roar of laughter sounds around me as I struggle to put it into words. I settle for throwing up my hands and leave the clubroom with the intention of going up to my suite. I think about taking a sweet butt with me to make a point, but truth is, my hangover still has its hold on me and my cock isn't interested.

Yeah, right. When has that ever stopped me before?

"Blade! Wait up."

"Not now, Peg," I say, tiredly. Not ready for more words of wisdom from the sergeant-at-arms. Seems to me, if someone gets hitched and their old lady's dropped a baby, they think others can only be happy if they're in the same situation.

"Not going to have a go at you. You," he points to me, "I," he points to himself, "have places to go."

My eyes sharpen. Yeah. Give me shit to do. That's what I need. Too much fucking introspection if I'm left on my own, and too much temptation if I see Tash. "Where we going, Peg?"

"Drummer's suggested we pay Cobb a visit."

"Isn't that showing our hand?"

"Not if your woman is right. Can't see any fucking reason why he would go running to Lawson. If he does," Peg shrugs, "then we'll lose a job we were gonna jack up anyway."

I bristle at his reference to my woman, but let it go. I'm more eager to get on my bike and ride. But looking at the sky, and the desert where sand is already billowing in the distance, suspect that I'm not going to get that freedom today. "Storm's blowing up, Peg."

He looks up and sniffs. "We'll take the SUV."

Now I love living in Tucson, but summer monsoons are shit. First you're likely to be caught in a sandstorm, then torrential rain falls mercilessly for a while. After that, there's often a steady drizzle, then when the black clouds pass over, everything dries as the sun comes out, blazing overhead as if asking, what happened, I only went away for a short nap? It's the kind of weather it's best not to be caught out in on your bike. Only a fool would keep riding in near zero visibility.

Hating the cage, I sit beside Peg, holding on to the oh-shit handle as he handles it competently, but not dis-similar to the way he rides his bike. The sandstorm hits us before we arrive in Tucson at least forcing him to slow down, then comes the thunder and lightning accompanying the rain which falls in earnest, proving we were correct selecting this mode of transportation.

Making slow progress, we arrive at a street which currently resembles a river. Peg grimaces as he gets out, like me pulling his jacket up over his head to try to keep off the worst, as we run towards the house which luckily has a covered porch. I shiver, the temperature having dropped about thirty degrees, warmth of the summer for the moment dissipated.

Whether it's because the storm's raging around us, or Cobb is normally not cautious, the door is quickly opened after Peg's heavy finger hits the bell.

"Oh shit!" Cobb tries to close the door as he sees two burly bikers on his doorstep, but Peg's boot maintains the gap, and his weight easily pushes it open.

"Anne. Call the..."

"No calls." Peg nods at me.

I push past, quickly finding the wife in the main room rummaging in her purse. Her eyes widen as I take it from her. Inclining my head toward a sofa, I say one word, "Sit."

Peg's hand on his shoulder, Cobb comes in, his face white, and when instructed, parks his ass down beside his wife.

"If you want money," Cobb starts, "you're damn out of luck." Yeah, Mouse had already checked his financials, he's already re-mortgaged his house to pay for legal assistance.

"Don't want your fuckin' money," Peg snarls. It's more or less his normal tone. I'm used to it, but Cobb shrinks back.

Doesn't stop him talking though. Taking the hand of his wife, he asks, "Did Lawson send you?" Then adds, almost to himself, "What more does that fucker want from me?"

Taking a chair opposite, I make myself comfortable, crossing one leg over resting my ankle on my knee. "Why go there? Why immediately finger Lawson?"

Cobb's lips thin. "You're Satan's Devils. You're working for him."

Peg glances at me and doesn't bother to confirm or deny anything. Like me, he sits, arranging his legs so he can lean forward. "You do what you're accused of?" He gets straight to the point. "Put your hands on those women?"

"Of course not," Cobb protests.

I'm examining him carefully. His response would have come whether he was guilty or not. What I want to see is the truth underneath.

His wife's eyes shoot daggers at Peg. "My husband would never do such a thing." It's the small smile of support that she gives him which convinces me. Or, if he had, she knows nothing about it. He's got a woman who loves him the way the old ladies in the club do their men. There's no doubt at all in her mind, that's easy to see.

"And you know that, how?" Peg arrows in on the woman.

"Probably beyond your understanding, but we were childhood sweethearts. I've never been with another, and neither has he." Another curve of her lips toward her husband. "Raul's a good man."

"My reputation doesn't matter," Raul turns to her sadly. "We've discussed this, Anne."

"Tell me," Peg instructs, "exactly what you're accused of." Mouse has already briefed us, but like the sergeant-at-arms, I want to hear it in his own words.

"I'm a defence attorney, you know that?" He huffs, "Or I was. Nobody wants me now. I prepare witnesses for court. Two women, at separate times, have come forward to say I touched them inappropriately."

"You did meet with these women?"

"So my records say. You must understand that I meet with hundreds of witnesses, and these cases were from eight and ten years ago."

"You stepped away from the election as soon as you were accused. Why not stay on and fight if you're innocent?"

"Oh, I'm fighting." His face darkens. "But in today's climate, women tend to be believed. Don't get me wrong," he adds hurriedly, "that's not wrong per se, just when it's you, and you know that you're innocent. I've got to find a way to clear my name, and I prefer to do that out of the limelight. It was getting nasty. Those women were appearing on television, going into all manner of details. All I could say was it wasn't me, and that I hadn't done what they were accusing me of. What other embellishment was there for me to use?" He breaks off, and squeezes his wife's hand. "Reporters cornered Anne at the store, would follow her putting microphones in her face. Asking what she thought of the revelations, whether she was going to stand by me. I didn't want her dragged into it."

"So you stepped down to take the heat off? Did it work?"

Cobb's face is grim. "It worked. The prosecuting attorney is still considering whether there's enough evidence to take it to court, but the press have lost interest. The women no longer make a good spectacle on TV. Accusations against a lawyer not so gossip-worthy when he's no longer a potential candidate."

Peg nods. "Did you know Lawson would get the nomination when you stepped down?"

"No." Cobb's expression darkens further. "I thought Ray would be a shoe-in. He should have been, but then he died."

I nod. Raymond Ferguson had appeared to be popular. "You got any suspicions about how he died?"

"The police said it was an accident."

"What do you think?" I press.

He shrugs. "I'm an attorney. I have to work with the evidence at hand. There's nothing to suggest it was anything other than an unfortunate set of circumstances that led to him driving off the road." Suddenly he turns the tables. "I don't understand why you're here, or why you're asking these questions. I don't think I want to say anymore."

Peg raises his chin to me, I nod back. He clears his throat. "You said we're working for Lawson, and you're right. He's asked us to provide extra security now he's got pole position. Whatever people might think, nowadays the Satan's Devils run a clean club. We're talkin' to you as we like to know who we're dealing with and make sure they don't come with baggage we'd rather not touch."

He's clearly not a stupid man. It's almost possible to see gears whirling in his mind. "You think Lawson might have cleared his own way to the top?"

"You sayin' you don't have any thoughts in that direction?"

Cobb's mouth slams shut, and his eyes shutter over. Understandable. He's a legal man, he wouldn't say anything he can't back up.

Peg stands, husband and wife get to their feet. Copying their actions, I rise as well. As the sergeant-at-arms holds out his hand, Cobb's good manners ensures that he takes it. "Thank you for talking with us."

His head shakes in confusion. "I still don't understand why you think coming here today could help."

"Just trying to understand who we're dealing with," Peg replies.

Chapter 29

Tash

I stayed with Mouse as long as I could, finding some sanctuary in the computer guy's office. Having answered his questions to the best of my knowledge, Mouse seemed happy for me to stay while he started to dig into the information I'd imparted.

I'm stunned, my head reeling, thoughts barrelling around in my skull, one by one each surface to the top, then another pushes it back down again. Knowing the reason Blade's the way he is doesn't mean I understand it, but I suppose the death of his brother and desertion of the one parent he had has certainly left a lasting impact. I feel so sorry for him that he's sentenced himself to a lonely life.

I could be pregnant. I'm embarrassed that everyone knows. Why do I make these bad choices? First Seb who turned out to be someone totally different to the man I thought I knew, and now Blade, who's never lied to me, but just the same, he'll leave me to deal with any repercussions alone.

The tapping of Mouse's fingers on the keys is like music playing in the background, only noticeable when it stops. Glancing up, I see him looking at me.

"Six days prior," he says. He writes something on a piece of paper, and hands it to me.

"What?" I ask for clarification.

"It might not be accurate then. But that's the earliest test you can buy and use it six days before your next period is due. I checked it out for you, thought you'd want to find out as quickly as possible."

My face flushes red. I'd thought he'd been looking into what I told him, not researching pregnancy tests. But I am grateful. "Thank you, Mouse."

He leans back in his chair, pushing his stunning black hair over his shoulders. He's a handsome man, his wife, Mariana, is one lucky woman. "I've known Blade a long time, Tash. He's not as hard as he wants people to believe. Don't give up on him."

"He can't trust me, Mouse." I give a sad frown. "He's told me why. It runs deep."

"He trusts the club, Tash. Every one of us in it. It's not that he hasn't the ability, just that outside of his brothers, he's never been able to rely on anyone else. You serious about him? You've got to break down those walls. Someone determined enough and worthy of him would be able to do it."

The club is made up of men. I'm female. It's very different. I can't even tell him why I'm shaking my head. Blade entrusted his story to me and I'm not going to betray his confidence for a second time in one day. As Mouse had said, he's known Blade a long time, but doesn't seem to know his background. If he did, he'd understand what I'm dealing with. I look down at the note I'd been given. Almost two weeks to go until I can see whether I'll have a lasting reminder of the man.

Mouse seems to realise there's nothing more he can say. "Well, thank you for giving me all the info. I'll start looking into it."

That's a dismissal. I stand, start to leave, then turn back. "I'm getting a bit bored. You wouldn't have a spare laptop I could use, have you?" My eyes roam the numerous monitors both on his desk, and those behind him on the walls. He's got a couple of laptops in front of him, as well as a tower PC.

"What do you want it for?" His eyes narrow.

"I'm an author. I write."

"Yeah?" He stares at me for a moment, then opens a drawer. Taking out a laptop, he taps on it, then passes it to me. "I've disabled access to the internet. So you can't email, go on Facebook or any of that shit, okay? Just looking out for you, Tash."

I wouldn't try to make contact with the outside world so it doesn't matter that there's yet another man here who doesn't trust me.

I leave his office hugging the device. At least there's something I can occupy myself with now. Keeping my head down, I walk through the crowded clubroom, not wanting to get into conversation with anyone. Although conversations seem to falter as I walk past, I make my way to the door without being stopped.

"Rash?"

"Hey, Tommy. Want to play pool?"

"Yay!"

I don't recognise who called out; I'm just grateful they distracted him and helped me escape. Perhaps when a couple of hundred years have gone passed, I'll be able to face the men and women here again without my face glowing red.

At last I reach the privacy of my, *Blade's*, suite, go inside and close the door.

I've got two choices. I can continue to worry about things I can't control, or get down to work. Opening the laptop, I'm pleased to see that it's got the word processing program I use installed. Plugging in the power cable that Mouse had also given me, I start to type.

Outside the afternoon sky grows dark, lightning flashes and thunder growls and barks, giving me an idea for my story. Words flow from my head onto the screen in front of me. The room lightens again as the storm passes, and I roll my head on my neck realising I've been concentrating so hard, I've stiffened up, and must have overused my still recovering shoulder, as it's paining me.

A shower. Yeah, that will help. It does. The water is hot, the shower is powerful, massaging my sore muscles. It's only when I turn the water off that I realise I haven't brought any clean clothes in with me. In fact, I haven't any to wear.

Eyeing the clothes I've just taken off with distaste, with the towel wrapped around me, I go back into the bedroom. I'm bending over one of Blade's drawers, looking for a t-shirt, when the door opens.

"Fuck!"

Flustered I stand, pulling the towel quickly down over my bare ass, yanking it too hard so it falls exposing my breasts. Wet and heavy, I fight to get it back into position, turning to find Blade standing there, smirking at me.

"I didn't expect you," I try to explain.

"Came to get some clothes." He steps closer.

"Blade?" I ask as his hand reaches toward me.

His finger traces the exposed skin above my breasts. Huskily, he asks, "You trying to tempt me?"

His closeness makes my breathing speed up. "No. I didn't think you'd come back."

"It's my room," he says reasonably, as his touch moves a little lower, his forefinger and thumb gently but insistently moving the towel down. The intense look in his eyes challenges me to stop him. I'm almost hypnotised and do nothing to prevent him lowering my covering, exposing my breasts to his gaze. It's not cold in the room, but goosebumps rise on my skin as his fingers trace around my nipples. "Didn't pay much attention to these before, did I?"

My nipples grow erect even though he hasn't touched them. I feel his breath caressing my bare skin. *Don't let him do this.*

Have some self-respect. But while he's barely touching me, my whole body feels alive.

Leaning in closer, he breathes in deeply. "Fuck, you want me, don't you?"

I can't deny it. But know this is a mistake. Blade's never going to be offering a future. "Blade, we can't." I take a step back.

He follows me. Suddenly his arms are on my shoulders, turning me so fast I lose my grip on the towel which falls to the floor. Pulling me tight against him, my back to his front, he lowers his hands, covering my breasts. As his fingers begin to toy in earnest with my nipples, I feel myself weaken.

"Blade," I say his name again, but whether in encouragement or admonishment I'm not able to tell. His touch is sure, certain. He's playing me like an instrument he's played many times before. The thought pulls me up. *He doesn't go back for seconds. Except for the club whores.* Catching him unawares, I pull away from him and run to the bathroom, thankful there's a lock on the door. I pull on clothes I'd been wearing earlier and that I'd discarded in a heap on the floor, taking my time, hoping that when I go back out, he'll be gone.

No such luck. He's sitting on the bed with his head in his hands. When he hears me, he draws his fingers down his cheeks and looks up. "You're right," he says, with a grimace. "Shouldn't complicate this anymore than it already is." He glances down, then back up. "You okay, Tash?"

I shrug, not knowing what he's asking. I'm unsatisfied, I know that for sure. But I couldn't let him continue. Knowing he's no threat, I sit beside him. "I don't want to be used. I'm not that type of woman."

"I know you're not." His hand covers mine and squeezes it gently. "I wish I was a different man. But I'm not going to try to be something I'm not. I can't be there for you, Tash."

"I don't expect you to be," I respond. While knowing, I'm wishing things could be otherwise.

He nods over to his desk. "You worm your way around Mouse?"

He's spied the laptop. "Yeah," I grin quickly. "It's not connected to the outside world, but it's been good to do some writing again."

He starts to stand. "Mind if I take a look?"

"Be my guest."

"Babe, I think it's you who are mine."

I grin. He's got a point. This is his suite after all.

I watch as he opens the laptop. I'd saved, but not closed, the document I was working on, so it's staring him in the face. I watch, biting my lip as he reads. Soon he's grinning, chuckling, then laughing.

"You want I should do some illustrations for this?"

"You'd do that?" He's surprised me.

"You know my secret now. Can't see it would hurt. I'd enjoy doing it."

There'd be complications though. "You'd get a share of the royalties, Blade. Which means we can't make a clean break."

"Don't want payment, Tash. Saves you paying someone else, and if, well, if things work out that you are pregnant, I'd be paying maintenance for the kid in any event."

Taking a moment to think it through, I give him my answer, "No, Blade. It would be great, and I think you'd do an amazing job, but I don't want to stop there. I'll be doing a series and need an illustrator who'll stick with me." He gives me an odd look. I feel I need to expand. "In the likely scenario that there are no implications, I'll be leaving here when it's safe. You and I need never see each other again."

My answer seems to have come as a surprise. His hand brushes back his hair. "Have you thought of where you'll go?"

"Probably back to my hometown in any event. I'll need to get a job, get back on my feet. I could do with someone in my corner."

"You miss your mom and dad?"

"Dad and stepmom," I correct.

"Won't they be worried about you? You must have been out of touch for some time."

I shrug. "Not unusual. We're not that close. Not since Dad remarried, even before really. My mom died when I was just a kid, he did what he needed to, but that was about it. Now my stepmother doesn't like being reminded he's got grown-up kids. And my sister is wrapped up in her own family. We haven't been close for a while. I've got friends there though, they'll let me stay if I'm in a bind."

"Family, huh?" He shakes his head. "Blood always lets you down."

"I think we're just unlucky, Blade. I've seen families who seem happy enough, that just wasn't the straw I drew. What's up?" I frown at the way he's staring.

"So you'll definitely be leaving Arizona."

I nod.

Suddenly he gets up, kicks the chair violently, places his palms on the desk then leans over. I jump when he snarls, "Fuck."

"Blade?" I ask, confused, wondering what I've said. Something has struck a nerve, but I'm not certain what.

CHAPTER 30

Blade

I breathe deeply, trying to calm down the rage that suddenly rose inside me. As Tash has been talking, the mantra's been going around and around my head, *can't trust bitches. Can't trust them.*

"You're fuckin' leavin' without a backward glance. Been there, done that, got the fuckin' t-shirt?"

"What?" Her voice sounds from behind me. Christ. She can't even see what she's doing wrong.

"You're walkin' out on me." The cold tone of my voice should warn her. "Why wait, hon? Why hang around? Go find one of my brothers to keep your bed warm." Pushing away from the desk, I go to the door and open it. "Get out. Get out now."

She stands. Comes toward me. Then, instead of walking out, her hand comes up and for the second time, she slaps my face. Then showing how brave she is, pulls the door out of my grasp and slams it shut with her still on the inside. Instead of being scared, she's furious. I swear sparks are coming out of her eyes.

Before the echo of the slap fades from the room, she's screaming at me. "What do you fucking want, Blade? What is it? You don't want me; you've made that clear. You don't want a kid with me. I'm giving you exactly what you asked for. Once I'm safe to leave, I'll take myself away and you'll never have to see me again. That's what you said, isn't it? You made it clear you didn't see us in a relationship, but now I'm letting you down somehow?"

"Tash…" I rub my cheek. It's hot and stinging. *Fuck, she hits hard.*

"I'm getting fucking confused here, Blade. No wonder you can't trust anyone. They'll always let you down if you keep sending out mixed messages. I thought I was doing exactly what you wanted me to do."

"I…" My mouth opens and shuts. She's right. I told her I wouldn't have anything to do with her whether she's pregnant or not. What other expectations should I have? That she'd sit around and wait in case I changed my mind.

Which I wouldn't have done. No. I'd have kept my eye on her, had my brothers watching her, making sure if she had my kid that she was looking after it right. Being satisfied I could step in if needed. That had been my plan.

Instead she's challenged me. She's not going to wait for me. No, she's going to get on with her life. I've made her no promises. Why should she stay close?

Her chest is heaving with her fury. Her cheeks show two twin spots of red. Her eyes are bright and flaring.

I offered to illustrate her books—she turned me down. Throwing it back in my face as that would tie us together. I took that as an insult when it was exactly what I told her I wanted.

I thought I couldn't trust her while she was doing exactly what I asked.

Somehow I've moved and am blocking the doorway. "Open the door, Blade. I'll go find one of your brothers like you suggested. See? I'm doing what you told me to…"

That's it. I step forward, my hands on her biceps, pushing her back to the bed. Her knees hit it. Lifting her, I throw her down then move over her, my palms either side, imprisoning her head. For a second I hold myself back, then, leap over the edge of that cliff.

Growling I lower my lips, taking her mouth, kissing her as though my life depends on it. She bites my lip. Drawing back, I lick the drop of blood away, grin, then kiss her again, thrusting my tongue into her mouth. My cock's rock hard, grinding against her as she tries to buck me off.

As her hands flail against me, I take both of them in one of mine and hold them over her head. The other I put against her voluptuous breast, kneading it. And still I'm kissing her. My tongue sliding against hers. She's trying hard not to respond.

Raising my head gives her a chance to speak. "What the fuck are you doing, Blade?"

"I'm thinkin' I'm about to make the biggest fuckin' mistake of my life," I respond harshly.

"Don't fucking make it then," she throws back.

"Or," I still my body, but remain with her helplessly captured beneath me, "make the best decision I've ever taken."

"What decision?"

I swallow, the words almost sticking in my throat. "The one where I claim you."

She stops wriggling. Her eyes widen. "*Claim* me?" The squeak shows while she probably has no idea of my meaning, she gets the gist. "What if I don't want to be claimed?"

One handed I unfasten her shorts and using my hand and hooking a foot into the waistband when it's low enough, manage to slide them off her legs. I unfasten my jeans, freeing my cock, then, pushing her panties aside, line myself up.

"Blade, no." It's the worst time for her to move her hips again, it almost makes me slip inside.

"Tell me you don't want this." Her body does, she's dripping wet.

"Condom," she gasps out, confirming her rejection isn't the act itself, but that for the first time ever, I had forgotten to glove up.

"That boat might have already sailed." I've never gone without in my life. Now the thought of claiming my woman without latex between us is all I can think about. Removing all doubt, trying to get her pregnant for real. The thought of seeing her body ripe with my baby being a turn on, not a turn off.

"It might still be in dock," she retorts.

Leaning my mouth next to her ear, I whisper, "Let's make sure."

"You're going to send me away."

"Think I need to explain something. I claim you? You're mine for life. This pussy," I press my cock in an inch, "is mine and only mine."

"And your dick?"

"Is yours."

She scoffs, "As if you could be faithful."

"I can do faithful. Can you?"

"Blade. This is crazy. I don't even like you."

I hadn't considered that. Arrogant bastard that I am. Jeez. I'd been working on the assumption I was a catch for any woman, running away from them, keeping them all at a distance and not allowing them to get close from some stupid notion any one of them would want to get their claws into me. My cock starts to deflate as reality steps in. *She's making her plans to leave not to spite me, but because she can't stand to be near me.*

I release her hands, put my palms flat on the bed and start to push myself up, as her arms come around me. I could easily break her hold, but I don't. Instead I relax, shifting just a little so I'm no longer crushing her.

"Blade, I'm in uncharted territory here. I thought I felt something for Seb." As the growl comes into my throat, she nuzzles her lips against my mouth. "But no, I didn't. I was fooling myself. Thought he was the right kind of man for me. Thought we fit. Accepted what I believed was an upstanding citizen as the type of person I should spend my life with. Turns out I was wrong on every count."

The mention of Lawson has deflated my cock completely. "He isn't, wasn't, the man for you."

"He wasn't a man at all. He was a poisonous snake. Turns out the man I want is an outlaw biker."

"Who you don't even like."

She continues as though I hadn't spoken. "When I was pregnant, I thought of having *my* baby. Never Seb's. Now, when I could be expecting *your* baby, all I can think is, if I am pregnant, I'd have a piece of you in my life. A child with your blue eyes. It's stupid, isn't it? You rescued me, brought me here. Treated me dreadfully. Were arrogant, conceitful. Immensely annoying. Never pretended to be anything you weren't and offered nothing to me. I must be crazy as I'm already more than half-way to loving you."

"Christ you make me sound fucked up."

She chuckles. "That makes two of us, doesn't it?"

Her hands come up and now she's the one cradling my head, angling it, bringing it to her so she can kiss me. I respond. As our tongues dance, my cock predictably shows his interest again. When she taps at my chest, I ease up, giving her room to remove her shirt, and then I help her with her bra.

The urgency gone, I take my time, feasting on her gorgeous breasts, teasing those nipples into peaks. My hand joins my mouth as I toy with one, then the other. Her little moans of satisfaction, her hips writhing against my groin betray how sensitive her tender nubs are. I use my teeth, she gasps. I pinch with my fingers, she jerks. Every response she makes is ramping up my arousal again.

But this time I'm going to go slow. I told her I was claiming her, I hadn't lied. I didn't want another man to have her, I didn't want her to move away. I'd been running from the truth, that I wanted her in my life. Now I've made my decision I'm not letting her go. I've got to persuade her to give us a chance.

I'd give her my baby to prove it. I'll cover my dick if that's what she wants. She's half-way in love with me? I've got an emotion bubbling inside me which I can't put a name to. I've hit my brothers for her and wanted them to hurt for thinking they could step in and take her. The men who I love and who've filled the hole caused by the loss of Jonah. The realisation I put her above them shows what depth of feeling I have for her.

"Blade," she cries out, "I want more."

I love that she's not too shy to encourage me. And I love I have the power to drive her wild. I move down her body, taking time to kiss her stomach, when my hands touch her sides she jumps and covers them with her own.

"Not going to tickle you, babe. Trust me, okay?"

But she holds her breath until I pull my hands away, then gasps again, this time with pleasure as my tongue rims her pretty sunken navel. Then I'm kissing down over her mound, finally, flicking my tongue over her clit.

I breathe on it, lick it and suck it. As she starts to tighten, I raise my head and rest my chin on her mound. She raises her head to look at me, scornful of the interruption.

"Want you to come with me inside you, darlin'."

A quick look of frustration at the delayed satisfaction, but she dips her head in agreement. I sit up, lean over, and opening the drawer, take out a condom. It had been a stupid idea to try to anchor her to me. She'll stay of her own free will, or not at all. "Ain't gonna pressure you, Tash."

Her hand rests on mine, our eyes lock. She swallows, moistens her lips, then gives a little nod. A moment of indecision and, I suspect, thoughts running through her head along the same lines as mine. *Neither of us want to trap the other.*

I smooth on the condom, a fleeting disappointment that I'm not feeling her skin on skin, not planting my seed inside her, then I glance down and position myself. Capturing her eyes once again, I push slowly in, examining every expression crossing her features. *She likes that. Ah, that's the spot that my piercing's touching. Yeah, that right there.* Backing off a little, then pressing back in. *Yeah, that's it.*

I try a slightly different angle and am rewarded with a puffed-out breath. Quickening my pace gets a sharp inhale.

"Wrap your legs around me."

When she immediately obeys, I slip in deeper. Now her inhales and exhales come closer together. Her face begins to scrunch up. Using one hand I gently pinch her clit. It's enough to send her over. *Christ. She's strangling my cock.* She screams, but it's my head that's thrown back as I desperately try not to follow her. Her internal muscles grip hard then ripple, my cock is all but impossible to control, and I'm breathing almost as fast as her.

Her eyes had closed. She opens them again. They're crinkled at the edges as she offers the most beautiful smile.

"Did you…?" She looks confused.

For an answer I push in hard, startling an 'Oh' from her. Then I start thrusting again, hoping to take her over for a second time.

She's moving with me; I can tell she's surprised herself when her muscles start gripping all over again. This time I allow myself to let go at the same time, pumping and filling the condom. *Why have I never gone back for seconds before?* But perhaps it's her, learning her, knowing how responsive she is. *If she agrees, we'll have a lifetime of this. Rumours are, it can only get better.*

Drained in more ways than one, I drop my forehead to hers, then let our mouths meet, tongues now gently gliding in joint appreciation of the pleasure we've just shared. Then, with my cock still half-hard, I carefully pull out and go to dispose of the condom.

When I return, she's lying there, her arm thrown up over her face. I sit down beside her, my hand resting gently on her naked stomach.

"How's this going to work, Blade?"

"How d'you mean?"

"If we're going to see how this goes?"

"First, we get dressed and I'm going to get my woman fed. Need to keep up your stamina."

Moving her arm, she grins at me. "Actually, that sounds like a plan. I'm starving."

CHAPTER 31

Tash

Blade has my head spinning in circles. I thought he wanted nothing to do with me, but the threat of me leaving the state caused him to make a one-eighty. He's now talking about claiming me. What the hell does that mean? Does he see me as a piece of lost property? Deep down I know it's more than that, but I'm wary. Whatever it is between us has gone from zero to full speed ahead.

I've had relationships before, nothing serious, and before that disastrous attempt with Seb, where my hopes were based on false promises, none where I saw a long-term relationship developing. Thinking at my advanced age of thirty that I was running out of time, when I met Seb he seemed to tick lots of boxes. Looking back, that's all it had been; the perfect match on paper.

Using the same criteria, there's nothing about Blade that would indicate he'd be a perfect partner. I certainly wasn't looking for an outlaw, an enforcer whose hobby is collecting knives, whose job is torturing the truth out of people. But whatever paper matching exercise I'd done wouldn't have prepared me for my heart getting involved. I'd told Blade I was half in love with him. Already, for some inexplicable reason, I think it's more than that, which is the basis for my plans to leave state. I knew, should I stay in Tucson, I'd always have been watching for a certain biker to drive past, or be hoping he'd realise his mistake in letting me go. If anyone asked me to list the rationale for my feelings, it would sound ridiculous. I love that private part of him so few people know, the artist inside that he showed me. I love his self-confidence, his arrogance, while it should be a turn off. I also admire him for overcoming his past and want to help that little boy still locked inside who's afraid to have faith in anyone.

That he's decided to give us a try, that he wants me around, well, I'm honoured it's me he's putting his trust in.

As we walk down to the clubhouse, Blade puts his arm around me. When we walk through the door, he doesn't let me go.

Beef notices first. "You claiming her?" he asks, stepping in our path. I can't read the expression in his face. If I didn't know better, I'd think it was disappointment.

"Yes," Blade answers. I know enough to keep quiet and hold back that I've not yet agreed.

Mouse is leaning on the bar. He winks at me and raises a bottle in salutation. I take it as congratulations.

"Never thought I'd see the fuckin' day," Wraith, bouncing a baby in his arms grins widely.

"Language," Sophie admonishes him sharply.

Blade waves them all off. Worried, I look at his face, but he's grinning, and looks… happy. It makes him appear even more handsome. My stomach clenches realising this man could really be mine.

It seems to take forever to get anywhere close to the kitchen. Each man we pass seems to have something to say to Blade, ribaldry or some sarcastic comment, but Blade shrugs it all off like the proverbial water off a duck's back. It's another side of him I haven't seen before. The only comments that come close to riling him are a couple of personal comments at me. Like Marvel saying he'd have tapped that if Blade hadn't got there first. Blade was quick to draw a knife from somewhere, and his brother had backed off fast as he'd held it at his throat. It probably shouldn't have, but it made me laugh. My chuckle drawing a look of admiration from Blade.

When we finally reach the kitchen, Sam's directing a couple of scantily clad women who are sullenly cleaning up.

She rolls her eyes at Blade. "'Bout time we got new prospects," she observes. "I'm all for patching men in, but who's left to do the work?" A shake of her head as she eyes her unwilling workers leaves us in no doubt what she means.

I see Blade wink as he replies, with a glance at the reluctant and inappropriately dressed kitchen hands. "You got that right. Any food going?"

Sam smiles my way. "There are some leftovers I can heat up. We made tons of fried chicken I've just wrapped and put in the fridge. That's if Tommy hasn't already eaten the lot."

My mouth waters. "Don't go to any trouble for me, Sam. I can do it myself."

"Nah, it's no trouble. Looks like you need to keep your strength up." As she speaks, and I blush, she opens the fridge and takes out some wrapped food, then, after turning and giving us a pointed look, takes out another pack. It's not long before a mouth-watering aroma is filling the room. "So," she starts, "you two are a thing, now?"

"Not official, but yeah," Blade informs her, pulling out a chair from the table and indicating I should sit.

The two women cleaning turn to each other and huff. Sam sees them and her eyes narrow. "Another one off the market, girls." I take it these are the club whores I'd heard about, but hadn't yet met.

"That's what we're worried about," one points out.

But the other, comes over. As her hand rests on Blade's arm, I find myself wanting to slap it off. Blade though, does it for me.

"You deserve someone, Blade," she murmurs quietly. Then glares at me. "Just don't hurt him."

"Thanks Paige," Blade replies, while raising his eyebrow in my direction. Yeah. He's right to question how I'm feeling. This is someone he's obviously fucked. As the club girl moves away, he leans in and speaks softly to me, "Know what you're thinking. But I've never touched her the way I've touched you." As though he knows he has to give me more, he shares something I hadn't appreciated. "Before you, I'd never kissed a woman, okay? That's yours, and yours alone. Means a fuckin' lot. You hear me?"

As Sam puts a plate of food in front of me, I glance at the club girls, and then back at Blade. Of course he's got a past, I just don't like it being right in front of my face. It's me he appears to want though. Probably the sooner I accept that the better.

Instead of leaving us, Sam shoos the other women away, then sits down, a cup of coffee in front of her. "You know how Drummer got his name?" she asks conversationally, taking a sip of her drink. When I shake my head, she continues, "Because he used to bang everything in sight. Club girls, hangarounds, stray women," she chuckles.

"Wouldn't call you a stray Sam." Blade winks at her. "Gave it all up when he met you." He finishes her story for her. He bites off a lump of chicken, chews, swallows, then carries on. "Thought he was a fuckin' idiot. Never understood how one pussy could be all that a man would want."

I shoot Blade a look, wondering whether I'll be able to satisfy him. As if he knows what I'm thinking, he leans close and reassures me, "It's me who was the imbecile. It was you who made me understand. Already addicted to you, babe."

"How did you cope, Sam? With everyone around, throwing it in your face?"

Her face tightens for a second. "It's not easy at first, but what you've got to tell yourself is that your man chose you. Whatever happened is in the past, and it's the future you've got to worry about now. Oh and don't be frightened to tell the whores off if they get too close. Old ladies trump sweet butts. Am I right, Blade?"

Blade nods. "You're right."

Sam's approach is the right one. But it's not easy when Blade and I walk back through the clubroom and I get an eyeful of the club girls doing their stuff. One is with Road on the sofa, and the way she's sitting on his lap, her short skirt up around her ass, leaves nothing to the imagination. Marvel's not even attempting to hide that he's fucking another on the pool table. A third is playing bartender, at the moment, staring wistfully over the bar, making eyes at Beef. The way he's staring hungrily back at her suggests what she'll be doing when her work is done.

"Did you do that?" I ask, as to my relief, we walk out into the open air. I touch Blade's arm and hold him back, his face briefly lit by a flash of lightning from a distant storm.

"What? Fuck in the open?"

I suppose the way I averted my eyes and almost ran through the clubroom gave my thoughts away. "Yes."

"Babe." He turns to watch the heaven's light playing over the mountains, gathering his thoughts before he turns back. "The whores are there to be used. Ain't pretending to be a saint. Been upfront with you, Tash. Yeah, I fucked them. Sometimes in public, more often in the crash rooms." Suddenly he swings me around, pushing me up against the wall of the clubhouse. "Never fucked a sweet butt in my suite. Never kissed one. Ever."

His eyes blaze into mine, wordlessly stressing the difference between me and the women whose sole purpose is to service the men.

When I nod, his hand reaches down, going to the top of the leg of my shorts, his finger pushing it aside as well as my panties. I know he'll already find me wet for him.

"This pussy," he tells me, his voice hoarse, "this is mine. Fuck, woman. Why would I think of going to another when I've got this right here just for me? Comin' inside you? Best fuckin' feelin' in the world. Don't need to go lookin' for another." Pulling out his hand, he licks his finger clean. My stomach clenches. "Trust me, babe."

Trying to keep my mind on the topic that's worrying me, and not simply dragging Blade back to the suite for another round of the most amazing sex I've ever experienced in my life, I reply seriously, "It works both ways, Blade."

His lips curve slightly as one hand reaches out and is placed palm flat against the wall by the side of my head. "I suppose it does. Fuck, Tash. I can see why you have doubts about whether I'll be able to be faithful."

"And you have doubts about me, just because I'm female. All we can do, Blade, is promise not to knowingly do anything to hurt each other." I place my fingers against his heart, feeling it beating. "That's what being in a relationship is about. I already know I'd never do anything to cause you to have doubts about me. I respect and feel far too much for you to do that. I'll never leave or walk away." I pause, then look into his face. "Unless you do something to deserve it."

He shrugs and offers a self-deprecating smile. "And you wonder why I stayed away from havin' an old lady before. This shit is complicated."

"No," I refute, "it's easy. It's just respecting the other person's feelings."

"Never had to consider someone else."

"Yes you have." Again, I disagree. "You do it every day with your brothers, Blade. You think about the club all the time. Being with me is just adding in one more person."

"Or two," he reminds me, his free hand, moving to my stomach.

"Is that what you want, Blade?" The ominous rumble of thunder punctuates my words. "Is all this because of a broken condom? Is it the possible child that makes you think you want me?"

Both of his palms come around my head. "Never wanted kids, Tash. Didn't see them in my future. Tolerate those of my brothers, but never saw any with my blood. But you? You were born to have children, weren't you? If I'm with you, it's sort of a package deal. But it's not the reason I changed my mind and claimed you. Would have done that anyway once I got my head out of my ass."

"Blade…"

"Nah, stop what you're thinkin'. Now it's a possibility, it doesn't frighten me. Hasn't made me break out in hives or want to run in the other direction. Meant what I said earlier, hey, you're going to find that out about me. I'll always give it to you straight. The thought that it might not just be you, that we've already started a family, gives me a warm feelin'. A completeness. That's why I don't mind if we're careless." He breaks off as this time the thunder is louder, almost drowning him out. "I never had a family. Even before Jonah died, it was only him and me; Mom didn't really count even when she was there. No idea what we're doing. I can't say I won't fuck up, all I know is what not to do. But that's got to be a start."

"I'm not much different. Got no good reference point to refer to. But there are examples here around us, Blade. Your brothers, their wives and their children."

"Yeah." He smiles. "Could do a lot worse than copyin' them."

A drop of water falls from the heavens, so large it makes a plopping sound as it lands. It's quickly followed by another. Blade looks up to the sky, then, suddenly, picks me up, throws me over his shoulder in a fireman's lift. As a laugh is startled out of me he slaps my ass, then starts to run up the incline.

CHAPTER 32

Blade

"Peg. Blade. Mr Lawson will see you now." Turner waves us in through the open office door.

Lawson's head's down, scribbling something on a piece of paper, as his campaign manager motions us to the two seats in front of him, then returns to his normal station behind us, leaning against the door. A minute passes, then another, before the politician deigns to acknowledge our presence.

"There have been no sightings of Emmalina Fielding. Have you found any trace of her at all?" he asks, his brow creased in annoyance.

"No," Peg replies economically and truthfully. I nod, adding my confirmation we've found no one using that name.

Lawson breathes in sharply. He smashes his fist against the top of the desk. "I thought the Satan's Devils were better than this. How hard is it to find one woman? With the sort of contacts you have, I'd expected better."

I don't need Peg's cautionary glance to remind me to stay calm. The implied criticism of the Satan's Devils is infuriating, but I content myself that Lawson's got it all wrong. Our associates are more likely to be businessmen nowadays, and not the drug dealers and pimps that he's suggesting. But then, he is right. Were we searching for Emmalina, we would have found her. Well, actually we already have.

I notice Lawson's particularly twitchy today, his mask starting to slip as his concern deepens. The closer he gets to his prize—winning the election—the more he's fretting about being exposed for the fraud that he is. I'm not going to console him by admitting Tash wouldn't go anywhere near him and that he's got nothing to worry about. Instead, I poke the beast. "You've got that big rally coming up at the end of the week. Are you worried about her turning up there and causing a disruption?"

"It's possible. Mr Lawson would rather take preventative measures. He'd prefer to talk to Ms Fielding prior to the rally, to try to persuade her to drop these ridiculous stories."

I nod over my shoulder to Turner. Then turn back to the man sitting behind the desk. "It seems to me she'd do better to go to the press at any time to tell her story. Easier for her than trying to accuse you in public."

"She's got no proof of anything. If she goes to the press they'll ask for my side of the story, and I can explain she's not right in the head, and that her accusations are pure fantasy."

"And I'd remind them about publishing anything libellous," Turner butts in. "Mr Lawson's in a good position at the moment. The latest polls show the electorate seems to be swaying his way. They like his policies, his direct way of talking, and the press are mostly onside, everyone likes a story of an outsider reaching pole position. They'd likely dismiss her."

"At a rally," Lawson takes over, "people might listen to something salacious without hearing both sides of the story. Of course, my wife will be there, and she doesn't deserve anything thrown in her face."

"I was wondering," Peg starts, "about searching Emmalina's apartment if we're able to get in. It's possible we might find some clue that would suggest where she might go. A friend or someone you haven't thought of."

Again Turner says his piece first, "We've looked. Couldn't find anything."

"But the Satan's Devils might have different methods, Neil. It's worth a shot, isn't it?" Suddenly Lawson looks hopeful.

"Grant left it in a bit of a mess," Neil admits.

Peg grins an uncommon smile. "We wouldn't worry about that. We're quite used to… messes."

Lawson slides open a drawer and takes something out. The next moment he slides it over the desktop.

"You've got a key?" I say wonderingly.

"Yeah. I helped her get the apartment. She left one with me in case she ever got locked out."

He had one cut, more like. For when he was fucking her. I work hard to stop the disgust showing on my face that this sorry excuse of a man had her before I did. What did she ever see in him? A façade he's not bothering to present to us today.

Peg pockets the key and stands, I do likewise. "We'll check it out. Follow up any leads. But if she remains in the wind, we'll have our boys there in force on Friday, all on the lookout for her to turn up." Yeah, I inwardly smile. Fucking easiest gig ever. All of us looking for someone who hasn't the slightest intention to appear.

And when she doesn't, how is Lawson going to explain that? The snake's going to find himself caught in a trap of his own making. I wonder exactly how long he's going to have us chasing our tails to stop the truth getting out.

"She's a bitch." Lawson suddenly stands, his control lost. His eyes flare and his face grows red as he adds, "She wants to ruin my life with her lies? Well I'll fucking ruin hers. If she turns up on Saturday, or if you find her before, take her back to your compound. I don't give a fuck what you do to her after that. I just don't want her walking the streets of Tucson."

"What the fuck do you mean?" Peg snarls.

"You've got contacts with the cartel," Turner speaks for his boss. "They might be able to… use… a woman like her. She's quite attractive."

My fists clench at what they're suggesting. Peg sends me another warning glance. We were right all along, Lawson doesn't want us to be his security, he thinks the reputation we once had still reflects us. I send Peg a slight chin lift, his message has been received and understood. Lawson's shown us the first piece of rope, now we've got to get him to unwind more until it's long enough for him to hang himself.

"I'll discuss it with the prez," I assure him, proud that my voice is steady and calm. As if selling a woman off into the slave trade was an everyday occurrence.

"Christ I need a drink to get that taste out of my mouth," Peg tells me as we go to the bikes.

"You and me both, Brother," I agree. "But at least we've got the key to her apartment."

"Now's the time to see whether Lawson knows exactly what she has on him."

"Or," I put in optimistically, "Grant didn't find anything, and the evidence to bring him down remains where she said it would be."

We waste no time. A short ride later and we find her apartment is a fucking mess. Lawson hadn't been lying. No attempt had been made to tidy up the damage Grant had done. I suspect it had been left this way to support the original story of a home invasion for if her absence was ever reported. The only thing put back in its rightful place is the skillet she'd presumably used to brain Grant. Shame she hadn't killed him.

Just inside the door, Peg tilts his head slightly, then says loudly. "This is a fuckin' mess, Brother. Come on. Let's get started."

I'd expected to go straight for the floorboard Tash had told us about, but Peg's words warn me. Flicking my eyes quickly I see exactly what he's seen. *A camera.* I quirk my mouth toward Peg, receiving a slight shake of his head. *Amateurs.* If we were going to film anything, we'd use shit Mouse could get that wouldn't be seen. But then, if Tash had returned, she probably wouldn't have noticed it.

We waste time going through paperwork that's already been searched and left strewn around. I find the loose floorboard where Tash had indicated, but make no attempt to pull it up.

After a while I whistle to get his attention. "Going out for a smoke." I pull my cigarettes out of my cut for emphasis.

"Sure."

Once outside, I do indeed light up, but get down to my main purpose fast, swapping my lighter for my phone. "Mouse? Need you to cut into a feed for me. Fuckin' cameras in Tash's place. In the main room and bedroom. Can you cut in and put it on a loop or something? Yeah? That's great. Give me a call if you're able to do it. Yeah, that would work as a backstop."

I go back up. Peg and I spend another half hour making it look like we're doing a proper search, then loudly exclaim we can't find anything, and leave. We go to a nearby coffeehouse.

"Mouse thinks he can do it. He's going to try to track down the feed."

"Must be something Lawson's put in." Peg looks grim. "Do you think it was there while Tash was in residence? Or recently installed, in case she went back?"

I shrug. "Could be either. But with the camera in her bedroom, I'd say he was a fuckin' pervert."

My phone rings. It's Mouse. He's done what he needs to, has put footage of the empty rooms on a loop. Abandoning our unfinished coffee, it doesn't take long to return, lift the floorboard, and extract what we really came for.

Back at the clubhouse I take it straight into Mouse, thanking him for his help today. His eyes light up when he sees the USB key Tash had told him about.

"Blade?" Having left Mouse to do what he does best, when I return to the clubroom, Heart catches my eye and calls me over. "Had a bit of luck today. You know Amy's starting school in the fall?"

I didn't, but then I don't really notice anything to do with the kids. Hmm. Perhaps I ought to start paying attention. "She old enough?"

"Almost six," he tells me proudly. "Anyway, Marc and I went there for an open house. You'll never guess who we met there."

"Go on," I prompt, wondering why the fuck he's telling me. Preparing me to play happy families, perhaps?

"There was a woman there without a husband, ugly mother-fucker with her instead. Obviously security. Thought she looked familiar, so got up close when she was registering." I circle my hand to encourage him to get to the point. "Lawson's wife." He waits for that to sink in. "I had a quiet word with Marc. She targeted her, bit like separating a steer from a herd, must be her cop background." Heart smirks. "Christ, my woman's smooth. Anyway, she ended up chatting with her. New to Tucson, no friends. Marc got her phone number and suggested they met up on a playdate. Amy's not far off her daughter's age and it looks like they'll be in the same classes."

Now it's me grinning broadly. If Marcia can get her alone, she's the best to find out what's going on. Being an ex-cop she's used to conducting interrogations, and reading between the lines of what people don't say.

"Good work, Heart. Can she arrange something soon?"

"Thursday work for ya?" Heart casts a fond and proud glance his woman's way, who responds with a wave of her fingers, and a smile so full of love it makes me yearn to get that kind of response from Tash.

As Heart walks off to join Marc, I stand pinching my nose. *Both ways. It works both ways.* You have to give love to get it returned. I've got to let Tash in if I want the kind of relationship my brother has got.

That's what I want, isn't it?

Eli, Prez's toddler son runs into the room, trips and falls over, letting out such a scream it sounds like he's done serious damage. Even I start to go over, but Sam's already there, picking him up, placing a kiss on his knee. Suddenly it's all better.

Kids. Hell. What if that's already in my near future? Someone I could lose. Just like Jonah.

"Hey." Tash's arm comes around me. "You're looking serious."

I hug her close as the memory of Lawson's suggestion of what we should do to her comes into my mind. No woman deserves to be treated like that, and least of all, my woman. My gut churns at the thought, if Lawson had his way, she could be taken from me. Perhaps this is the reason I'd stayed alone all my life. It's not just a child that would make me vulnerable. Already she's got under my skin, and I know, losing her would be like losing my brother all over again. Breathing in the perfume of my soap she's still using; I wonder how I could have been sucked in so fast. What is it about her that above all women, she's the only one I feel I could invest my future, my happiness in? Even as I wonder whether I'm making the biggest mistake of my life, I realise, it's too late. I've already given her the power to hurt me.

"What's up, Blade?" Her eyes shine with the same expression I just envied when I saw Marcia looking at Heart. Fuck. I'm already a goner.

It's the wrong place, the wrong time, but when is something like this right? I lean down and speak into her ear, "I love you, Tash."

"Blade," she squeals, hearing the words I never expected to feel let alone utter. She literally leaps into my arms. When I support her, she wraps her legs around my waist, her arms around my shoulders, and fixes her mouth onto mine.

"Get a fuckin' room. There are kids here," yells Beef. But I see him grinning.

CHAPTER 33

Blade

It was like something had broken within me, but in a good way. The moment I told Tash I loved her, I knew it was right. I'd opened my heart, or rather taken it out and given it to her for safekeeping.

That she loved me back was incredible. We'd fucked, no, made love. There's no other way to describe it. We'd talked right into the night, discussing what we wanted from life and making plans for our future. I was going to draw the illustrations for all her books, she wasn't going to be working with any other artist. Fuck me, I'll be the enforcer for an outlaw MC, and a children's artist to boot. The thought of how that would be received from my brothers made me laugh until my sides hurt.

As we'd lain together, now in comfortable silence, my mind returned to how I'd first seen her, and I made her a vow. As soon as she could safely leave the compound, I was going to take her to the Wheel Inn for a proper meal, and one she didn't need to forage out of the waste bins.

For the next few days we settled into a routine. I loved going back to my suite knowing she would be there, usually bent over that computer as she writes the rest of her book. I'd watch her giggling to herself as the cartoon dog, Grunt, got up to something stupid. He'd gone from learning to ride a motorbike to starting up his own club. An American pit bull terrier had become the sergeant-at-arms, and I couldn't wait to get started on that illustration, Peg certainly came to mind. A Rottweiler was the enforcer, a Great Dane the treasurer.

There were some adult jokes that children wouldn't understand creeping in, some had me in stitches. The bitches, well, yeah. Those for a start.

Marcia had managed to get a playdate between Amy and Sally, Lawson's wife and her daughter Eliza, but on Friday, not Thursday, and I was hoping to hear an update at church later.

Knowing I've got to leave now to avoid being late, I stand, reluctant to go, watching Tash typing away, waiting until she looks up from the page before interrupting her. Wondering what a lucky fucker like me did to deserve her.

"Got church. Want to come and party after?"

Her eyes narrow. "I'm not sure if I want to see any more of your brothers' asses."

I certainly don't want her to look at them. The only ass she's going to see is mine. "It's usually PG for a while, the other old ladies will be around."

"Do you think there'll be any problems?" she frowns. Well aware tonight I'll be telling the club I'm officially claiming her.

"You worried? You shouldn't be. Anyone said anything to make you have doubts?" Fuck, Wraith, Drummer, everyone knows we're together. Getting it recorded is just a formality.

She shrugs. "They haven't, but…"

"I'll let you know as soon as I can babe." I grin. In anticipation, I've had Sam pick up a cut and get a property patch put on it. Can't wait to see her just wearing that leather tonight. Knowing I've no time to linger, for now I content myself taking her mouth in a punishing kiss, her bruised lips will have her thinking about me all night.

Problem is, I bruised mine too. And my cock has predictably thickened at the thought of her wearing my patch. It's not just her who's going to have an agonising few hours of waiting. Ruefully I walk down to the clubhouse, grab a beer and enter church.

I adjust myself, then sit.

"Christ, stop playing with yourself, fucker. You've got a woman for that." Peg roars at his own joke, watching me over the table.

"Anyone missin'?" Drummer walks in, his eyes scanning the chairs' occupants, nodding when he satisfies himself no one is. All seats are filled, including Drifter's at the end of the table. He looks on intrigued by his first church.

"First, over to Dollar."

I listen, we're making bank which is all to the good. Bullet gives a quick run-down of progress at the mall. Foundations are laid and everything appears to be going smoothly.

"Talking of the mall," Peg takes the floor after a chin jerk from Prez. "Drummer and I have met the two hopefuls who'd like to prospect for us. We've suggested they come as hangarounds for a while. They're going to be here tonight so you can all meet them."

"Names?" I ask.

Shooter grins and answers from the end of the table, "Hound and Roadkill. Hound's always chasing tail, and Roadkill looks like he's been run over most days."

So they come with readymade road names. To be seen if they make the grade. "If we take them on, we going to consider bringing Matt to the table?" Rock asks. "He's given a lot to the club. Does everything without complaining."

I nod in support. Especially now when he's the only prospect we've got. From other dips and rises of heads, I'm not the only one thinking that way.

Viper raises his hand. "There's another man, no road name, just called Bertram. He overheard and wants to come see what we're about too. Thought it wouldn't hurt letting him tag along as we'll already be geared up for the others." He means shit not meant for prying eyes will be kept under wraps.

Prez thinks for a moment, then nods. "Yeah, can't hurt Viper, we'll be on our best behaviour anyway. No discussions about where we bury the bodies." As laughs follow his words, I reckon he's only half joking. "Right. Moving on. Blade, want to get your business out of the way?"

There's only one thing Drummer can be asking. "Yeah, I'm claiming Tash."

Prez raises the gavel. "Any objections?"

Peg's hand starts to rise, then he winks at me and scratches his head.

"*Bastard,*" I snarl, getting a round of laughter.

Drummer smirks and brings down the gavel. "And another brother goes down."

"Probably what persuaded her."

I waggle my tongue at Rock.

"More sweet butts to go around," Beef observes.

"Not if we keep bringing new fuckin' brothers to the table," Marvel grumbles. "Can't we get any fresh meat, Prez?"

"Allie is getting a bit old."

"You would fuckin' think so." Shooter's, what, twenty-two now? "Should appreciate her experience. Ask her for a few lessons. Probably still don't know where a g-spot is."

As Shooter growls and looks like he's going to launch himself at Jekyll, Prez bangs the gavel. "Let's get this meetin' back on track. You recorded that Heart?" A nod indicates he indeed has. I've officially got myself an old lady. "Sticking with Heart, you want to fill everyone in on Marcia?"

"Yeah. Marc met Sally. Amy and her daughter Eliza are going to go to the same school. Marc played on the fact it would be nice for the girls to get to know each other, make a friend before the semester starts. Don't expect them to be bosom buddies for long though with her father being Sebastian Lawson. Reckon he'll put a stop to it when he finds out Marc's relationship to us." There are a few sneers of agreement. Yeah, knowing what type of men Lawson believes us to be, Heart is probably right.

"What did she get from her, Heart?"

"About what we expected. Sally Lawson had a fucker called Grant with her. Mean-looking chap. Always in earshot so Marc had to be careful. She did manage to drop in discreetly that she used to be a cop, and gave Sally her number to call if she ever needed another woman's ear."

"So it was a waste of time." Peg shakes his head at me.

"Not at all," Heart contradicts. "Marc has been trained to spot people's tells. I didn't want to influence her, so hadn't told her our suspicions. It was interesting she came back and said her view is that Sally's married to an abusive fucker. She was sporting a bruise that Marc could see through her makeup."

Growls and objections go around the table. None of us have time for men who lay their hands on a woman.

"So why's she gone back to him?"

"Obviously there's a story there. But I expect money's behind it." Drum strokes his beard. "Prestige or power? Her family got a tame politician in their pockets. Heart, Marc's done well. See if your ol' lady can foster that relationship."

When Heart indicates he will, Mouse is the next to speak. "That shit Tash had hidden? Lawson was up to his neck in bringing Raul Cobb down."

As I suck in a breath, Drummer sits forward. "You sure, Mouse? Can we get that info into the right hands?"

"I'm sure, Prez. But there's a bit of reading between the lines. Got him on tape encouraging both women to come forward, offering money to ease their way. Unfortunately, nothing to say there wasn't already a story, and he just encouraged them to step up."

"So we get to the women directly. Find out the fuckin' truth." Dollar cracks his knuckles making me flinch. Fucking hate it when he does that. "If they made it all up, get them to retract their story."

"I believed Cobb," Peg says. He nods at me. "I know Blade probably has doubts because he's a distrustful fucker, but Cobb's woman's standin' firmly beside him. You can't know anyone from a short meetin', but from what I saw I preferred him to Lawson any day."

"Those women who lied about him? We go put the fear of fuckin' Satan into them," I suggest. "Get them to tell the fuckin' truth." Women lie and let you down. I frown slightly. Tash is the exception, isn't she? Peg was right, my mistrust is ingrained. It doesn't take much to make me have doubts, wondering whether I've made a dreadful mistake. *Nah, Tash is straight. I feel it in my gut.*

"Yeah. Someone needs to go talk to them," Drummer agrees. "One is out of state. Overnight trip for whoever's going."

"I'll go," I say.

"Best take someone with you who won't be tempted to use his knives on them." Peg chuckles.

"I'm up for it," offers Beef. I nod my thanks. Yeah, he can charm the pants off of any woman. Beef looks puzzled. "We get them to talk, what happens now Lawson's the nominee? Can they take his name off the ballot?"

"Way it works," replies Mouse, "if he wins but can't take his place because he's dead or something, it goes to someone else in the same party."

"Dead," I echo, spinning my knife. "Sounds pretty good to me."

"We're not in the business of murdering in cold blood, Blade."

I shrug. "It's fucking hot for me, Prez. He wants us to sell off my ol' lady to the cartel."

We chuck around ideas of the practicalities involved in getting close to the ladies who've fingered Cobb. Mouse is going to do some investigating with Marcia's help. For the moment there's not much else to do.

"Prez," I raise my hand to remind him. "Got that rally we're supposed to be at tomorrow to protect Lawson from Tash." I break off to allow the laughter to die down. "I said we'd have a good contingent of brothers there."

"Fuckin' political speeches? Rather stick my head in an oven," observes Beef. But he sticks up his hand and volunteers anyway, as do most of the rest.

Prez frowns. "Think we ought to get moving on the other shit. Blade, you and Beef skip out on the rally and go visit the out-of-state bitch. The rest of us will be enough to dissuade a woman, who we know is not going to turn up, from protesting."

Chuckling, I raise my eyebrow at Beef. He's on board, not seeming bothered in the slightest that he's missing out on having to listen to a politician spouting false promises. For the benefit of the rest, I clarify the time and the arrangements that had been agreed with Turner, assuring them all, it's a late-afternoon, early-evening affair so shouldn't waste too much time, and they'll soon be back getting their throats and dicks wet.

Then, as there's no other business, with a final bang of the gavel, church comes to a close.

Tash has come down from the suite, and is sitting with Sam, Sophie, Ella, Darcy, Marcia, Becca and Mariana. Tommy and Drew are playing pool. Surprisingly there are no children, but Sandy and Carmen are missing. Sandy's grandma to Eli and Zane, and Carmen is an honorary one too. Guess they're taking on babysitting duties for a while, giving the mothers a probably much needed break. I watch as Becca stands, arching her back, and grimacing. Rock's pushing past and going to her, looking concerned.

Sam catches my eye and tilts her head. When I nod, she gets up from the couch and disappears from the room. Tash stares over as though trying to read the expression on my face.

I beckon with my finger. With a grin, she stands and walks around the girls and comes straight toward me. The expression of longing on her face, the way her eyes fix on mine and on nobody else, means as soon as she's close enough I take her into my arms, placing my lips against hers. Of course, that isn't enough. My tongue demands entry, she allows it. I lose all sense of time and place as I devour her mouth, her giving as much as she is taking.

A barked laugh reminds me where I am.

I pull back, slowly, keeping contact as long as possible, then peck gently at the tip of her delightful snub nose before letting her go. My eyes catch those of Allie who's standing behind the bar. Her brow creases, then her lips curve and then slowly, she nods. With this woman in my arms, I'm another who won't have the need for sweet butts anymore.

Behind her I notice the door opening and see, as we'd discussed in church, the three hangarounds, wannabe prospects, walking in, looking around the clubhouse in amazement, their first time in a biker's den. But I've no time or inclination to find out any more about them tonight. Not when I've got something more important to do.

"Blade," Sam's voice interrupts. When I turn, a brown sack is placed in my hands.

I pass it straight over to Tash. "Open it."

Perhaps I should have waited until we were in the privacy of my suite, but I'm too impatient. It's only when she's taking the leather vest out that I suddenly have a fear she won't like it.

I watch as she extracts the soft, feminine shaped leather garment, unfolds it and looks at it in wonder. Then she turns it over, and reads the words on the back, 'Property of Blade'. "Really?" But her eyes are sparkling as she slips it on.

Catcalls, whistles, cheers and congratulations sound all around us as I lean in, unable to resist tapping the tip of that nose which I love so much. "You've been claimed."

Her hands reach out, grab each side of my cut, and she says firmly, "So have you, Blade."

I wouldn't have it any other way.

CHAPTER 34

Tash

There are no words to describe last night, and what happened when we returned to the suite after Blade had given me his property patch. I realised how much it had meant to him when he demanded in a gravelly voice which went straight to my lady parts, that I strip everything off and lie on the bed wearing nothing but the leather vest he'd just given to me.

To say I'm exhausted today is an understatement, and sore in the most glorious ways. He'd been a beast, an animal, and I'd loved every moment. As it had been another lengthy session, he'd even stopped to change the condom halfway.

He's gone this morning, and will be away all day, returning tomorrow. Not completely joking, I'd told him I didn't mind, I needed the time to recover.

When I pictured myself with a life partner, it hadn't been someone like him. How I saw the years ahead of me, it wasn't spending it being part of the life that he's living. But these past few days have shown there couldn't be anyone better for me. He's nothing like I expected, attentive, caring. Supportive of the author I want to become.

Although I appreciate how hard it is for him, I think he trusts me. I suppose to what extent it remains to be seen. The knowledge that he has no faith in women does worry me, causing me to walk as though on eggshells, analysing everything I do or say.

That's the only downside to our relationship, I suspect that he's waiting for me to fail.

It's that thought that's leading me down to Mouse's office today.

"Am I interrupting?"

"Nah, Tash. Come in." Mouse stubs out his joint. It's a thoughtful gesture, but probably doesn't help much. The air's already thick with smoke.

"Have you remembered something else to tell me?"

I press my lips together, feeling awkward, out of place. "It's nothing to do with Lawson, Mouse."

His eyes sharpen as he settles back, stretching out his long limbs. "What can I do for you, then?"

"Look, it's Blade. I need to know something about him."

His brow furrows. "Know you're new to this, Tash, but brothers don't get in between them and their old ladies. You want to know anything? You ask Blade yourself. Up to him whether he wants to tell you."

"It's something he doesn't know," I say hurriedly.

Again, he doesn't let me finish, shaking his head. "Shouldn't have secrets between you, Tash. Not going to go behind my brother's back."

I'm starting to get frustrated. "You know knowledge is power, don't you? And that saying, what you don't know can't hurt you?" Of course he will. He'd even have words to describe it, *club business*. Somehow I've got to get around that wall and make him help. "Mouse, in this case I wonder whether what Blade doesn't know is definitely paining him."

"You know something he doesn't?"

My head moves side to side. "No. And I could be completely wrong to be looking into it. Maybe it will be something Blade's best not knowing in the end. But on the other hand, it could give him answers. Give him closure at least." My teeth worry my lip again. "I love him, Mouse. He says he loves me, but that could easily come crashing down."

"Never thought Blade would take an ol' lady," he admits. "You're good for him."

"I'm going to fuck up, sometime Mouse. Everyone does. Most people clear the air then move on. But Blade?" I leave the question about his reaction hanging.

He gives me an assessing look. He knows his brother better than me. What I've said is the truth and he can't deny it. At last he speaks, "Fuck, woman. Doesn't sit right, feels like I'm makin' a huge fuckin' error, but to hell with it. Tell me what you want. I'll either do it or not."

Taking a breath, I begin, "Blade's got no family. His brother was killed when Blade was twelve."

"Know that," Mouse agrees.

"His mom disappeared the day after, didn't even go to her son's funeral. Blade never saw her again."

"Didn't know that." His face hardens. "You know, Blade's not going to be happy you're talkin' to me. Giving me information he didn't want shared."

"Well, now you know. And you can't unhear it," I challenge.

Leaning forward with his elbows on the desk, he steeples his hands. "You want me to find her? Woman, you're mad if you think that will mean fuck all to Blade." He swipes back his long hair that's fallen forward over his face. "What you've said? She abandoned him at the worst possible time. He's not going to forgive her when it's shaped his life all these years."

"Mouse, I know it's a long shot, but what if she didn't leave voluntarily?"

"Long shot?" he snorts. "If it was any longer I'd be able to reach out and touch the fuckin' moon. You're seekin' answers which aren't there, sweetheart. What you've got to do is find ways to deal with it. His mom leavin' cut him up bad, anyone can see that. Rather than getting answers to questions better not asked, work out your coping strategy."

"What the fuck do you think I'm doing?" I snarl, losing my temper. "The odds are against finding anything to help, I *know* that. But because I love him, I want to try anything I can to make his mind easier."

"You do know I'll tell him?"

I'd expected that. These men are close. "I know. But just not before we know the answer. Please."

He closes his eyes. When he opens them, his hand automatically reaches for his joint and lighter. Then, with a shake of his head which gets his hair flying around him, he puts them back down. "When can you find out if you're pregnant?"

"End of next week." His question seems unrelated.

"I'll do it. If, when, I find her, you can do what you like with the information. But one tip, sweetheart, for fuck's sake don't try to talk to her. Woman walked out on her kid? Didn't hang around to see her other son buried? What fuckin' excuse could she have for that? Blade would fuckin' hate you if you tried to bring her back into his life. He's managed without her for more than twenty years."

But there might be an explanation of why she left as she had. Maybe there's a reason she'd thought it was for the best. Perhaps she'd had a mental breakdown or something. Truthfully, I don't know what I'll do with whatever Mouse finds out. I'll think about that when he gives me some answers.

I leave Mouse's office deep in thought. As I'd said to Mouse, knowledge is power, but there's a niggling feeling inside me that says lack of it has strength too. Not knowing why she'd left has affected Blade all these years, shaped him when he grew into a man. I've got a temper. What woman hasn't? Especially at certain times of the month. What if I walked out on an argument?

Would that be enough for Blade to confirm his mistrust in women had a basis?

That's the fear that worries me in the middle of the night.

"Hey, Tash. Hang on a minute."

Swinging around, I see Joker. He's waving a box at me. "Blade left this for you."

Crossing over to him, I take the box. Inside is a brand-new phone. With a quick shake of my head, I explain why I'm not taking it, "Joker, I can't make calls. I'm not crazy enough to give myself away."

He grins. "Blade's already programmed his and our numbers in there. The old ladies too. And Mouse has done some shit with it which means it can't be traced. Blade wanted you to be able to contact him if you had to."

I should have realised he wouldn't have left it if there was a risk. Though I'm still wary about using it. I'm sure Mouse has set it up right, but still, why take a chance if I don't need to?

"Blade's out all day. Think he just wanted you to have a way of getting in touch. Place is going to be pretty dead tonight. Most of the brothers are going out later."

"I won't ask where." I grin at the jovial man.

When he slaps my back, I stumble forward a step. "Already making a great old lady, aren't you?"

"I'm a quick learner," I grin back.

"Rash!"

Swinging around I see Tommy. "How you doing? You getting on okay?"

"Tommy's been helping Matt," he informs me, seriously. "We've been clearing the firebreak. Tommy's hot."

Hmm. Yeah. Well, he certainly looks sweaty. I eye the prospect who's come in behind him.

Matt leans into me, confiding, "He's a good worker. Never complains either. Did twice the work most people could have done in one morning."

It has to be good Tommy's keeping useful. I make a mental note to ask Blade what they are going to do with him. For now, it appears, they are letting him stay.

"You hungry, Tom boy?" Matt asks, slapping his helper's back.

"Tommy hungry." That characteristic gesture of rubbing his stomach accompanies his statement, making me smile.

"Well, let's go eat then."

I could do with something too, so I follow them into the kitchen where I find the other women.

"Hey, Tash. You have a good time last night?" Sam winks at me. I blush. Before my cheeks redden completely, she returns to the conversation I'd interrupted. "What did you make of the hangarounds last night, Soph?"

"Couple of them seemed willing enough. One gave me chills."

Unashamedly interrupting, I ask, "What are hangarounds?"

"Hangarounds are normally women who come to our parties wanting to shag a biker," Sophie explains, "but they can also be men hoping to prospect for the club. Three came along last night, they're here today too. Seeing if they make the grade," Sophie replies. "You probably didn't notice as you were too wrapped up in Blade at the time."

"Literally." Sam bumps her hip with the VP's old lady and laughs. Then expands on the explanation I'd been given. "They'll be given all manner of shit to do. If they stay the course, then they'll be made prospects."

Seems there's a lot I've got to learn about how the club works. I stay for a while to be sociable, then decide to take myself off to Blade's, *our*, room, and get some writing done.

But as I walk through the clubroom I notice Tommy is now sitting on a couch, a bottle of soda in front of him. I've noticed that while he's well past the legal age to drink, he doesn't partake. Probably to the good, who knows what he'd be like as a drunk? Hard to handle, that's for certain. I'm about to pass him, when I notice his expression. Or, lack of. He's staring vacantly into space.

"Hey, Tommy. You alright?"

He comes straight back to himself with a jolt, and a huge smile. "Rash!"

"You doing okay?" I sit down opposite him.

"Tommy good." He nods his head up and down fast. "Good place here, Rash." Then his face falls.

"What is it?" He's worried about something.

Now his head is moving left to right. "Tommy doesn't want to go."

I bristle. I'd heard nothing about him leaving. "Who's said something?"

"No one. But this is too good, isn't it, Rash? Food, bed. Bikes."

I lean forwards and take his hand in mine. "Just take it as it comes, Tommy, eh? We'll look out for each other. Like we did on the streets, yeah?"

"Rash and Tommy?"

I nod, and offer a smile. "Rash and Tommy. Yes." I consider him for a moment. "What happened to you, Tommy? How did you come to be living rough?"

Tommy's brow furrows and his face once again goes blank. A hand lands on my shoulder. Looking up, I see the slim biker called Lady.

He bends and speaks quietly into my ear, "Tried asking him myself. Our Tommy here, well, he lives in the present. He doesn't like to think of the past. Not sure he even remembers it, or not too far back anyways. Reckon we shouldn't push him." He turns and glances over his shoulder to where his partner is standing. "Some things are best left buried."

"You ready to beat me this time, Tom boy?" Drew strides in. Tommy changes like a switch being thrown.

"Tommy win!"

Drew chuckles as Tommy lurches over to the pool table. Satisfied he's in good hands, I stand and resume my interrupted walk to the door.

Back in the suite it's not long before I'm engrossed in what I'm doing, and, as usual when I'm into my writing, lose track of the time.

I hear thunder, *no, not thunder*. A large number of motorcycles revving up and leaving. Guess the brothers are going out to do what they have to do. None of the women knew what was going on, but surprisingly, they hadn't seemed worried. It's apparently par for the course of being an old lady.

When my phone rings I jump out of my skin. It's been so long since I did something as normal as answer a call. Laughing at myself, I spy Blade's name on the screen. Happy that he's checking in with me, I accept the call, putting it to my ear, and saying in greeting, "Hey, you."

A horrible chuckle, one I know only too well, snarls sarcastically into my ear. "Emmalina. It's so nice to talk to you after all this time."

My heart's beating fast, my palm's so sweaty I'm in danger of dropping the phone. *Don't talk to him.* I'm about to cut the call when he says, "Emmalina, I know exactly where you are. And I'm talking to you on your boyfriend's phone. I think you better listen to me, don't you?"

I stay silent while chills go through me. *How the hell does he have Blade's cell?*

"You do know Blade works for me, don't you? And that he who pays the piper calls the tune."

"The Satan's Devils might take your money, but you don't own them." I cover my mouth with my hand, not having wanted to give him the satisfaction of speaking to him.

"Listen to me, Emmalina. I know they've double crossed me which has made me very angry. When I'm angry, you know what I can do. I have Blade's phone. I have Blade too. If you want him left unharmed, then you'll come to me, and I'll exchange him for you."

What? He's got Blade? Rapidly thoughts run through my head, unanswerable questions tumbling one after the other. *How does he know anything? How does he know I'm here? How does he know my relationship to Blade? Has someone told him? Has he tortured the information out of the enforcer? To do that, he must have seriously hurt him. He's bluffing. He's got to be. He might be.* But he knows too much it shouldn't be possible for him to know. How do I play this?

"Why do you think Blade means anything to me?" I try to sound nonchalant. If he thinks he can't use Blade as persuasion, maybe he'll let him go.

"Oh, he clearly thinks a lot of you. He gave you his property cut, and from the display in the clubroom last night, you return his feelings. I think I've got you right where I want you, Emmalina. I know everything, you see."

How does he know what went on in the clubroom? Is someone in the club a traitor? One of the women from Tucson, perhaps? No, that can't be, I hadn't seen any arrive before Blade brought me up to the suite for our own private celebration.

I picture the scene again in my head. As we'd walked out, I had noticed strangers there. I hadn't connected the dots when talking to Sam and Sophie. "One of the new hangarounds," I whisper, putting it together.

"You see, that was something I liked about you. You could always add two and two." Suddenly his voice changes and goes from mocking to hard. "Think on this. You get out of the compound. I'll have Grant waiting at the end of the track; he'll bring you to the house. Don't tell anyone. Most of the Devils are at the rally tonight providing me," he snorts, "with protection in case you appeared to cause a disruption. There's hardly anyone left, so you should get out without being stopped. You bring the cavalry? Blade dies. You know what will happen if you tell just one person, they'll all come running to rescue their friend. He'll get a bullet in the head at the sound of the first motorcycle engine. You keep your mouth shut, or Blade's dead."

"How do I know you won't kill him anyway?"

"You don't. But it's a certainty that's what will happen if you refuse to follow my instructions. You want to be selfish and keep yourself safe, then you'll never see Blade again."

The proof he's not bluffing is that he's talking to me on Blade's phone. Blade would never have just handed it over. Putting myself back in Seb's hands would be signing my death warrant, yet, if I don't, I'll be signing Blade's. When I found he'd already killed Ferguson, that's when I realised what he's capable off.

"It's past time we spoke, Emmalina. You've got no choice. Not if you want to keep your man breathing." Seb sounds like he knows he's winning.

I don't know what to do. It's unthinkable that I'll never see Blade again. I can't consider sacrificing him for me. Seb's right, most of the men have left the compound, from what the women said, there'd only be the prospect left behind, and the hangarounds, one of whom is a traitor.

But what can they do? Seb will kill Blade anyway if I get anyone else involved.

"You better get moving. And I suggest you run down that fucking track. Grant will only wait so long for you, then it's goodbye lover. I'll kill him, Emmalina, I promise."

"You'll kill me too. Maybe both of us."

"Maybe not. Maybe I will. But one's a certainty, the other? Well, perhaps you can persuade me my action needn't be so extreme. Now get moving and get your ass down to the main road."

He hangs up. For a second, I'm frozen. I don't know what to do. Then I look up to the display on the wall. The idea hits fast. Although the temperature is in the low hundreds, I change into jeans, hiding a small blade in my shoe. I've one in an ankle sheaf, like I've seen Blade wear, and a couple of flick knives in my pockets. Grabbing my phone, and with one look of regret at my property cut sitting on the back of the chair, I leave.

One of the new hangarounds is manning the gate. That he's the one who gave me away I become certain of, as he opens it for me without question, and with a leer.

Then I start running, not knowing how long I, or rather, Blade, has left.

CHAPTER 35

Blade

I wouldn't say I was sorry I was going to miss out on Lawson's rally later in the day, quite happy to skip out on the babysitting gig, where all the Satan's Devils were going to be on the lookout for a girl who wasn't going to appear.

Instead Beef and I will be heading over to Nevada to meet a Virginia Parsons, one of the women who's pointed the finger at Cobb. We'll be spending tonight at the Las Vegas clubhouse. I'm particularly looking forward to catching up with my counterpart there, Twister.

When I'd agreed to go, I hadn't given a thought to Tash. This relationship stuff is all new to me. When I realised the implications, that both she and I would be sleeping alone tonight, it hit me how much I didn't like leaving her. However, I couldn't back out on a promise to my brothers, but at the last moment thought to get a phone sorted for her. At least I'll be able to call and wish her goodnight.

"Tonight will be a piece of piss, as Sophie would say." Peg nudges my arm as he walks out of the clubhouse.

Yeah. There certainly won't be much too it. "Unless that place gets filled to the gills. Lawson could have other protestors there."

"Can't see that many people wanting to listen. Better things to do on a Saturday."

I agree with the sergeant-at-arms. Must lead a pretty sad life if you've got nothing better to do than go to a political rally on the weekend. "Who's going with you?"

"Pretty much all the darn club. Most being nosy, wanting to get a look at Lawson for themselves. Joker and Lady are stayin' to keep an eye on things, Matt's going to be keeping his eye on the hangarounds."

"That wise? Having them here?"

"Joker and Lady know to make sure they stay out of places they shouldn't be looking. Matt too. Think he's going to give them the shit jobs, cleaning the pool."

"Get used last night?" I grin. It was a hot evening. I'd be surprised if there wasn't a condom or two in the water to fish out.

"No idea," Peg grins. He too will have been with his old lady, but he knows what the single brothers are likely to have gotten up to.

Taking out my phone I glance at the time. "Better get a move on, Peg. Got a long ride ahead. You take care tonight."

"Take care, yourself, Brother."

As Peg slaps my back and moves away, I tap in my code and send a quick text to hurry Beef up, then replace my phone in my cut. My eyes fixed on the clubhouse watching for the big man to appear, I don't notice the man who knocks into me until too late.

"Hey, sorry, man. I tripped."

No harm done, just took me by surprise and made me stumble. I let the hangaround off with a growl, then, happy Beef's at last appeared, waste no time going to our bikes.

I'm glad once we get out onto the open road and are able to get up to speed, the air rushing past at least keeps us cool. Above, the skies are completely cloudless, hopefully we'll escape riding through a monsoon today. It's been a while since I've been on a long ride; I sit back, twist my throttle, and settle in to enjoy it.

With the larger tanks on both our bikes, we've got three hours under our belts before, glancing to my left, I notice Beef's got his arm out to his side and is pointing to his fuel tank. I nod. I'm fairly low on gas too. He catches my eye and with closed fingers puts his thumb to his mouth. Fuck, trust Beef, the big fucker to always be hungry. Seems we're going to have a break.

First thing I do is remove my cut and start folding it to place into my saddlebag as we're out of our territory. It feels lighter somehow. I pat the pockets. *Where the fuck is my phone?* Jean's pocket? No, it's not there either.

"Beef? Do me a favour, will you? Call Peg and see if I dropped my phone at the compound? Lost the fucker." I hope it didn't fall out on the road.

"Can it wait until I've had a piss?"

"Yeah." Wherever it is, it's not with me and I won't be reunited anytime soon.

Beef rings Peg when he's emptied his bladder. Peg says he'll have a look by the bikes as that's where I thought I last had it. Whether it turns up or not, I realise I won't be calling Tash tonight. While I'd given them all her number, I won't give my brother a chance to joke I'm pussy whipped.

Damn. I hate being out of contact. Beef, of course, jerks my chain for losing it. We get back on the road, the rush of the air putting thoughts of my lost communication device behind me.

It's early evening by the time we arrive at Virginia's house. I let Beef take the lead. He's a big fucker, but can be a lot less scary than me.

The door is opened by a man, his receded hairline and deep lines etched on his forehead betray his age. He's distracted, laughing at something that's been said behind him. He rears back when he sees Beef on the doorstep.

"Whatever you're selling, we don't want any." He tries to close the door.

Beef's heavy biker boot is in the way. "We'd like to speak to Virginia, please." He sounds pleasant. Polite. Well, for a biker anyway.

"Ginny? Someone for you?"

A forty-something woman appears behind him. "What do you want?" Her eyes narrow suspiciously. "I don't know you."

Beef steps in. The weedy man takes a step back. Following, I close the door behind me.

"Get out, or I'll call the police," Virginia threatens.

"I wouldn't do that if I were you. Think telling lies is a crime and they might be very interested in what we have to tell them," Beef drawls, lazily.

"Lies?" Her voice is so shrill it hurts.

"About Cobb?"

Interestingly, it's the man who reacts, his eyes flick to the left, looking anywhere but me. I catch on fast. "How much? How much was it worth to ruin a man's career?"

"You Mr Parsons?" Beef asks.

When the man gives a hesitant nod, adding, "I'm her brother," I see the familial resemblance.

"We'll get Mouse checking the financials. Reckon the payment came in your name, didn't it?"

No one says anything. But it explains why nothing suspicious was found in Virginia's bank account. They'd indeed been paid, but her brother took receipt of the payment.

Virginia suddenly speaks. "It wasn't my idea. Clyde made me do it." She glares at her brother who mumbles.

"Didn't take long for you to agree."

Only needing confirmation for now, a money trail is always a good lead, I ask, "Lawson approached you directly?"

As if she knows the game is up, she breathes out and sighs. "It was a man called Neil."

Neil Turner. Who replaced Tash as Lawson's campaign manager.

"Please, please don't hurt us."

Beef's face turns almost as scary as mine. "Not going to hurt you. Yet. You won't see us again as long as you tell the truth. Retract your story. Say you were mistaken as to who the man was. Say you got fuckin' confused. Don't care how you do it. We're going to prove you were paid. If you don't do something voluntarily, we'll give the cops the details. Won't take long for them to come knocking, and after they've finished with you, we, and our brothers, will be back."

"I got confused," she says, slowly. "If I say that, you won't do anything?"

"You be straight with us? You'll not see us again."

Clyde doesn't look happy. "Will we have to pay the money back?"

When I ask, "What money?" he cottons on and looks happier.

"How much does it take to buy people like that, Beef?" I wonder aloud as we return to our bikes.

He leans forward on his tank. "Mouse will be able to find out. Not sure as I want to know. Ruins my faith in the human race. She fuckin' lied, brother. Just to sweeten her life without givin' a damn how she was sourin' that of an innocent man."

She's female. That's what they do. It doesn't surprise me at all.

"Hey, while we were in there, I got a text. This will cheer you up, brother. Peg's found your phone. It was kicked away to the edge of the parking lot. Fuckin' Tommy found it, he wouldn't give up searchin' for it. Persistent fucker when he's given a job."

I chuckle, pleased. I suppose I could ask Beef to get Peg to check what Tash's number is, but then I'll have to give them the passcode. Oh, why the fuck bother? I made no promise, she won't be expecting me to call. She calls me? Peg can answer, he can deal with anything she needs. I eye the small house again, knowing it's harbouring a reminder of just how untrustworthy women can be. I've got a good one though, haven't I? Tash is the exception to the rule. She understands she needs to be straight with me, as I will with her. We'll be alright.

"Not all good news, Blade. Looks like you probably dropped it outside the clubhouse, then someone must have run over it. It's totalled, Brother."

Shit. But it's only a phone. I can replace it.

It takes an hour to get to the Vegas clubhouse. We park up and walk into the converted warehouse, the noise of the Saturday night party in full swing reaching us even before we open the door. Red, the president, is holding court by the bar, a hopeful sweet butt hanging onto his arm. The breeze we've let in from the outside must catch their attention, as Twister swings around.

"Blade, you asshole. Get over here." Grinning widely, I saunter over.

"How's it going, man?"

Beer in my hand, I'm happy to share stories with him. Going back over old times. Twister's one of the good guys. Don't see him much, but when I do we get on. Guess we have things in common.

"Hey, Brother," I say when we run out of the normal topics. "Remember Mouse?"

"Yeah, he's our Keys, isn't he?" Twister nods behind him, their computer guy, hearing his name, raises his hand.

"You know he's half Native?" When he nods, I lean in. "Showed me how to scalp a man."

Twister's eyes widen with professional interest. "Really? Was it hard? How?" His eyes scan the room. "Here, Scrapper." As he shouts out the name, an eager youngster with a cut bearing the word Prospect on it runs over. Twister bends his head down. "Need you so Blade here can give a demonstration. You'd do anything for your patch, right?"

Scrapper gives an eager nod, then the whites of his eyes appear when he sees me take out a particularly evil looking knife.

"Well," Twister continues, "Blade's going to show us how to remove the scalp from your skull."

The prospect gives a nervous giggle, then frowns. I force all emotion off of my face, and step up, my fingers taking a tight grip of his hair making him gasp.

"Man, you're not really gonna…"

"You want your patch," Twister thunders, giving me a wink over the prospect's head.

"Don't nod," I warn him. "Keep very still." Then to Twister. "You start here…" I proceed to show him where he would be removing the scalp, tracing my blade so the prospect can feel it, but not pressing hard enough to cut. "Then," I finish up, "you tug, hard." My fingers dig in, the prospect gasps in air sharply as his hair is yanked, but to his credit makes no sound.

I let him go. Twister slaps him on the back, and laughs. "Will have to try that sometime." He thinks for a second. "How did you get the fucker to keep still?"

As I launch into an explanation, I notice Beef walking off with one of the club girls—Pixie I think her name is—clearly intending to enjoy some private time in one of the rooms.

Twister notices where I'm looking, then glances around. "Hey, Angel, come here."

Angel's pretty enough, her skirt barely covering her ass, her top so low the brown of her aureole can be seen. Her waist is narrow, her legs long, encased in thigh-high boots. In the past I would have been tempted. Now, my cock stays asleep.

It's time to let Twister in on one more thing. "I've got an old lady."

"Well I'll be fucked." His eyes go wide. "Fuckin' Tucson brothers. There is definitely something about that place. You've given up free pussy?" I lower and raise my chin. "You got her knocked up as well? Seems all you Tucson lot do is breed."

There are some things you don't go into. My lack of response and shrug has him roaring with laughter. "Well, if you're not fuckin' because you've got a ball and chain to go home to, best get some liquor into you instead. Rosa? Give us a bottle of the good stuff, will you?"

Despite Twister doing his best to get me hammered last night, I limited my alcohol intake, taking sips while he was throwing back shots. Beef had spent his time fucking his way through the whores rather than taking solace in a bottle, so we're both up relatively early. I'm itching to get back on the road but not, for once, solely for the enjoyment of feeling the pavement rushing under my wheels. I'm anxious to get back to Tash.

Justifying my urge to see her is because my cock stayed firmly in my pants last night, I have a suspicion that it's more than that. When I'm not with her, when she's not in range of my touch, I miss her. It's not just sex, she needs to be there for me to feel complete. The depth of my feelings for her scares me, with the realisation that by letting her in, I've got so much to lose. I've not felt like this for anyone since Jonah.

Now I understand how my brothers feel about their old ladies. Why they'd go to the ends of the earth in order to keep them safe.

Beef twists his throttle to keep up with me, a curious look when I increase my speed yet again. The miles pass by beneath us as we shave vital minutes off the eight-hour journey across two states.

Having left at the crack of dawn, we arrive back early afternoon. I kick down my stand and all but run into the clubroom, my eyes seeking the one person I want, need, to see. They aren't rewarded. So I go to the kitchen. Other old ladies are buzzling around, but not the one I'm seeking.

"Sam. You seen Tash?"

She frowns, and looks at the others. "Actually, I've not seen her today."

She must still be up in the suite. My long legs carry me there quickly, and I throw open the door, an image in my head of her lying there waiting for me dressed only in her lingerie, but I'm to be disappointed. The bed's made, and the room is empty. Her property cut is lying abandoned on a chair.

Where the fuck can she be?

It's a hot day. Perhaps she's gone to the swimming pool? That's the next place she might have gone. But that too, proves a disappointment.

I return to the clubroom intent on questioning everyone I see.

"Hey, Blade. Here's your phone. Last night…"

"Peg, not now. I'm looking for Tash, have you seen her?"

Peg shakes his head. Noticing the expression on my face, he suddenly bellows out, "Anyone seen Tash?"

His roar causes the room to go quiet. Anxiously looking around, I see everyone shaking their heads. Sophie and Marcia look concerned.

It's the ex-cop who speaks. "I saw her yesterday; around lunchtime I think. She was going up to your suite. I haven't noticed her since."

"Well she's not fuckin' there now," I shout.

"She must be somewhere," Heart offers, reasonably. "She wouldn't have left the compound. Come brother, I'll help you look."

"I gave her the phone, Brother. Have you tried calling her?"

Swinging around I look at Joker, about to give him an earful when I realise he probably didn't know. "My phone's busted," I tell him.

Peg starts to get his out, but Beef's already calling her. I remember I'd given them all her number. I glance at him. He frowns. He taps on the contact again.

He doesn't have to say anything. "She's not fuckin' answerin'," I snarl.

"Blade, calm the fuck down. She must be here somewhere." Marvel's hand comes down onto my shoulder, and squeezes, a gesture of support. I shrug him off.

Calm? As if I can fuckin' do that. I breathe in deeply then out, then do it again. Around me my brothers jump into action, arranging themselves into search parties. They search that darn compound, me along with them, but she's nowhere to be found. Every suite, occupied, empty, being built. Every nook and cranny. As their concern grows, my anger begins to take hold. *She's left me.*

I fucking knew I shouldn't trust her.

CHAPTER 36

Blade

When all return to the clubhouse empty handed, I'm so blinded with rage I can hardly see, let alone think.

"Church, now," Drummer snarls. He comes up behind me, his hand grasping my shoulder. "We'll find her, Blade."

"Don't fuckin' bother," I roar back.

"Whoa." Drummer's eyes go cold. "Whatever you're thinking, Blade, we've got to talk through the possibilities. You claimed her, that makes her one of ours. We need to know she's safe."

"Where's Rash?"

"Not now Tommy." For a moment Drummer's eyes soften as they land on the man with tears on his face, shifting from foot to foot, agitated. This is one search where he'd come up empty-handed. Bitch has not only left me; she's caused the man she'd called her friend distress. Prez raises his chin towards Sam, who comes over and takes Tommy away to distract him.

"I'm un-claimin' her, Prez. Bitch has betrayed me."

There's no gentleness in his eyes as he turns back to me, and his fingers, still on my shoulder, bite hard into my skin. "Church, now, Brother."

They want to talk about her disappearance? I'd rather take a bottle of Jack back to my suite. But Prez won't let me get away with that.

"Can't fuckin' understand you, Blade," Peg comes alongside. "Your fuckin' woman's gone missin', and you're immediately givin' up on her? What the fuck did you say to her before you left? She's in danger if she leaves the compound, she knows that. Something fuckin' serious must have gone down for her to take herself off. If you did anything to that girl to make her run away, I'm inclined to take a swing at you myself."

"I didn't fuckin' say or do anything." It's hard to keep my fists at my side. *Why are they blaming me?*

"Church," Prez repeats coldly. With his grip and Peg crowding me, I don't have much choice.

I kick out my chair, almost knocking it over, righting it and then put my ass on the seat. When my brothers are likewise sitting, I explain, "I gave her a phone. Fuckin' stupid." Or right. Best I find out what a liar she is before things go any further. "She must have been lying all the time. Called someone to come collect her. Took advantage of the compound being near deserted."

"Hate to say this," Rock sends me a look of apology, "but with us all gone yesterday, it would have been ideal if she wanted to leave. And for the first time, she was able to communicate with someone on the outside."

At least he believes me. I raise my chin toward him.

"But why would she want to leave?" Peg supplies, his brow furrowed. "She liked it here."

"Blade just claimed her. Maybe she didn't like being thought of as property," Beef suggests.

"Then she should have fuckin' talked to me." I slam my knife down on the table.

"Property patches mean something else in the civilian world. Maybe she thought you'd stop her leaving," Beef says so reasonably, I want to throttle him.

"Who did she call? Who'd come and help her?" Mouse is shaking his head. "Blade have you tried ringing her?" I glare at him as though he's the idiot, and don't answer. It doesn't faze him, he just continues. "Okay, so where was the phone?"

"How the fuck should I know?"

Now it's Mouse's eyes widening as they stare back at me. Then, without another word, he opens his laptop and starts checking. "Thought this was the first thing you'd have fuckin' done, Blade—checked 'Find a Phone'. Fuckin' programmed her details into yours." He's almost mumbling to himself, while I'm thinking he's being unfair. Yeah, technology might be his go to, but it's not mine. And why the fuck should I care where she is now?

After only a second or so, Mouse looks up. "Her phone's at the end of the track. Suggest we get Matt to go down there and check she's not with it."

"You think that's where she is? She's running away on foot?" Surely I would have passed her on the way back.

Again, Mouse's long hair flies around his head as he shakes it. "Let's wait until we hear what Matt has to say. I'll brief him, Drummer."

With that, he leaves the room, then, almost as if there wasn't a break, he resumes when he returns. "Matt will either find the phone, or her. If it's just the device I can check out the phone records, to see who she might have called. But it seems strange; if she had someone who she trusts more to keep her safe from Lawson than she does us, why did she spend so much time living on the streets? It simply doesn't add up. And if a friend collected her, why discard the phone?"

"She could have chucked the phone as she rightly thought you could track her." To me, it fits. "She's a woman," I rasp. "Since when do bitches make sense?

Peg, Wraith, Drummer, Rock and Slick all send me looks of contempt. Heart's shaking his head, Bullet and Viper look incensed.

Even Mouse's face is set. "I was probably one of the last to see her. She came to talk to me. Raised some fuckin' questions as she was concerned about you, Blade."

"See?" I throw up my hands. "She was talkin' to you behind my back. She needed to know anything about me? She should have asked me direct."

Mouse looks like he's going to say something more, but Peg raises his hand and waves him back down. He strokes his long beard. "Apart from Beef's suggestion she didn't like being labeled property, anyone have the slightest suspicions she wanted to leave?" I have to admit, I don't. Christ knows she enjoyed my type of fucking well enough. When silence answers him, the sergeant-at-arms continues, "With all due respect to my Brother, I think we should consider she was lured away. Taken against her fuckin' will."

"Not possible," I refute immediately. In my mind, she's already been tried and convicted. "I gave her a chance, she blew it." Like all bitches do. Sooner or later.

It doesn't stop Peg. "Blade lost his phone yesterday. Tommy found it some hours later, smashed as if a bike had ridden over it. That's what we put it down to, we all rode out. If he'd dropped it, it's possible."

Now our technical man's lips purse. Leaning forward, he exchanges a glance with Peg. Then his cold, dark eyes find mine. "Go get it, Blade."

"What? It's smashed up. Unusable." My eyes flick to the prez pleading him to intercede. It's her we should be discussing, not my carelessness in letting my phone fall out of my cut. Besides, I just used it to call her. *No I didn't, that had been Beef.*

"Get your phone and give it to Mouse," Prez directs, no sympathy in his face.

What the fuck has my phone got to do with Tash going missing? But I do as I'm asked. It takes only a minute before I've retrieved it from the box outside the room. A technicality I put it in there, it's not exactly usable. I pass it over to Mouse with a shrug.

Mouse takes it, turning it over this way and that. "Looks more like a something pointed hit it. I could be wrong, but I'd place a bet it wasn't the victim of a bike tyre."

I shake my head. "I don't understand. Why would anyone deliberately break my phone? That's what you're suggesting, isn't it, Mouse?"

"Take me through what happened yesterday," Drummer requests without waiting for the Native American to answer. "Everything. Leave nothing out. How did you lose your phone?"

What the fuck has this to do with Tash walking out on me? Exasperated, I think back. "I must have dropped it when I took a call outside the clubhouse. I'd taken it out, sent a text to hurry Beef up, then one of the new hangarounds bumped into me..."

Mouse's eyes sharpen. "Step through it slowly. You unlocked it to send a text, yeah? If he was close enough, he could have seen the code you tapped in, then used it himself. Too many things don't add up here, Blade. Which new hangaround was it?"

My features are tight. We're getting into the land of fantasy here. "I dropped my fuckin' phone, okay?"

"Which hangaround, Blade?" Prez's eyes burn into me.

Christ, this is all too far-fetched. "Bertram," I answer reluctantly. *She walked out, took her chance to leave me.*

Why are they focused on the fucking phones? Tash walked out. Didn't she? A small seed of doubt that Tash left of her own accord comes into my head. "Who was on the fuckin' gate, yesterday?"

"Blade." My eyes turn to Joker. "Lady and I were the only ones here, apart from the prospect and the hangarounds. Bertram offered to man the gate."

That seed starts sprouting. Enough so I want to know more. It's clearly a no brainer. "Let's get fuckin' Bertram in here, then. Ask him some fuckin' questions." Looking around, I'm surprised no one's jumping into action.

It's Lady who answers, "Bertram left. In fact, he was in and out a couple of times during the day. Thought nothing of it at the time. But before the rest came back from the rally he came to talk to Joker and me. Didn't like what he was being asked to do. Thought joining would be all about riding bikes, not actually having to lift a finger to work." He shrugs. "Didn't think anything of it. Just wrote him off as not being a fit for the club."

"Shut it, Blade," Drummer growls as I open my mouth. "I'm not fuckin' interested in your accusations any more. You might not care enough to worry about your woman, that doesn't go for the rest of us." He raises his chin and looks around. When no one contradicts him, he carries on, "To sum up, Tash, a woman we've taken under our protection is no longer on the compound. Somehow she left while conveniently most of us were babysitting the man who wants to get his hands on her. A man who knew there would be hardly anyone here. Another convenience, a man we have no knowledge of was manning the gate. Viper, you vouched for him?"

"He seemed okay, Prez. He's a good enough worker, and he was only a hangaround. Didn't research his fuckin' political affiliations."

"Don't want any more hangarounds here until Mouse does a full background search. Okay?" Drummer smooths his hand over his beard, fixing his steely stare on me. "But it's too late to shut that stable door now. Blade lost his phone which seems fuckin' suspicious. If that was my woman, Blade, I'd climbing the fuckin' walls by now."

However she left, perhaps I've had a lucky escape. Should never have let my emotions get the better of the good sense in my head. Women, fuck. The bane of my miserable life.

Tash might have been lured off the compound. Lawson might have her. She might already be dead. Or hurt. She might be carrying my kid.

I look down at the knife I'd been idly spinning in front of me. When I look back up, all eyes are on me. They're waiting for me to say something, my rightful place as I'd claimed her. Just one word, and they'd give their lives to help me save her. *If she's in trouble, that is. Could very well be the thought of being my property which had made her run.*

There's fog in my head and I can't find a way through it. Jonah dead, my mom disappearing. It's like history repeating itself again. I relied on a woman, she left me. My brother's reactions tell me I'm wrong, but I'm frozen. My hands are cold, my heart almost stops beating, still I can't make myself move. In that moment, I hate myself, but the idea she didn't leave by choice won't take root in my head. *She's left me, left me, left me...*

Suddenly, there's a sheet of paper in front of me. "Wasn't going to give you that until we were alone, Blade, but it's the answer to the question Tash asked. The question you've been fuckin' asking for twenty-four years. Well, there's your answer." Mouse's voice is flat.

The paper is face down. My hand hovers, reluctant to turn it over. Raising my gaze, I look at Mouse instead. "What can history have to do with Tash going missin'? The answer to why she left is to be found in the past?"

"Nah, Brother," Mouse replies, his voice quiet, "but it might help to get your fuckin' head together."

I force myself to turn it over. Disinterested, I glance down. It's a copy of a death certificate. *Traumatic head injury.* The date of death is a week after my brother's funeral. The death certificate is my mother's.

Uncertain what I'm reading, I look again at Mouse. He nods across to the paper in front of me. "Your Mom was hit by a car the day after your brother died; walked out into the road without looking according to the reports. She was in a coma, but never regained consciousness."

I can't take it in. I look at the certificate again, then back up at Mouse. The table has gone silent. Time seems to stop while I try to comprehend, to rewrite everything I've thought for more than twenty years. *My mother didn't abandon me. She didn't attend Jonah's funeral because she couldn't.* Everything I've believed has been wrong. Well, she was a shit mother, but not guilty of what I'd been accusing her of. What I'd thought were her actions, the yardstick against which I'd measured every other woman.

Suddenly feeling sick to my gut, I rise and leave the room, my hand over my mouth and tearing out of church. The fog in my head disappearing so fast clarity reappears in a blinding flash which hurts.

"Didn't want to lay that shit on you, Blade. Not like that."

The last thing a man wants is his brother watching him vomiting up his guts. "Get out of here, Mouse."

No sound of footsteps to tell me his obeyed my instruction. "Like I haven't seen you puking before," he scoffs.

I might as well take the advantage while he's here. Pulling on some sheets of toilet paper, I wipe my mouth. "Why did no one come for me?"

Mouse instinctively knows what I'm asking. "You fell through the cracks. Took a while to identify her as far as I can tell."

"She'd have had her purse with her."

"Maybe she was mugged? Attacked? Maybe she was escaping? Fuck knows, whether the cops did a thorough investigation."

It's probably too long ago to find out all the answers. "Why did Tash come to you? Were you going to tell me, Mouse?"

"Yeah. I told her that I'd let you know she was asking, but agreed she did have a point. Tash was convinced there had to be a reason why your mom disappeared."

Probably because Tash would never dream of abandoning a child herself. *Because she's a good woman.* She'd never up and leave without word.

I feel sick again, but this time manage to keep the bile down. Can't afford to waste any more time. "Tash didn't leave of her own volition."

"Nah, I don't think she did. Drummer's sorting out how we're going to search for her. You want to be involved, or stay here feelin' sorry for yourself?"

I stand, flush, then round on him, my face set in determination. I nod. "I'm gonna find my ol' lady."

White teeth appear as he grins. "Glad to hear you say that. Fuckin' glad to hear it."

My hand goes to my fly. "Gotta take a piss first."

"I'm out of here, Brother. Don't need to see your junk."

As the door closes behind him, I relieve myself. In reality, needing a moment to try and get my thoughts together. Will take longer than that to process what I've just heard, to rethink what I've allowed to shape my life. Jonah's still dead, nothing will change that, but I can no longer blame my mom for disappearing when she was actually dying or dead. Can't argue she didn't have a good reason why she never came back. Going to take more than a minute to rethink the last two-thirds of my life.

I've no time to be selfish. Need to find that woman of mine. But how do I go about getting her back?

Returning to church, I find a gap on the opposite side of the table. Casting a glance at Drummer, he explains, "Matt's back. Mouse has gone to talk to him. One thing I can tell you, Blade, he hasn't found Tash. If he found her phone, she wasn't with it." His lips purse, then he continues, "I'm working on the assumption that Lawson's got Tash. I'm also thinkin' we don't have a lot of time."

"Fuckin' suspicious Bertram could have got hold of my phone, and was the one to let Tash out of the gate. Then, disappeared himself. I want to have words with this Bertram." I nod at Peg. I think he's on the right track.

"Fucker was there on Friday when I made a show of giving Tash her property cut." I pinch the bridge of my nose. "Could be he's working for Lawson. A plant. Lawson could have become suspicious of us."

Prez takes a deep breath. "The danger she's in is from Lawson. My vote is for going after him first. Bertram may well have been working for him, or have some kind of connection, but there's no other reason for her to leave." He glances at me. "You got your head out your ass now?"

I nod. The idea that Tash left of her own volition seems the least likely option now. And while I'd like to torture the truth out of Bertram, finding Tash takes precedent. The only person looking for her is Lawson. It's a good bet, find him, we'll find her.

"What we need to know," Prez resumes, "is where Lawson's got her. Then we go in heavy. Don't give him any option other than giving her up. Ideas on where he'll be?"

The door bangs open. All eyes go to Mouse. "Matt found the phone. Blade's phone, before it was smashed, placed a call to Tash's number yesterday afternoon." He nods at me. "Only time I've been thankful you're a suspicious fucker, Blade. I set Tash's phone up to record all calls." He places the device on the table, and presses play. Suddenly we're listening to Tash's voice, and Lawson's.

The silence around the table after the call ends is deafening. *She left because she thought I was in danger.* Reasonable assumption, Lawson had my phone. What was it Lady had said? The hangaround kept disappearing off the compound. Easy for him to take the phone to Lawson, then bring it back and destroy it. I couldn't have found out it had placed a call in the meantime, and Tash couldn't have known its owner had become separated from it.

Christ. *Has all the air been sucked from the room?* I can't fucking breathe. My heart thumps as though it's going to burst out of my chest. *She didn't leave me. She went to fucking save me. She hadn't been thinking of herself, her thoughts had all been for me.*

While I'd had my head up my ass, blaming her of things she was so far from being guilty of, it's ridiculous. Now she might be hurt, dying or already dead. And what had I been thinking? I'd shut her out.

For a moment, I've been numb. Now all feeling floods back with a whoosh that feels like a physical pain. *I could have lost the only woman I ever loved. The only woman for me.* Because I was an ass who didn't even want to look for her. I hadn't seen what was right in front of my face. Tash hasn't a disloyal bone in her body.

My eyes, flaring wildly, find those of the prez. I'm paralysed with fear.

Prez is regarding me, half with sympathy, and half with disgust that I'd allowed my past to influence my actions and thoughts today. But it's his words that at last break the spell my fear has over me.

"His house. Ready to roll?" There's no need for a verbal response, his answer provided by everyone, including me, standing at once. "Five minutes to get your shit together, then we go."

Focus Blade. I might have failed her earlier; I can't fail her now. *I need my knives.* Using those precious minutes, I rush to my suite. It's only then I notice what I'd missed before. Several knives are missing from my display, the smaller ones, those which can be discretely hidden. Ankle sheaths too.

Now I don't jump to the conclusion I might have done before. *Tash is no thief. My brave girl's gone prepared to fight.* I know instinctively, it's for my life as well as her own.

I cast off the remnants of my fear. I can't allow anything to blunt me now. I focus until all my senses feel sharpened, the pain, loss, misguided sense of betrayal have to be put behind me now.

Hold on, Tash. I'm coming.

CHAPTER 37

Tash

Grant leers at me when I get into the car. The last time I had the misfortune to see him, I'd smashed a skillet into his skull. I only wish I had one handy right now.

"Phone." He holds out his hand.

Seeing no alternative, I pass it over. He opens the window and immediately throws it out. Yeah, well I hadn't expected it was going to be that easy. Shame, but that lifeline is gone. It's probably not wise, but I want to remind him he doesn't always have the upper hand. "How's your head?" I ask, snidely.

"My head's fine. Better than yours is going to be." His hand wanders and rests on my thigh. I slap it away, as much worried about him finding the weapons I'm carrying, as it rising inappropriately higher. If he finds one, he'll probably check for more.

He chuckles, and turns with a smirk. "We've got unfinished business, you and me. And I, at least, am going to enjoy it."

Not when I've put a knife through your dick, you won't.

"You don't know who you're dealing with. Me, I can disappear and I doubt anyone would miss me. But Blade? You realise the Satan's Devils won't stop until they find him?"

Another chortle, but he says nothing more. There's no point in having a conversation. No point trying to escape the car. *They've got Blade.* I can only go where he wants to take me and hope that I can take both him and Seb by surprise. *And free my man.*

Of course, I'm scared. My worst nightmare has caught up with me. But now isn't the time to allow myself the luxury of letting fear overwhelm me. I need to channel all my emotions into rage. My hands link together over my stomach, the thought it might not just be me they're going to kill bolsters my courage to go on the attack. No, they haven't the slightest suspicion that they'll be faced with a potential mother bear wanting to protect her young, and save the man she's in love with.

When I was with Seb, I was first the meek employee following instructions as expected. Then I became the girlfriend, wanting to impress. Imperceptibly my lips curve; he's got no idea of the woman who lies underneath, having made no effort to understand me. He's going to find out, you don't mess with a Satan's Devil's old lady.

Could I kill them? Or will I chicken out at the thought of a blade slicing through flesh? Apart from the incident with a skillet, I've never hurt anyone in my life. That incident I remember more for the jolt it sent through my shoulder than the sight of the man collapsed on the floor. Looking sideways at the man driving, I realise I could definitely hurt him again. He makes no bones of what he wants to do with me, and if sticking a blade into him is the only way to stop him, I'll do it. Inwardly I grin. Perhaps there's an innate violence inside me. Maybe that's why the enforcer and I work. That thought, at least for today, doesn't disturb me. Better that than weak.

As the streets and roads go past, I recognise we're coming up to our destination, Seb's home which I've only been to once before. It's a huge gated mansion, and I try to remember the layout. *Where could they be keeping Blade?* But all I remember is the direction to the master bedroom, Seb hadn't wasted any time taking me there. I doubt that's where he'll be holding my man.

Grant punches in a code and the gates open; in the side mirror, I can see them closing behind. I tamp down the sudden thought I might never see anything outside of them again. I squash that negativity fast. *I'll be fighting. I will survive.*

He pulls up in front of the large double fronted doorway. "Get out."

I only pause a second, before I obey. Time to put my plan into action. *Find Blade, give him a weapon, then side by side, we can fight our way out.*

Seb's man pushes me in front of him as he steps up to the door, which is opened as we approach. We're clearly expected. But then, to think otherwise would be stupid. Seb had pushed all the right buttons to get me to give myself up.

What I hadn't expected was to see a woman, Seb's wife, who I recognise from having seen her on TV, hovering in the large hallway. I send her a plea with my eyes, she shakes her head and turns away. *Bitch.* She must know, or have suspicions, about a woman, clearly reluctant, being pushed into the house. She's just ignoring anything odd. *Unless Seb has a habit of bringing other victims in and she's used to it.*

The man who'd opened the door steps aside. "Mr Lawson is in his study," he addresses my companion, not me. I just note there's another person who I'll need to get through to get out.

Am I really in danger? This man, Seb's wife; would they condone a murder happening right under their noses? And a rape, if Grant gets his way. Surely that won't happen here? Maybe they'll take me somewhere else, a place it might be easier to escape from. *Where are they holding Blade? Here?* Or at another location.

Grant raps politely on the door which presumably leads into Seb's office. There's a strange disconnect between what's happening now, and my life just a couple of months earlier, when I'd be entering not dressed in jeans and armed with knives, but in a suit carrying a sheaf of business papers. For a second it's disconcerting when in a normal tone a voice calls out, "Enter."

Even more so when I find Seb looks just as he used to, dressed in sharply pressed slacks and a button-up shirt, top button undone, and wearing no tie. A politician's casual attire. "Ah, thank you, Grant. You can leave us now."

Us doesn't just include me. I'm disappointed to see the man who'd taken over as campaign manager, Neil Turner, also in the room. When I'd worked for Seb, there had been something about him I hadn't liked.

Seb's mouth is pursed in disapproval. My hair has grown out. I hadn't yet taken Carmen up on her offer to style it, Blade seeming to want me to grow it longer instead. I'm wearing no makeup and still have only the borrowed clothes. For a second I shift awkwardly and want to make an excuse, then I remember having to run and leave everything I own was down to the man in front of me. I owe him nothing.

I decide to take the initiative. No way am I going to give a hint of being cowed. "Where's Blade?"

His eyebrows rise at my audacity to speak first, to avoid the necessary polite small talk. "Straight to the point, I see," he responds. "To answer your question, I've got no idea."

That response is unexpected. "You've got him somewhere," I insist. "You told me you had. You spoke to me on his phone."

"His phone, yes. I had that. But not him."

"But...?" His phone call I start to say.

"He was careless, it was easy to take his phone from him. Then, he disappeared without even knowing it was gone." He nods at Neil. "Must reward Bertram for his initiative and pickpocketing abilities."

Neil nods as though he's making a mental note at an ordinary business meeting.

"I was lucky," Seb now speaks to me. "There were a few people that I've entrusted to look out for you. People who came to my attention at rallies. They were, shall we say, rather enthusiastic in the way they supported my views. The societal element that comes in handy, those who aren't afraid to use violence to get their way. Just the sort of people who'd ride with an outlaw motorcycle club."

"The hangaround." He'd been responsible for more than enabling my escape.

"Stroke of luck him deciding he wanted to prospect for the Satan's Devils. Soon as he spotted you, he reported it back. Allowed us a chance to hastily put together a plan. God must indeed be on our side as it went like clockwork." His eyes become hooded. "Oh, my dear, I had no idea how far you'd fallen. You allowed a criminal to claim you? Yeah, Bertram held nothing back."

That's another name on my list of people I'm wanting to kill. *Christ, I'm becoming bloodthirsty.*

"Luckily as it happens, the Satan's Devils are working for me tonight." Seb huffs a soulless laugh. "They've no idea I know who they're watching out for will never turn up. Of course, I'm not going to enlighten them. What a joke. Me insisting on them attending in numbers meant the compound was left empty. The perfect opportunity to get you away. Bertram only had to volunteer for gate duty, and you got out without anyone knowing. I suppose I should admire your loyalty for wanting to exchange yourself for your biker. And, my dear, you must be relieved to discover, the only person in danger, is yourself."

Neil shifts position, moving a step into the room. "Sir, we need to know what she's told them."

Seb's lips press together again. "You've been claimed as an old lady. That doesn't happen overnight. Neil's right to be suspicious. What exactly have you told the Devils? They're supposed to be working for me. Looking for you. Yet they're acting as if they don't know you. I want to know why." He tilts his head. "Were you reporting back to them all along? Did you run straight to them? And if so," he wonders, almost to himself, "what were you doing looking like a crone when Grant ran into you."

I'm not going to give him the satisfaction of answering his questions. There's only one thing he needs to know. "They know everything about you." I can't see the harm in admitting it. "If anything happens to me, guess where they'll be looking? And even if you take me out, they've got the evidence and will use it. You're finished, Seb." I take great delight in the pronouncement.

"Tut tut. You must know by now; nothing ever sticks to me. Grant's got ideas how to make you disappear. I don't even want to know. I'll be at the rally as if nothing has happened. Even if they've got suspicions, there'll be nothing they can prove. As far as they know, you've taken the opportunity and have simply run away."

"Might help to pass her photo around again. So the Devils know who they're supposed to be looking for," Neil helpfully puts in, a not very comforting grin on his face.

"Indeed. Make them think I'm still searching. Get more printed out, will you?" He turns back to me. "You were on the compound, then you weren't. Why would they think that had anything to do with me?" He barks a laugh. "In fact, they'll be my alibi."

I suppress my reaction. Try not to show the cold that's come over me. I'd left. So worried he'd hurt Blade, thinking he must have done so already to get hold of his phone, I hadn't said a word to anyone, or even left a message. I'd just disappeared. Exactly what Blade's mom did to him. Why would Blade want to find me? He wouldn't. *I'm on my own.*

"You think the Satan's Devils are as dirty as you. They're not. They've got enough knowledge to bring you down. Whatever you do to me, that won't change a thing. You think you'll get elected? No chance. They won't let that happen." My tone is icy.

Seb's up and around the desk so fast it stuns me, and before I can evade it, he's backhanded me across my mouth. Immediately I taste blood flowing. "Bitch," he spits. "No one's going to take me down. You think anyone's going to listen to a bunch of criminals?"

"Sir." Neil gets his attention. "We've got her. What if her old man wants her back? Maybe enough to keep quiet?"

"They're not getting her back." Seb parks his hip on the desk, and puts his head into his hands. "Though it might be depriving Grant of some of his pleasures, we could consider keeping her alive a bit longer. An insurance policy should they start to make waves. Just until after the election, of course. Then we'll find a way of bringing the Satan's Devils down. There's city money going into that mall, I'm sure we can find a way of proving they're siphoning it off."

"Can't understand how they got that contract in the first place. Criminal gang like that? I'm sure you're right. We'll be able to find something on them. Or plant evidence if we can't."

Whether Blade will believe I left him and not look for me at all, I won't let them take the Satan's Devils down. I've got to get out of here and warn them. They've given no thought to searching me, apart from Grant having taken my phone. Inwardly, I laugh. Seb always put me in the box of a good little woman who knew her place. It shames me now that I ever let him believe it. But it helps too. They think I've nothing to fight with or for, but I have. Even if Blade thinks I've deserted him with no right to redemption, I may be carrying his child. Just the chance means I'll give all I've got.

As they deliberate what to do with me, I start to plan how I can take them down. I'll have to separate them, needing the element of surprise on my side. Two would get the better of me, but one I, and my hidden weapons, can surely handle. I feel no guilt or disgust at what's going through my mind. Seb's shown himself to be so evil, that I don't mind the thought of leaving the bodies of anyone condoning him behind. He's admitted Grant is going to kill me, and Neil, didn't say one word to discourage him.

As I mentally plot his death, Seb picks up a pen and starts tapping it against his teeth as he thinks of mine. "We'll keep her as I was saying, but after what she's put me through? I deserve payback. No, take that look off your face. Already been there and done that. Don't want in your nasty cunt again, not now you've let all the bikers at you. You're nothing but a dirty whore now. But Grant, well he won't be as fussy. He always wanted in your pants. Will certainly take the smile off your face if I let him have you."

"Not right now," Neil reminds him. "We need him at the rally tonight. Just in case the Satan's Devils are suspicious. Want to have a strong fucker at our side."

Seb rolls his eyes. "He'll probably find a woman to fuck there, either that or get high. But he'll have his prize sooner or later." His eyes snap back to mine. "Don't worry about that."

I don't bother saying he can wait until hell freezes over for all that I care. I'm sure my expression speaks for me.

Seb presses a buzzer on the desk, and the man who'd opened the front door comes in. "Sir?"

"Take Emmalina to the… guest room."

Expressionless the man nods. He's equally unaffected when, taking a firm grip on my elbow, he frog marches me to a room at the back of the house. *Should I try and take him now?* But it's my right arm he's got a tight hold on. Extracting a knife would be awkward, any hesitation or delay, an opportunity for him to shout a warning. *Best wait.* Like a weak woman, I allow him to push me into a barely furnished room. All it contains is an uncovered mattress on a bedframe, a half bath with no door which holds a plain toilet and sink. As I examine my new quarters, I hear a key turn in the lock with a loud snick.

Alone, I allow no despairing thoughts to intrude, framing what I have learned in terms of positives. Blade's safe and, for the moment, so am I. It sounds like I've got a reprieve from Grant, time to consider how best to kill him.

Ruefully I rub my mouth where Seb hit me. Another plus, no teeth were knocked out. But it's sore. I huff a laugh, doubting anyone would offer me a painkiller.

Chapter 38

Tash

Seb isn't a stupid man. He'll know all the tricks in the book. One of them would be his victim sitting alone in this soulless room, knowing eventually that door will open and it's likely that it will be my potential rapist who'll appear. I try not to give in to fear, but it's not easy. Terror builds as the time passes. The sun sets, and while lightning from a distant storm plays outside the locked window, I keep my eyes fixed on the entrance, worried that if I close them, I could be taken unawares.

I've prepared as best I can, keeping two of the knives on my person, placing the others under the mattress at strategic points. If I can't get to one, maybe I can get to the other. The knowledge I'm armed is comforting. When despair threatens, I pat the steel warmed by my body heat and feel determined.

As night turns into morning and still no one appears, I'm going crazy wondering what's going on, whether anyone's looking for me, or whether I've been forgotten already. Does Blade know I'm missing? Or is he still travelling? When he finds out, will he come searching? He never looked for his mother.

Yes, because he loves me. I love him too. He must believe that and that I'd never walk away from him. The man I've come to know, he wouldn't be satisfied until he found me.

He has to come. What man leaves a woman he cares for in danger?

But there's no one to tell him what happened. Another man wouldn't be satisfied, but Blade's been abandoned before. That's why I'm the first woman he's trusted. Will he think my unexplained absence just serves to confirm he was right not to have faith in a woman?

I have to believe he'll be moving Heaven and Earth to find me. I jumped at the chance to save him. Surely, he won't be satisfied until he knows the truth?

That's what I focus on. To believe otherwise would destroy me.

Minutes, hours seem to go both fast and slow at the same time. When I eventually hear footsteps, at first I jump, uncertain. It takes a second to spring into action, taking my planned position behind the door, the procedure I've practiced in my head all night long. Knives appear, one in each hand. I'll have one chance and one only. Grant's a big man, fast, and all too familiar with using his fists. If I don't get the better of him on his entry, he'll easily overpower me.

The key turns in the lock, the door opens. He steps in. For a second he pauses, clearly confused by the empty-looking room, but must cotton on fast as he turns to close the door, realising the only place I can be is behind it.

"Emmalina, I know where you are," he all but sings out.

You sure do, fucker. I aim for his neck with one knife, his chest with another, getting him as soon as he turns. The flick knife is torn from my hand, but I still have the blade I pull out of his chest and stab him again.

"Bitch!" he roars, one hand covering the blood streaming out from his neck. He launches himself at me, seeming not to care he's pushing himself further onto my knife that's lodged between his ribs.

The hilt hits my stomach, making me gasp, his weight crushes me against the wall. I can barely move, but I try to twist my wrist, the one still holding my weapon. Blood is spilling from his neck, dripping onto my face, the warmth and faint metallic odour making me gag.

His hand comes up, he's grabbing at me, ripping my tee. Then, with eyes glazing over, slowly, tortuously slowly, he starts dropping to the floor. As he slides away, my knife, wet and sticky, at last, comes out of his chest.

I stand, my rib cage heaving, trying to get air into my lungs as a large pool of blood begins to spread out from the man now lying on the ground. My eyes are transfixed, watching his chest, hearing a gurgling as he struggles for air. Then he goes still, no movement at all. No sound.

It's one thing imagining him dead, quite another to see it. Knowing how much I hated him, even though I was all too aware he'd have shown me no mercy, it is more disturbing than I'd expected to watch the life fade out of a body and know I'm responsible for it. I feel no pleasure at my accomplishment. Disgust at the bloodiness, but strangely, no actual remorse. Maybe it will hit later.

I stand, knife dripping with blood pointing down to the floor in my hand, unable to take my eyes away from the corpse at my feet. *Get moving. Pull yourself together. You can't stay here.* My pep talk to myself takes a couple of minutes to have an effect, but eventually, my legs start working. I ease around him to get out of the door. Then I think for a second. I hate to touch him, but he's blocking the entrance, anyone walking past would see him immediately. It takes a lot of effort to move him, my hands having difficulty gripping clothes which have become slippery, but at last it's done and he's out of the way. Collecting the other knives I'd hidden, I go out into the corridor, closing and locking the door behind me.

I can't relax. I need to get out of the house. Need to get a message to the Devils. Shit. Perhaps I should have searched

Grant to see if he had a phone. I hover for a moment, unwilling to go back and search his corpse. Even if I found his, I don't know Blade's or any of the other Devils' numbers. I can't call the police, I just killed a man and am covered in his blood. I'm on my own.

Is there a back entrance? Damn, I don't know. Last time I was here, I wasn't checking out escape routes. That seems another lifetime ago. Before I knew what a bastard Seb was, and that he already had a family.

His wife's around here somewhere. Seb himself? Probably. Neil? Can't rule it out, they seem to live in each other's pockets. And Lurch, of course—the name I've mentally given his manservant—the man who'd locked me in that room.

The house seems claustrophobic and airless as I walk down the hallway, retracing the path I'd taken the day before, trying to keep the image of Grant's dead body out of my mind. Shock is starting to set in, I'm shaking like a leaf, but I refuse to break down and give in to it. Time for that once I've escaped the house.

On tiptoe, keeping to the wall, I approach the entrance hall. I hear voices in the office where Seb and Neil had confronted me yesterday. I pause a second outside to see if I can distinguish who and how many. Then, horrified, I see the door handle turning as someone prepares to come out.

In a split second I determine the front door is too far away; my only option is to slip inside another room that's right behind me. Immediately I do, I see it's a large kitchen, with what looks like a pantry. I head that way, quietly opening it and stepping inside, closing the door behind me, and not a moment too soon.

"Mrs Lawson. I was about to start dinner," I hear Lurch say. "How many will there be tonight?"

Seb's wife has obviously entered with him. "The children are still away with their grandparents. It will just be Seb and I this evening."

"Mr Turner's not staying?"

"I don't think so. Not today. He left just now."

"Right, ma'am. I'll get a start on it."

"Um," she starts hesitantly. "What about our guest?"

"Guest?"

"The woman who came yesterday."

There's a gap, then Lurch says, "I don't know if Mr Lawson wants her to have a snack or main meal. I'll talk to him and see what he says."

Don't feed me, please. If they go and find Grant dead, they'll turn the house upside down trying to find me. I'd rather they let me starve. They haven't fed me so far today; it seems Sally Lawson is the only one to consider my comfort in this place.

I presume she's left as I don't hear her voice any more, but I do hear pots, pans and plates. Crossing my fingers, I hope he doesn't break any and need a dustpan and broom. Just in case, I have my knife ready.

I'm squashed and in an odd position. After a while my muscles start to protest, but it's my life that's on the line, so I ignore the pain. There's been silence for a while, maybe Lurch has gone away?

Daring to crack the door open, I peer out. He might be working for a corrupt man, but there's an amazing aroma in the kitchen that's making my mouth water, but except for a pot bubbling, I'm alone. Right, time to get out of here.

Where the hell's the back entrance? There's a utility room, but I don't want to get trapped there if there's no way out. Main door it is. Carefully, I exit the kitchen the same way I went in.

I've chosen the exact wrong moment. Seb is stepping out of his office, Lurch just behind him. I run to the front door, but can't open it, it must be deadlocked. Seb's only a step away when I spin and launch myself toward another door, throw it open, jump inside, and slam it behind me. Just my luck! There's no freaking key to lock it.

A scream announces I'm not alone. Sally is getting to her feet, her hand covering her mouth in horror when she sees me covered in blood.

I've only got a split second to do something. Throwing myself toward her, I spin her around so her back is against my chest, and have a knife held against her jugular just as Seb slides to a halt inside the door.

"I'll call the police," Lurch says, pulling a phone out of his pocket.

"Throw that over here, or she's dead." The voice coming out doesn't sound like mine at all. But the tone convinces him I mean it. The squeak from Sally as I deliberately prick her neck, doesn't harm my case either.

He looks quickly at Seb, who swallows and nods, and the phone's sliding across the floor toward me.

"Yours too." I challenge Seb to tell me he doesn't carry one. He doesn't bother. In a second I have another shooting my way.

"You're not going to hurt her," Seb says. He clearly hasn't guessed what I've already done today. I choose not to enlighten him though the blood sticking as it dries on my clothes and skin should provide some clue. His next words show he's not as blind as I'd first thought. "Grant? I presume you and he have already had… words. I can't think you've managed to get the better of him." Oh, so he's not as clueless as I thought. Still, I keep quiet. Let him think Grant's only injured, and will bring the cavalry to save the day.

What do I do now? It seems easy on television where the hero escapes using a hostage as a shield. I don't like frightening people, but… "If your husband or Lurch there make one move to stop me leaving this house, I will hurt you," I tell the woman shaking in my arms.

"Lurch?" The manservant looks puzzled and quickly looks around as though expecting to see someone else.

I shrug. "From the Addams family."

A slight grin curves Seb's lips. I can't allow that. I want him frightened, knowing I'm serious. He cared enough about his wife to bring her back to Arizona, he needs her. He can't want her dead.

Seb stares, then barks a laugh. "I have to admire your spirit, but you're not going to get out of here, Emmalina. You're holding no cards at all. Threatening Sally? Nah, not much of a threat. Go ahead, kill her. You'll be doing me a favour. I get rid of two annoying bitches at once." *Okay, so maybe I was on the wrong track.*

"Seb!" Sally's stilled in my arms. She goes rigid as the implications set in, then she squeals, "Seb, please."

"Oh shut it, woman. I hate it when you beg. Or whine. Or spit out kids I don't want. Yeah, go ahead and kill her, Emmalina. I'll be rid of my burden of a wife, and you'll be locked up for murder."

"I won't hurt you," I murmur into Sally's ear. "Just trying to make it look like I will."

"He'll kill me himself and make it look like you did it," Sally offers equally quietly, shaking with fear. "He's just using me for appearances. A grieving widower might get more sympathy than a husband with a loving wife."

"What are you two talking about?" Seb takes a step toward us, I draw Sally a step back.

"Can I trust you?" I ask out of the side of my mouth, trying to process what's going on and calculating my next move. Wondering if I'm doing something stupid, when she, carefully due to the blade that's at her neck, nods her head and I admit to her, "A Lawson is going to die today; do you understand me?"

"I hate him." The tone of her voice, the slight relaxation of her body in my arms, suggesting she doesn't see me as the greatest threat, makes me believe her.

"I have a spare knife in my right pocket," I hiss softly, almost under my breath.

Seb takes another step forward. "Go on, kill the bitch."

I feel Sally's hand probing my front pocket. "Back one," I correct, as she reaches around me. I feel her take it out. "Press the button, it's a flick knife." I hear the snick which means she's done as I said.

"Sir. I don't think you ought to go closer," Lurch nervously suggests, as Seb comes even nearer. His eyes transfixed at the knife I've still got pressed to Sally's throat. "Sir, I don't think she's joking."

"I don't think so either." Seb's face has lit up. It looks like he's salivating at the thought of me spilling his wife's blood.

Lurch suddenly proves he's got a backbone. He moves fast, putting himself in front of his employer to shield him. As he does, I've already begun the motion of setting Sally free and stepping to her side instead. My threats haven't worked, there's no way I'm going to hurt her, which means I've got to take on Seb. My hand itches to gut him like the pig that he is.

It happens so quickly. All Lurch can see is that I've set Sally free. He leaps with a clear intention to get her out of harm's way, not realising she's brought her knife around to the front to defend herself from her husband. It sinks into his chest.

Immediately he looks downwards, and his hand goes to the hilt. Not wanting what could be an innocent man to die, I scream, "Leave it. You could do more damage pulling it out." I've not really got a clue, but watched enough ER to know that.

Sally's standing stunned. It's Seb who's moving. He hasn't the same compunction to keep his man breathing, pulling the knife out of his chest and approaching his wife with it.

Now it's Sally standing behind me.

My blade had been one I'd had in an ankle sheaf. It's longer than the flick knife Seb's holding. But he's stronger. *Quicker? Luckier? Deadlier?* That remains to be seen.

He's approaching. Sally is dragging me back, but she's not helping. There's nowhere for us to go. *I've got one chance at this.* I hear Blade's voice in my head, feel his hand on mine, guiding me, showing me the best place to stab with the knife. I raise it.

Seb starts dancing on his feet. A step this way, then that, the knife he's holding going back and forth. It's like watching a snake preparing to strike. I bend slightly, anticipating the moment he'll stab forward…

A burst of thunder as if the heavens are providing a symphony in the background. *But it's not thunder making the windows rattle.* It's not a storm sent by Mother Earth. Instead it's bikes.

It's the Devils.

CHAPTER 39

Blade

Mouse had unlocked the gates with some gadget of his, and we followed Drummer up the sweeping driveway, not wasting a second pulling around and parking backed up against the front of the house. I'm off my bike fast, but Drummer's there first, his meaty fist banging at the door. When there's no answer, he waves Peg forward, and the rest of us back.

Peg takes aim and shoots out the lock.

"Now search this fuckin' place," Drummer snarls. "We find Tash, or someone to tell us where the fuck she is."

"I need the office, see what other shit Lawson might own, and where he could have taken her." Mouse reaches for the door closest to us. But on opening it, instead of walking in, he freezes. "Blade. I think you'll want to see this," he throws over his shoulder, before stepping inside.

I can't tell from the tone of his voice what to expect, so my heart's in my mouth as I go to the doorway, tense, preparing myself to find Tash dead. I come to a halt, my eyes wide when I see my old lady standing there with one of my knives in her hand, facing off against Lawson, who's also got a blade. On the floor is a man in a pool of blood clutching his chest. Behind Tash is a cowering woman, who I think is Lawson's wife.

"Guns trump knives." Mouse, faster than me, is already there, a gun to the politician's head. "Drop it," he growls.

His words spur me to move. Never taking my eyes off Tash, who's still got that knife in a death grip, I take a zip tie out of my back pocket, and soon have Lawson's hands fastened behind him.

"What the fuck's going on?" Drummer steps into the room. He eyes the scene, including the man bleeding. Then raises an eyebrow at Tash. "Your handiwork?"

I cross to her, noting someone has obviously hit her in the face, her mouth is swollen with dried blood on her lips. But that's nothing to the blood covering her body. "Are you hurt?" I question harshly, fear that she's seriously injured making me tense, scared to touch her anywhere in case it hurts. My hands hover uselessly, not knowing how to help.

Looking down, as though seeing herself for the first time, she shakes her head. "No, it's not mine. It's Grant's."

I glance at the man on the floor as I gently take the knife from her trembling hand. "This Grant?" I ask gruffly.

"No, that's Lurch."

"I did it," a quiet voice says from behind Tash. "It's not her fault, nor mine. It was an accident."

Beef is on his knees examining the man on the floor. "Think we need to call an ambulance for him. Lurch, isn't it?"

"I'm not fucking Lurch. My name is Malcolm," the man on the floor spits out in a voice that's more spirited than I expect from someone whose blood is soaking the carpet. He can't be too badly hurt.

I glance at Tash who shrugs, showing no remorse. "Well he looks like Lurch to me."

I grin, suddenly remembering the manservant from the Addams family. Then I study her carefully. My old lady is standing there, dried blood on her face and in her hair, her t-shirt soaked and torn, her complexion pale, but defiance still shining from her eyes, and I can delay no longer. I pull her into my arms, loving the way she immediately relaxes into me, getting a sense of peace now she's back where she belongs.

"Tash, you alright?" Drummer's stepped up to us. "Need to talk to you."

"What about me? I'm dying here."

"You're not dying," Beef declares, "but you might be if you don't shut up."

Tash pulls away from me, just enough to fix her eyes on the prez. "I'm okay, Drummer. Well," she offers me a small smile, "I am now."

"Come with me." Drummer turns and leaves the room. With my arm around Tash, I lead her out into the hallway. Once there, Prez asks, "Need to know what's happened here so we can sort out the best way of dealing with this."

Tash raises and dips her head. I feel a change in her, a tension, notice a tear rolling down her face. The adrenaline rush that's powered her is obviously fading. My hand caresses up and down her back in a tactile gesture of encouragement.

I feel her take a deep breath, then she starts, "Seb got me off the compound. Brought me here. Earlier he sent Grant to rape me." My arm tightens around her. It takes enormous effort not to run back into the other room and slice Lawson open myself, but I don't. I'm not going to fail my old lady, and right now, she needs me. She's hesitated, waiting to see how I'd react.

"Go on," I murmur softly, giving a small nod to the prez. *I'm in control. Just.*

"I'd taken some of your knives, Blade—they hadn't bothered to search me—didn't expect me to be armed. I managed to get the drop on him." She waves down at her clothes. "This is his blood. I'm pretty certain I killed him."

"Where is he, pet?" Peg, who's stepped closer to listen, growls.

"In one of the back rooms, down that way." She waves with her hand. Peg goes off in the direction she's indicated.

Drummer points to the room we just left. "And in there?"

"I was trying to escape." She swallows, and her eyes flare as she seems to be reliving the panic she'd experienced. Her words are rushed. "I couldn't open the door to get out. Seb, well, he saw me. I ran into the nearest room, Sally, his wife was there. I threatened her with the knife, told him I'd kill her." She glances up at me. "I couldn't have done that."

"I know, sweetheart, I know." Ignoring the blood, I nuzzle her hair.

"Seb told me to go ahead. He wanted us both dead, Drummer. Either that, or me locked up for murdering his wife."

She's shaking so hard as she begins to come down fast. I want to get her out of here, but Drummer still wants answers. "Lurch?"

"I gave Sally a knife to defend herself. It's all a bit confused, but I think he thought he was protecting her. He managed to throw himself on it."

"Drummer, I'm gonna take Tash outside." I'm the enforcer for the club. Normally I'd be all over this shit. But my concern for my old lady tops my desire to seek vengeance. Realising I'm abdicating my responsibilities, I stare steadily at the prez, surprised to see his face soften.

"Yeah, get Tash back to the club. I'll sort things out here."

When Tash steps out into the fresh air, she raises her face to the sun and breathes in deeply. It's then I realise how fucking scared she must have been. Threatened with being raped, killing a man, thinking she'd soon be dead herself. Knowing, if we hadn't arrived in time, it was going to be Seb against her. That's she's not a crumpling wreck on the ground reminds me just how fucking strong she is.

"I called Mariana," Mouse's voice behind me makes me jump. "She's bringing Drew's car."

I'd been thinking of her arms around me as I took her for the first time on my bike, but Mouse's foresight has reminded me Tash is covered in blood. Hard to hide if we're seen by the cops. Last thing I want is to get pulled over today. Turning, I thank him.

"Low on prospects, aren't we, Mouse?" My comment needs no answer. But as Matt will be needed by the prez for clean-up, I'm more than thankful Mouse has thought to call his wife to give us a lift. After what Bertram did, none of us are in any hurry to trust hangarounds.

Tash and I wait in a shaded spot. I hold her close, reluctant to let her go.

"I was worried, Blade…"

"Hush, sweetheart. Of course you were." My arm tightens around her as I consider that to be the understatement of the century.

A shake of her head tells me the obvious wasn't where she was going. "Seb gave me no time. He said he had you, and that you'd die if I didn't go that moment. I was in a blind panic. I was desperate to get to you. That's why I brought the knives. So you'd be armed."

"Darlin'," I close my eyes for a second, experiencing the pain she must have felt. Similar to mine when I knew she was missing. Her first reaction had been to run to me. Mine, I'm ashamed to admit, had been to run away. Something I vow to spend my life making up for.

"I didn't know if he'd already hurt or killed you. I just ran, Blade. I had to get to you."

Knowing what I'd first thought, I almost can't bear hearing her side of the story.

"Then," she continues, "when Seb told me he'd stolen your phone," a distraught sob escapes her mouth, "I thought you'd think I'd just disappeared on you just like your mom. That's why I did what I did, why I was so desperate. I thought I had no one to rely on but myself. I was going to kill Seb, Blade. In just another minute..." Her pause tells me she was going to have a fucking good try, but knew success hadn't been guaranteed. "I didn't think you'd come to my rescue." Another loud sniffle, followed by more, "I couldn't wait. I thought all I could rely on was myself." Her hand slides down and rests on her stomach.

Fuck! She thought I'd abandon her and my child too. I sweep my free hand through my hair. I feel sick to my stomach as I acknowledge I can't even contradict her. That's exactly how I reacted. Christ. How alone must she have felt? Being threatened with rape and a painful death without even the comfort of knowing that I'd be moving Heaven, Earth and the bowels of Hell trying to find her. Holding her to me, I just let her tears fall, powerless to find any words of comfort. Unwilling to lie because she's exactly right. Unable to tell her the truth as that would only hurt more.

All I can do is resolve to do better. To never let her down again. To always be there for her. My whole life has been turned on its head, for two-thirds of it, I've been living a lie. It's going to take time to become a new person, but for her, I'll try.

But it's when she turns and grips my cut, looking straight into my eyes and saying, "Thank you. Thank you for coming. Blade, I dreamed, but never hoped." There's the beginnings of a smile as she adds, "Now I know how much you must love me."

Bowing my head, I realise I need to tell her the truth. Can't have secrets between us, not of this magnitude. Can't start the rest of our lives on a lie. But will she ever forgive me? "You asked Mouse to look into my past," I say, casually.

Her eyes no longer meet mine. "I'm sorry," she whispers.

"Nah, babe. Don't apologise. Best fuckin' thing anyone's ever done for me." I grimace. "Played my cards too close to my chest. Should have investigated myself years ago."

"He found your mom?"

Taking a deep breath, I explain exactly what Mouse had discovered. Her reaction is what I'd expected from her.

"Oh, Blade. I'm so sorry. I know you said she wasn't the best mom, but to find out you lost her, and didn't even know…"

As her hand rests on my face, giving me comfort, I don't dismiss her concern. It's going to take time to sort things out in my head. Tash, without needing to talk it through, understands. Time to stop prevaricating and admit it.

"You weren't wrong, babe. I nearly didn't come," I say at last. "Thought you'd walked out. Lumped you in with my mom. Was going to give you up. But…" as I feel her hand lift away I cover it with my own, holding it tightly. That understandable flash of hurt in her eyes showing me her palm may well have made contact for a third time with my cheek if I hadn't done something to prevent it. "Listen, babe," I say hurriedly, "No excuses for me at all. But even though I was a dick, and wasn't going to come looking myself, I knew you weren't going to be abandoned. While my head was stuck up my ass, Drummer wasn't hanging around. He was preparing to come for you, and would have, along with my brothers, even if I was too blind to see what was in front of me."

Fresh tears start to trickle down her face, and there's a sad shake to her head.

"Babe, I'm trying. I'm gonna spend all my fuckin' days trying. That slap around the face you wanted to give me just then? May end up deserving a few more. I've spent too long unable to trust any woman at all. It's my go-to kick-off point, the idea that I can't get hurt if I always believe the worst."

"You can trust me, Blade. I thought I'd proved that."

She's battling with the idea I didn't care enough to come to save her. I tap my heart. "Know that, darlin', in here. But here?" My knuckles rap my forehead. "Might need you to knock some sense into me after all." Raising her hand, I touch the palm against the side of my face. I'm rewarded by a weak smile.

Then her brow furrows. "Why, Blade? Why did you say Drummer would have come anyway? Why would Drummer care?"

I chuckle softly at the confusion on her face. "Because you're one of us now. I claimed you." She considers that for a moment, so I add, "Even when I'm being an asshole, my brothers will always have your back."

Another contemplating stare, then she wipes the last of her tears from her eyes. As a familiar car sweeps in through the gates, the old banger I helped Mouse buy for Drew, she glances at me, looking a little chirpier now that her ride away from this house of horror has arrived. She even gives me a smirk. "There are some benefits to being your old lady, then."

I lean in close. "Let's get you home, and I'll show you a few more."

Mariana gets out and runs over as I hold out my hand and help Tash to her feet. "Oh my goodness, are you okay?"

Tash gives a sassy grin, the expression reassuring me more than anything else that she's coming back to herself. "I'm fine. The blood's not mine. Just need a shower."

Mouse's woman has to be curious, but knows enough to bite her tongue and not ask. "Well let's get you back to the compound." Mariana opens the passenger door, seeming surprised when Tash gets into the back seat. "You coming too, Blade?"

I'm not leaving Tash alone. Not today. Not for a moment.

Mariana's style of driving is frustrating when I'm in a rush to get home, anxious to start showing Tash just what benefits she's entitled to by being my old lady. But she obeys every speed limit, slowing at traffic lights just in case they go red. Curbing my impatience as she's doing us a favour, I satisfy myself with a glance over my shoulder. Tash's eyes have closed. Now in the safety of the cage, removed from the bloodbath we've just left, she seems, at last, able to relax. My lips thin, thinking she can't have turned off for a moment since she left the compound.

I must have been right, and she'd been dozing. She's a bit groggy as we arrive at the compound. Mariana drives up to the clubhouse to let us out before she'll be taking the cage back down and parking it behind the auto-shop. I help a dazed Tash out of the back seat and lead her directly up to my suite. Hers, too. It's going to take a while to get used to saying that, but fuck me, it feels right.

Once inside, I leave her for a second to get the shower going, then return. As her hands go to her shirt, I stop her.

"Let me. Just relax now. I'll do all the work."

"I'm just so tired, Blade."

"I bet you didn't sleep."

"Would you? Knowing a man was going to come and force you to do things you didn't want?" She shudders. I take it as a rhetorical question which doesn't need a response.

"You're here now. Let me take care of you."

I pull her bloody tee over her head, then unbutton and unzip her jeans. For once there's nothing sensual or sexual in what I'm doing. I've never touched a woman like this before, when it wasn't a prelude to sex. Suddenly it feels like ice cracking inside of me as I discover parts of myself that were hidden. Wanting to take care of my woman, in any way she needs it.

Once she's naked, I quickly divest myself of my own clothes, and lifting her, carry her into the shower. She makes no protest as I wet then shampoo her hair. Washing and rinsing it three times to make sure all trace of the blood has gone. Then I turn her to face me, upset to see tears streaming down her face.

"Sweetheart, what's up?"

"Blade." One word, then she's clinging to me. Sobbing so hard it feels like my own heart will break.

"You're safe. I've got you. I've got you now." Over and over I voice platitudes while the water pours over us, washing those tears away. Finally, *thank fuck* the sobs becomes sniffs snuffled against my chest. Gently I take the sponge and wash her body, rinse us both then turn the cascading water off.

A clean towel is waiting, I wrap it around her, grabbing another quickly for myself and towelling the worst of the water off, before my attention is one hundred percent back on her. Still dripping, I carry her to the bed, then lie, pulling her into my arms.

Uncaring we're dampening the bed, I rock her, telling her I love her, then repeating it, willing her to believe me. She begins to relax, her head nestling into my shoulder.

"Sleep, sweetheart."

She does.

The moment I feel her deadened weight and know she's succumbed to her fatigue, no longer fully focused on getting her on the road to recovery from her ordeal, images begin to flow into my head. *Mouse calling me into that room, seeing Tash standing with my knife in her hand, in a stance that said she was prepared to fight for her life.* That picture is etched in my mind; I don't think I'll ever forget it. If we'd been minutes later, she might have fought. Might have lost. Stuffing my hand into my mouth to prevent a cry escaping, events from the day continue to assail me. *The fear I'd felt when I'd seen her covered in blood. The thought she could be badly injured. Sometimes, in the heat of a fight people don't know they've taken a fatal blow until it's too late.* I could have lost Tash. If our arrival had been delayed, it would have been my fault for having my head so far up my ass, I couldn't separate past and present.

I'll never let you down again, Tash. I vow it.

She'd put herself in danger to save my life. How could I ever not trust her?

My body is trembling as I think how close I came to never holding her in my arms again. She sleeps on, I stay awake, unwilling to miss a moment of time with this woman. The woman who I'm not letting go. Ever.

Would my life have been different if I'd done more twenty-four years ago? If I'd tried to find my mother? Knowing the truth then would have changed me. But what could a twelve-year-old have done? It had been the system that had failed me, not a person. A simple twist of fate that meant my mom had died without identification. She'd been identified at some point, else the death certificate wouldn't bear her name, but presumably, by then, I had disappeared.

Do I want to know the answers? Mouse might be able to find out more. Probably not. It wouldn't change anything.

It's going to take more than a minute to rewrite my life, but I can do it, with Tash beside me. Not knowing the truth has blunted me all these years. Now I've let her in, I feel I've been sharpened, able to feel all the emotions I've hitherto kept buried.

I lost Jonah. Lost my mom too, though I didn't know it. It took Tash to make me step off that cliff. Tash, who was my safe landing.

She sleeps on. I want to be nowhere else but here with her.

CHAPTER 40

Tash

ey." Slowly opening my eyes, I see Blade's stunning blue pupils staring into mine.

"Hey, yourself, babe." His fingers gently trace my mouth. I flinch. "Sore?"

"A bit."

His face darkens. "I hope Drummer made him hurt."

I'm confused. "Don't you know?"

"Nah, I've stayed here with you." He reaches over to the table on his side of the bed and picks up his phone. "You've been asleep for six hours."

"And you been here all that time? Shouldn't you have been doing enforcery things for the club?"

"Enforcery things?" he chuckles. "Babe, not sure I like it being called that. And no, the club can handle shit without me for a while. You're most important right now. My brothers will have my back."

That is so not what I expected from him. Like a cat, I stretch. Suddenly I realise I'm not wearing any clothes and lying next to an equally naked man who's sporting a very aroused cock. "Hmm," I murmur, turning, and rubbing myself up against him.

"Someone's woken up horny," he grins. "Not that I'm complainin' of course."

"Mmm, mmm." It's hard to form words when the fingers of one hand are trying to coax my nipples into peaks, a job which I admit isn't very difficult, and his others are trailing their way down my stomach. I'm writhing, already anticipating the destination that hopefully they'll reach quickly.

Very gently, he leans and places a light kiss on my swollen lips. Even though they're bruised, I push against him, trying to make him give me more.

"Uh uh," he waggles his head side to side. "But as I can't kiss there…"

He slides down my body, and well, who am I to protest? Instead I start making unintelligible sounds when he commences to more than make up for the caress he couldn't apply to my mouth. Propping my head on my arm so I can absorb the sheer eroticism of the sight of his head busy between my thighs, I settle in to enjoy the ride.

Oh my God he's so talented. Any thoughts of not being an active participant disappear when he slides his tongue inside me, lapping at the wetness I can already feel. Then a slow glide to my clit, which he teases with small circles, avoiding applying direct pressure. His head raises a fraction as he huffs a warm breath, even that is enough for my fingers to curl into my palms.

Whether it's the knowledge I'm here and safe, whether it's to do with the overwhelming fear I experienced when I'd been literally fighting for my life, or it could simply be Blade's expert touch, he's making me reach levels of arousal I hadn't realised were possible.

He hoists one of my legs over his shoulder, then the other, opening me to him even more. Now avoiding my throbbing clit, he pushes his tongue inside me, the sensation only pushing me to greater heights, until I feel like a compressed spring. I moan. In this position, I've no option but to take what he's giving.

Then he pulls back. Opening my eyes, I frown as I see him staring. "Blade," I wail. Trying to buck my hips to get him to do something to relieve my overwound sensation.

"Never thought one cunt would be able to satisfy me, but yours, babe? Prettiest I've ever seen in my life." He leans in closer, breathing deeply. "Your perfume, best I've ever smelt."

"Do you think the compliments could wait until later?" I protest.

He chuckles. "What do you want, babe? Some of this? Want my fingers inside you?"

I don't care how he does it. Each time he speaks, my over-sensitised skin feels the exhaled air as a caress, keeping me on edge. "I want you," I cry out again.

"You want to come, don't you, babe?"

His fingers abruptly invade me. The unexpected, but welcome intrusion, forces a wail out of my mouth. His lips curve as he sees my flush which betrays he's got the right spot. At last he lowers his head, and now fingers and tongue work me expertly. The build-up of anticipation has me screaming as my body again starts tensing, my stomach rolls with euphoria, and my muscles clench, seize, then pulsate as the strongest orgasm I've ever experienced washes over me.

He wastes no time, rolling a condom on quickly, then, before I've come down, he's thrusting inside me, driving into me so hard it's almost punishing as he reaffirms his ownership of my body. There's no denying it belongs to him. My response to his onslaught takes me to heights I've never known, would have thought it impossible for any man to make me feel this way.

As I start tightening all over again, I interpret what I'm experiencing. It's my love, my emotional connection to Blade that's intensifying this experience, taking what we're doing far out of the realms of fucking and into lovemaking.

"Blade!" I scream his name.

"Yeah babe, I'm with you. Come for me."

Christ, I can't take it. I can't breathe, can't see; I swear I pass out for a moment as the intensity of my response floods over me. When I finally start to descend from my peak, I feel Blade's short little stabs, as he empties his all into the latex, his pumps gradually slowing as he gives me everything he's got.

Then his head is on my chest, his breathing is jerky, lungs heaving in unison with my own.

"Fuck, woman. You're going to kill me."

"Back at you," is all I can say.

He lowers my legs from his shoulders, I'm incapable of moving myself, then collapses forward. We lie like that, both recovering. I don't know how long it is before I'm aware of other things, the air conditioning blowing cold air over my sweaty skin, the weight of him covering me, and the tears in my eyes.

"Babe, what's wrong?" He sits back on his haunches, his hands carefully securing the end of the condom as he pulls out of me, removing it, tying the end and discarding it in a bin by the bed. "Tash, speak to me." One hand caresses my cheeks as concerned eyes stare into mine.

My arms go around him, pulling him to me as I let out a loud sob. Then I'm crying in earnest, and Blade's tugging me up, manoeuvring me, then rocking me gently. "It's okay, babe. I'm here. I'm here, you're here. You're safe."

"I killed a man." I weep against his chest. The moment when my knives went into Grant's neck and chest coming back to me. The horrific recollection of his blood pouring out, soaking my hair, my skin, my clothes. It's as though I'd suppressed everything inside me, until the physical release had brought it out. "I killed him, Blade."

"It was you or him, Tash. You shouldn't waste one moment of sympathy on that man. He had none for you. You did the only thing you could. If you hadn't, you wouldn't be here now. You get that, Tash? You hearing me? You put down an animal."

He keeps talking, keeps trying to find ways to reassure me. But none of it really sinks in. It's as if my soul's been blackened from my actions.

"Tash, look at me." He turns me to face him. "You know what I do, don't you babe? I don't have to hide myself from you, you know what I am, inside. I'm no killer, yet I maim, torture and end lives for the club." He's never said it so plainly before, but from his title, I'd inferred what he did was something like that. "I'm no killer," he repeats, "I'm an artist. What I do goes against what I feel, here." He places my hand over his heart, I take strength from the way it beats beneath my fingers.

"How do you cope, Blade? How can you do what you do?"

"My club is my family. I do what I wish I could have done to save Jonah. I fight for them. I have never, ever, hurt a man who didn't deserve it, Tash. That's how I cope. Knowing I've removed evil from the world, and have protected my brothers. That's what you did. If Grant had lived, how many more lives would he have ruined? How many women would he have raped? Was his life worth more than yours? Nah. It wasn't. It would have been you or him babe, and I'm fuckin' glad you were the one who survived."

"But I still took someone's life."

"Tash." The sharpness in his voice gets me to meet his eyes. They flare with the intensity of his words. "Are you now going to go out on a killing spree? Kill for the sake of it? His blood given you a taste for more?"

"Of course not," I snap.

"You're no murderer," he repeats. "It was self-defence, babe. Believe me." His palms cradle either side of my face. "Tash, I'm fuckin' proud of you. Fuckin' in awe of how you went there to save me." He leaves one hand on my face and moves the other to rest on my stomach. "When you have my baby, whether you're pregnant now, or months, years ahead, you're going to be a fuckin' lioness with a cub, aren't you?" There's admiration in the tone of his voice, which I don't think I deserve.

But there's one promise I can make. "I love you, Blade. I'll always do anything I can to prove it."

A shake of his head, then a hushed, "I don't deserve you, babe, but I'm not fuckin' lettin' you go." Then his expression changes and he taps my ass. "Get up, get dressed."

My eyes narrow at his sudden desire for action.

Seeing my confusion, he leans in, placing his lips to the tip of my nose, the part of me I've always hated, but he seems to have a fascination with how it turns up at the end. "I love you too. Don't doubt that for a second. But there's one thing that's missin'."

Now it's me moving my head side to side, not understanding.

"You, you're my ol' lady. But you've never been on the back of my bike. Gonna rectify that now, babe. We're going for a ride."

"But surely we should find out what's going on? Have the police been told? Will they want to question me? What's happened to Seb? To Sally, and to Lurch? What…"

His mouth curves as my questions spill out, and he places his hand over my lips to still them. "Babe. I trust my brothers. They'll have everything sorted. Now you need the wind in your face, blowing your bad memories away, and I need to feel you behind me on my bike. Never had a woman riding with me before; that's something that's only yours too. We'll ride out, get something to eat. Think about us and our future. Time enough to deal with the shit when we come back."

"Can we do that? Just up and disappear?"

Another tap to the end of my nose. "We can do that. It's what you, *we* need."

"What time is it, Blade?" When he replies, I'm amazed it's early the next morning. My sleep, our lovemaking, had turned yesterday into another day. Despite my horror at my own actions, his enthusiasm for us going out, wipes some of the effects away.

We shower, dress. I slide on my property cut, not missing how his eyes blaze as he sees me wearing it. We walk down the incline to where his bike, obviously recovered from Seb's residence, is waiting for us outside the clubhouse.

Wraith comes out. I expect the VP to challenge Blade, to tell him he's wanted elsewhere, but when Blade simply calls out, "Getting some wind therapy, VP," Wraith grins and nods. When Beef steps out, the VP holds him back with his arm and a quick word into his ear.

I still don't understand how Blade can just ride away, leaving so many questions unanswered. Like what's going to happen to me for killing a man, and how they're going to deal with Seb. Or why he doesn't feel the need to be part of it.

Until he turns on the engine and the Harley begins to rumble and vibrate between my legs and all thoughts other than holding on tight go out of my head. Blade's instruction to hang on is superfluous. I've never ridden a motorcycle before, and my hands take an iron grip around his waist, terrified I'm going to fall off. But when we turn out onto the open road, wind rushing past my face, my hair streaming out behind me, it's as if my worries, my fears, my apprehensions are being blown away, and like the view behind us, fading in the rear.

Blade turns onto the Catalina Highway up Mount Lemmon. I lean with him as he takes the curves, hiding my face in his shoulder at the steep drop-offs. But as he handles the bike so competently, I have no qualms that he's a good rider, and that he'll keep me safe. When we eventually park at the top and I have to get off, I'm a little disappointed.

When I dismount, Blade laughs and reaches out to steady me as I stumble, unused to the feeling of being astride the bike. I bend over, placing my hands on my knees, still feeling the vibration going through me. Then I glance at my man who remains sitting astride his bike, and I smile broadly. "Best feeling in the world, Blade."

He grins that smirk at me, the one I used to think was too arrogant, but now I know he's entitled to wear it. "Loved having you on the back, babe. You're a fuckin' natural."

Stepping forward, I place my hand on the handlebars, and really look at the bike for the first time. Suddenly I meet his eyes. "Can you teach me to ride? Can I have one of my own?"

Whatever he expected me to say, it wasn't that. His face goes blank as though I've stunned him.

"Well," I start, placing my hands on my hips. "Sam rides beside Drummer. Marcia's got her own bikes. Why can't I have one too?"

"Christ," he says, laughing. "I've created a fuckin' monster, haven't I? One ride, and you want to be up front." At last getting off the bike, he curls his hand around the back of my neck and pulls me into him. "You know what? I fuckin' love it. Yeah, I'll teach you to ride babe." His lips crash down onto mine.

When, finally, we part, I look around me. The view goes on for miles. "Wind therapy, that's what you called it?"

"Has it cleared your head?"

"Yes." I've still got that uneasiness inside me. Still worried about the person I've become, and whether what I did yesterday has changed me, but he was right. Getting away, clearing our heads before facing all the issues again, was just what I needed.

Turning back from the view, I eye my man instead. There are depths to him, complexities I haven't even begun to explore yet. Now I've got a lifetime to discover the Blade he keeps hidden from the rest of the world. The future that Grant wanted to take from me.

He extracts a pack of cigarettes from his cut and lights one, careful to stand downwind. Looking out over the same vista that I'm admiring, he inhales, and blows out smoke. After a moment, he turns, saying seriously, "Fuckin' needed this babe." His hand reaches out and taking mine, squeezes it. "I was scared, yesterday babe. Fuckin' terrified. I thought I'd lost you. Couldn't bear that. Never want to feel like that again."

I stay quiet. I can't make promises fate might not allow me to keep. But I turn my hand so I can squeeze his fingers too.

CHAPTER 41

Blade

Having left without eating, hungry as we missed dinner the previous evening, we decide to grab brunch at a restaurant overlooking the ski slopes. I'd been worried about Tash's understandable breakdown in the early hours of this morning. Recollecting the events of the day before had blown up in her head, hitting her hard. I could sympathise, having felt much the same way the first time I dispatched a man to meet Satan. It hadn't got much easier over the years, but I've developed coping mechanisms. Usually the pavement under my wheels and the wind blowing in my face does much to lessen the impact. That, as I hoped, it appeared to have had a similar effect on Tash had been gratifying.

Fuck me. Now she wants her own bike. Hell, yeah. I'll help her learn to ride one. As we wait for our food to arrive, I'm considering buying a nice little Sportster for her. An 883. We can always bore that out later once she's got used to the power and if she wants more. It makes my cock jerk to think of her riding beside me.

She seems content to stare out at the view, watching the chair lift taking tourists up to the summit and then back down again, enabling me to just soak her in. As I do so, I think what I know of my old lady. Somehow I suspect it's not only a request to ride a bike that will surprise me during our lifetime together. It will probably take years, if ever, before I know everything about her. But so far I've learned she's the only woman I want beside me in my life. She's strong, she had to be, to survive on the streets, instinctively knowing how to evade capture. Brave enough to escape when she was caught. Loyal to the extent she was prepared to sacrifice herself to rescue me. For a moment, I grow cold at the thought of how I so nearly deserted her, but even then, she was prepared to save herself. Caring for me made her risk my displeasure and approach Mouse, and in doing so, discovered life-changing information for me.

She's a strong fucking woman, but also so tender, with a great sense of humour as can be seen in her writing. Once everything's behind us, we'll get to work on those books. My artist's hands are itching to pick up my pencils and watercolours. I wonder if the joint team of Jack and Tash Sharples will become famous. Yeah, she's going to take my last name, and soon, if I have anything to do with it.

"You look thoughtful. Oh, thank you." Her statement for me, her grateful thanks for the server who's just brought our food.

"Just thinkin' how fuckin' lucky I am." I start my attack on the ham and eggs. It's tasty, and I'm hungry.

"Yeah?" she speaks around her mouthful.

"Yeah. I was remembering that wretch I caught stealing food from the Wheel Inn."

She giggles. "Can you steal something that's already been thrown away?"

Smirking, I tell her, "It's owned by the Satan's Devils, babe. Even Tommy knew not to go there."

"What's going to happen to Tommy?"

As her head tilts in worry, I reassure her, "Not sure, yet, babe. But we'll figure out something." Tommy belongs in the real world which we'll be getting back to soon enough. For the moment, I'm just enjoying this peaceful interlude.

But all good things come to an end. Stomachs filled, bill paid, we return to the bike. This time, she's a little more reluctant to get on behind me. I know how she feels. Once we get down off this mountain, we'll be in the middle of the shit once again.

I love the way she rides behind me, seeming to know instinctively how to lean into the curves, of which there are many on this road, not once making me feel she's unbalancing the bike, so different from the last time I'd had someone, Tommy in fact, riding pillion. Tash rides as if she'd been doing it all her life, a natural. Another confirmation, if I was in need of one, that she's a perfect old lady.

The miles seem to pass by all too fast, although we have been away a fair few hours. It's mid-afternoon by the time we arrive back at the compound. She dismounts, I back into my parking spot, then kick down the stand.

"Time to face the music?" Her face is pinched.

I take her hand. "You and me, babe. Together. Okay? We've can take on anything." I hate that her eyes have lost the sparkle they had a couple of hours ago.

"You're back. Good." Wraith appears, leaning against the door to the clubhouse. "Waiting on you to start church." Tash pulls away, but Wraith calls out, "You too, Tash." As I raise my eyebrow at him, he continues, "You'll want to know some shit. Best you hear it first hand, then Blade having to go through everything with you after."

Her eyes meet mine; I nod in reassurance. "Come on."

Her lips press together, then a look of determination comes over her face, and I put my hand on her back and give her the gentle encouragement she needs to walk into the clubroom, across it, and into the meeting room where we hold church.

Drifter, showing some quick thinking, has brought in a spare chair, and already has it placed at the bottom of the table. Ignoring it, I take her up to the top, seating her in Dollar's, next to my own. When the treasurer comes in, he startles, then smirks, and then nudges Beef who gets up and hits Viper on the shoulder. I chuckle as one by one all the brothers move down to make room for her. Then, clasping her hand in mine, place our entwined fingers on the table top.

"You and me, babe. Together," I whisper into her ear.

Beef overhears, and puts two of his fingers into his mouth, pretending to gag. "Fuckin' lovebirds make me sick."

As Prez walks past to take his seat, he gives his approximation of a smile, and a nod in approval. All eyes go to him as he bangs the gavel.

"Welcome, Tash. This is an exception, so don't get used to your ass being in that seat." He waits for the rumble of laughter to die away. "Right. While Blade and Tash were out gallivanting today, we've been cleaning house." Drummer looks straight at me. "Matt's guarding Lawson in the storage shed."

"You want me to question him, Prez?"

"Nah, did that myself." Drummer cracks his knuckles loudly. "Seems I haven't lost my touch."

Peg grins across the table. "Didn't even need to put a mark on him. Pansy boy gave it all up when he saw the tools of Blade's trade laid out."

Tash glances at me, I smirk back. "Mainly woodworking tools, babe. Innocent hammers and saws." I don't explain it's what I do with them that isn't so harmless, but I expect she can read between the lines.

Drummer grins, then grows serious. "Now we've got to decide what to do with the information he gave. Tash, nothing you haven't already surmised and told us. Lawson arranged for Grant to take out Ferguson. He also approached those two women to come forward with lies about Cobb. Cleared his way to get the nomination, just as we thought."

"But I killed Grant..." Tash interrupts.

"All cleaned up," Prez reassures her. "It will look like Grant left the state to avoid getting arrested in connection with murder and collusion."

"His disappearance could be convenient," Mouse agrees.

Prez raps his fingers on the table top. When his steely eyes scan the table, finally settling on Tash, they soften. "We've been talking this through," he informs us, his gaze moving from her to me, then back again. "Lawson can't be allowed to get away with stealing the election. We're all agreed on that."

"Still think we should take out the trash ourselves," Peg interjects.

Drummer sighs. "Been through this, Peg. He's too visible. Grant's disappearance is easy to explain, Lawson's? Not so much." His eyes focus on Tash again. "Going to have to ask you to come forward. Report what you know."

Tash starts, her hand, still held in my own, grips me tightly. "How do I explain why I didn't go to the cops before?"

Prez fixes her with his stare. "We're not suggesting you approach the cops first, though they will eventually get involved. What we're talking about is giving your story to the press."

"Yeah," Peg joins in. "The journalist who came to the compound when we had that business about us supposedly kidnapping Ma. He was pretty impressed with us. We'll explain how we took two more sorry people in."

Tash first bristles, then relaxes and shrugs, giving a self-deprecating grin at the way he described her. But she's not leaping at the opportunity. "I don't trust the press."

Prez nods in understanding. "Don't much care for them either. But this is one way to get your story out there, and I think it's the best. Cops won't be able to ignore it and will have to act on it."

"Then my question stands. The one about why I didn't involve them earlier?"

Heart's the one to speak. He smiles reassuringly. "I've already spoken to Marc, talked her through what went on. She said the truth's the best way to approach it. You weren't in a position to come forward before. You were threatened by Grant, in fear of approaching the wrong person, and didn't have evidence to back up your story until you managed to return to your apartment. You were Lawson's campaign manager; you were in a position to know all his secrets. Marc knows the right cops to approach, ones she can guarantee won't be on Lawson's payroll or who are looking to benefit from him getting elected."

Tash doesn't look convinced. "If I tell the whole story, and it gets published, they'll think I'm just trying to get back at him. He'll go free, and I know how vindictive he is. I'll live my life looking over my shoulder."

"For a start Tash, you won't be going to the press or the cops on your own."

Beef raises his hand. "Don't forget Sally Lawson." We both look surprised as we turn to him. "Yeah. I've been talkin' to her. We were right. He was an abusive asshole, but she was pressured by her family, and his, to return to him when he got the nomination. She wants nothing more than to be free of him for good and allowed to raise her family without his interference. She's prepared to back up Tash about how Lawson got her to his house to," Beef puts this in air quotes, "persuade her not to go to the authorities."

"She knows I killed Grant."

"She might think it, but doesn't know it. All she knows is that you had his blood on you, and that he's disappeared. Anything else would be conjecture, and we made sure no evidence was left. I don't think she'll say anything Tash, and if she did, there's nothing to back that up."

Seems to me, Beef's spent a long time talking to Sally. I wonder if anything's going on, especially when he continues, "Heart's old house is still standing empty. I thought maybe we could let Sally and the kids stay in it until she gets herself sorted."

"It's a good idea," Prez starts after a moment's thought. "We can watch over her and give her the support to tell her side of the story without influence from her parents or in-laws. For the moment, Lawson will need to be on the loose, and she may well need protection. Any objection, Heart?"

Heart shrugs. "Yeah, it was bought for me and Crystal, but we just rented it. Club officially owns it. I won't want to go back."

"What about Lurch?" Tash asks suddenly. All eyes look at her in confusion. My lips turn up. Having met the man, I think her name for him suits him. "Malcolm," she corrects, finally recollecting his proper name.

"Seems he's got a soft spot for Sally. Told the hospital it was an accident and he'll live. We can play on his sympathy for Lawson's wife. Reckon he might know which closets to look into where we might find more skeletons."

Beef's face has gone red. Hmm. If you ask me, I'd think Lurch might not be the only one with a soft spot for Sally.

Prez raises his chin. "Seems all everyone's got to do is to tell the truth. What will help, of course, is if Lawson turns himself in."

Now my eyes go wide. "Not a hope in hell." Then I catch the look on Drummer's face. "Is there?"

"After my chat with him, which, I'll have you know, left no marks on him. We didn't even use handcuffs…"

"Though he did need a new pair of slacks," Peg interrupts. A little gleefully in my opinion.

"He said he would give himself up." Prez glares at the sergeant-at-arms. "It was his outdated view of the Satan's Devils that made him come to us in the first place. I must admit, I didn't do much to change his opinion."

"But even if he doesn't," Mouse grins, "we've got all the evidence."

"What about Neil Turner?" Tash frowns. "He could support Seb's side of the story, say he's innocent."

Prez raises his chin as though impressed. "Currently in the wind, Tash, but we're looking for him. If he reappears, I'll have the same conversation I had with Lawson, if not, well, his disappearance is telling."

Tash bites her lip. "From the way he was in Seb's office, and what I knew of him, I'd say he aided and abetted, but wasn't directly responsible for what went on."

"Interesting," Prez nods. "Maybe we'll be able to get him to rat his boss out. Either way, I don't see he's a risk to you coming forward."

Tash moves her gaze to me. When I give an encouraging nod, she looks back to the prez while squeezing my hand again. "I'll do it. I'll speak to the reporter."

I lean closer to her. "That's my girl," I tell her quietly.

"Thanks, Tash. That's all we need you for. We've got a few more things to discuss…"

She takes that as her cue to leave, rising from the chair. No argument or discussion. Another sign, if I was looking for one, that she'll make a great old lady.

Once the door has closed behind her, I take my knife out of my cut and place it on the table in front of me. My fingers toy with it, as my expression becomes the cold, enforcer's mask. "I want Bertram."

"Knew you would. Already found him. Got him tied up and gagged in a corner of the storeroom. His, discomfort, shall we say, was helpful in getting Lawson to talk."

I raise my eyes to the sergeant-at-arms, and my lips start to curve nastily. Peg stares back steadily. Bertram betrayed me, my old lady, and the club. He's in for a whole world of hurt.

Chapter 42

Tash

Nominee accused of conspiracy to influence the Election

*L*ocal businessman, Sebastian Lawson (38), and aspiring law-maker has been accused of using nefarious methods to obtain his recent nomination.

Two women, his previous campaign manager and self-professed one-time mistress, Emmalina Fielding (30), and his wife, Sally Lawson (34) have stepped forward with a raft of evidence that casts doubt on whether Raymond Ferguson's death was an accident, and suggest the accusations which caused Raul Cobb to step down have no basis in reality.

This reporter has obtained tapes and documents that suggest Lawson at least knew about, if not ordered a hit on Ferguson who it's thought lost control of his car and went over the edge of the mountain. Police are now investigating whether his vehicle could have been tampered with. They are trying to locate Grant Locosta, known in some circles as Loco, who acted as Lawson's bodyguard and fixer. Locosta has disappeared and so far has been unable to be reached to answer questions.

Virginia Parsons and Gillian Patron, however, have both stepped forward and have withdrawn their statements alleging Cobb subjected them to sexual abuse. While they allege the abuse happened, they are no longer confident they identified the correct man, the incidents having taken place ten years ago, and both *women now state their memories were faulty. On at least one of the dates given, Cobb was out of state. It appears both women came forward after receiving money from Lawson which they suggest had triggered false memories.*

This reporter has also seen evidence that Lawson procured the abortion drugs mifepristone and misoprostol illegally. Ms Fielding alleges Lawson pressured her to take these drugs after she became pregnant during her brief affair with him. Lawson is running on a strong pro-life platform.

At the time of their affair, Ms Fielding was unaware of Lawson's marital status. Mrs Lawson had been living out of state and had had an agreement that they would live separately due to Lawson's violence toward her and the children. When it seemed likely that Lawson would get the nomination, he approached the wife from whom he had been separated for years and asked for a reconciliation. It appears his reason was to promote himself as a happily-married man. Hospital records confirm the serious injuries received by Sally Lawson prior to their separation.

When approached, Mr Lawson was eager to tell his side of the story. In his opinion, Ms Fielding was an incompetent campaign manager who he sacked and replaced with Neil Turner (42) when it appeared he was going to rise to prominence. Lawson points to two facts in his favour, one Ms Fielding was tardy coming forward with her information, and secondly, the events of last Sunday.

Mr Lawson alleges that Locosta was killed by Ms Fielding. Though he did not see a dead body, and none was found in the house, there are witnesses confirming Ms Fielding appeared covered in blood. On her part, Ms Fielding explains that the blood was hers, coming from a blow to her face. When asked why her bloody clothes were not available, Ms Fielding explained it wouldn't have been possible to clean them and discarded them instead.

Mrs Lawson had been a witness; she claims her husband had turned violent and had gained possession of a knife. She alleges Lawson planned to killed both her and Fielding. Another witness, Malcolm Lyons (32), was hurt in the altercation when he tried to protect Mrs Fielding. Police are still investigating the incident.

Sebastian Lawson, who comes from a moneyed family, is still protesting his innocence and remains a candidate in the election, but legal experts say the amount of evidence against him could see him imprisoned on charges of murder and attempted murder. The police have taken Mr Lawson in for questioning.

It is too late to remove his name from the ballot paper, but if Lawson is charged and convicted, Raul Cobb, who's withdrawn his concession, will likely be named winner of the election instead if Lawson comes top in the ballot.

Lawson is currently held in police custody.

"You holding up, Tash?" Beef interrupts my perusal.

I put down the newspaper. I'd had a second chilling day of questioning by the police. The newspaper had passed the evidence Mouse had given to the reporter on to them. Lieutenant Diaz, who Marcia had introduced me to, seemed a fair man, but thorough. Luckily, apart from having to be slightly inventive about Grant's disappearance, I could tell the truth, and it was hard for them to slip me up. It helped Sally had come clean about everything, preferring the protection of the Satan's Devils to returning to her family. We've become friends, both having been taken in by the same man.

Beef laughs softly. Leaning over he taps me on the forehead. "You've got a lot going on in there, haven't you?"

I have. More than he realises. I just nod.

"You need someone to talk to? Any of us here would help."

I smile and thank him. I've come to like the big man who it would be easy to dismiss as shallow. He has indeed become someone I'd call a friend. Now Blade has in that caveman way what they call, *claimed* me, he seems less jealous of me talking to any of his brothers.

Beef raises his chin, then stands and walks away, joining his brothers in church. My thoughts having been interrupted, I look around, surveying the clubroom instead. The women with children are herding them up and disappearing to follow their bedtime routines. Only Carmen and Sandy remain and are sitting with drinks in front of them. They wave me to join them, but I shake my head. I'm not being rude, just content to be on my own, waiting for Blade to come out from the meeting room.

Tommy's at the bar, cleaning it so hard the top looks like a mirror. He grins broadly when he sees me, and within moments of me sitting down, has placed an open bottle of soda on the table in front of me.

"Rash okay?" he asks, his normally smiling face looking concerned.

I know how much he'd been worried when I went missing, so I brush it off, saying breezily, "I'm fine. And you, Tommy? How are you doing?"

"I'm busy." There's pride in his voice. I doubt he's ever been made to feel useful before. Again, I worry what's going to happen to him now there's no need for him to be here.

I should have said something on that rare occasion I'd been allowed into their meeting. But I had been awed by all the brothers around me. I'm ashamed to say, Tommy's predicament hadn't come into my head.

"Tommy?" Both mine and Tommy's heads turn at Drifter's loud voice. Tommy leaps up and rushes over, then disappears into church.

My stomach drops. After the newspaper had printed the article, and the police had spoken to me the first time, Seb had been taken in for questioning. There's no reason now for

Tommy still to be here. He can tell who he likes I'm with the Devils.

My teeth worry my lip as I wonder if they're tying up all loose ends. If that's the case, I hope Blade will stand up for him, hating the thought of Tommy being turned out from the one home he's ever really known, left to fend for himself on the streets again.

I'm on edge, annoyed with myself. I should have spoken to Blade. Perhaps we could get a place ourselves in town and have Tommy stay with us. There must be something we can do.

I'm still thinking of ideas and ways I could help, when the men start pouring out of church. In amongst them is Tommy. And he's… I stand to get a closer look. When I see what he's wearing a startled gasp comes out of my mouth. He's got a brand-new leather cut, with the word Prospect on it.

Blade's grinning widely. Making a beeline my way, when he reaches me he pulls me to him and his hands go around my waist. He nods toward Tommy. "He won't be able to patch in," he explains. "Wouldn't trust that fucker on a bike. But he'll be happy enough having a home and he's a good fuckin' worker. We'll have to see how it goes, but he might be able to take on more as he finds his place."

"Did you do this?" I ask in wonder.

"Club vote, babe."

Yeah, it would have to have been. But Blade's got a soft spot for the man who kept me alive on the streets. Underneath his hard exterior, my man's got a tender heart. Hmm. I'm certain he would have had a lot to do with it. To show my appreciation, I put my arm around his waist and hug him, while watching Tommy, who's revelling in being the centre of attention. As brothers slap his back, a drink is placed in his hand. A soda.

Looking up, he catches my eye and points to his new cut. "Tommy's a Devil Man, Tash."

"He called me my proper name." I nod to the man beaming with pleasure, but my words are for Blade.

"Er, I might have schooled him," Blade replies with a smirk.

I kiss him to thank him, which ends up meaning we don't spend long at Tommy's party, making our excuses as soon as we can, and heading up to our suite for a more private affair just for two.

The next morning, I'm up behind Blade as we head down into Tucson, Marcia's riding one of her own bikes beside us. I try to quash my worries by dreaming about a time when I might be riding alongside my man instead of up behind him. I watch the ex-cop with envy as she competently handles her bike.

All too soon we're arriving at the precinct where I'm to have yet another meeting with Lieutenant Diaz. As always, I help as best as I can. It's there I hear news which bolsters my spirits. Neil Turner has turned himself in, and, in exchange for leniency for his part in the proceedings, has made a deal to give the cops all the dirt on Seb. He had, as Drummer so sagely predicted, turned rat.

The next few days pass in a blur. Seb is arrested for murder and other conspiracy charges for fraudulently trying to influence an election. Now there's a new reason I'm glad to have gone to ground on the compound—the press keep trying to talk to me. I thought I'd be free once he was arrested, but until the story dies down, I'm as captive as I ever was.

I've got company. Sally is also being hounded by various newspapers and even the TV stations so she, and her three children are staying with the Devils as well. It amuses me that Beef never seems far from her side.

I'm starting to feel like I'm settling into this new, but strange, family. Becoming more a part of it as each day passes.

It's the end of the week when Blade enters the suite and passes me a package. "It's time." He kisses the top of my head.

It doesn't take long to do what needs to be done. When I exit the room, Blade cocks his head at me.

"Negative," I tell him.

I can see him visibly relax, breathing a sigh of relief. That hurts more than it should.

"It might be too early, and it's a false result."

He comes over to me, taking my hands in his. "I hope it's not."

I move my fingers away, and turn around, unwilling for him to see the pain in my eyes. The cramping in my stomach warns me the test is probably accurate. I'm not carrying his baby inside.

"Tash," he starts softly.

"I'm okay, Blade, I'm alright."

"Babe." As I won't turn around to face him, he pulls me back against his chest. "Listen to me. I'm glad you're not pregnant, and you're going to listen to me as to why. If you had been, I'd have been happy. But now we've got a chance to do this right. I want to throw those fuckin' condoms away and love you every hour of every fuckin' day until I put a baby inside you. Do it because that's what we want. Not have a second of doubt we're coping with an accident."

"You'd throw them away today?"

"If that's what you want. I know I do."

My brow creases. "Every hour?"

He chuckles against my ear. "Maybe twice."

"You're going to kill me." I doubt I'd be able to keep up.

"Want to have my baby, Tash? Here's a thing, I'll sweeten the deal. You'll be able to get the full effect of my piercing without latex." His warm breath caressing my skin as he speaks directly into my ear, the words he's saying, combine to make my toes curl.

But I don't tell him that. "You trying to bribe me now?" I try to sound nonchalant, I'm not sure I'm succeeding.

A nuzzle to my neck, a nibble of my ear lobe. "Is it working?"

It certainly is. "I'm not sure I can turn that offer down."

EPILOGUE

Another burst of laughter rings out across the clubroom.

"My book, Mommy. Mine." An indignant Amy tries to take it from Marcia's hands.

"Oh, this is too good, Tash." Marcia wipes tears of mirth from her eyes as she reluctantly relinquishes control of the book to her adopted daughter. "And Blade? Never knew you could draw like that."

"It's already been nominated for an award," Tash says proudly. She's delighted as she believes it's my illustrations that had garnered the interest it had. Me? I think it's down to how she crafts her words.

Husband and wife team. That's what we are. I'm proud as fuck of my wife, and wish Jonah could have lived to see what I've become, a man I'd like to think he'd be impressed with, in more ways than one.

Tash passes out more copies of the book we only received ourselves this morning. They're snapped up fast. Rock's taken one to show Becca, who's rocking week-old Rose in her arms. Though she's too young to appreciate it, they're pointing out the pictures to her. I chuckle quietly, remembering Rock's horror when he found out he had a daughter. Wraith had commiserated with him, and there might have been some discussion about which shotguns were to be recommended. Rose has utterly stolen and melted Rock's heart, and I have to admit to being smitten myself, and the tiniest bit jealous.

Wraith's laughing as Sophie shows him a copy of our book, a real deep belly laugh. Then he gives Tash and I a thumbs up.

Even Drew's lost his sulky look as he flicks through the pages. I see Mouse's grin is tinged with a touch of relief as he take's Mariana's hand and feel some sympathy for him. The lad wants a promise he'll be allowed to prospect for us; Mariana remains dead set against it. It hasn't been settled in the past few weeks, and looks set to be an argument that will continue. I've no idea where Mouse stands on it, but suspect he'll lean toward whatever his wife wants. Yeah, women have a way of affecting us like that.

Pulling Tash onto my lap, I give her a hug. Wondering whether last night I put a baby inside her, if not, it has to be soon. Maybe I was slightly optimistic when I thought my stamina might hold up to fucking her hourly, but it's come darn close at times. I just can't get enough of her darn pussy. I love her so much. It seems right the books we're making together should be read to our own child. Relaxing back, I watch my brothers around me, glowing with pride that they're finding pleasure in Tash's and my achievement. That they've accepted I can be two men, the enforcer, as well as the artist. My creativity with a paintbrush hasn't blunted my skills with a knife, in fact, it seems to have sharpened them. Loving Tash has given me an edge, even more reason to protect all I stand for.

This is my future. With Tash beside me, I can be who I want and be proud of it. *Jonah, hope you're looking down on me.* My only regret? That my brother hadn't lived to see me happy.

A door bangs behind me. I spin around at the heavy sound of feet, and a throat clearing. My eyes take in the scene in an instant, pushing Tash off my lap, and getting to my feet. Darcy's in floods of tears, barely able to stand, propping herself up on her man. Peg, himself, has moisture in his eyes. *No. Don't say anything's happened to their kid, Noah. Don't let it be that.*

Drummer, coming in alongside them, looks shaken himself. It's unusual to see the normally controlled prez looking upset. His eyes find those of Peg, and hold them for a moment, before looking around the room, which is brimming with brothers and old ladies.

Walking forward, he goes to the bar. The whole room falls silent, brothers reading that look on his face. Imperceptibly I pull back my shoulders. *What the fuck are we up against now?*

He doesn't waste time before enlightening us. "Brothers, old ladies. There's no easy way to say this. You all know about the fires in California that our brother Truck was fighting? How he's stayed down there as more broke out?" He pauses for us to catch up. I freeze, recognising that look on his face. "Truck was being a fuckin' hero, as expected. Tried like fuck to get a woman and her child out of the path of the fire, saved their lives, but part of a structure fell on him. Trapped him."

Gasps sound all around me. A loud sob comes from Darcy's mouth. She's known Truck longer than any of us. Worked alongside him for years. Knows all too well the dangers of fire-fighting, being a firefighter herself. No wonder she's distraught.

It's Sam who approaches her man. "Drummer, is he, is he…"

Drummer's eyes soften as they land on her. "I'm so fuckin' sorry. All I know is that he's alive, but in a very bad way. Extensive burns all over his body." He hugs her, then his attention is on the rest of us. "If you're into praying, suggest you offer up a few now. It's touch and go, apparently."

There's not a brother with an old lady who doesn't scoop her into their arms. Those with children hold the kids tight too.

Truck's our brother. He's hurt, badly. Maybe not going to make it. Shaking my head, I say loudly, "Truck's got this, Brothers. He's not going to fuckin' let go. He's got too much to live for. He's one of us." I pause, then I start our chant off, "Satan's Devils Ride Together. Ride, Satan's Devils."

At first my sole voice rings in the air, then my brothers pick it up and shout it on repeat. Fists thump over hearts. If good wishes carry weight, our brother will be receiving them in California.

For now, we can only wait and hope for good news.

Truck's in God's hands now, not the Devils'.

DEMON'S ANGEL

Up to the time Nathan had died, Violet had been the annoying child who'd followed us around everywhere. When she became a teenager, she'd developed an annoying teenage crush on me.

My promise to my best friend had been to watch over her, a debt paid when she moved out of state and was grown and settled.

Ten years later she's back in my town, this time with a baby. Now twenty-five, she's the one who's got me twisted up in knots.

But she's Nathan's sister. She needs help, I can give it. In the role of replacement big brother of course.

She'd be horrified if she knew what I'd really like to do to her.

Violet

*It's embarrassing to remember last time I'd seen Demon I'd flirted
with him incorrigibly.*

When we meet again, I realise I still want him.

*He doesn't see me that way, treating me just like he would a sis-
ter. Stepping into Nathan's shoes to help me out of trouble.*

*I do need someone's help. But that shouldn't be down to a man
who's doing nothing more than keeping a promise made to my
dead brother.*

*I've become involved in a war. Now, because of the debt Demon
thinks he owes, I'm dragging the Satan's Devils into it with me.*

*But nothing is more important than keeping my son safe and out
of the clutches of his real father.*

Satan's Devils: Colorado Chapter #2
DEMON'S ANGEL

OTHER WORKS BY MANDA MELLETT

All books can be read as a standalone.

SATAN'S DEVILS MC ARIZONA CHAPTER

#1	*Turning Wheels*	Wraith & Sophie
#2	*Drummer's Beat*	Drummer & Sam
#3	*Slick Running*	Slick & Ella
#4	*Targeting Dart*	Dart & Alex
#5	*Heart Broken*	Heart & Marc
#6	*Peg's Stand*	Peg & Darcy
#7	*Rock Bottom*	Rock & Becca
#8	*Joker's Fool*	Joker & Lady
#9	*Mouse Trapped*	Mouse & Mariana
#10	*Blade's Edge*	Blade & Tash

SATAN'S DEVILS MC COLORADO CHAPTER

#1	*Paladin's Hell*	Paladin & Jayden

Coming in 2019:

* *Demon's Angel* (#2 – Demon & Violet)

Blood Brothers

A series about sexy dominant sheikhs and their bodyguards

#1	*Stolen Lives*	Nijad & Cara
#2	*Close Protection*	Jon & Mia
#3	*Second Chances*	Kadar & Zoe
#4	*Identity Crisis*	Sean & Vanessa
#5	*Dark Horses*	Jasim & Janna
#6	*Hard Choices*	Aiza

Sign up for my newsletter to hear about new releases in the
SATAN'S DEVILS MC and **Blood Brothers** series:
http://eepurl.com/b1PXO5

GLOSSARY

Motorcycle Club – An official motorcycle club in the U.S. is one which is sanctioned by the American Motorcyclist Association (AMA). The AMA has a set of rules its members must abide by. It is said that ninety-nine percent of motorcyclists in America belong to the AMA.

Outlaw Motorcycle Club (MC) – The remaining one percent of motorcycling clubs are historically considered outlaws as they do not wish to be constrained by the rules of the AMA and have their own bylaws. There is no one formula followed by such clubs, but some not only reject the rulings of the AMA, but also that of society, forming tightly knit groups who fiercely protect their chosen ways of life. Outlaw MCs have a reputation for having a criminal element and supporting themselves by less than legal activities, dealing in drugs, gun running or prostitution. The one-percenter clubs are usually run under a strict hierarchy.

Brother – Typically members of the MC refer to themselves as brothers and regard the closely knit MC as their family.

Cage – The name bikers give to cars as they prefer riding their bikes.

Chapter – Some MCs have only one club based in one location. Other MCs have a number of clubs who follow the same bylaws and wear the same patch. Each club is known as a chapter and will normally carry the name of the area where they are based on their patch.

Church – Traditionally the name of the meeting where club business is discussed, either with all members present or with just those holding officer status.

Colours – When a member is wearing (or flying) his colours he will be wearing his cut proudly displaying his patch showing which club he is affiliated with.

Cut – The name given to the jacket or vest which has patches denoting the club that member belongs to.

Enforcer – The member who enforces the rules of the club.

Hang-around – This can apply to men wishing to join the club and who hang-around hoping to be become prospects. It is also used to women who are attracted by bikers and who are happy to make themselves available for sex at biker parties.

Mother Chapter – The founding chapter when a club has more than one chapter.

Patch – The patch or patches on a cut will show the club that member belongs to and other information such as the particular chapter and any role that may be held in the club. There can be a number of other patches with various meanings, including a one-percenter patch. Prospects will not be allowed to wear the club patch until they have been patched-in, instead they will have patches which denote their probationary status.

Patched-in/Patching-in – The term used when a prospect completes his probationary status and becomes a full club member.

President (Prez) – The officer in charge of that particular club or chapter.

Prospect – Anyone wishing to join a club must serve time as a probationer. During this period they have to prove their loyalty to the club. A probationary period can last a year or more. At the end of this period, if they've proved themselves a prospect will be patched-in.

Old Lady – The term given to a woman who enters into a permanent relationship with a biker.

RICO – The Racketeer Influenced and Corrupt Organisations Act primarily deals with organised crime. Under this Act the officers of a club could be held responsible for activities they order members to do and a conviction carries a potential jail service of twenty years as well as a large fine and the seizure of assets.

Road Captain – The road captain is responsible for the safety of the club on a run. He will organise routes and normally ride at the end of the column.

Ronin – A biker who travels alone, sometimes wearing a patch denoting he's Ronin. Not affiliated to any club, but often bearing a token which will help ensure safe passage through territories of different clubs.

Secretary – MCs are run like businesses and this officer will perform the secretarial duties such as recording decisions at meetings.

Sergeant-at-Arms – The sergeant-at-arms is responsible for the safety of the club as a whole and for keeping order.

Sweet Butt – A woman who makes her sexual services available to any member at any time. She may well live on the club premises and be fully supported by the club.

Treasurer – The officer responsible for keeping an eye on the club's money.

Vice President (VP) – The vice president will support the president, stepping into his role in his absence. He may be responsible for making sure the club runs smoothly, overseeing prospects etc.

Brothers protecting their own

ACKNOWLEDGEMENTS

All we've really known about Blade up to now was that he was the enforcer who enjoys plying his trade using knives. In the last couple of books though, we've found out while he's an expert at getting men to disclose their secrets, he's not as hard as he looks.

Why? What happened to turn a man with a sensitive interior into the enforcer for the MC? Why does he keep the softer side of himself hidden? When Blade started talking to me, I was intrigued to find out his past, and then search for a way to marry that up with his future. I hope you like the man when you discovered what he was hiding underneath. Though yeah, throughout a lot of the book, he's an asshole. I will give you that.

Tash? Well, she's two people too. How she got caught up with Sebastian I could well understand. Don't we all have someone inside us, a persona we act as at work? She was good at her job, performed it to the best of her ability. Having an affair with her boss? She wasn't her own person then, too used to working under his instruction. Not that she's submissive, but because that was how she thought she should be, she was doing what she thought was expected.

I loved bringing the tougher side of her out. Giving her the guts to survive, then putting her up against Blade which brought out more of her inner strengths. Blade needed someone to stand up to him, he wouldn't have fallen for a weak woman.

I loved writing the interactions between her and Blade. Especially when she ends up slapping him. I hope, like me, you feel he deserved it.

And the ending? Oh, I'm a tease, aren't I? What I will say is that there is going to be one more Satan's Devils' book about the Tucson chapter. Yup. At the moment I'm just planning one. But who? Hmm. You'll have to wait to find out.

As this section is for acknowledgements I better get on with them. When I finish the first draft of a book, I need help to polish it and make it the best it can be before I press that button and publish it. So now, as always, I have to thank the team who are behind me.

My editor, Maggie Kern. This is the fourth book we've worked on together, and it's an honour to work with her as we knock my initial words into shape. I particularly like her comments when she says parts make her laugh out loud. As that was the effect I was going for, I'm so pleased it works.

As ever, I have to offer my very grateful thanks to all my beta readers who are prepared to read a rough draft and pick up so many useful things. Danena, Colleen, Sheri, Terra, Zoe, Nicole, Alex and my husband Steve.

Blade was a very special character to me, and I spent hours looking through stock images trying to find the right person to put on the cover without success. There were a couple of possibilities, but none which were right. Then I browsed a photographer's site and there he was, staring at me. Thank you Paul Henry Serres for taking the photo, and thank you, Will Taylor, for being a spitting image of my character. It's all in the eyes.

Once again thank you Astronima's On Pointe Proofreading for proofreading the final version. I enjoyed working with you. You picked up some final consistency errors for which I'm extremely grateful.

Last but not least, I'd like to thank Tracy Wood for being my PA. She's helped so much over the past few months, keeping me organised, being active on my Facebook page, and even doing some graphics. Such a lovely person to work with.

As always, I've left the most important people to the end. So now please, every person who's taken a chance on this book, accept my heartfelt thanks. If you weren't buying my books, I wouldn't be able to write them.

You can help even more. If you liked this book, don't keep it to yourself. Tell a friend, hey, tell me. Every time a reader contacts me to express how much they enjoy any of my books, especially when they ask for more, it spurs me to continue writing. I appreciate every message you send or comment that you make.

Know what's even better? Leave a review. I don't care where. Just one or two words is helpful. Reviews help authors make sales, sales allow authors to pay editors, models and photographers, cover designers etc, and put food on the table.

To anyone asking the question, while the Tucson chapter may soon come to a close, there are still the other chapters.

One thing I can promise you, there'll be another Devil along very soon.

STAY IN TOUCH

Email: manda@mandamellett.com
Website: www.mandamellett.com

Connect with me on Facebook:
www.facebook.com/mandamellett

Sign up for my newsletter to hear about new releases in the Blood Brothers and Satan's Devils series:

http://eepurl.com/b1PXO5

ABOUT THE AUTHOR

Manda's life's always seemed a bit weird, starting with a childhood that even today she's still trying to make sense of, then losing her parents in the late teens. Going from the tragic to the bizarre, who else could be unlucky enough to have had two car accidents, neither her fault, one involving a nun, and another involving a police woman?

There isn't enough space to list everything that's happened to Manda, or what she's learned from it. But by using the rich fabric of her personal life, psychology degree, varied work experiences, and amazing characters she's met, Manda is able to populate her books with believable in-depth characters and enjoys pitting them against situations which challenge them. Her books are full of suspense, twists and turns and the unexpected.

Manda lives in the beautiful countryside of Essex in UK, the area's claim to fame being the Wilkin's Jam Factory at nearby Tiptree. She can usually find jars of jam which remind her of home wherever she goes. As well as writing books and reading, Manda loves walking her dogs and keeping fit. She lives with her husband of over 30 years, who, along with her son, is her greatest fan and supporter.

Manda is thankful that one of the more unusual, and at the time unpleasant, turns her life took, now enables her to spend her time writing. Confirming, in her view, every cloud has a silver lining.

Photo by Carmel Jane Photography

www.ingramcontent.com/pod-product-compliance
Lightning Source LLC
Chambersburg PA
CBHW070344170726
48291CB00001B/173